REGNUM VITA

NAIM SADEER

Copyright © 2013 Naim Sadeer

The moral right of the author has been asserted.

Apart from any fair dealing for the purposes of research or private study, or criticism or review, as permitted under the Copyright, Designs and Patents Act 1988, this publication may only be reproduced, stored or transmitted, in any form or by any means, with the prior permission in writing of the publishers, or in the case of reprographic reproduction in accordance with the terms of licences issued by the Copyright Licensing Agency. Enquiries concerning reproduction outside those terms should be sent to the publishers.

Matador
9 Priory Business Park,
Wistow Road, Kibworth Beauchamp,
Leicestershire. LE8 0RX
Tel: (+44) 116 279 2299
Fax: (+44) 116 279 2277
Email: books@troubador.co.uk
Web: www.troubador.co.uk/matador

ISBN 978 1780884 042

British Library Cataloguing in Publication Data.
A catalogue record for this book is available from the British Library.

Printed and bound in the UK by TJ International, Padstow, Cornwall
Typeset in 11pt Minion Pro by Troubador Publishing Ltd, Leicester, UK

Matador is an imprint of Troubador Publishing Ltd

REGNUM VITA

For my brother, who is my best friend,
For my mother, who is my hero,
For Audrey, who came in my life when I needed her,
For the two sisters, who will always amaze me.

Regnum Vita is the signification of Kingdom of Life in Latin.

Prologue

Vita was a world where fairy tales were not a myth but a reality. It was a world full of magic and a time where kings and queens were the absolute rulers. Dragons, goblins, orcs, and many creatures lived amongst the humans, and together, they shared a harmonic life. However, humans were dominant and took away everything from the others. The dragons were hunted down, and the other creatures were being oppressed. Soon, there was one thing that stood up against the ultimate reign of mankind. It was the one thing that was feared and mostly misunderstood by them: magic…

Thirty years ago magic was a forbidden art, and something feared in Vita. It was against the law to be born with magic, let alone practice it. Those who were unfortunate enough to get caught were condemned to death. And so, a revolt between magicians and the people of Vita began. It was a war that brought both sides terrible losses and much grief.

Fourteen years later, the Queen of Heartsas, named Keira Fulgura, brought peace and freed the magicians from this abominable law. She was the most remarkable woman that ever lived on Vita. But there was one sorcerer who could not forget about the past. This sorcerer tried to open the demons' world. Anyone who opened it was granted an army of undefeatable monsters. Aware of the disaster it would bring to their world, the royal family of Heartsas fought against the sorcerer. They had won the battle, but at a terrible cost. The queen was dead and her husband's body was never found. It was a tragedy rather than a victory. Because of this terrible loss, a lot of the people hunted down the magicians and went against the law. The magicians had no choice but to isolate themselves from the people. The only chance they had to live amongst everyone resided in a two year old girl who was Keira's daughter.

Many did not wish for a two year old to rule the kingdom, and so different sides were created: those who stood up for the princess and those who wished for a democracy. But it was a short lived conflict. The heads of all the kingdoms around Vita had chosen to give the princess ultimate powers once she reached her seventeenth birthday. The people agreed. It would make much sense to be led by a woman who had developed wisdom throughout the years rather than a little girl who could barely walk.

For fifteen years, the kingdom was led in a democratic system. It was the first time on Vita that a kingdom was ruled in this system. But it was only a temporary measure, and the years had passed. Prudence Fulgura was no more a baby but a seventeen years old woman. She was the princess and the new ruler of the kingdom.

However, a dark face was lurking around. And this face had no intention in submitting itself to a young woman. It was not clear who was hiding in the dark, but one thing was sure: this individual was waiting for the right moment before making a move.

And so, Prudence's journey was about to begin, on a fateful day, where her life was about to take a twist.

Chapter One
A Princess on the Loose

It was a wonderful and radiant day for the people of the kingdom, the sky was blue, the sun was magnificent and the scenery faultless. Heartsas Castle was entirely decorated; the walls were shining like diamonds. A royal red carpet was set up from the entrance of the castle to the throne; and petals of flowers were disposed on the ground as if a wedding was taking place. An immense crowd was standing outside under the watch of different soldiers. The soldiers were fully equipped with beautiful armour and armed with swords.

Whilst everyone was impatiently waiting for the event to take place, a young girl was standing by her window, staring at this crowd and feeling intimidated. She was of an average height, a skinny brunette with short hair and chestnut eyes. Her white skin was as pure as the snow. She was a cute woman with an innocent look. She had a small breast but it did not prevent her from looking astonishing in a dress. Her hair was coifed flawlessly and her lips were pale red. She was dressed with a long and mesmerizing white dress that made her look like an angel.

As she looked down on the crowd, she took a deep breath and gently closed the red curtains. 'Do not fear Prudence, you will do fine for the sake of the kingdom.' The young girl was murmuring to herself, as she was leaving her tidied room.

While she was walking down the immaculate stairs of the castle toward the hall, she noticed something rather unusual. The servants of the castle were all gone and emptiness reigned within the very walls of her abode. She knew the soldiers and the knights were outside assuring the well-being of the event, but the servants were her only friends and they were not present for this important day.

'Where is everyone?' questioned the young lady. 'Have they left me behind? On my coronation day?' The more steps she was descending, the more bizarre the castle seemed to be. The princess did not however trouble herself with the unpleasant feeling she felt, she went down and approached the crowd with her beautiful appearance in order to complete her coronation.

Prudence took a deep breath one more time, before holding the gate's knob.

'I shall make Father and Mother proud... '

Prudence opened the door and the whole crowd had gone. She was shocked and thought that the people of the kingdom were making a suprise for her. But something felt wrong: was she right about the unpleasant feeling?

The princess walked slowly toward the entrance of the castle which led to the forest; there was still no sign of life, it was as if the whole castle had been deserted. As she was inspecting, she heard a noise from the bushes.

'What is going on? Please... is anyone here?' the princess shouted, terrified.

There was no answer, only a much louder noise. This time a branch cracked behind her. She knew she was not alone and she had no way of defending herself, yet still she took a stand with a confident and arrogant posture.

'I shall not abide by this mockery; if you do not wish to be harmed I suggest you answer to me when asked. Who is there?' said the princess.

'Rather foolish of you... ' a voice said out of nowhere. 'A common and reasonable choice would have been to run... do you not realize what has happened here?' The voice kept getting louder and louder, pretty soon the weather turned gray and rain dropped out of the sky. 'I shall enlighten your foolish mind... ' the voice went silent for a while, Prudence knew there was no choice but to run, it was not a friendly voice but rather a sinister character who did not wish her well.

Panicked, the young girl ran toward the castle's gates where she thought of being secured: how wrong she was. As she got inside, she closed the gates firmly with an incredible speed and ran toward her room, which she firmly barricaded after getting inside.

'What has happened to the courageous and arrogant tone? Princess…' the voice managed to enter the castle; it was faster than Prudence had imagined. 'You cannot escape your fate… as it is sealed today… but you shall not worry… your demise will be the beginning of a new era,' the voice claimed with a gentle tone.

The poor defenceless princess was petrified in fear, she could see the furniture that served as a barricade being slowly moved away with some sort of magic. She was not safe, she could not jump out of the window for it was too high.

She desperately looked around but there was no exit, and, soon, the door was the next to move. The knob was gently and delicately turned and unlocked.

'This way princess!' a familiar voice was heard by Prudence, and a wall opened out of nowhere in her room. At the same time, the door was opening.

'Sir Slade!' The princess sighed, relieved.

The knight used a form of magic and sealed the door, which prevented the evil doer from entering the room of the princess.

'Magic?' Prudence gasped. 'But it is forbidden…'

'It will not last long; you have to leave the perimeter as you are in grave danger.'

The knight opened an inside tunnel to get the princess out of the castle; it was a tunnel that had been made during the time of the construction of the castle, when the possibilities of being attacked by close neighbours was considered. It was an escape door that led to a village. However it was dark, and since there never were any attacks, the door was never used and dust, spiders, rats and humidity made their way in. The visibility was poor; it was barely possible to distinguish the silhouettes of the knight and the young lady.

However, escorted by the brave knight she had known since childhood, she feared not. She knew she could rely on the bravery of this man. Sir Slade was around eight feet tall and intimidating, he was big but not fat and his face had an attractive yet menacing look. He looked in his forties with a fine beard and a short coiffure which made him look younger. The knight knew the family and was considered the godfather of the princess.

'Do not worry, we shall rest once arrived,' he calmly said.

'It's been four months since your birthday on 1st August… you are indeed growing up. How old are you now?' demanded the knight with a teasing attitude.

'I thought you would have known, you have witnessed my very birth… seventeen years old sir,' responded the young woman with a disappointed tone. 'Have we arrived?'

'Aye we have arrived,' the knight said, while opening a trap door strengthened from above. 'This shall take some time, how about you tell me,' Slade grunted, 'about what have you been doing during my absence?' the knight asked politely.

'I am not an ignorant; you are hiding something from me… ' Prudence sighed. 'Tell me, what is it that you are not saying?'

The knight did not answer back, he opened the trap door that led to a house and went silent for a while.

Once in the house, he offered a chair to the princess near the chimney, and went toward the kitchen to find bread or anything good to eat. The young lady was calmly looking around the house, which was rather small but well tidied. Everything in the house was made of wood apart from the walls, which were made of bricks. The house was surprisingly well cleaned, the floor mopped, the kitchen in order, and everything was arranged perfectly, however this masquerade was soon irritating the princess. She needed to be sure of what was happening, but Slade was not saying anything and it was making her impatient.

The princess jumped off her chair angrily and rushed toward the kitchen, where Sir Slade was gently slicing bread. With nerve she took the knife from the knight's hand and threw it away, she then approached his face and demanded an explanation to all of this.

'What are you hiding when I have already been put in the middle of this? I have been attacked in my own home yet you still hide from me?' the princess cried in anger. 'I shall not allow this ridiculous act to last any longer, nor shall I abide this irritating silence!'

Soon, the knight would confess, he dared not upset the princess since she was like a daughter to him. He asked the young woman to sit down so he could explain everything to her.

'There are some things that – how do I put this?' The knight was lost in thoughts, 'I should have known we would one day have this conversation!' The man kept on muttering to himself.

'Enough sir, what is it?' asked the princess.

'Have ye ever heard of a story?' as the knight asked this, the princess nodded her head, irritated: she was not a child and a story was something she'd hear often. 'Anyway… this is not any story – 15 years ago, when your parents died, there was that man.' The knight was slowly yet carefully putting his words right. 'That man claimed to possess the highest powers in all Vita… and of course, ye guess he made proof of it. That man violated everything in our world and as a king your father could not let it happen.' He paused. 'With his wife and a couple of knights, he decided to end the fear that was menacing Vita and eliminate the threat. He succeeded but at a terrible price.' Prudence was so intrigued and captivated by the story, she was impatiently and deeply looking at the knight's face.

'What has happened?' Prudence asked curiously.

'Your mother died and your father disappeared. I had sworn to your parents that I would take care of you, but Vita is not safe anymore… ' said the knight.

'But I don't understand,' said the princess. 'Earlier, when I had taken a look outside the window everyone was present. The crowd, the soldiers… in a blink of an eye they were gone… '

'He must have used magic to fool you. I would not be surprised.'
'But you said he was… '

'Somehow, the spirit of that evil man managed to survive – gathering a group of dangerous assassins to bring him something that lies in your family.'

The knight then held Prudence's hand and squeezed it tightly. 'You have to run away as far as you can; I will try and divert their attention. I would not be surprised if they are on their way here.'

He did not wish to show it, but his eyes were full of terror: a great danger was threatening Prudence and the existence of Vita.

As Prudence learnt what was happening, she could only remember that she possessed the family's necklace. Might that be what the evil man's looking for? She could not know; she was unsure about everything. She only knew she was in danger and she had to run: life was not safe in Vita, but where would she go? Many questions were striking her mind but she could not think of a solution.

Suddenly, as she was deep in her thoughts, the door started to be hammered by a powerful force. She could feel the ground and the walls trembling through the impact, the door had not long before been smashed.

'Take this!' The knight offered a sword to Prudence. 'Get under the trap door, turn left as soon as you get down from there, hurry to the woods. I doubt they will search for you there!' Sir Slade said in a hurry, as he was arming himself. 'Farewell, princess, and good luck,' the knight said, as he was ready to face his fate.

'We shall meet soon enough Sir Slade… ' the princess said, while she was opening the trap door.

The door had been destroyed and soon a group of creatures entered the house. Prudence could only hear what was happening, the cries were horrible, the blood was spilling, she could only think of negative thoughts as she was running away.

Soon she would hear one last blow and a horrifying cry of agony from the knight. Was he dead? Had she failed to protect the man who had protected her since her birth? She could not help but feel bad; no matter, she had to honour the will of Sir Slade and save herself.

'Forgive me!' the princess cried out in tears, as she was running.

Time had elapsed since the attack in the house; the princess was out of breath and still inside of the tunnel. She could not see what was in front of her and her feet were hurting. She then decided to take a short break, however, she was not alone in the tunnels, as she would soon realize.

A horde of goblins were in pursuit; they were small and ugly looking with pale green skin and razor teeth that could rip out anything. Their hands possessed only three fingers with sharpened claws and their odour was abominable.

'Go that way! If we don't bring a dead body our boss will kill us!' ordered one of them as he was searching around. 'Damn these old tunnels! And stop eating would you? You are on duty!' complained the same creature.

'When he gets what he wants, I want to be the one to rip her skin with my teeth! Princess blood tastes good apparently!' another goblin said with enthusiasm.

Hidden, the princess was near them. She could feel them approaching, one noise and she would be located by these evil monsters. 'I need to leave fast…' Prudence murmured.

Shortly after, a goblin found a pile of bones covered in dust; the prints on the skeletons were inflicted by a powerful bite that ripped inside the skulls. It was as if a sledgehammer had slammed a person multiple times until they died.

'What is the meaning of all this rubbish?' the goblin said with vulgarity, as he was analysing the bones. The princess and the goblins were not the only ones in the vast and dark tunnels. Another creature was observing what was happening; with a predator's instinct it was slowly and without noise getting closer to the group of goblins, ready to devour them.

One of the goblins then took a map, wondering where they were and where the tunnels headed. With terror it realized their location. 'S… Sir!' panicked the goblin. 'We… we are! We are in…' It was so scared it could not formulate a phrase without trembling and stumbling with its words.

'What is it that you want, imbecile?' the leader asked furiously.

'We are… we are in the… ' stuttered the goblin in terror.

'Give me that!' The leader snatched the map out of the hands of the goblin, and punched him in the face. 'Could you not say we are in Tarantula's Lair?' the leader shouted in anger.

'Are… are you not scared sir?' the goblin demanded while stuttering.

'Only morons like you would believe in such idiotic stories! Tarantula is a myth! Now get on with your work before I kill you myself!' the leader shouted, after throwing the map in its worker's face.

'Si… Sir! Be… Behind you!' the goblin shouted, petrified.

'What is it now?' The leader turned around angrily.

It was the very last second of the goblin's life, as he saw an enormous spider with fangs three times bigger than a human. It was hairy around its legs and saliva was spilling from its mouth; its eyes were of a bloody red and its skin colour was of a black that was advantageous for camouflage in those tunnels.

It seemed as if it was the guardian of the tunnels and anything that met its path would end up as dinner. With incredible speed it ate the leader and swallowed its body in one sip. All the goblins panicked and were trying to run for their lives. However, a spider is commonly known for throwing webs and paralyzing its victims.

Prudence knew she would also end up as lunch for the monster. She had to run away now, as she was slower than the goblins and the spider. This was an opportunity for her to save herself and escape her pursuers.

She was unsure of the path she was taking but it did not matter;

the cries and the noises Tarantula was making, while ripping the skin of the goblins, convinced her to not look back. Blood splattering and agonised shouts echoed in the tunnels. There were no doubts that the spider liked to play with its victims before devouring them.

The princess kept running but quickly fell down and ripped her dress, injuring her knee. Fortunately it was not a deep wound and it did not prevent her from walking or running, but the smell of human blood was the spider's favourite and without knowing it, Prudence had become the new prey.

'I have to hurry!' the princess said, panicky and out of breath. She kept on running and finally saw the light of the woods. She was safe… or so she thought.

As she was crossing the last corridor of the tunnels, Tarantula was right behind her and was faster, so fast that it could easily grab the princess in a blink of an eye. Prudence ignored the spider's approach and kept running, thinking she was alone and safe, but at the very last second the spider wove a web and blocked the exit.

With terror, the princess shakily turned around. She grabbed her sword but her hands were trembling so much she could not keep a stable posture.

'What do I owe the pleasure of this meeting?' the spider asked quietly. 'Goblins are not the most enjoyable feast… but humans…' Tarantula seemed impatient to eat Prudence. 'Tell me child… before I remove the life from your corporal form… what is it that you were looking for here in my lair?' the spider gently demanded of Prudence.

'I… I… nothing… I,' Prudence could not formulate a phrase, she was paralysed in fear, words could not come into her mind.

'Nothing… that is rather an uncommon answer… nothing shall you get… ' the spider said, while approaching the princess. 'I shall calm my thirst for human blood with yours… after all, I did not come to you… you came to me,' the spider said sadistically, while touching the princess with its legs.

Tarantula then opened its large jaw but felt a new presence in its lair; someone else was here and it was rather preventing the spider from enjoying its meal. 'We cannot eat peacefully in this world!' Tarantula grunted. 'But later on I shall, after I have taken care of this fool!' as it was saying this, Tarantula trapped the princess in a web that prevented her from moving.

Prudence tried her best to move but it seemed futile. The web was so strongly glued to her that she could barely feel her own skin.

'I cannot end this way... no, my kingdom needs me!' the princess kept on muttering, while trying to find a way of escaping the infernal trap.

It was hopeless, nothing worked, her legs were too stuck in the wall and her arms heavily stuck with the web. Desperately, she looked down and thought of imminent death. She could not find a way and the sword was unreachable, if only she had something that could rip the web off.

She then remembered her family necklace; it was a tiny sword replica, with a dragon surrounding it. The edge of the sword and the dragon's wing were sharp. With haste she took it out with her teeth and started moving up and down to cut the web. If it could help her move her right arm, she would be able to reach her sword and get out.

Meanwhile in the tunnels, Tarantula was observing its new victim. The spider wanted to get back to its formal meal. With growing impatience it quickly approached its new prey.

A man was standing with a stick in his left hand. He was old and had a long beaked nose with long sideburns but no beard. He had long white hair that fell above his shoulders. The way he dressed was smart; he was wearing an English gentleman's outfit with a hat and a black cape. Everything he wore was black as the night, only his shirt was white. His eyes were grey and his smile was horrible. He looked like a demon incarnate. But with an old appearance, he did not stand high in the spider's esteem, and seemed to be a much easier target than the princess was.

'Old fool – I shall kill you fast!' claimed the spider, as it approached the old man.

'You shall not, as I have an absolute advantage, you stupid creature,' the man said arrogantly.

'Fool! You dare enter my lair and threaten me? Your carcass will rot in this very wall!' the spider snarled, as it jumped to devour the man.

'Rather pathetic,' the man chuckled, as it paralyzed the spider with magic. 'You creatures think with your hunger and not your brains…' The man took a knife out of his pocket and approached the paralyzed spider. 'Now now, allow me the pleasure of introducing myself. I am Reaper. Surely you have heard of me, since I love to rip apart anything that dares resist me.'

The spider tried to move but its efforts were in vain. The magic the old man used was very strong and awfully painful.

'Magic is forbidden! You shall pay with your life once the heads catch you!'

'The heads are hypocrites… ' the man laughed. 'Even they make use of magic, yet forbid anyone else from using it.'

'What is it – that you want?' demanded the spider, in pain.

'A young woman made her way here, where is she? Speak fast and I will terminate your existence now, refuse to speak and I will take great pleasure in watching you empty yourself of blood.' The man laughed, as he was licking the point of the knife.

'She is mine to devour… I do not share – you shall rot in hell,' the spider grunted in pain.

'Oh I do know of a couple of tricks that would indeed make you beg for death.' The man chuckled. 'Like this one for instance… ' He clicked his finger and his paralysis attack changed into a sort of torturing magic. 'Aha! Suffering is just the most pleasant spectacle!' the man laughed in a Machiavellian manner.

The princess could hear the cries of the spider. She managed to get a hold on her sword and ripped the web that trapped her. Once done, she could only think of escaping and cut out the wall of web that

Tarantula had woven earlier. The light of the woods was a wonderful sight; she only had to step outside and she would be out of this tunnel. However, hearing the cries of Tarantula pained her. How could she walk away from this? She had to help; it was the noblest thing to do. After all, she was the one who had entered Tarantula's lair. Armed with her sword in her hand, she ran to help the creature.

The spider was lying on the ground; it was badly injured and sad to look at. Prudence was hiding behind a wall that gave her a good view of what was happening. She could see the man... he seemed unusually familiar. She wondered where she had seen his face, but she had no time for questions. She seized her sword firmly and raised it to prepare for an attack.

The man then grabbed his knife and advanced toward the injured and defenceless spider.

'It was indeed good entertainment to witness your pain, however – I am a busy man. It is OK, I will make sure you do not suffer much when I finish where I began.' As the man was about to stab the spider, Prudence left her hiding place and jumped out in front of the man.

'I forbid you to commit such an act!' the princess yelled.

'Oh – such a pleasant surprise, it is the princess. You do not know how much it saves my time not having to look for you and bring you to him,' the man said with a gentle manner, he then put away his knife and raised his hand.

He was trying to attack Prudence the same way he had the spider, but something was off. He could not for some reason use magic on the princess. The spider then managed to get back on its feet and grabbed Prudence, before hasting to the exit of the tunnel. With an incredible speed, the spider brought Prudence to the woods.

'I cannot go any further, my wounds need healing...' the spider groaned in pain. 'I shall always remember your act of kindness... I will do my best to slow down the demon... run, run princess!' The spider snarled.

Prudence did not wait long; she was worried about the spider but nevertheless she had to move on. She may be safe from the magic of the man, but she was still vulnerable as he was not the only one after her.

The woods were dark and the rain made Prudence slip more than once. She had no idea where to head towards. The trees were grey, the grass slippery and dark green, she could barely distinguish a flower. Prudence had a hard time just moving within the woods but she managed to find a safe place to take a break.

She was out of breath, exhausted, and her beautiful white dress was ruined; it was all wet, grey and covered in dirt. She was shivering, as she had nothing warmer on her. The princess was out of strength but mostly out of courage, she did not know how long she could endure this.

Suddenly, as she was resting near a tree, something spoke. 'Hello dear – what gives me the pleasure of meeting the Princess of Heartsas?' a kind voice said.

Prudence looked around but she saw nothing, she was frightened and kept shivering.

'You do not have to fear me, I wish you no harm,' the voice said.

'Do show yourself!' Prudence shouted, terrified.

'Oh but I am right here, your hands are so cold and it pains me to see you in this state,' the tree said in a kind way.

Prudence jumped, surprised. She knew magic and fantasy reigned in her world, yet she had never met anything like a talking tree. It was not astounding; she may have grown up on Vita but she did not know anything about the outside world. A princess was not allowed to get away from her castle for fear of abduction or a coup d'état. It was a hard task to live in one place and never see the outside life. The only way she could have seen the outside world was when she was reading the books of adventurers and imagining their journeys.

'What… what are you?' the princess demanded nervously.

'Aha, I am a tree my dear. But you can guess it. My name is Fraisier,' the tree said kindly.

'How is… but… I do not have time for that… I am obliged to run and find refuge somewhere,' Prudence muttered to herself.

She then realized she had been rude to Fraisier, who had politely introduced himself. After blushing in embarrassment she bowed and presented herself.

'But I know who you are princess. You do not need an introduction, we creatures of the forest know what is happening… you are in deep danger,' the tree said kindly yet darkly.

'I am aware of that… Sir Slade – he… ' Prudence went silent for a short time. 'I have been informed of what is happening, but I do not know where to go.' The princess clenched her fist.

'We cannot hide you here in the woods forever.' Fraisier paused. 'However, we will make way to a place no living creature outside this forest knows of. But I have to warn you… ' The tree took a dark tone. 'This path is dangerous. We do not know of what is hidden over there, no human has managed to come back from it, thus it is secret,' Fraisier said while spreading its branches.

'Aw stop worrying the lady, ye imbecile! A princess is not like those idiotic adventurous people! Take it from me m'lady; you ought to do just fine by yourself! Blimey! Fraisier talks rubbish!' Another tree proclaimed this much comforting speech.

As they were discussing, the trees had felt someone's presence nearby and they knew it was the dangerous man. He was approaching with good care, as if he knew the forest was alive. The trees then gathered their branches together and formed a circle around the princess.

'We shall open the secret path… remember to be careful princess,' Fraisier said, concerned.

'I will be fine; it has been my pleasure to have made your acquaintance,' the princess bowed in respect.

The trees formed a magical portal which glowed a magnificent yellow; it was so bright and so shiny that it could not go unseen. Prudence suspected the evil man to discover her whereabouts. Fortunately for her, the trees had made sure they prevented the light of their magic from being seen by using their branches. 'Good luck, Princess!' a tree said, as they finished creating the portal.

Prudence looked down at the portal; she was frightened about crossing it. Where would it lead? Would she be able to breathe? Then she realized she could not afford to think of the risks; in Vita, she was already in danger.

'Here I come…'

Prudence took a deep breath before jumping inside the portal.

It was all yellow inside, stars were shining around her and it was so bright that the light was blinding her. She could only feel the wind that was dragging her down. It was as if she had jumped off the top of her castle. Incredibly fast and frightening, she could not help herself but to scream throughout her descent. She then felt a faint pain and lost consciousness: she had crashed on the ground.

Chapter Two

A Strange Day

London is known around the world for being a beautiful and rich city. It is the place where a lot of young spirits want to learn and aim far in life. It is also the city where a normal boy lives. Ryan was eighteen years old; he was around 5 feet 8 and quite skinny. He had blonde hair with a fringe that covered half of his face; his eyes were so obscure people could not guess their colour, but they were mainly brown. He was half Mauritian and half English, which gave him a natural surfer's tan; it was more than enough to make the girls fall for him. He had a friendly smile and a cute appearance. Ryan liked to look classy or casual; he would rarely wear things like a hood or tight jeans. His tastes were quite old school and he preferred shirts and black pants or casual jeans. He tended to smile whatever the circumstances.

He was appreciated by many and hated by a few; he was a boy who had a lot that others desired. He never seemed to know what it was; he was just being himself. He was not rich and he struggled a lot to save money to buy himself something, so he knew it had nothing to do with his financial status. Ryan was focused when it came to honour and self esteem; everything he did or said had to be meaningful and honourable.

A lot of his friends thought it had to do with his French background, since he had grown up there. Or perhaps it was his Belgium heritance, since he was born in Ixelles during a family trip. Everyone looked at him as a foreigner, yet Ryan was English by his mother's side, and he always looked at himself as being part of the world instead of a country. He believed that the world was home, no matter the place or the land.

Deep inside Ryan always wondered if he belonged in the life he had or if he was meant for something else. At some point in his life, he used to sleep at night thinking something would happen, as if a magical event would bring him to another world.

But foolish he was not, he knew that there was no way he'd ever end up in another world, or live the life of a knight. No, he had to get back to his reality, where he was just a teenager wanting to join the police. That was all he had in mind, spending his life protecting the weak and righting the wrong.

December 13th 2010 – that day was about to change many things in the destiny of the young man. It all started in a normal way, or rather a cold and snowy day in London. Children were playing with the snow, having snowball battles or making snowmen. It was a joyful atmosphere, since snow is rare and only happens to fall at this time of the year.

Ryan was at his home packing up his bag and preparing for what he was about to do that day. 'Got to grab my bottle of water, then take the train…' he muttered while planning his day. 'Got the keys…' he checked his pocket. 'Yep! Err…' he then took his wallet out of his pocket and maniacally checked everything was there. 'Good, I haven't forgotten anything,' he kept on muttering to himself. He then grabbed his jacket and left his house, checking if he had closed the door by pushing it twice. Once happy; he left toward the town where he would get the train.

The town was shining with all the lights and the decorations of Christmas. The young man stared at the shop windows as if they surprised him.

'Is the spirit of Christmas really back?' he mumbled to himself for some reason.

During his walk to the station, he felt in a strangely pleasant mood. Was it the lights of the shops, or the music he was listening to that made him happy? Ryan did not know, the only thing he was certain of was that he would have a good day. At least that was what his heart was telling him.

The young man took the first train to Sutton. Once in Sutton, Ryan received a message. He took his phone out.

"Classes dismissed for today, we apologize for the inconvenience but due to the weather, a lot of teachers cannot make it for today's lessons. The library will however be open for revision and coursework."

The young man was annoyed. He groaned in exasperation after reading the message. It was not because he loved university; no, it was the annoyance of taking the train back, which was a half an hour journey.

'Damn it!' Ryan grunted, after kicking a pile of snow. 'I thought it'd be a good day!' he sighed in disappointment.

For some reason he did not feel like going back home. He decided to leave the station and visit the town he was in.

The shops were all lit up surprisingly well; the products in sales were all displayed at the shop windows, whether it was a video game or a clothing shop. They all had the perfect presentation that pushed people to get in and buy something. "For someone special" to "A day like no other", the shops all had their banners and their own way of getting the attention of the people.

Ryan was used to looking at the shop windows and wondered with whom he could share Christmas Day when it came to love, and then a thought struck his mind. He gently yet sadly smiled and looked down on his feet. He felt sad because he wondered if love was meant for him. He'd never had a girlfriend, and it was not because he was shy; on the contrary, he was quite relaxed when it came to speaking to women. He then looked up and glared at the window before leaving the shop centre.

'I'm a fool, seriously – I need to stop thinking about it…' Ryan laughed wryly to himself.

As he walked toward the train station, Ryan felt as if he was being followed. It was strange, was it a robber?

Instead of looking behind his back, he started to slow down as if he was waiting for his follower to show up.

'So, courageous, or is it ignorance… ' a voice said out of nowhere. It was a woman's voice.

'Huh… who's that?' Ryan asked, after he turned around.

The woman wore a hood. Ryan could not see her face, she seemed young and he could only see her beautiful lips. They were of a light red and her skin was of a pale white. Ryan thought she was made of snow because her skin was so radiant. He could not see her eyes or her hair, but she seemed beautiful. Who was she? And what did she want?

'Who are you? And what the hell are you on about?' Ryan politely yet abruptly demanded.

'You shall soon enough understand. There is a lot to discover… your journey will soon begin; I shall witness your very accomplishments and failures,' said the woman. 'Well… until we meet again. I bid you farewell.'

As she said that, she disappeared. It was as if she had used magic, but magic did not exist. Ryan thought it was the fruit of his imagination playing tricks.

'What a weirdo,' he mumbled to himself, as he headed out to the train station. 'That was just weird… ' he kept mumbling.

'Are ye all right boy?' an old man offered his hand.

Ryan did not understand how he had ended up on the ground. When did he fall down?

'It is horribly easy to fall down. Hope you're doing all right? Blimey, snow! Yesterday got me self into an unfortunate accident. Felt my butt really cold.' The old man chuckled and laughed in reminiscence.

'Tell me about it, I feel like I have been sprayed with cold water,' Ryan said, as he was shaking down the snow which was inside his clothes. 'The thing is, I don't even remember falling down, what the hell is wrong with me today?' Ryan shook his head dazed. 'Did you happen to see that woman with the hood? She may have been the one who pushed me, that… ' Ryan abstained himself from cursing the woman.

'Nah did not see anyone here. Just saw you from the bus stop, you slipped – and you were not moving for a while. You got me worried, so I came to check up on you,' the old man said.

'Oh I see. Well erm, cheers! It must have been my imagination… ' Ryan said gratefully. He then started to check his pockets to see if everything was there. 'All right got everything… ' he said reassured.

He then looked at the time on his phone and decided to go back home.

Chapter Three
An Unexpected Encounter

The young man reached the station, and the train had arrived. After a short day which drastically changed from good to bizarre, Ryan was finally home. The young man was lying on his bed and still thinking about what he thought he had seen. Who was that woman? And what did she mean? Ryan kept repeating to himself that it was tiredness that may have caused him to hallucinate and imagine things.

However, he just could not believe it was tiredness or imagination. It happened, he knew it had. 'Arg! Get out of my head!' he groaned, annoyed. He then grabbed a tiny ball and bounced it on the wall. 'I know!' he said loudly. 'I'll just tell Nash when he's back!'

Ryan's parents were in Paris for the whole month because they had business meetings to attend, it was only him and his brother for Christmas. The door then opened and slammed; his brother was back from the university.

Nash was about the same height as Ryan, only slightly taller and muscular. He was twenty one years old and quite a lone wolf. He had black hair and brown eyes, and an Italian tan which made a lot of women fall for his charm, but not as much as Ryan. He was handsome and did not seem to know how to act around women, which was quite the opposite of his younger brother. Always on his own, Nash was the type of person that did not waste his time or efforts socializing with the people he met. The only time he did bother working on relationships with others was when he found a girl interesting.

Ryan and his brother were really far from understanding each other; people often described them as rivals. As his big brother went upstairs to the bedroom, Ryan jumped out of his bed and went straight away to tell him what had happened.

'And then that woman disappeared! It was just weird! I swear I didn't fall,' he said excitedly. 'Come on Nash, don't tell me that doesn't make you want to say something?' Ryan impatiently waited for an answer from Nash.

'And you want me to say what?' Nash said arrogantly, like he did not care.

'Well well, here is Mr I Don't Care About Other People's Problems. Guess what, when it's you I listen so suck it up and hear me out would you?' Ryan responded. 'That woman said some stuff, the way she spoke, it wasn't rude at all… just eloquent. And you know people don't talk in such a manner.' Ryan kept on talking about the woman.

'Well, Mr I Talk A Lot… what did she say?' Nash asked while taking a glass of water. 'You know what, save it for later. Got to go to the bank and then I have to go to buy some things. Do you want anything? Like chocolate?' he asked Ryan in a polite tone.

'No, I'm going to the town in a bit; I'm meeting up with Mia. I can get what I want there… '

'Okay then, suit yourself… ' Nash said, as he took his car keys.

Ryan grabbed his jacket and decided to go out for a while before meeting up with his friend. It was cold outside and snow was falling from the sky; a white Christmas was to be expected this year.

Of course, this kind of weather could really end up as a nuisance; the traffic was slower and people could not risk running or they would end up falling. It was pretty much the kind of weather that would convince anyone to stay indoors. Ryan did not want to admit it but he had no interest in meeting up with his friend. All he cared about was that mystery woman who would not leave his mind, even if he had only seen half of her face.

The town was small; it was really easy for him to go around it in thirty minutes without missing out anything. After making a tour, he did not find the mystery woman.

Disappointed, he then sat down for a while on a bench where he was waiting for his friend. As he was looking down, he started to laugh wryly.

'I'm such a fool,' he sighed ironically.

'There you are!' a nice and cute voice came out of nowhere. Ryan looked to his left and saw his friend.

'Hello Mia!'

Mia was quite short but of average height for women. She was about 5 feet tall, skinny with a cute Japanese face. She had long hair that was slightly orange, and a fringe that covered her forehead. Her accent was quite funny but at the same time adorable. Ryan was really fond of her and considered her his best girlfriend.

She was dressed in a casual way, with tight jeans and medium heel boots. She wore a nice dark magenta coat and a scarf that matched.

'You do realize you're late,' Ryan said with a smile.

'Wow, doesn't seem to bother you. And I am not late for your information,' the girl replied joyfully.

'Aha, so what are you so joyful about?' Ryan asked curiously. 'Is it because you get the chance to hang out with a stunning bloke like me?'

'Oh yeah, it's a privilege! Wow, I will never get a chance of meeting someone that cute!' Mia replied sarcastically.

'Oh I know, I know – anyway, enough with how cute I am. I mean yes, it's a fact, but I've something big to tell you. I saw a woman today… '

'Wow… so did I,' the girl chuckled with a mocking tone.

'No but that's not the point, I mean of course you did. But that woman disappeared right in front of me! She said something about my destiny being about to start and all kind of stuff.' Ryan seemed pretty serious as he persisted with how strange it was. 'Then apparently I fell down, but I don't even remember falling down.' He kept on going with the story.

'Look honey, you may have hit your head hard when you fell down,' Mia replied, not convinced by what her friend was saying.

'Well I didn't hit it that hard,' Ryan scoffed, annoyed. 'Let's go do something; staying on this bench makes me feel old,' he added in a bored way.

The two friends decided to go around the town until they felt tired; all the shops were still open and looking at the products they were selling was quite interesting for a while. But it was just the usual articles, which were nothing fascinating. Mia then insisted on visiting a clothing shop, the worst nightmare for Ryan who could not care less how popular these jeans or these shirts were.

'Argh, do we really have to come here?' the young man grunted.

'Well duh, it's soon Christmas; I'm best showing you what you ought to buy me eh?' Mia laughed happily.

'I suppose, that is a fair statement.' Ryan nodded.

Mia had tried all sorts of dress; she was really difficult when it came to clothes. She would even make Ryan give a score out of ten. Finally, she found a dress that met her criteria, it was a princess gown. The gown was white with nice ribbons around the waist; it was undeniably the most beautiful dress in the whole shop.

'Don't I look like a princess?' Mia laughed joyfully, as she was posing in front of the mirror.

'Yes, you sure do… so, happy? Can we leave?' demanded Ryan.

'No, I cannot… I mean, this dress is so beautiful, if I leave it here some old hag is going to buy it before me. I have to get it!' The young girl did not wait long before getting money out of her wallet.

'There we go again, and then you're going to complain on how much you have spent at the end of the month,' Ryan sighed.

The young man was mesmerized, but at the same time scared by how women could act when in the presence of beautiful dresses or clothes. 'Women,' he scoffed.

As he looked around, he saw her, the woman he had seen earlier. She was standing right in the middle of the crowd; she was dressed in the same way and had the same smile on her face as before. Ryan tried to approach her but she was gone; she had disappeared again.

Mia had finished looking around and bought the beautiful gown she had found. The two friends had nothing else to do and decided to call it a day. Ryan walked the young lady home. Frustrated but at the same time curious, Ryan decided to go around the town once more before heading home – maybe the mysterious lady would make an appearance. Determined and hoping to see her again, he headed out to the shopping centre where she had appeared earlier.

There was nothing, only the same shops which were now closing. A lot of people were in a rush to leave the town, before the snow got any worse. It was starting to get dark outside, Ryan looked around the shops but found nothing, and it was time for him to go. The young man sighed in disappointment; a part inside of him strongly believed it had been the beginning of something. Feeling absurd, he went home, thinking how ridiculous he had been today. Maybe Mia was right, maybe he had fallen down and hit his head.

As he was on his way home, a light glowed around a footpath. It was of a bright yellow, and Ryan saw it but thought he had gone mad.

'What the heck? Now there are yellow lights in a footpath!' the young man scoffed, feeling completely laughable.

Tempted to walk away, he nevertheless decided to go on and check; after all, if it was his imagination then he would find nothing. He approached the dark footpath; the darkness made it hard to perceive anything and the snow was thick. Not seeing anything, he shook his head and laughed to himself. 'Guess I do need to sleep…' he said whilst turning around. To his surprise, someone was lying on the snowy ground; a young woman who coughed and groaned in pain. Without haste he went to the woman.

Ryan was captivated by the beauty of the young woman. He stared at her for a while, before offering his hand to help her to stand up on her feet. The girl was shaking with cold; she stood up but kept shivering.

With a noble gesture, the young man gave his jacket to the lady who was dressed in a rather unusual way. She wore a princess dress and her jewels seemed tremendously expensive. Her pendant, bracelets, earrings and the ring on her right index were made of diamonds.

Ryan looked at her and assumed that she was English. The way she looked made him immediately think of English women. He could have been wrong… maybe she was French, or from another country of Europe. No… actually, he was convinced that she was English. If she was not… then she was from another world. Because only English women looked the way she looked. Of course, Ryan never judged a woman's beauty because of her country or background. He always felt that each country in the world had their own unique touch that made every woman special. But this girl… she had this English look. Ryan just loved English women. They had a strange attractiveness and grace that made them unique to him. Perhaps that is why he deducted that the girl was English. It was mainly because of this gracious and mesmerizing beauty she had. It was just unique.

'Are you okay? What is your name?' Ryan demanded softly.

'I… I am fine… thank you for your kindness. Do you – do you not know of me?' the young woman asked to the young man.

Ryan heard her voice and she had a lovely and posh English accent. The young man then realized that he did not answer her question and shook his head.

'No… it is only the first time I have met you,' he replied. 'My name is Ryan, nice to meet you.'

'I am Prudence; it is a pleasure to make your acquaintance.' She bowed in respect.

'Woah… where are you from?' he asked, surprised of her noble manners.

'Heartsas, it is my kingdom, have you not heard of it?' she asked proudly.

'Erm, no… ' he answered confusedly.

The young man could not help himself but to stare at her eyes. She was so beautiful and it was rare to meet a woman with such hypnotizing eyes. The more he looked at her, the more he wanted to kiss her; it was as if she was compelling him to do so, just by standing in front of him.

Ryan then realized he was staring and tried to think of something to say.

'Where do you live? I can take you home if you desire… you know the streets are not safe at night, especially for young beauties like you. I can protect you.' Ryan chuckled nervously, convinced he had made a fool out of himself.

'My home is far from here… I do not wish to trouble you with it,' Prudence responded.

She could not stop looking around her and noticing how things were strange and different, and then she stared at Ryan's eyes. His eyes were of a profound darkness, the more she looked at them, the more she wanted to look deeper. His eyes were full of mysteries, she felt charmed at first but she looked down, her cheeks were getting red and her eyes were lost on the snowy ground. She hesitated to look at him again, her feelings were mixed up between desire and intimidation. She felt as if she wanted to look at his gorgeous face yet she was afraid how he would react.

'I live right by the street there… you don't have to say yes if you don't want to… but if you do live far and… well it's dark… I uh… I could take you in for tonight… ' Ryan said, while struggling with his words. 'I know it's completely absurd for me to ask since we just met, but… ' he kept on struggling with his words.

She did not know of him and was scared, but, somehow, when she looked at him and saw how gracious he was, she just wanted to trust him. It was an odd feeling, she could not explain it and the more she thought of it, the more confused she ended up. She was silent for a while, then she saw Ryan looking around and scratching the back of his head. He seemed nervous and his cheeks were getting red. Was he embarrassed? Did she say something that made him look away and bite his lips? She then realized that she had not said anything, thus the reason of his nervous posture.

'I thank you… let us be on our way, the snow is intensifying.' Prudence bowed.

'You don't need to bow you know. It's completely natural to take you in when it's so cold and… ' Ryan saw the blood on Prudence's knee. 'Oh my God you're bleeding… what happened?' he gasped.

'I have been in an unfortunate accident.' She looked away and tried to cover up her wound. 'Could we go now? I do not mean to be rude or to intrude on your home. But I am indeed cold… ' she said, as if she was trying to evade the subject.

'Sure, I'm sorry for making you wait and talk in this kind of weather… ' he laughed nervously. 'Come on; let us be on our way then,' Ryan said while guiding her to his house.

They had crossed two roads and marched for about two minutes; Prudence kept on looking around, she had never seen houses treated with such great care. All of them were polished and beautiful; it seemed that everyone in this village were rich.

She then heard a horrible noise, it was so loud and getting closer, she could barely hear what Ryan was saying. Then she was flashed by a bright and intense light that was coming from nowhere, with fright she jumped on Ryan and held his arm tightly. It was a red monster, a dragon which looked different to its kind, it could light up from the inside, and people that had been devoured were visible in two different places of its body.

'What… what is wrong Prudence?' Ryan demanded of the lady, as he was looking around.

'Here! It has devoured those people!' she pointed out toward the monster. 'It is the first time I have met one of them! Is it a dragon? Why do we not run? Will it come after us?' she kept asking, frightened.

'Erm… well we do not need to run since it won't come after us. I mean unless we pay the bus driver then sure… he might take us somewhere.' Ryan laughed with amusement.

'Pardon me? Where would it take us?' Prudence demanded, puzzled.

'Nevermind, let's just get inside and we will talk about it later… I'm surprised you have never seen a bus before.' Ryan laughed.

'I hope I did not make a fool out of myself.'

Prudence kept looking around; she could see many buses that were smaller and asleep, all in front of different houses and of different shapes. She was surprised that humans would dare adopt monsters and use them as transport.

She could see Ryan smiling. She did not understand why; she then looked down and realized that her hand was firmly holding Ryan's. She was embarrassed but it felt surprisingly good. It was the first time she had held someone else's hand while walking.

'Here we are… ' Ryan dropped Prudence's hand gently, before taking his keys out of his pocket. 'The car is not here, that means he's not back,' Ryan muttered, as he was opening the door.

'I'm sorry, but who is not here? And what is a car?' the princess politely asked.

'Do not worry about that. Erm, let's just say that we will have to keep a low profile, it is convenient that my brother is not here. Anyway, welcome to my humble house,' the young man said, while gently pushing the front door.

It was a beautiful house, everything was well in order and the furniture was in such a great state. A nice perfume resided in the house and it was warm without the chimney being lit up. She was charmed by the beauty of it.

'I can't hide you like you are a pet and I just brought you home… that won't work,' the young man said. 'Oh yeah, please sit down… ' Ryan offered the princess to sit on the sofa.

The young man then left to a room that was brighter and different from the living room. When he returned, he had a small bottle, with a small box upon which was written *bandages* and a sort of tissue in his hands.

'It is a nice home you possess… are you from a noble family?' Prudence asked, as she sat down.

'Aha… no, it's called having a job and working hard.' Ryan laughed. 'It's my parents' property; they are working really hard to feed me and my brother while paying for the house,' Ryan said in a proud way. He lifted up Prudence's hurt leg. The young man's facial expression turned to surprise after seeing how long Prudence's legs were. She had long feet and long legs for a woman. 'This is going to sting a bit… ' he gently warned her before disinfecting the wound.

'You are quite handy… did your mother teach you how to be so gentle with women?' the princess asked happily.

'No, that is called going to college and learning first aid. To tell you the truth, I thought I'd wasted my time that day.' Ryan laughed, as he was applying a bandage.

Chapter Four
The First Bond

While the two individuals were getting along magically well, in Vita darkness had risen up. The weather was of a dark grey and the rain kept falling from the sky.

Two people wearing hoods were at the top of Heartsas Castle. One of them was wearing a blood red hood with a robe. The other, had dark armour and a cape along with his hood to hide his face. They were staring at the rainy sky and the scenery it was offering. A familiar face then appeared out of nowhere, it was the old man from the tunnels.

'Were you successful in your mission?' The red hooded person demanded.

'I have failed in finding her. However, I have an idea of where she might be,' the old man responded.

'You have failed, my Lord… bow in presence of him you ingrate!' the red hooded said in a hateful tone.

'You did not hear me well, my Lord… I do know of where she could be hiding. I have searched all of Heartsas Kingdom, yet I have not managed to find her. This has only one meaning… ' the old man explained himself.

'She is no more in Heartsas. It does not matter, she will come back… I shall make sure of it. After all, Reaper… she has set foot on a world she barely knows. Vita may be her home… it is still a dangerous world for a princess,' the dark armoured man said.

'My Lord… I shall kill her for you.' Reaper bowed.

'That shall not be our priority. With her gone, I can gather my army… everyone will believe in the princess's death since she is no more in Heartsas. This is an opportunity and when the time comes… she shall bring to me what I desire… ' the armoured individual said in an evil tone.

'We cannot tolerate another of your failures… should you fail, it will be an imminent death,' the red hooded man said grimly.

'I do understand – worry not, I will not fail you again.'

The old man disappeared again after those words; he was clearly aware of how much he had to lose.

'Can he be trusted?' the red hooded individual demanded.

'Do not worry; he is but a mere pawn in my vision.' The dark armoured man paused. 'One of many I have… he shall be useful for a short period.' He laughed in a sinister way.

'I have taken the liberty of selecting two new recruits… I shall warn you my Lord, they are not intelligent creatures. They only believe in bloodshed.'

The red hooded individual clicked his fingers and two monsters dressed in a rather unusual way made their appearances. They were hideous; one of them was taller than a common human being, while the other one was short. They wore leather clothes. Their pants made them look like eighties rock stars and so did their hair. They were similar to goblins apart from their corpulence and their skin colours, which were of a dark brown.

'You called boss?' the bigger one said.

'We are the most dangerous killers of all Vita!' the short one claimed.

'I have a request for the two of you – I need you to find the Princess of Heartsas and kill her. Then bring her body to me, or what is left of it. Succeed and you shall be amply rewarded. Fail… and your heads will be the ones to drop,' the armoured man said.

The two brothers nodded their heads, unafraid of the warnings, they seemed blindly over confident with their skills.

'Where should we look for her my Lord?' the small one asked.

'London…' the dark armoured man said darkly.

'London? What is London? Is it a creature?' the tall one asked in a confused way.

'Turax! You are the disgrace of this family!' the small one snapped. 'London must be a river!'

'Surrounded by imbeciles...' the red hooded individual sighed.

'London is a world beyond Vita... or precisely, a city,' the dark armoured man said.

'Allow me to accompany them.' The voice of a woman was heard.

'Cheryl...' the dark armoured individual said quietly.

Cheryl was mesmerizing; she had dark red hair that was so well coifed and fell extraordinarily well above her shoulders. She had unnatural glowing yellow eyes. Her skin was of a pale white, and something else was strange with her: she had a wolf's tail.

'She is so pretty!' Turax chuckled, as he was dribbling.

'Ugh... out of my sight,' Cheryl grunted.

'Why would you have an interest in venturing in London?' the red hooded person demanded.

'Because I live to serve you, my Lord,' she replied.

'You are a Humolf!' the red hooded individual snapped. 'You cannot be trusted!'

'Indeed... you shall accompany these two imbeciles.'

'But, my Lord...'

'I work alone.' Cheryl said quietly. 'Lone wolf, I am.'

'Not this time... Wolf,' the dark armoured man said.

'Feel privileged, the emperor has acknowledged your request... Wolf,' the red hooded person scoffed.

'Bring me the head of the princess, and you shall be fully rewarded.'

The dark armoured man then opened a portal with a magical stone. It led to London and had a clear image of the city. 'Once you find her...' he paused. 'Use the fairy dust to trap her in another dimension... that way magic will not be exposed.'

'How do I make it back?' Cheryl asked.

'Use this stone. There is one from Heartsas to London, and

another one from London to Vita… ' the dark armoured man presented a stone. 'I have to warn you… should you lose it, and the journey back will be impossible for you. So be careful… it takes years and years to forge a teleporting stone.' He threw the stone to Cheryl, who caught it easily.

'Noted… ' she said after looking at the stone.

Cheryl then took a sort of small sack and slipped it inside her pocket. She then bowed and jumped inside the portal, accompanied by the two hideous monsters.

'She is a wolf… she should not be trusted.'

'I am aware of it,' the dark armoured man answered. 'But she shall bring the princess's head to us… I am fairly convinced on that,' he said darkly. 'After all… she has revenge to take on the royal family… '

Meanwhile in London, Ryan and the princess were both talking a lot to each other. Prudence was evasive when Ryan asked her questions about her origins and where she came from. But Ryan was quite smart; he somehow played with her mind to get answers he wanted to hear.

She was hypnotised by his charm and found it hard to hide from him. Why did her eyes want to look at him so badly? Why did she want him to look at her? It was so confusing. His voice was echoing inside her head, everything he said made her heart beat faster. What was the meaning of it? She tried her best to avoid eye contact, but she could not. It was hard to resist his gorgeous face and those mysterious eyes.

'You were running – then you fell down, that explains the bleeding on your knee,' Ryan said calmly. 'I want to protect you… ' he claimed.

'Why? Why do you wish to know about what has happened to me? And why do you wish to protect me? You do not know of me… ' Prudence asked confusedly.

'I… ' Ryan was about to answer, when the door opened and Nash made an entrance.

'Who is he?'

Nash looked at Prudence and dropped the plastic bags on the floor. Prudence did not understand why he was staring at her. He was a handsome man and his face was well shaped. His eyes were light brown and his smile was kind. His dark hair was neatly coifed and he was tanned. But she did not look at him the same way she was looking at Ryan. Instead, she could only focus on how Ryan was feeling and how she could get his attention.

'Hey I'm Nash Snowangel, nice to meet you.'

'Prudence Fulgura, it is a pleasure to meet you.' She bowed.

'The pleasure is mine.'

'Yeah yeah… do you mind?' Ryan spoke abruptly. 'We were having a conversation, so if you have nothing better to do… how about you go and take a nap?' he said.

'What happened to your knee? Are you hurt?' Nash demanded to Prudence, while ignoring Ryan.

'This is what I'm trying to find out, so… ' Ryan clicked his tongue. 'Off you go.'

'I apologize, it is an honour to meet you but I feel tired… ' Prudence said calmly.

'I'll let you sleep in my room, I'm used to the couch after the numerous times I've slept on it,' Ryan said with a persistent tone, as he glared at Nash.

'It was nice to meet you Prudence,' Nash chuckled.

'The pleasure was all but mine… ' Prudence replied with courtesy.

Ryan was annoyed by his brother, he did not say it but it was clearly visible from the way he was suddenly acting. He was deep in his thoughts as he was climbing up the stairs. Prudence abstained herself from saying anything as she saw how upset he was. Ryan then opened a door; he did not say a word to Prudence and just showed her to his room. He went inside and lay on his bed.

'Do come in,' Ryan said to Prudence, as she was standing besides the door.

The princess entered the bedroom of the young man. It was a nice room and everything was tidied apart from the desk, which had a lot of papers and other items on it. Prudence could not help but notice that different books in plastic covers were nicely arranged in a pile.

'Do you like reading?' Prudence asked, as she kept on looking around to objects she never saw before.

'Me? Reading?' Ryan scoffed. 'No way would that happen… I spend most of my time drawing and writing.' He went quiet for a short time. 'Hey listen… ' he paused, trying to find the right words to say. 'I'm sorry for acting so weird earlier… I just don't like it when my brother comes in and assumes that my friends are his friends,' he said apologetically.

'I accept your apology, although it's unnecessary. I do not know the history between you and your brother; therefore it is not my place to take sides,' Prudence said in an eloquent manner. 'It is such an extraordinary room you have. All the books, and what is this dark mirror's utility?' she asked, mesmerized by everything around her.

'The dark mirror… oh you mean the TV?' Ryan chuckled. 'What world are you from? I love the good manners you have.' He paused. 'But not seeing a TV, confusing my games and DVDs with books and now the TV for a mirror?'

Ryan was surely lost on where Prudence had grown up. He did not understand her lack of knowledge in things of the era.

'I – well it is hard to explain… ' she looked down, embarrassed.

Ryan had to break Prudence's secret; she was hiding something that intrigued him. He took the TV remote controller and switched on the TV. A romantic film was playing. Prudence was so surprised and shocked that she fell on the floor.

'Are you all right?' Ryan asked her, while offering his hand to help her to get up.

'What… what is the meaning of this? Why – why did you trap those people inside your mirror? Are… are you a warlock?' She jumped out, frightened.

'Sorry?' Ryan asked feeling dazed. 'Prudence, I think you play too many video games. Honestly, if you call me a warlock for switching on a TV, then everyone is a warlock.' He laughed nervously.

'How did you do this magic?' she asked, terrified.

'I just used the TV remote controller.' Ryan laughed. 'By the way… what were you doing with a sword?' he asked curiously.

Prudence was lost. She did not know what to say to him. He was really talented at making people confess things about themselves in a short time. She tried to think of something, and then she saw a DVD titled *From Royalty to Democracy*. She made up a story that was partially true.

'I am from a royal family, which explains why I have not been outside much… ' She paused, trying to find a good story that added up. 'Since I was born, I was raised as a princess.' She looked down and bit her lips. 'Thus the reason, I have not ever seen a "TV".' She swallowed. 'And for the sword… it is a family tradition to wield one.'

'OK… fair enough,' Ryan said with a confused tone. 'That explains the noble manners I suppose.' Ryan then opened his wardrobe, and gave the princess warm clothes. 'You'll still look nice even wearing men's clothes. They'll keep you warm,' he offered kindly.

'Thank you Ryan – but may I ask you why you are being so gentle to me?' Prudence asked, puzzled by Ryan's gentleness.

'Do I need a reason to help someone?' he asked. 'You are kind, fragile and you do not strike me as someone who wishes me harm. This is the reason why I put my trust in you.'

'You are the same as me… we are both naive… ' she muttered to herself.

'OK, I'll let you change your clothes, it must be cold and tiring to wear that dress all day. Call me when you are ready. I'll be downstairs getting us something to drink and to eat,' he said before he left his room.

A short time had elapsed; Prudence changed her clothes into what Ryan had given her. She was wearing a comfortable and warm navy blue sweater and blue pants. The pants were too big for her, but she had nothing else to wear. The clothes' textures were really nice; she spent most of her time touching the sweater just to feel the quality of it. She was relieved to see that it was not fur. Prudence loved animals and she could never understand why people were being so cruel to them. The smell of Ryan remained present; not that he smelled bad, on the contrary, it was a nice perfume and it made her think of him. It felt rather nice and for Prudence it was the very first bond she had made outside of her kingdom.

Someone knocked gently on the bedroom door; Prudence turned around and heard the voice of Ryan. 'Can I come in?' he asked indistinctly.

'Yes you may.'

'I was right; you do look nice in my clothes.' Ryan chuckled, while opening the door. 'I must say, you are beautiful.'

'Thank you very much. It is always a pleasant thing to hear.' She smiled.

'I uh… I brought us some food and drinks, crisps, and some chocolates.'

Ryan entered the room while making sure he closed the door behind him.

'Crisps? Chocolates? What are those?' Prudence asked, at a complete loss.

'Aha – you will find out soon enough,' Ryan laughed. 'I warn you though; chocolate is my favourite food so I'm really attached to my dear chocolates. However, because you are such an attractive goddess, I will make an exception and share for this time,' he said, with a smile that made Prudence feel comfortable.

For about two hours, the two friends spoke and shared a great time together. Prudence did not understand what it was that she felt, but whenever he smiled she wanted to smile too. And whenever he said her name, it made her feel warm inside. She was lost and confused about the feeling she was experiencing. Somehow he made her forget about her problems. It was strange and unrealistic.

How could someone she had met a couple of hours ago, make her feel that way? She did not know, but it did not matter. She loved the way she felt.

'Well, it's time to go to sleep, eh? I'll let you rest. Starting tomorrow you shall learn the way of London and how we rock and roll,' Ryan said, after getting back on his feet.

'Would you be kind enough to allow me to sleep on your bed?' Prudence demanded.

'Of course, where did you expect to sleep?' Ryan asked loudly. 'Come on, Your Majesty, what kind of man I would be if I made a woman sleep on the floor?' he chuckled with a friendly tone. 'Do not miss me much.' He laughed, as he was leaving.

The princess could barely believe her luck; she had found refuge where it was warm and where she was not bound with obligations. It was a place to call home, even in unfortunate circumstances. But above all, she had found someone with whom she shared a bond that kept on growing stronger by the minute.

Chapter Five
Revelation

A loud noise was heard, it was echoing in the room. Alarmed, Prudence opened her eyes and saw a glowing red light. There was a sort of strange symbol displayed on it. Ryan pushed the door gently and turned the sound off.

'Sorry about that,' he whispered. 'I'd forgotten that I programmed it for 7:00 am.'

'What is going on?' Prudence groaned. '7:00 am?'

'Sorry princess – looks like it's time to wake up,' Ryan chuckled, as he opened the curtains. 'Come on, we have a lot to do today,' he said with an enthusiastic tone.

Prudence did not understand what he meant. Ryan then clapped his hands. 'Chop chop!' he said loudly.

'Could you be kind enough to enlighten me please – what is it that you meant – when you said we have a lot to do?' she asked him, confused and with closing eyes.

'Wow, you sure look tired,' Ryan laughed. 'I meant that today we are off to London. I wanted you to meet a couple of friends of mine and we'll go to the arcades later on,' he replied. 'Bet you have never been to the arcades.'

She was even more lost. What was an arcade? She looked around for her dress but did not find it. Ryan then informed her that he put it in the washing machine. But what the heck was a washing machine? This world sure had a different type of magic.

The young man then gave her some clothes that looked nice.

'They are my mum's clothes – so be careful with those.' He chuckled. 'But don't worry, we'll go around and buy you some clothes for yourself. I saved up some money from my previous birthdays.'

'I thank you – but I feel uncomfortable taking advantage of you.' Prudence replied.

'Ah it's nothing,' Ryan said in a modest way. 'You're totally worth the trouble.'

Prudence was speechless at Ryan's tenderness. He was such a good person and so lovely. The young man then opened his wardrobe and took out a nice navy shirt and jeans.

'May I bathe before leaving?' Prudence asked Ryan. 'It is just that… yesterday, I have been suffering from the fatigue of my… erm… travel… and… '

'Oh, yes sure!'

'Where can I bathe?'

'Come downstairs, and I will show you… ' Ryan said, before leaving the room.

Prudence followed the young man downstairs. He then walked her to the kitchen where Nash was reading a journal, while drinking a cup of tea.

'Hello beautiful.' Nash chuckled, as he saw Prudence.

'Oh good day,' she replied.

'Yeah yeah… ' Ryan scoffed. 'There… ' he pointed to a door. 'Just call me if you need any help in using the bathroom.'

'Tut tut… Ryan, you are such a little pervert.' Nash laughed.

'Don't you have uni?' Ryan looked at Nash. 'I thought you had to work with your mates on a presentation?'

'Well yeah… '

'Aren't you late?'

'I can make an exception for once. You know, there is always a first time for everything, young man. Of course, I'm talking to a guy who always skips classes or arrives late.' Nash mocked his brother. 'By the way young lady, if Ryan wants to show off, remember that I am the one who bought the breakfast.' Nash then finished drinking his tea. 'Anyway… I will see you later on, darling.' Nash winked at Prudence.

Prudence looked down in embarrassment and pretended not to listen to the two brothers arguing. Nash left.

'Sorry about that… ' Ryan pushed the door of the bathroom. 'After you… '

Prudence entered the bathroom, and was met with a tremendous surprise. It did not have any boiler next to it… where was the water? All she could see were small knobs with a sort of round object hanging on the top.

'Ryan!' she called out to the young man.

'Yes?' he arrived in a matter of seconds.

'I do not know how to use your bath… ' Prudence whispered. 'I have always been given my bath by my female servants… '

'Erm… ' Ryan started to think. He then turned red and smiled in a strange way. 'I could… ' he paused and laughed nervously. 'I could help you take your bath if you wanted… '

Prudence would normally say no straightaway, but for some reason she gave it a thought. She then turned completely red and refused Ryan's offer. She wondered why she had even thought about it. She would never let a man see her naked if he was not her husband. The princess then asked him to give a quick explanation of the bathroom. Ryan looked down in disappointment, but laughed afterward. After ten minutes of explanation, the princess started to understand better how to use the bathroom. She demanded the young man to leave, before she got undressed and took her shower.

She opened the left knob, which was hot water, and then slightly the right knob, which was the cold water. Once well mixed, she lifted a small switch and water rained through the sort of round object. It was so good… so warm, and so pleasant.

After twenty minutes, she had finished to shower. She did not wait long before putting on the clothes Ryan had lent her. The princess then looked at herself in the mirror.

'I look different…' she said as she posed. 'Oh, nevermind.' The princess left the bathroom.

When she arrived in the living room, she could see the table was set up with different plates and goblets. '*Bon appétit!*' Ryan said, as he brought a long plate with bread, and a long transparent jug with yellow water inside of it.

'What is this water?' Prudence asked, as she saw the yellow mixture.

'Erm… orange juice?' Ryan replied. 'Have you never been given orange juice?'

Ryan poured some of the orange juice into her empty goblet.

'Try it, you'll see it is very nice.' He chuckled.

The princess gave it a go. Ryan was right; it was delicious and so refreshing. She poured more juice in her goblet and drank it all. Ryan glanced at her in a funny way.

'Wow, I never thought you'd love orange juice that much,' he said with amazement.

A good hour had passed. Ryan took out a small piece of paper which he called a ticket.

'Hold on to it,' Ryan said as he gave her the ticket. 'You'll need it if you wish to travel legally in London.' He laughed.

'I am a princess… the law is something I abide by,' Prudence said proudly.

'Well, hanging out with a sword was not really legal… was it?'

She did not know what to say. The rules of Ryan's world were a totally foreign concept to her. But in Vita, walking with a sword was not considered unlawful. And so, she did not feel bad about herself. To her, she had not broken any rules.

Ryan then opened the door and they left the house. She could see more of those ferocious monsters called buses. They were not glowing this time. Ryan kept laughing, she did not know why but it seemed as if he was enjoying himself.

They crossed the street, marched for about ten minutes and finally crossed two other streets ahead. Ryan showed Prudence how to use her ticket. It was rather an easy thing to do. Once done, the young man kept laughing.

'Is something the matter?' Prudence asked.

'Whatever happens, don't be frightened by the train.' he kept saying. 'I mean if you were scared of a bus...' he paused and cleared his throat. 'Let's just get on the train. If you're scared you can always grab my hand.'

'I shall not!' Prudence said loudly. 'Nor shall I abide by your mockery!' she said, upset.

Ryan placed his hands on her shoulders and looked deeply into her eyes. He then asked her to forgive him. How could Prudence refuse? His eyes were so compelling. She did not know why, she wanted to kiss him. But she was a princess, and a kiss meant everything to her. Nevertheless, she could not stay mad at him for long. Soon, her cheeks were turning red, and her heart was pounding like a sledgehammer.

'I – forgive you,' she said nervously.

'Cool!' Ryan chuckled and grabbed Prudence's hand. 'Come on! Or we will miss the train!' he giggled, and dragged her to the stairs that said *Platform 1*.

They had arrived at the Platform 1, and a horrible and strange monster was awaiting them. A lot of vapour was breathing out from it and a nasty noise was creaking as it approached them. Prudence grabbed Ryan's hand firmly and hid herself behind him. Why would humans venture into that creature's stomach?

'Aha – come on!' Ryan laughed, and dragged her inside of the monster with him.

She was trembling, and closed her eyes for a few seconds. Her body was shaking and so were her teeth. She was terrified, what would the monster do to them? She kept on shaking, and soon everyone in the monster's stomach stared at her.

'What are you lot looking at?' Ryan said loudly, as he addressed the people around him. 'Prudence darling...' he said softly. 'Look at me...' he said with a gentle voice.

Prudence looked up. The young man then wrapped his arms around her. 'I will not let any harm come to you – Your Majesty,' he said in a comforting manner. 'Now please – sit,' he said, as he pointed out a chair near to the window.

She could never understand how Ryan was doing it, but every time he looked into her eyes and spoke, she would always feel reassured and in good hands. She had only met him the night before, yet his presence was enough to make her feel safe and secure.

The monster started to groan and Prudence could see the scenery outside moving. Ryan laughed and explained to her that the scenery was not the one to move. She started to understand better. These creatures used in Ryan's world were a mobile way to move from one kingdom to another. It was fairly interesting.

An hour later, Ryan's pocket was vibrating. He took out a small and strange device.

'It's my phone, don't worry...' he said and looked at the screen. 'Oh...' his voice turned to disappointment. 'Guess it'll only be you and I for today... my friends ditched me once again.'

'Oh it is terrible...' Prudence said this, but deep inside she was relieved. She did not wish to meet people who would ask her about where she was from or how she met Ryan. And it was an opportunity for her to spend the day with Ryan alone. Prudence was also worried that the brothers would ask her when she would leave. But so far, they had not asked anything about it, so she kept quiet.

The journey lasted for about forty minutes and the train stopped for the eighth time. Ryan stood up and informed Prudence of their arrival. They were in London and Prudence could see a monumental difference of scenery. The city was bigger and extremely vast compared to Ryan's town. There were a lot more people walking in the streets and everything seemed unnaturally busy. Ryan advised her to stay close to him. The crowd could effortlessly separate them and she could get lost.

An hour had elapsed since the two individuals arrived in London. They had visited a lot of famous places of the capital and Prudence's stomach started to groan.

'Aha, I see you're hungry, eh?' Ryan chuckled. 'Let's get a romantic table for two.'

The young man brought her to a restaurant and they ate a large sort of pie called "pizza". The princess found it delicious. There were no uncertainties; Ryan's world had much more enjoyable food than in Vita. She ate as much as Ryan did and did not feel ashamed of not knowing the right fork to use. She followed Ryan's gesture and took the piece with her bare hands before swallowing it.

It was by far the best meal she had ever had. Ryan then got up and paid with a piece of paper. There were no coins used. The princess wondered why the people were not using coins to pay.

'It is because of the inconvenience the coins make.' Ryan chuckled. 'You bring a sack of coins in your pocket, and everyone will know you've got a lot of money on you… ' he said. 'Thus the reason why we use notes or cards to pay.'

After paying the bill, Ryan dragged Prudence to the arcades in Piccadilly Circus. But when they arrived, it was closed due to work constructions. The young man seemed gutted about it.

'I had an extraordinary time in your company,' Prudence said. 'We shall make do with what we visited for today.' she tried to console him.

'You're right! It was a great day!' he smiled cheerfully. 'Let us go home.'

And so they left to the station, unaware of the misadventure they were about to experience…

Ryan was surprised how empty the train station was. It was only 3:00 pm, yet the sky was already dark and no one was there. It was deserted, which was unusual considering the place and the time of the day.

'Something is strange,' Ryan said, as he looked around.

The train arrived. Ryan's town name was written on the small side of the train's front window. Prudence was the first one to get on it. She wanted to show to Ryan how unafraid she was of the trains now. Ryan demanded she got off. He had a bad feeling about this train.

'What is the matter?' Prudence asked with amusement. 'Not knightly enough?' she giggled.

Ryan heard the bell of the train ring. It was about to leave the station. He groaned and entered the train, knowing something strange was happening.

'Next stop we'll get off and wait for another train…' he said grimly.

'Why is that?' Prudence asked. 'You do reside in Epsom – don't you?'

'Yes – but this train is weird.' He looked around, worried.

'I shall protect you – do not fear.' Prudence chuckled.

Ryan approached the window and waited for five minutes. Normally, the train would stop at the next station.

'All right, five minutes are up. Get up – we are getting off this train.'

But the train did not stop, and started to speed up. The young man then pressed the emergency bell, but it did not work.

'I knew something was off!' he said loudly. 'Listen to me Prudence – we'll go to the front of the train and we'll tell the driver to let us out.'

The two teenagers advanced toward the first compartment of the train. The young woman did not understand why Ryan looked so worried. But as they approached the front, she saw some dust on the floor. She bowed down and took a small pinch on her finger. She then gasped in terror, realizing what it was. She jumped on Ryan, and grabbed him tightly from behind.

'What is wrong with you?' Ryan grunted.

'Let us enlighten your limited mind.' It was the voice of a woman.

Ryan looked behind him and saw a woman appearing from nowhere with two horrible creatures. But the young man was more interested in the woman than the rest. She was gorgeous, her face and her body were perfect. She looked like a model, and the smile she had made her easily desired. When he looked closer, he could see she had a wolf's tail. It was strange and unnatural.

'Who are you?' he asked.

'I am Cheryl – but you shall not live long enough to remember me,' she claimed.

'I am Troxia, the most fearful troll!' the small and ugly individual said.

'And I am Turax! The most fearful troll!'

'Huh?' Ryan said, baffled. 'It does not make sense – if the small one is the most fearful troll, then you cannot be.'

'You idiot!' Troxia jumped and slapped his brother.

Cheryl scoffed in annoyance. She then approached Ryan and the princess slowly.

'Hand over the princess – and I shall consider your life worth something.'

'Who are you people?' Ryan asked loudly. 'I get your names, but where are you from? And how come you have a tail?'

'Ignorant fool… she did not tell you anything,' Cheryl scoffed.

'Ryan I – there is something you have to know…' Prudence stuttered.

'A bit late for that…' Ryan sighed.

'I understand if you wish to hand me over – but know that I – I thank you for the time we shared together…' Prudence's voice was shaking.

'Stop it!' Ryan shouted. 'We will discuss it later on – I have no intention of handing you over to these funny people!'

Ryan kept Prudence behind him; he wanted to make sure she was safe. Cheryl did not seem happy at all. She advanced with frowning eyebrows. Her teeth were showing angrily. She had small fangs like those of a wolf.

'Hand over the princess – before I end you,' she threatened Ryan.

'Prudence, run – I will try and preoccupy them,' Ryan whispered to her.

'So be it,' Cheryl scoffed.

The woman ran at an incredible speed, Ryan could not believe it. She then punched him in the face, which knocked him down next to a chair. The strength she had was the equivalent of at least ten men. Ryan grunted in pain and got up, but he was so stunned by the hit that he could barely see straight. Everything was blurred and moving around.

'Now – it is time for you to die.' Cheryl advanced toward the princess with a sword in her hands. 'I shall witness your very demise now!'

The trolls then stopped Cheryl.

'She is ours to kill!' they claimed.

'Out of my way you imbeciles!'

The trolls and the woman began to argue. They had forgotten about the princess and the young man. Prudence held Ryan's hand and discreetly, they were taking few steps back from the three antagonists. Ryan was still stunned, but he was slowly recovering. He could not see well or understand what was happening, but he trusted Prudence's lead.

'You two shall die by my hands!' Cheryl snarled.

'You Humolfs never scared me!' Turax shouted.

'Let's kill her bro!' Troxia said enthusiastically.

Cheryl had had enough of them. With a vicious speed, she snapped the small troll's neck.

'Brother!' Troxia yelled furiously.

He was so furious; he went berserk and started to smash everything with his immense axe. Cheryl tried to kill him, but he was too strong and unreachable. Soon, he had managed to corner her in one side of the train.

'Darn… ' Cheryl grunted. 'I should have killed you first.'

While Troxia was dangerously approaching Cheryl, Ryan had recovered, and was witnessing the big monster advancing with a thirst for blood toward the young woman. She seemed somehow defenceless, even with the impressive demonstration she had given earlier.

'We have to help her… ' Ryan said calmly.

Prudence refused, she wanted her dead. Why would she help someone who wanted to harm her? She demanded Ryan to not help her, but the young man could not sit back and watch.

'How could I not help a beautiful damsel in distress?' he asked. 'Wish me luck,' he smiled before running to the woman's rescue.

Ryan grabbed Turax's axe and approached Troxia carefully from behind. The young man's hands were shaking, he was breathing slowly and harshly. One traitorous noise would be enough for Troxia to slice Ryan in half. He swallowed calmly and when close enough, he jumped on the hideous troll and stabbed him repeatedly in the back.

Troxia was battling to survive, but eventually, he collapsed on the floor and ceased to move. Ryan panted before letting go of the bloody axe. Prudence ran to him and saw how shaken he was. He may have been incredibly courageous but he seemed demoralised and psychologically affected.

'All my life –' he breathed scarcely. '– I wished of magic... but I never knew – that it would happen.'

'You saved me –' Cheryl said calmly. '– It seems that I am indebted to you.'

'Just stay away from Prudence,' Ryan said sharply.

'You do realize I'm not the only person to be sent after her?'

'I figured... ' Ryan said, still shaken. 'But you do not seem evil to me.'

'Who sent you and why?' Prudence asked Cheryl.

'Mmhm... this is not important,' Cheryl scoffed. 'However, you do realize that you are losing your bet?'

'My bet?' Prudence asked. 'I do not understand... '

'By the night of the 24th, if you have not reach Heartsas and defeated its new ruler... ' Cheryl paused. 'You will lose all the memories of Vita and Heartsas and in addition to this... you will lose your rights as a princess,' Cheryl said grimly.

'What says you are not lying?' Prudence asked furiously.

'Try and remove your necklace my dear... '

Prudence did as asked, but her necklace could not be removed. She tried her best to take it off but it was stuck.

'The necklace will only be removable once Heartsas is freed. If you fail… the necklace will disappear and it will take your memories with it.'

Cheryl then took out a small sack from her pocket.

'The countdown begins now, princess… ' she laughed.

Cheryl then threw dust around her, and she disappeared. The train then stopped. When Ryan looked outside, he was in his town station.

'We have arrived… ' Prudence said calmly.

'Let's get out of here – you have a lot to tell me, once home.'

'What about the two bodies?' Prudence asked.

When Ryan looked down, he saw nothing. They had disappeared. It was surely better this way. No matter to him, he just wanted to go home. Prudence could see how furious he was, but at the same time frightened by what had happened on the train. Maybe he was trying to figure out if it was a dream or reality?

Ryan had been completely silent throughout their walk. He did not say a word or even look at her. Prudence thought he was mad at her, and an unpleasant thought crossed her mind. What if he wanted her out? Where would she go?

She felt ill, as if she wanted to vomit. She could feel the stress building up inside of her. All she wanted was to hear Ryan's voice. She knew he would not forgive her for lying to him, and it was easily conceivable that he did not wish to be part of her disastrous misadventure. After all, who would?

They had arrived in front of the young man's house; he unlocked the door and pushed it gently. He asked Prudence to step in the house before him. She entered the house, still scared of what he would say to her. The young man then stepped inside and gently closed the door behind him.

'Sit down,' he ordered her, as he pointed out the sofa.

She did as told. He then grabbed a chair and sat down right in front of her.

'What was that back there?' he asked with a calm yet intimidating tone.

'I – I am not from this world…'

'Gee, really?' he asked sarcastically. 'Be sincere, and tell me the truth.'

Prudence grabbed his hand, and confessed about herself. She told him everything, from the very beginning. Ryan was quiet throughout her whole talk. He did not say anything and only contented himself to hear what she had to say.

'And this is how I met you,' she concluded her story. 'I will understand if you wish me gone.' She looked down with a breaking voice. 'And I apologize for the trouble I have caused you.'

Ryan then grabbed her hand.

'Look at me,' he said calmly.

Prudence looked into his eyes weakly.

'I will not let you go – especially after the incident in the train.' He smiled. 'We are in this together, from now on. Let's just hope there won't be any more of them after you.'

Prudence could not help it. She wrapped her arms around Ryan and cried. It was so reassuring to hear Ryan stand by her, even after what had happened. The thought of her not being alone made her cry in happiness.

'We have to figure out how to save your kingdom,' Ryan said quietly.

'I do not even know how to go back…' Prudence looked down. 'And even if I do, I am not strong enough to beat an entire army…'

'We will figure it out… we still have eleven days before us…'

Prudence had found a strong ally, no, she had found a friend with whom she could share her burden. Ryan Snowangel, a young man who was only a normal citizen of London, had become the first true bond she had ever made.

Chapter Six
A Magical Trick

A week had passed since Prudence found refuge at Ryan's home. The incident on the train was still on her mind, but whenever she was with Ryan, she always managed to forget about it and what was after her. Maybe, the evil had forgotten about her too. And perhaps that was the reason why she had been living a peaceful life for a week.

The young man and she became really good friends. And even if she was lost with all the technologies and everything that belonged in Ryan's world, she felt much more responsible and independent. The princess was learning the simple things of a normal life which made her feel happy.

Ignoring what was flying above her head, she kept on doing what felt right to her. It was the 21st of December; Ryan kept on telling her what an exceptional day the 25th would be. Yet she did not understand, she could feel the enthusiasm of the young man and somehow it made her feel the same way. She was doing so well that she even started to forget about her old life; it was only a week but it did not matter, she did not wish to keep in mind or think of what she had before she had met Ryan.

However, she knew she only had three days before her kingdom banished her for good. So, Prudence went to look for books that could help her to reach Vita, but she found nothing. She tried different libraries and Ryan even went to look on the internet, but it was in vain. Vita did not exist in Ryan's world.

She did not want to lose her place on Vita, but somehow, she felt happy to not find anything. It was a good excuse to stay on Earth.

Was it so wrong for her to be selfish? She wanted to make her parents proud, but deep inside, all she cared about was her new life.

Three days… was it enough? And even then, where would she find the strength to fight the evil controlling her kingdom? She did not know what to think, but above all she did not know what was right: a selfish life that she would find enjoyable to live or the miserable life of a princess who fulfilled her parents' wishes?

Yes, all her life had to be decided within these three days, the Humolf had warned her. But even so, Prudence had no way of getting back to Vita. She decided to sleep on it; perhaps she would find a way soon.

It was the morning; the princess was listening to an invention that captured the voices of different people. Ryan then entered the room hurriedly; he seemed to have been looking for something he had misplaced. Prudence was under the duvet and pretending to sleep, but she was curious about what the young man was searching for.

'I know you're not sleeping, my beauty,' he said while searching inside his wardrobe. 'Why don't you give me a hand?'

'Now I am awake,' Prudence moaned 'What is it that you have misplaced?' she gently asked, while getting up from the bed.

When Prudence looked at Ryan, she was mesmerized by how good looking he was. He was wearing a nice white shirt with casual jeans and black casual shoes. His jacket was the same as the day they had met; it was a black jacket with a dark grey hood. But the way he looked in it was sublime. He then looked at her, and his eyes seemed lost on her. Prudence wondered if it was because her hair was a mess, or if she did not look good.

'Wow, I forgot how magnificent you look; anyway I cannot be distracted by your beauty. Have you found a wallet?' Ryan demanded. 'It was on the table and it contains things that I need for today. It's grey and it has a red logo on the middle.' He described the object while searching.

'Oh yes, I do know of what is it that you are requesting.'

'Do you know where it is?'

'Yes, as a matter of fact I do… however, I shall hand it to you on one condition,' said Prudence.

'Aw come on… seriously? You'll do this to me?' he grunted.

'May I come with you, to wherever you're going?' she asked.

'Mmhm… yes sure, why not? I wanted to make the surprise for tomorrow, but what the heck. That way you won't be disappointed. Just hurry up, get changed because the crowd outside is mental when shopping at Christmas time.'

'Thank you!' The princess jumped out happily.

A while after, the princess and the young man had left the house. They were both heading toward the town.

The brothers had been very kind to her; they had bought her a lot of comfortable clothes that made her fit in with the other girls outside. She did not feel like an outsider at all; on the contrary, she felt as if she was part of Ryan's world.

She was dressed up in what a lot of women from Ryan's world would call casual. She was wearing a dark red coat with black gloves and a black scarf. Most of what she wore was black really. Her cotton tights were black and even her small heeled shoes. However, even though she was dressed like others, she was looked at by many on the street. Whether it was the other girls or boys, they were all staring at her. It felt pleasant. For once, people looked at her without knowing who she was. Prudence could not help but feel happy about her life. It was for once calm, with no obligations or expectations. However, this calm was also unusual. Deep inside, she knew that something was happening, and the calm was just a camouflage.

The calm was indeed hiding the tempest that was coming towards them. In Vita, chaos had taken control. Word was out that the princess had fallen and Heartsas was now the property of a terrible tyrant named Daemn.

Acknowledging the menace in Vita, all the kingdoms were unifying their forces to combat the evil that was born. However, in only one week, Daemn had gathered an army of orcs, goblins and other creatures that were oppressed by the humans. This strategy had given an absolute advantage to Daemn in leading his propaganda of fear within all of Vita.

As a result, one by one the nearest kingdoms had renounced to defy Daemn. Instead, they were all secretly praying not to be the next ones to follow Heartsas's fate. Soon, even children were to join the army to defend the walls of their homes in case of an attack.

The emperor was sitting on the throne of Heartsas. It was the same armoured personage, however, he did not wear a hood but a monstrous helm which made him look like a demon. By his side, a man, with the same red hood from before, was standing up.

A short time after, Reaper made his entrance. His immaculate white shirt was covered in blood; he seemed rather frightened by the emperor. 'My Lord,' he said, whilst approaching the throne.

'I presume you have failed me again in finding the princess?' the Emperor said calmly.

'I – I have been searching throughout all Vita. No signs of her… maybe she did perish in her foolish attempt at running away?' Reaper suggested while stuttering.

'She did not; she is the Princess of Heartsas. I firmly believe that she had the help of some living creatures,' the red hooded man said.

'I beg your forgiveness my Lord – allow me to search Vita once more,' Reaper begged on his knees.

'I shall grant that to you – however, do not search in Vita. It is a futile attempt,' the emperor ordered.

'I do not seem to understand my Lord – where am I meant to search?' Reaper demanded, puzzled.

'London. I do recall you coming from that place. This shall be where you will look for her. Remember, I want her alive or dead with a full body – but do feel free to kill whoever you wish on your way.' He laughed. 'Especially the Humolf who has decided to hide… she possesses the stone, you shall need it to make your journey back,' the emperor stated. 'Now out of my sight, I have other obligations to attend to.'

'My Lord, I will not fail you,' Reaper said before leaving.

'Too noble of you, my Lord. An incompetent like him should have deserved a death sentence,' the red hooded man said grimly.

'If I see fit, I will give him one chance to prove himself worthy. I would have ended his miserable existence, however, his loyalty towards me has allowed him to survive for today.'

'Will you really kill the Humolf? After all she is… '

'I do know of this,' Daemn interrupted the man. 'The trolls were evidently facing their demises. But the Humolf shall deserve a fate worse than death,' he said darkly. 'Just like her mother, she will beg for death once I have what I need… ' Daemn took a dark posture and started to mutter to himself. 'After fifteen years in the dark… my face shall come back to history, with the death of the princess.'

Meanwhile in London, the roads were full of life; people were pushing each other to get their hands on their Christmas presents. Prudence was surprised by how the crowd were reacting; it was unbelievable and hardly natural.

Ryan held Prudence's hand to make sure he did not lose her on his way to the women's shop. He knew how packed it would be, especially when it came to women clothes. 'Here we are, finally,' the young man said, relieved to be in front of the store.

'I do not understand why have you brought me to a woman's shop? I do not have any money on me… ' the princess demanded, baffled.

'Well, you wanted to accompany me today… so here we are, we will pick something you like. Do not mind the price, my lady. It's on me,' Ryan said with a smile. He seemed content to have Prudence with him.

'It is so generous and noble of you Ryan, I do not know what to say. I am touched by the affection you have given me since we met,' she said courteously.

'Well just say that you are indeed happy, that you will get a nice and expensive gift and I would not mind a kiss on the cheek for gratitude.' He chuckled.

'There you are!' a familiar voice shouted out of nowhere.

When Ryan and Prudence turned around, it was Mia, who seemed furious. She was so angry she could barely articulate what she had to say to Ryan. Instead, she just contented herself with slapping Ryan in the face.

Ryan was shocked; he did not understand what was going on. It was surely uncalled for and Prudence stepped in for Ryan. 'I demand an apology,' Prudence dared.

'You're the one he has replaced me with! How dare you come in my way and act all posh?' Mia yelled angrily.

'Ladies, please…'

Ryan tried to calm down the situation but was easily ignored.

'Quiet you!' Mia yelled at Ryan.

'You do not possess a valuable reason to act in the way you are. I do not know of you, but I surely do not appreciate how you are behaving.' Prudence was awfully big-headed. 'On your knees, I order an apology,' she said to Mia.

Mia scoffed. She could not take the princess seriously. She mocked her and demanded an explanation from Ryan. The young man did not know what to tell her. After all, how could he tell Mia that Prudence came from another world?

'I am your best friend, and you did not bother to let me know that you had found a girlfriend! What kind of friend does that?' asked Mia.

'Woah, you've got it all wrong! Prudence is not my… she's my fiancée!' Ryan claimed.

'Huh? But I…' Prudence gasped, surprised of Ryan's advances.

Ryan's words made her heart beat faster than usual; her cheeks were turning red and somewhere inside of her, she loved the thought of his allusion being true.

'Relax, I'm just kidding princess…' Ryan chuckled. 'She is new to town, she does not know anything. So I volunteered to educate her on how we basically live here and I gave her a tour. It's all innocent. Plus Mia, you are so not my girlfriend or my mother,' he scolded.

'OK I forgive you this time, and what's up with what you just said? Why call her a princess?' Mia questioned Ryan.

Ryan made up a story about Prudence. He was really believable, and the way he spoke made Prudence looks like a goddess rather than a simple princess. However, Prudence could not help but look down at her feet. She seemed ashamed of the way she had behaved earlier; it was rude and unworthy of a princess.

She could not help herself, she had to apologize to Mia, and so she did.

'All is good... I should not have slapped that idiot in front of you. Accept my apologies too...' Mia smiled. 'Hey, I actually have an idea. Why don't we just go in there and I'll help you pick whatever you're buying? I'm a pretty good customer, so you might get discounts.' Mia giggled, as if she was pleased to shop with another girl for once.

While the princess and her friends were having an eventful day, a man was observing them from a hiding spot. It was Reaper, somehow he had found Prudence. He was observing her discreetly and knew that he would be recognized by her if he approached her. He then took out a small sachet from his pocket, which was firmly closed with a gold ribbon. He gently opened it and bright dust was glowing inside, he took a pinch of it and closed the sachet.

'This ought to be amusing,' he said grimly, after throwing the bright dust to his face.

A short while after, his skin started to transform; his pale, old and wrinkled face changed and became younger; his grey hairs altered to a much polished blond. His beaked nose readjusted to a much younger and nicer form and his old teeth became of a shining white. His voice changed to a rather innocent and enjoyable tone and his skin metamorphosed to a fine tan, as if he had been sunbathing.

Unaware of the danger approaching her, the princess was enjoying the company she had. Reaper knew he would not be able to interact with the young girl with Ryan around, he had to do something to get her somewhere by herself, where she would not suspect anything abnormal.

He then discovered the perfect disguise; wearing the clothes of one of the employees inside the shop would give him absolute discretion. Reaper entered the shop from the back door which he managed to unlock, then waited in the staff room.

An old man who was working in the clothes shop entered the room, not conscious of the fatal encounter he was about to make. Reaper waited for the old man to come close, and when the man was close enough, Reaper got a hold of the old person from behind and broke his neck. He then dragged the lifeless body to the corner of the room where no one would find it for a while. It gave him the right amount of time to complete the task he had been given.

'It is such a humiliation to wear those horrible clothes,' he muttered while putting on the clothes.

Reaper had managed to enter the clothing shop without being spotted by the princess or anyone. He had indeed found the ideal costume, no matter who he'd had to kill. He could see the princess and the other girl; they were both trying on a lot of clothes and both amusing themselves. 'Hey, excuse me sir?' Someone gently tapped his shoulder.

'Yes?' Reaper answered after turning around. 'How can I help you?' he asked gently.

'I was wondering if you could tell me whether you have the size 7 for these shoes?' a woman demanded with her hands full.

'I do not know of how to check the system for you my lady. I do apologize for the inconvenience. May I invite you to verify this enquiry with one of my colleagues? I am fairly certain they would gladly answer your problems,' he graciously and courteously said.

Ryan was near to them when he heard them speak; it was rather strange and rare to hear a young man around his age talking the way he had done. Then he remembered Prudence. It may have been a coincidence but Ryan had to find out one way or another.

Meanwhile, in the fitting room, Prudence and Mia were having a good time talking and trying on the clothes. They kept on complimenting each other and a lovely friendship seemed to have developed between the two of them.

'So, now that we are between girls… any boy you fancy in your life?' Mia asked Prudence, while helping her to zip the dress.

'I do not know… I have this kind and warm feeling every moment I am in Ryan's company. However, I do not know the meaning of it,' Prudence replied bewildered. 'What about you?' she asked.

'No one, I'm the rock star… I like to be single and focus on my goals in life, and having a boyfriend could easily distract me. Take Ryan for example; he is kind, sincere, but sometimes he can really be an idiot. On top of that, I bet he has borrowed money from his bank account to pay for whatever he wants to buy you. It is really nice of him, but kind of stupid since he won't be able to pay anything back without a job.' Mia kept on going. 'But I can tell how much you like him. Gosh, you might even be able to fall for him!' Mia shouted enthusiastically. 'Got to tell you though, you are not the first lady who liked him then got turned down so be careful OK?'

Prudence looked down in embarrassment. She did not know what to say to Mia, since she could barely understand what it was that she felt. She had never felt this way before, and it was unique. It was a mixed up feeling, both nice and painful.

Ryan then opened the curtains of the fitting room, after making sure that no staff would catch him.

'Hey ladies, sorry to disturb you but we should head off. The crowd is getting bigger,' he said. 'So Your Highness, did you manage to find something to fit your interests?' Ryan asked with an animated tone.

'What the heck do you think you're doing? Imagine if she was undressed?' Mia yelled at Ryan.

'Then I would have hit the jackpot,' he chuckled, after closing the curtains.

'Ugh, men…' Mia scoffed in annoyance.

Reaper had heard Ryan; he had to make a move if he wanted to have the opportunity to capture the princess. He waited for Ryan to leave, and gently approached the two young girls who were leaving the fitting room.

'Excuse me ladies?' he asked. 'I am sorry to bother you but my team and I are doing a survey in our office. If you answer all the questions, you get anything from the shop that does not exceed £100. It is an offer that cannot be refused. So what do you say? Either of you two interested in doing it?' He tried to captivate the attention of the two girls.

'Well, I say I'm in!' Mia jumped out enthusiastically. 'What about you? Come on Prudence! That way Ryan won't have to use his money!'

'I am not sure we should…'

'Oh I do not mean to make you uncomfortable, my ladies. If you do not wish to participate in the survey, it is more than OK.'

'Please! Prudence, you have to come with me! If we don't do it, another group of girls might get the £100!' said Mia.

'Very well… I shall do it for you,' the princess said, convinced by Mia. 'But please, I do not want Ryan to worry. Could we at least let him know?' demanded Prudence.

'No don't worry about him, he can wait ten minutes,' Mia scoffed.

'Well ladies…' Reaper said, as he was showing the way toward the staff room.

The two young girls got inside the room; Reaper was smiling gladly, thinking he had succeeded on his mission. But he was wrong; as he was showing the two girls to the room, Ryan was following closely. The young man knew something was off and after the event on the train, his suspicions were easily confirmed.

'So where is it?' Mia sighed, annoyed.

'Here…' Reaper laughed.

Prudence noticed the hair of the young man changing to grey; his body was metamorphosing itself in an old and hunchback silhouette. His skin was aging and it was changing from a tan to a pale white. 'Mia! Run!' Prudence yelled in panic, as she recognised Reaper.

'It is too late princess!' Reaper said as he grabbed Prudence's arm.

'Want a bet?' Ryan jumped out of nowhere and punched the old man in the face. 'Run!' he shouted at the two girls.

Ryan did not wait long and knocked out Reaper after kicking him in the face, multiple times. The young man was trembling. He did not seem to be experienced in fights, no matter how confident he pretended to be.

The three teenagers then ran away from the shop. All three of them were heading out of the town and back to Ryan's place.

After a whole five minutes of running, the three teenagers were out of breath but soon at Ryan's house. The snow made it hard to run fast and the cold conditions were not favourable for the visibility. The wet floor and the frozen water managed to make anyone fall or glide. It was not the best time of the year to run. Ryan acted chivalrously toward the princess. Seeing how slow she was compared to him and Mia, he grabbed her and carried her in his arms.

The young man was struggling to find his keys in his pockets; he was searching everywhere but could not find them.

'Hurry up!' Mia yelled.

Ryan then recalled that he had left them with Prudence. He gently demanded the princess to look inside her pocket. Prudence did not hesitate in looking for them and handed the keys over after she had found them. Ryan inserted the keys in the locks of the house and rapidly unlocked the door. Mia pushed her way in, followed by the princess. Ryan wanted to make sure they had not been followed; he told the girls to lock the doors on the inside while he went around to mislead their pursuers.

'Are you out of your mind?' Mia yelled at Ryan.

'OK, you need to stop yelling at me young lady. I will be fine, just get in, lock the doors and do not open them, even if it's me who asks,' said Ryan.

'But how will you manage to come inside?' Prudence asked, scared.

'Your Highness, I have the keys… see? Now come here… ' Ryan hugged the princess to reassure her. 'You and Mia will be doing fine – if I don't come back, you can count on Mia to do her crazy karate. And you have to let my brother know about what is going on, he will be of a great help to you,' he calmly said, while caressing the hair of the princess.

Ryan then asked Mia to go in his room and get a certain sword that was left in the corner. The young girl seemed curious about it but did not ask any questions. She went to get the sword and brought it to her friend, as he requested. Ryan knew he would be arrested on site if the police caught him with this weapon, but he had to make sure Prudence was safe, no matter what.

Mia scoffed out of annoyance.

'Don't worry, he will be back. By the way, what the heck is going on?' she asked, frustrated. 'Go ahead Ryan, do your hero thing while "Your Highness" and I talk.'

'Good, you two enjoy your conversation,' Ryan said, after letting go of the princess. 'Do not worry my darlings; I will be back, and save me some chocolates!' he laughed, as if he was not afraid at all.

Ryan had left. Prudence knew how risky it would be to confront Reaper, but she trusted the young man. He would make it back; she had to believe this.

Mia closed the door and dragged Prudence by the hand to the living room.

'You and I will have a chat about what is going on,' Mia said, overwhelmed by what was happening. 'Who was that man? Or what was that? His face changed… and his hair! What the hell was that all about? And how come Ryan seems so confident and cocky and arrogant and unafraid?'

Mia spoke so fast and so panicked that the princess had difficulties in understanding her.

'I have not all the answers you seek about Ryan, I've only known him for a week. Yet he is kind, honest, fun, pleasant, and a lot of good things… I had never suspected how courageous he was.' Prudence seemed lost in wonder. 'But I'll answer one thing you asked; that man you saw is dangerous… I witnessed what he did in Vita… it was horrible,' she said darkly.

'Huh? Vita – what the heck is that?' Mia demanded puzzled.

'It is the place where I was born… my world. And my home – but I cannot go back. I only know of a story that I told Ryan but some dark and evil force wants my demise. I managed to flee and I met Ryan… ' the princess said calmly, but started to shiver, frightened.

'Tell me the whole story – as crazy as it seems. I saw crazier things today. Plus I bet Ryan believed your story straightaway… he is so fond of all the fantasy stuff. I would not be surprised if I went cuckoo because of him,' Mia claimed, as she sat down next to Prudence to comfort her.

'It all started a week and a half ago… ' Prudence began to tell her the story.

Chapter Seven
The Weakness Of Being Good

Meanwhile around Hook Road, the evil Reaper was getting closer to the location where Prudence was. He pushed a group of children out of anger. 'I shall kill her friends slowly once I get my hands on them!' he muttered in rage.

Ryan was around the corner, he did not suspect how quick the old man could be. It was unusual how fast he recovered, and his speed in finding where Prudence was. Ryan had no time for questions; he could only rely on a good diversion to protect the princess. But he was really scared. He did not wish to say it because of his pride, and he did not want Prudence to be worried, but he was terribly scared on the inside. He looked closely at the old man and discreetly marched towards him.

Reaper then stopped, he knew he was being observed by someone. He smiled and started to laugh evilly.

'I have been doing this job for a long time, young man. Killing has been my hobby for years now. I suggest you get out of your hide and apologize to me. I will consider a quick death for you,' Reaper chuckled, as he was getting a small knife out of his jacket.

Ryan bit his lips and took a deep breath. If he wanted to have a chance against the killer, he had to pretend that he was not scared.

'Well, well, grumpy has a knife. Careful old man, you might hurt yourself with something you can't handle,' Ryan said, as he was getting out of his hide.

'Aha – young flesh,' Reaper smiled. 'Always the ones to talk… It is the reason why I so like ripping their skins off. The louder they bark, the more pleasure I have in slowly cutting them.' He licked the blade of the knife sadistically.

Ryan walked towards the old man; he was presenting himself as a strong and fearless character, but it was a mask. Ryan was scared. Inside he was trembling and wanted to run away. He felt an ill feeling and stress getting the best out of him. His blood was freezing and his bones were slightly shaking. He was breathing slower than usual and carefully. Ryan had to do or say something for Reaper to walk away or disappear. It was his only chance of protecting Prudence and also for him to walk away unharmed.

'You talk big for an old carcass…' Ryan improvised. 'I will give you an invitation to dreamland, free of charge. What do you think of that, old freak?' he mocked Reaper, by making grimaces.

Ryan was hoping that Reaper would consider retreating, but it did not seem to work.

'You do not know of what you speak! You ignorant fool!' Reaper furiously thumped the snow out of rage. 'I will cut out your tongue before I kill you!' he claimed inhumanly.

'Ready… steady… go?' Ryan laughed.

Reaper had had enough of Ryan's attitude; he wanted him dead and dashed toward the young man with his knife. Ryan was good when it came to defending himself. His quickness and his fast reactions made him a lucky fighter.

The killer then tried to stab Ryan in the stomach, but failed and ended up caught in a submissive state. Ryan then smashed the old man's face on the snowy ground and broke his right arm. Ryan did not know how he had done what he just did, but it was pretty good reflex and technique. After getting back on his feet, the young man advanced toward the killer with Prudence's sword in his hands.

Ryan panted nervously, but edged the blade toward Reaper's throat. He did not seem to care of the neighbourhood around him; even if they called the police, he would do anything he had to protect the princess.

'Well, well, it seems you cannot talk much now, can you?' Ryan asked arrogantly. 'I bet you assumed that I would not harm you because I'm on the good guys' side… ' he paused. 'Well… I don't care – if I can have the pleasure of seeing you die to protect Prudence, then so be it!'

Reaper chuckled. It made Ryan nervous.

The young man could feel his blood boiling up and his nerves shaking. He was scared about what he was going to do. Could he even do it? He had killed a troll a couple of days ago, but it was the nerves and the heat of the moment which made him do so… Ryan was questioning himself, knowing that Reaper would kill him as soon as he could.

'Can you do it?' Reaper laughed.

Ryan's hands were trembling.

'You are weak!'

'Shut up!' Ryan shouted.

'Do it, coward!'

Ryan was about to cross the line and murder Reaper, but he was soon enough interrupted.

As he was about to stab Reaper; the old man used his magic and inflicted pain upon Ryan's brain. The young man was so hurt and paralyzed by the pain that he fell on his knees and screamed loudly.

'I shall take great pleasure in ending your miserable existence!' Reaper took the knife and approached the young man. 'No one will save you… I used fairy dust to make sure no one witnesses your death… sad little boy… '

Ryan thought it was the end of him… no matter the pain he felt, he had to try something. However, it was too overwhelming; even if he tried he could not manage to attack Reaper or to defend himself. For the first time in his life, he was defenceless and at his foe's mercy.

'Do not kill him,' a distinct voice said, before appearing in front of Reaper, who was about to end Ryan's life. 'Lower your weapon, we need him alive.' It was the voice of a woman.

'We do not need him; he is but riddance to the master's plan.' Reaper grunted irritably. 'And how dare you show your face to me!'

'I know the emperor is angry at me…' the woman paused. 'But I was planning on redeeming myself, by helping you to get the princess…'

'I do not need you… just like I do not need him!' Reaper raised his knife.

The woman pushed Ryan and went near him. Ryan could smell the nice perfume of the woman. He then felt a sort of animal tail softly caressing his face.

'He will serve as leverage, you imbecile. How will you get the princess out of her hide if you do not have something she cares about?' the woman scoffed. 'It is just like you men to work in barbaric ways. No wonder you accomplish nothing but countless failures.' She laughed.

'I do not have time to argue with you. Let's take him then!' Reaper grunted, agreeing with the mysterious woman.

Ryan could not see her. His eyes were affected by the magic used by the old man; he could only distinguish a blurred silhouette.

'It is a shame to do such a thing to a cute boy… oh well.'

The woman knocked Ryan out with a heavy slam from a sword's handler.

'Mmm… It is only because he is attractive that you spared his life!' Reaper grunted, as he was dragging Ryan to an unknown place. 'This is such a woman way… no wonder you do not kill enough!' he muttered, annoyed by the interruption of the woman.

'Hey, quiet! It pains me to see such a nice boy being dragged by such a hideous creature like you. Had I not being there, you would have killed him and the princess would have been harder to find,' the woman scoffed with pride.

Meanwhile in Ryan's house, Prudence had finished telling her story to Mia who seemed amazed by it. 'You really are a princess?' Mia asked, mesmerized.

'Yes I am…' Prudence looked down sadly.

'Why are you so down? I reckon it's cool to be a princess!' Mia seemed joyful. 'I thought Ryan called you princess because he liked you. Wow, I was so wrong…' The girl kept on going.

'I wonder where he might be… it has been quite a while,' Prudence said, worried.

The door opened and the two girls jumped from the sofa and hid themselves under a table.

'Now that you're here Eric, you and Ryan need to be careful not to break things in the house.' It was Nash's voice.

The two girls left their hide to greet Nash, who was accompanied by a young man.

'Oh hello, how are you Mia? And who is that pretty girl?' the young man demanded.

'Hello Eric, I see you're here for the holidays… this is Princess Prudence. You should bow in front of her.' Mia giggled.

Eric was a head taller than Ryan, he had black hair but he dyed it red. His eyes were darker than Ryan's but he possessed a friendlier smile. He had a Thai background and looked really sociable. He dressed smart, but not as smart as the two brothers.

'That will not be necessary; it is a pleasure to make your acquaintance.' Prudence offered her hand for Eric to shake.

'Oh the pleasure is mine!' he shook Prudence's hand, as he dropped his bag.

'I see… Ryan has taught you our ways…'

Mia seemed somehow disappointed that Prudence did not make a more noble gesture.

Eric was Ryan's closest friend; they had known each other since primary school. They could only meet once in a while since Eric lived in Paris, but once together they formed a great team, according to Nash.

'Where is Ryan?' Nash demanded while looking around.

'We don't know…' Prudence looked down.

'I think you should tell him,' Mia suggested darkly.

'Tell me what?' Nash asked curiously.

The princess was about to tell Nash what has happened and everything about her, but at the same moment Mia's phone rang. 'Hello?' she picked up her phone.

'I do wish you a good day, it was a pleasure to meet you, young lady, in the shop centre. However, I did not appreciate your friend's disrespectful manners,' a dark and sinister voice said through the phone.

'Oh my God, you're that hideous man from the shop!' Mia shouted.

'I am willing to strike you a deal… do not be foolish and listen to me. I have your friend here; well I cannot say that I did not have my fun in making him talk. But he refused to give me information, instead he kept on cursing me… you come with the princess in Horton Hill's park and we'll make the trade. I want the princess,' the man stated.

'I do not believe you; you might have found the phone.' Mia doubted the man.

'Proof… I shall enjoy this.'

'Mia! Don't give him Prudence! Do you hear me? Don't make the trade! Or I'll… ' It was Ryan's voice, shouting in despair through the phone, before a horrible shout of pain.

'Stop hurting him! I'll do it! Just leave him alone!' Mia panicked.

'Do not play games, or his death will be on your conscious. I want the princess before midnight!' Reaper ordered, as he hung up the phone.

'What is going on?' Nash demanded worried.

'He has Ryan… hasn't he?' Prudence sighed, feeling guilty.

'He wants to make the trade… tonight. Ryan doesn't want the trade to be made… ' Mia bit her lips anxiously.

Nash and Eric were confused; they did not seem to understand anything. The princess then sat down and told her story once more. 'And this is how I met Ryan… and now… he is in danger because of me.' She started to cry.

'I knew that...' Nash claimed. 'I heard you the night you came from London... I listened to what you were telling Ryan behind the door,' he confessed.

'You little...' Mia abstained herself from cursing Nash.

'Wait, hang on... You actually believe her, Nash? I mean seriously... big spider, old man with magic and all the kind of freaky stuff?' Eric scoffed, as if he did not believe any of it.

'Of course I do, I've always believed in magical stuff since I was a child,' Nash laughed.

'How dare you laugh when your brother is in danger!' Mia yelled at Nash.

'It is my fault; I wish to make things right... please...' Prudence said, distressed.

'All right... Eric, you will have to come as well,' Nash agreed.

'What? But I don't want to... I want nothing to do with that whole magical thing!' said Eric.

'Well it's either you come willingly or I will break your teeth until you accept the invite...' said Nash.

'Of course I am coming! What did you think? Eh! I'm Ryan's best friend!' Eric nervously laughed.

'Actually, I am, but whatever...' Mia mentioned.

Chapter Eight
A portal To Vita

Time had elapsed; it was nearly the time of the rendez-vous and Nash wanted to make sure they were prepared. No evil doer would play fair when it came to arrangement; he took out a box where a multitude of weapons were stocked. From nunchucks to Chinese swords, everything was there. Prudence and Eric were shocked and surprised by the brothers' hidden side. Mia, however, did not gasp with surprise; she knew Ryan and Nash were fond of martial arts and fantasy stories.

'Are those real?' Eric gasped, while pointing out a set of shuriken.

'Of course they are not... we bought it online, duh. They won't sell real blades. Everything here can inflict pain or impale but that's about it.' Nash chuckled, as he took out a sabre. 'Everything yes... except this and the bow.' Nash took a sword that was delicately and well preserved in a sheath. 'This is a sword Ryan and I found when we were kids... it cuts anything... it is an old sword... this is why...' Nash handed the sword to Prudence. 'I entrust this with you. You will need it more than us.' He smiled.

Prudence held the sword. It was light and easy to handle.

'Eric, take the bow...' Nash paused. 'Ryan bought that bow recently since he joined an archery class; this one is a real one. So don't go on shooting arrows if you can't aim, all right?' He gave the bow to Eric.

'It's time...' Mia said, after looking at her phone.

Prudence and her friends were scared. Nash presented a brave face and he did not want to admit or show that he was also afraid.

Everyone looked up to him, he was the leader and the smallest doubt he would show could affect the moral of the team. The park was just about ten minutes from the house. Nash decided to drive, even though it was close. That way, they could hide the weapons and not be stopped by the police.

Reaper and the woman from the train were both at the park; they had Ryan, who was trying to detach himself. 'Let me go, you freak!' Ryan kept on cursing the old man, as he was debating.

'Do shut up, bloody imbecile,' Reaper grunted angrily. 'Can we not kill him now?' he asked irritated.

'I dare you to!' Ryan glared at Reaper. 'Oh hello… ' he looked at the woman. 'Cheryl, was it?'

'Aha… ' Cheryl chuckled. 'You remember… '

'How can I not… it would be an insult to forget a beautiful woman like you.'

'All right that is it… I shall kill him now!' Reaper took out a knife.

'No, I want him alive… I plan on bringing him with us once we have the princess.' Cheryl laughed.

'Oh please woman, I knew you could not resist my charm!' Ryan paused after complimenting the lady. 'Heck, we could make a great couple.'

Cheryl began to blush. Her small fangs were perceivable and she kept on smiling.

'I like you already.' She giggled.

'Please, this is just ridiculous. You have not seen what a Humolf looks like in a full moon!' Reaper mumbled annoyed.

'I've seen my share of worst faces in the world, and yours has reached the top,' said Ryan.

Ryan's friends had arrived. It was dark but Reaper could sense Prudence's presence. Shortly after, the silhouettes of the four individuals presented themselves to the two antagonists.

'I am glad to see you value this fool's life.' Reaper chuckled, as Prudence and her friends got closer.

'Free him… I will not pose any resistance,' Prudence ordered.

'We do not take orders from you, princess… plus, I actually like him. It is a wonder you have not fallen for him by now,' Cheryl provoked Prudence.

Ryan started to smile. It was as if he had completely forgotten about being a prisoner.

'Always so modest, eh? Anyway, let my brother go or things will get ugly,' Nash warned Reaper and the woman.

'Oh please, seriously?' Ryan scoffed. 'That's all you could come up with?'

Reaper laughed, and used his magic to disarm Nash before inflicting him with a painful brain attack. Nash fell on his knees and screamed out of pain.

'Stop it!' Prudence proclaimed. 'I will surrender, just stop hurting him and release Ryan.'

Mia and Eric were afraid; it was magic they had witnessed. The two of them were tempted to run away, yet they could not because of the fear that was paralyzing them.

Eric was paralyzed in fear; he had never held a weapon in his life, let alone used one. However, somehow he managed to find the courage to aim. 'Just… just let… let him go!' he aimed at Reaper, while trembling in fear.

'Wow, it's really depressing how my only chance of escaping resides in you… ' Ryan moaned. 'Shoot him you idiot, if you don't do it he will attack you the same way Nash and I got attacked,' Ryan encouraged Eric to fire.

Reaper had had enough of the games the teenagers were playing; he advanced toward Prudence, knowing no resistance would be provided. Eric was too scared to fire; he closed his eyes and contented himself on shooting on a tree. Ryan could not tolerate the thought of Reaper hurting Prudence. He tried his best to break free, but he could not.

'The stone… ' Reaper turned to Cheryl.

Cheryl took out the stone from her pocket and used fairy dust on it. The portal then opened itself, presenting a forest and a castle.

'Heartsas!' Prudence gasped.

'It is time for you to die at home.' Reaper advanced toward the portal, as he grabbed Prudence.

'Let Ryan go! We had an arrangement!' Prudence struggled to push Reaper away.

'Yes indeed… the arrangement was a trade… since we did not need to trade, the arrangement is over. But since I am a fair man, I will let you decide. Who shall live and who shall die?' Reaper used his magic and tortured the two brothers.

Ryan could not take it anymore. He was so furious but he had no way of detaching from the ropes. 'Let go of Ryan…' Prudence softly said.

The princess had chosen to save Ryan, but Reaper was no fair man and progressively he was increasing the pain on the two brothers, until they would die. Cheryl took out a pinch of fairy dust and threw it on Ryan.

'Ryan, use your anger to trigger your magic!' she said loudly.

Ryan did not understand, but he gave it a go. He could feel a warm and blazing feeling surrounding himself. Soon, the ropes were burning from a fire that was coming from him. The young man was surrounded by a magnificent flaming aura.

'What the…' he looked at his hands and noticed they were on fire.

'You traitor!' Reaper yelled at Cheryl.

'I bid you farewell, old carcass!'

Ryan ran to Reaper and punched him in the face. The old man's cheek was burnt down and his skin was melting. 'What is this curse?' he shrieked. Ryan then advanced toward him as if he wanted him dead, but Reaper had enough time to crawl and jump inside the portal.

'Now…' Cheryl took out another stone and used its magic.

The scenery inside the portal was different.

'It is your only chance to succeed in getting your kingdom back.'

Cheryl looked at Prudence before she smiled. 'Well then… see you, losers.' She jumped inside the portal.

'Wait up!' Ryan shouted loudly, before he followed Cheryl.

Prudence and her friends could not stop Ryan. They had no choice but to follow him. Nash and the princess did not hesitate in jumping inside the portal, but Eric and Mia did. They were unsure of where it would lead and what was behind it. What if they crossed it and could never managed to come back home? Both had their doubts but as the portal was closing itself, the two of them panicked and jumped inside.

Chapter Nine
To Parisia

It was morning; Ryan woke up and realized he was no more in Hook Road's park. No, he was in a prairie and everything around him was of a bright green. A lot of trees and a lot of animals were present.

'What the...' he grunted in pain.

'Hey, how are you doing?' A familiar voice asked him.

'I'm hurting like hell...' he moaned, while getting back on his feet. 'Wow, Prudence you sure look worried...' he said after seeing her.

'Of course I am... you were not yourself last night. And – you...' Prudence went silent for a moment. 'How can you use magic? You created fire from your hands...' she asked, baffled.

'What are you talking about? A normal guy like me throwing fire... seriously?' Ryan said, as if he did not believe the princess. 'Come on, I just got angry, chased that idiot who managed to escape... and everything went blank for a while.' He chuckled. 'I black out when I get really angry and I lose control of myself... so you can guess that getting on my bad side is not a good idea.' He laughed.

'I am glad to see you are OK. I was worried about you.' The princess sighed with relief.

'Hey beauty, I would not fail like I did last time... you can count on me to protect you.' Ryan chuckled while making a ridiculous stance.

A short time after, Nash and Ryan's two friends showed up. Eric seemed frightened by the place; he did not feel comfortable at all.

Mia was speechless, she did not know what to say. Everything seemed unnatural to her.

'By the way... where are we?' Ryan asked Prudence, after taking a quick look around.

'We are in Vita... my world,' she answered calmly. 'I do not know of the place we are – I only know that forests like these are a good refuge if we do not stay here long.' She paused and looked worried. 'However, we should leave camp as soon as everyone is ready.'

'Why is that?' Eric asked, bothered by what the princess had announced.

'Forests at night... they have the tendency to hide all the creatures of darkness... you do not wish to meet a spectre or a monster,' Prudence said quietly. 'It is best we leave and find a town where we can rest and gather information on what is happening,' the princess said with a high confidence in her words.

'So we shall... Ryan, do you think you can make it to the nearest town?' Nash demanded of his brother, as if he underestimated him.

'Huh, like that's going to be a problem... don't worry about me. I'm fine and I intend on keeping it that way,' replied Ryan.

The two brothers were rivals. Both were naturally born to be leaders, and they both had strong tempers. Being in the same team made things challenging; Ryan did not want to listen to Nash's orders whilst Nash did not want to be led by Ryan. However, the main priority was how they would handle the team.

Mia seemed scared of Ryan; she was keeping her distance from him and seemed evasive towards him. Eric was really confused and worried, yet he was the most grounded person out of the whole group. Being worried was the most normal thing to do. They did not know where they were, Prudence was the only one from this world which she barely knew, and the two brothers were not on good terms. It was chaos within the group itself.

'I think we should leave, but Ryan and Nash... keep your distance.' Eric suggested.

'How are we even supposed to know if we can trust Prudence?' Mia scoffed. 'We don't know where we are, Ryan is one of those freaks… and we have no idea how to get back home!' she paused. 'I say we are doomed. We can say whatever we want; we have no idea about what to do or where to go. I should never have crossed that portal,' she lamented.

'Wow, calling me a freak? What do you think that makes you, grumpy?' responded Ryan.

'I think we should keep it together. Mia, I understand your frustration, it is even hard for me to come back to my world. But there is a reason for it. Besides, if Reaper could find a way to travel in both worlds… this only means that we can find a way to do so too. I promise you – once we find the way, I will help you to go back to your world safely,' said the princess.

'Let's go then,' Nash said, while leading the way.

Prudence and her friends were lost and scared. The princess knew the forest was dangerous even in daylight but she did not wish to scare her friends. She had read many books of different knights travelling places such as forests, mountains, and many other types of scenery. However, she had never personally visited them.

She was a princess after all, bound to stay in her castle and grow up there. The princess was unsure about a lot of things, she had promised Mia to help her to go back to her world, however even she did not know if they would be successful. She was not even sure of the situation in Vita to begin with.

Shortly after, the forest seemed somehow darker, the trees were scorched and the grass was covered in blood. There was no doubt that a battle had happened in those woods and it was recent.

'What the heck is that?' Eric gasped, as he saw the body of a green monster. 'Is… is it a… ' he stuttered afraid. The body of the creature was impaled in a tree, it had been stabbed at different places and one of its eyes was missing.

'A goblin, it seems… ' Prudence said coolly. 'We should be on our guards,' she said darkly.

'Don't worry princess, I will protect you,' Nash said, as he moved in front of Prudence.

'Thank you, it is really courteous of you,' she replied.

Ryan bit his lips angrily. He did not say anything but Nash getting ahead of him and acting the knight annoyed him. However, he stayed silent and just went along with the group.

It was not long before a horde of goblins made an appearance. Nash and Ryan had heard the horde coming; they were so loud that it would have been nearly impossible not to. Eric and Mia did not wait long before hiding in the bushes.

'Take Prudence and hide… ' Ryan ordered Nash.

'What are you planning to do?' demanded Nash.

'I'm just going to see how many there are… ' Ryan responded with a confident tone. 'Eric, give me the bow and the arrows,' he demanded.

Eric threw the bow and the sack of arrows to Ryan's feet. He did not wish to leave his hide.

'Thanks, I admire your courage,' Ryan said sarcastically, as he picked up the arrows and the bow.

'Please do not put yourself at risk… ' Prudence held Ryan's hand. 'I do not wish any harm to come to you.'

'Mhmph, you worry way too much princess. Just leave the job to me, I will not disappoint you. Just hide with the knight wannabe you have by your side,' Ryan chuckled.

'At least one of us is not suicidal,' Nash responded to Ryan's provocation.

'I never said I was suicidal.' Ryan chuckled, as he had the last word. 'Hide! They're coming!'

Prudence and Nash hid themselves as Ryan had demanded them to do. The goblins were approaching; they were about two minutes from the location of Ryan and his friends. It was a small group of goblins, about five of them and well equipped. They looked hideous, and they walked in a strange and ridiculous way. They did not seem clever at all.

Ryan was surprised by how ugly and disgusting they looked. He was in a good position to fire with his bow. Actually, anyone, even a beginner could, effortlessly shoot down all the goblins. It was such a good spot, and Ryan was very confident in taking down the goblins from there.

'Wait!' the leader of the group said after stopping the march of its team. 'I smell something.'

'Sir, it might be your pants,' one of the goblins laughed.

'You certainly have a death wish you stupid mongrel!' the leader replied vulgarly. 'Kill that imbecile!' he ordered one of its soldiers.

The goblins had no respect or loyalty. They could kill each other for no reason and were naturally barbaric. They would even obey one of their own to have the pleasure of ripping the flesh from a living creature. The goblin who laughed about its leader was stabbed and left to die in the forest.

'Let us be on our ways!' The leader spat on the grass, as he was resuming the march of its group.

However, Ryan had other plans for the leader. The young man shot an arrow and pierced the leader's leg. All the goblins were in a combat guard and looking around; they did not see anything. A second arrow was shot and another goblin went down.

'Show yourself!' one of the creatures shouted.

Ryan shot another arrow and injured another one of the goblins, he seemed really agile with a bow and his aims were perfect. Only one goblin was left unharmed. It was so scared that it dropped its sword and started to run. However, Ryan did not want to let it go and shot an arrow around its ankle. All the goblins were down.

'All right – that's done!' Ryan jumped from a tree. 'Eww, really ugly they are,' he paused. 'Now you – we have some questions,' he advanced toward the goblin leader.

Ryan took a goblin's sword, and edged the blade toward the leader's throat.

All of Ryan's companions got out of their hides; they were mesmerized by Ryan's accomplishment. The princess could barely keep her eyes off Ryan; she seemed to care a lot more about the young man than what was around her.

'You are really good with a bow,' said Prudence.

'Wait till you see what I can do with a sword,' Ryan chuckled. 'Anyway, let's question this thing here.'

Ryan had questions that needed to be answered. The best way for him to know what was happening in Vita was to get information from a living creature that lived in this foreign world.

'You're too cocky, plus you could have put yourself in danger,' said Nash.

'Come on, how would those idiots have realized the arrows were coming from the top of a tree? There was no way I would have been spotted,' Ryan scoffed.

'You're kind of careless Ryan… but hey, I admit you were pretty cool!' said Eric.

'Stop encouraging him, that was only luck. You're in a world you don't know and you act so carelessly. If you want to die, then go ahead and die, but don't put Prudence in danger. I won't allow it,' Nash stood up to Ryan's face.

'You need to back off… I've been patient with your annoying remarks. But right now, I will not let you get in my way,' Ryan answered seriously, and in a threatening posture.

'Please do not fight… we need to gather information as you previously suggested,' Prudence said, while separating the two brothers.

'Yes, you are right.' Ryan glared at Nash's face.

A few minutes later; all the goblins were immobilized, they could not move or make any attempts to run away without hurting their injured legs. The leader was separated from the others. Prudence wanted to question it.

'Let me go!' the leader shouted in pain.

'I am sorry for the pain that has been inflicted upon you – however do understand that it is not personal. I am Princess Prudence Fulgura from Heartsas,' Prudence introduced herself. 'I wish to know what has happened. Why are a group of armed goblins allowed to march in the forest?' she demanded politely.

'Ha! Princess of Heartsas, who are you trying to fool? The princess is dead, everyone knows that!' it scoffed, while spitting on the grass. 'You can go to hell!'

'Please – I assure no harm will be done to you if you cooperate. I wish to know who has taken Heartsas,' demanded the princess.

'The Emperor Daemn has allowed every creature to walk equally. You humans deserved what happened. I will not say more than that, otherwise I will be killed,' the goblin said darkly.

'Emperor Daemn?' Prudence seemed troubled by her thoughts. 'Which direction is the nearest town?' she asked the goblin.

'I will not tell you. You can go to hell.' The goblin spat toward the princess.

'Listen, earlier I was being nice and I missed you on purpose,' said Ryan. 'But I could be really clumsy with this sword and kill you right here if you don't cooperate.' He paused. 'I suggest you answer wisely.'

The goblin looked down.

'There is – there is a town near of here.'

'Good, now keep talking.'

Ryan was intimidating the goblin, but Prudence knew that he would not kill it. If he wanted to do so, he would have killed all the other goblins in the first place.

'The town of Parisia – it is in the south east from here.' The goblin shook the sweat out of its face.

'Good, now turn around, Prudence,' Ryan demanded of the princess. 'I'll end its suffering.'

'But Ryan… I gave him my word that… '

'I know you did – I'm just going to… '

Nash pushed Ryan. 'You can't do that, she gave her word.'

'Again – you stand in my way.' Ryan grunted.

'Ryan is right, we should not let it live,' said Eric, siding with his friend.

'Hang on a second – I'm not going to kill it!'

'Then what were you going to do?' asked Mia.

'I was about to remove the arrow that I shot in its leg,' replied Ryan.

Prudence sighed in relief. She then looked at Ryan and was happy to see that he respected her decision.

'Thank you, Ryan,' Prudence smiled. 'You are very kind to do that.'

'Why would a human spare us?' the goblin asked.

'There is no point in killing if it's unnecessary,' said Ryan. 'That is what separates us from evil.' He paused and sighed. 'I hope that you will learn from us.'

Prudence was mesmerized by Ryan's kindness and the strength of his words. It took a few minutes, but Ryan and Nash had decided to remove the arrows from all the goblins' legs.

'All right, that's done,' Nash clapped his hands. 'Shall we go now?'

'Yes, let us go,' replied Prudence.

Nash then led the way toward Parisia. The indications of the goblin were right; they could see a sort of signboard indicating *Further South Parisia*.

Chapter Ten
Mademoiselle Delacroix's Tavern

An hour later, they had arrived in Parisia; it was a town that was full of life. However, goblins, orcs and many creatures were not permitted to visit it. Only elves, dwarves and humans were allowed to walk the streets of this beautiful town. It was a big town and well decorated, where the walls and the roofs of the houses were intricately painted.

The people of the streets were not shy in saying hello and the guards forced compliance. It was a marvellous town and the *joie de vivre* reigned in every house.

Ryan and Eric were both talking quietly. They were surprised and intimidated by how the people were looking at them. The dressing style of Ryan and his friends was more than enough to draw the attention of the people in town.

'Where are we going?' Ryan asked loudly. 'Because we've been walking for quite some time, but I don't see anywhere to stay,' he grunted.

'Do not worry Ryan; we shall arrive at an inn soon. I just need to find the nearest tavern,' Prudence said while leading the way.

'Why is that? I mean, why are we looking for a tavern?' Mia asked curiously.

'Rumours spread a lot in taverns, especially in towns like these. Everyone has a story to tell and to share,' Prudence answered.

'Mhmph, as long as there are pretty ladies in there, I won't complain.' Ryan chuckled.

Prudence went silent after hearing this; she felt a faint pain around her heart but did not know what it was.

'He is always like this, but don't worry princess I will look out for you,' said Nash. 'I think this is it.' He pointed out toward a big house.

'*Mademoiselle Delacroix's Tavern.*' Ryan read the sign out loud. 'Yep, this definitely says tavern,' he said enthusiastically. 'Who on Earth is Mademoiselle Delacroix?' he questioned.

Prudence and her friends entered the tavern; they needed to gather information on the emperor, but also a way to cross a portal which led to Ryan's world. However, they could not afford to bring too much attention to themselves. Prudence was still the target of the emperor, and a lot of the people who hang out in a tavern are up to no good most of the time.

The tavern was quite unwelcoming, it was dark inside with only a few lights were present. It had been installed this way so everyone could enter and stay in the dark if they did not wish to be recognized. It was the perfect place for rumours to be spread by individuals who wanted to remain anonymous.

'Sit there, I will try and ask around about any rumours that have been spoken. I will be back in an instant,' Prudence told her friends, as she was walking toward the barman.

'I'll come with you – it's not safe for a girl to go around and ask things that may cause problems for some people,' Nash said, while walking closely next to Prudence. 'Ryan, why don't you look around for some women, thought you were interested in flirting.' He laughed.

Ryan glared at Nash, his eyebrows were frowning and he was turning red.

'Leave it Ryan. Let him be,' Eric tried to calm down Ryan.

'Watch out, he might burn all of us down,' Mia scoffed.

Ryan closed his eyes and took a deep breath. Without saying a word, he did as his brother advised, and went to look around to see if he saw any woman that pleased him.

While Ryan was out searching, Prudence and Nash went toward the barman. The man was big, quite fat and unattractive, he had a big bump on the forehead and his eyes were so small they could barely distinguish his emotion. He had an angry look and an immense body. A lot of the people in the tavern were scared of him, because of his extraordinary appearance.

'Excuse – excuse me?' Prudence nervously asked the man.

'Yes what is it?' he grunted after seeing Nash.

'We need information.' Nash did not hesitate, 'Have you heard of a rumour or anything that involves the Emperor Daemn?'

'I suggest you to turn around and walk away from this tavern,' the barman advised Nash.

'So you do know of something?' Nash muttered.

'You should go before any harm is made to you. I am saying this for your own good, kiddo. You should leave this tavern. I will pretend that I never heard what you asked me,' the barman nicely advised the young man once more.

'Sorry we bothered you,' Nash said while backing out. 'We should go and sit with the others,' he suggested to Prudence.

'But I need to –'

'We'll talk about a plan which is the safest with the others,' he whispered to the princess after interrupting her.

Nash and Prudence went back to sit with their friends; they were quite frightened of the people who were inside the tavern. All of them were armed and aggressive looking, one of them even had a long scar instead of a left eye, and golden teeth.

One stare and they could take it the wrong way; it was best for everyone to keep their heads and eyes down. Once seated, Nash looked around him but couldn't see Ryan. Eric had told him about Ryan's little quest of finding an attractive woman, which made Prudence bite her lips in jealousy. Mia was quite silent throughout the whole time; she was not feeling right about anything that happened in Prudence's world. It was just too much, and she was surprised by how the brothers were reacting to all of it. It was as if they'd been here before, which was not normal at all.

While Nash and Eric were discussing, Ryan was on his own

table, trying to calm down. He needed to find peace of mind and, with Nash around, it was rather a hard task to do. The young man was drawing in the dust on the table. He was quite artistic and drawing was one of his hobbies.

Then, out of nowhere, a young and attractive woman approached him. She was dressed in a mini skirt, in a nice attractive outfit, which made parts of her body visible such as her belly and her neck. When Ryan looked up, it was Cheryl.

'May I serve you something?' she asked with a cute smile, as she bent toward Ryan.

'Erm, no thanks I don't drink.' Ryan stared at the young lady, amazed by her pretty face. He then looked down slightly and stared at her breasts. 'Nice ones… ' he whispered.

'Would you allow me to sit with you?' Cheryl asked the young man.

'Why?' Ryan asked her.

'Because I may have some answers to your questions. And I saved you, remember?'

'Fine, sit,' Ryan said coolly. 'Huh?'

Ryan looked at her once more, but she did not have any tail. He then asked her about it.

'Aw, a boy who likes to discuss… this makes things better.' The woman giggled. 'I used fairy dust. Only humans, elves and dwarves are allowed here. So Humolfs can stay out.'

'Humolf… what the heck is that?' Ryan asked her.

'My species… I would not talk much about Humolfs if I were you.'

Ryan asked the young Humolf a lot of questions. She was really cooperative, considering the circumstances.

The two individuals had gotten to know each other well, they were quite compatible and they had a good relationship. It was quite a nice time Ryan had; he forgot about Nash or his friends, he only cared about the instant he was living. His arrogance and his ego made him confident.

'I'm going to ruin this but I have no choice,' Ryan sighed, after getting up. 'Would you know anything about what is going on in Vita, or how I could get my friends home?' he asked, convinced that the woman would either laugh or turn him down.

'About Daemn... I know a lot,' Cheryl confirmed. 'But it could cost me my life, so you understand... ' she whispered, as she got up. 'And for the portal – only Heartsas possesses one that leads to London. The other kingdoms' portals lead to other worlds. This means that you will have to go through Daemn if you wish to go back to your world.' Cheryl then took out a stone. 'There are the stones too, but each are made to a specific destination, just like your tickets in your world. This stone here.' She showed the stone to Ryan. 'It can activate a portal from London to Vita, it is the one I used to bring you and your friends here... '

'Oh I see... ' Ryan looked interested.

'I am sorry. But if it is of any consolation, I had a good time.'

'Me too, you are gorgeous, charming and my kind of rock 'n' roll girl.'

'Rock 'n' roll?' Cheryl asked, puzzled.

'Aha, don't worry about it. Let's just say you're really memorable.' Ryan chuckled.

The woman then approached Ryan's ear. 'Pretend to kiss me on the neck... ' she ordered him quietly.

Ryan did what Cheryl asked him to. She then whispered to him something that would help get the information he was looking for. It was a name, Alexandra, but who was she? Cheryl only mentioned her name, and pointed out a back door that was firmly guarded with five men, completely armed. 'I have to go now... the dust is fading away,' Cheryl said, before she left.

'Wait, I wish to know if I will see you again.' Ryan held her hand, as if he did not want her to leave.

'We will meet again, I promise you,' she said softly.

Cheryl had left... Ryan decided to retrieve his friends and tell them about the information he had gathered. He would of course brag about the woman with whom he had a chat and how good looking she was.

Prudence and the rest were all sitting down quietly and discussing serious matters. 'Since Ryan is not here, it will be easier to discuss things that need to be discussed,' Mia rudely said.

'You should not backstab Ryan – he did not do you any harm. Why are you being so mean to him?' asked Prudence.

'Because Mia is a backstabbing b… ' Eric was about to insult her when she kicked him.

Mia was being childish and did not try to put herself in Ryan's shoes. It was not long before the young man arrived and told his friends about the information he had managed to gather.

Nash was on his guard and did not wish to trust Ryan. To him, it was yet another way of getting into trouble and putting the princess in danger. Ryan was really out of patience and punched the table in anger. The young man had had enough of his brother dictating everything and pretending he was the knight of the princess, when he was nothing. Ryan decided to go through with his plan no matter if his friends agreed, those who wished to follow him were welcomed and those who refused to acknowledge him were good riddance to him.

'Prudence, you choose – know that I won't force you or even try to convince you. But if you want to stay here and wait for a safe yet uncertain opportunity, then so be it. I will go on my own way for now… Nash will be your knight since he thinks he is one,' said Ryan.

'I wish to be by your side – I am always in danger. With you, I feel much safer,' Prudence said, with a smile and a deep sign of affection.

'Fine, I'm in. Tell us what you know… ' Nash moaned.

'I don't trust what Ryan has to say,' Mia scoffed.

'Well get lost – I don't need to hear any more of your rubbish. If you want to go solo, then go ahead little girl, you can count on a sure death,' Ryan snapped.

Ryan knew he was mean but it was time to cease Mia's annoying behaviour.

'You were a bit harsh…' Eric hesitated but spoke his mind.

'I know and I'm sorry, but we don't have time for all these childish things.' Ryan clicked his finger. 'That's how fast we can all lose everything in this world.'

'OK, enough with the boundary time – what is the plan to enter the door that is barricaded by these big guys?' asked Nash.

'We could fight our way through with a front attack, but we could die, since they are better equipped than us. Or we could use a little distraction and surprise them. This would give us a much better chance on bringing them down.'

Ryan briefly introduced his plan.

'You are brilliant,' Eric said loudly.

'You never fail to surprise me,' Prudence giggled.

'OK, Mr. So Brilliant, how do you plan on surprising them?' Nash asked, annoyed by everyone looking up to his brother.

Ryan expanded on his plan; he was great at managing a team and building up the confidence of it. Everyone, even Mia, was charmed by the way he was briefing his plan. The plan was risky but it was the best they had. Ryan counted on Eric's mentality to lower the guard of the men protecting the door. Prudence and Mia would enter the door with Nash, whilst he and Eric had to find a way to get the guards out of sight. It was planned but not guaranteed. Prudence was biting her lips and picking her nails nervously. She was unsure of the plan but she needed to put her faith in Ryan.

'Right – Eric, you're ready?' Ryan asked his friend, while approaching the guards.

'Well, erm… yes… I think!' Eric stuttered nervously.

The two young men were right in front of the five guards. They were all big, strong looking and with a scary posture. Their faces were covered in tattoos and scars; one of them had a missing eye and had to cover it with a pirate eye patch.

'What is it ya want?' one asked aggressively, as he saw the two boys approaching.

'We're here to see Alexandra,' Ryan claimed, with high confidence.

'Walk away lad,' another said immediately. 'You don't need to meet her.'

Ryan gently elbowed Eric to give him the signal of his act.

'Yeah, how would you know? Big man, I bet you have no brain!' Eric insulted the man. 'You all look so ugly, no wonder no one wants to approach you!'

'Eric calm down, you're being rude. These idiots might have ears you know!' Ryan added.

'You little children need to run away before we end your miserable lives!' one of the five men said.

'Oh and we can count on you to do that? Bet you can't even do a shoelace!' Eric said loudly.

'You will be sorry you said that!'

'Stein, what is a shoelace?' the eye patch man asked.

'O-M-G he doesn't even know what a shoelace is!' Ryan laughed. 'Sorry, I bet you do not know what O-M-G stands for; I'll enlighten your limited minds. It means oh my God.'

The five men had had enough, they were losing patience.

'Gary, get him!' Stein ordered furiously.

Gary tried to grab Eric but Ryan knocked him down with a sweep kick. Eric then kicked the head of the man to knock him out. All the men got up and started to rush toward the two teenagers.

'Catch me if you can, you idiot!' Ryan provoked, while running around the tavern.

Eric and Ryan had managed to run away and get two men to chase them; while one was knocked out, it severally lowered the guards of the two who remained. However, even then this would not be enough to enter the door without risking their lives; Ryan had to make sure he could get the two left to chase them.

'Eric – step two!' Ryan shouted while running.

Eric ceased running and crouched, the man who was following him hit himself on Eric's back before being projected violently on the ground.

Ryan made sure the man who chased him was close enough so he could elbow him hard. With the speed of the run, the man was violently smashed on a table; the impact was so brutal that the table broke itself in two.

'Well played mate!' Ryan congratulated his friend. 'Now, step three!'

The two remaining men in front of the door were furious, they could not tolerate two young boys standing up to them and mocking them. 'I will kill you! Little piece… ' the leader yelled in rage, he got his sword out and started to rush toward Ryan, blinded by his anger.

'Here we go!' Ryan said loudly, and waved his hand as if he was giving a sign.

Nash then threw the bow to Ryan but missed, the bow fell on the ground next to Ryan's right foot.

'Ah! Nash, you are an idiot!' Ryan gasped, panicked, as he reached for the bow.

'Die!' the man was about to slice Ryan's neck.

'Enough!' a woman shouted out of nowhere.

Stein stopped the blade of his sword right at one millimetre from Ryan's neck.

'Wow, that was close,' Ryan chuckled nervously, after moving away from the blade.

Prudence ran toward Ryan, the fright she had was unexplainable, and it was as if her own life had been threatened.

'Who are you? I heard a lot of noise and I have to admit, it was rather annoying,' the woman said, while approaching Ryan and his friends.

When she left the darkness they could distinguish her. She was gorgeous, about twenty years old, with dark blonde hair which was slightly curly on the sides and mysterious brown eyes. She was tall for a woman, the same height as Ryan and her body was neither skinny nor fat. She had the body of a goddess and her lips were lustful. The way she was dressed was unusual; she wore a pirate outfit, which was sleeveless and attractive. A pistol was inside a holster and a rapier on the opposite side and she wore black boots with medium heels.

'I'm Ryan – nice to make your acquaintance my beauty,' the young man said to the woman. 'But for you, my dear, I could be anyone.'

'Mhmp, I'm not interested with your advances,' Alexandra said coolly. 'What do you want?' she asked after drawing out her rapier.

'We do not mean harm,' Prudence spoke, before Ryan would say anything that could escalate the atmosphere. 'We wish to know about the Emperor Daemn.'

Everyone in the tavern stared at Prudence and her friends, and then they started to talk indistinctly between them.

'I told them to leave… ' the barman stated, as he was cleaning a goblet.

'No matter, they will not live long enough if they go on the way they are,' Alexandra scoffed.

'How come you have a pistol?' asked Eric. 'Everyone in this crazy world, I mean goblins and all the freaks, have bows, crossbows, swords… why are they not using pistols or weapons that actually are easier to use and stronger?'

'Gunpowder is rare, but mostly pirates stole what was left of it a very long time ago… plus, only us know the secret of using it to create pistols. Of course, the emperor and other kingdoms have their ways of using the powder for their own methods,' said Alexandra.

'We wish to know – what has happened?' asked Prudence.

'You are being cryptic, lady,' Alexandra responded. 'But if it involves the emperor, I suggest you find another purpose in life.'

'Why is that?' demanded Nash.

'Because you fools are venturing into a death sentence.'

'The emperor will be sorry for what he did to Prudence, trust me, lady,' Ryan said sharply. 'He doesn't scare me at all,' he added.

'Then you are indeed foolish. Oh well – we have this in common I suppose.' Alexandra laughed quietly. 'OK, I am willing to hear you out; after all you have managed to beat my men. Come on in,' the woman said, while leading the way to the room that was firmly guarded earlier.

Chapter Eleven
The Myth Of The Sword

Prudence and her friends went inside the room; it was dark with a table in the middle. A window with bars was the only thing that allowed light to enter. The walls were quite old and a lot of spiders had woven their webs. They could even, at certain times, hear rats crawling; it was a place Ryan would never suspect a woman to live.

Nash was being bossy again and told Ryan to get a hold on his behaviour; of course, the remarks Nash was making were only aggravating the tension. Eric then got in the middle and separated the two brothers before one of them snapped in anger.

'So what do you wish to know about the emperor?' The woman sat down on a chair.

'Who is he? And why are the other kingdoms not doing anything?' demanded Prudence.

'What's in it for you?' the woman asked with nerve.

'I believe she asked you a question.' Ryan took Prudence's side.

'Leave her, you should not get involved,' said Nash.

'OK, that's the third time today you have thought you are the boss.'

The young man was irritated; he wanted to punch Nash so badly that his hands were trembling in anger.

'I like to play with fair players,' the woman chuckled. 'Fine, I shall tell you about the emperor.'

The woman began to tell the story; she explained how the emperor appeared as a tyrant and how fast his dominance had spread. She did not miss one detail, from the beginning to the end of it, she even mentioned the presumed death of the princess and how Heartsas had fallen apart since then. Every kingdom was on their defences and frightened by the emperor, thus the reason they did not defend Heartsas. Prudence could not believe what she was hearing. The master behind this plan must have been someone really experienced in strategic and military regiment, there was no doubt.

'Is there a way to defeat the emperor?' the princess asked.

'If you are foolish enough... '

'Come on Alexandra, I bet you will tell us.'

Ryan advanced toward the woman.

'So you do know of my name,' she chuckled. 'Fine, I've heard of something that scares the emperor,' she said darkly. 'There is a legend about a sword,' she began to tell the story.

'A long time ago, humans were oppressed by the orcs and the goblins. They were literally their slaves until one day when a man we all call King Leo, came out of nowhere with a sword in his hands. This sword eradicated a whole army of orcs with only one strike. It was presumed that the sword had disappeared when the king died. Of course, a lot of adventurers or fools went to look for it. If anyone could find it, they would ultimately become the ruler of Vita.'

'So the emperor fears that someone will whoop his sorry – ' Ryan deducted, before being interrupted by Nash, who punched him in his arm.

'So if anyone can find this sword... ' Prudence muttered to herself. 'Then we would be able to destroy him?'

'What's in it for you? I answered your questions – now I demand an answer,' Alexandra insisted.

'I need this sword – if I wish to free my kingdom and take my rightful place.'

'Aha – this is absurd. Do not mock me lady... the princess is dead.' Alexandra laughed

'We have what we came in for – I thank you, you do have my gratitude,' Prudence said, before she turned around to open the door.

'Wait... you need someone to escort you. If you wish to go looking for the sword, you should start where only royal blood is considered,' Alexandra claimed. 'After all, only those who were of non royal blood went to look for it.'

'What are you saying?' asked Nash.

'If she is who she pretends to be, then she will have no problem in entering the Dragon's Realm. Everyone knows only a person of royal descent may enter this realm. If she is a princess indeed, then she will be able to enter it.'

'Why would you help us?' Nash demanded, convinced Alexandra was hiding something.

'I am interested in the treasure.' The woman paused. 'And also, it is every pirate's code to go against the law. Since the emperor is taking the lead, I will rebel against him,' Alexandra said quietly. 'I am offering my help, however I demand a reward once you have freed your kingdom,' she stated her conditions.

'What kind of reward?' Prudence asked, puzzled.

'You must possess a lot of diamonds and gold. This interests me. So, do we have a deal?'

'I have not much choice.' The princess paused. 'I accept your terms.'

'We shall leave tonight; the boat will be ready by then.'

'Do you know anything about a magical portal?' Mia asked out of nowhere.

'No, I have never heard about such nonsense.'

Prudence and her friends left the tavern. They had the afternoon to relax before they departed at night time. They decided to rest in an inn for a while, since the town was safe from goblins, orcs and other creatures. Surprisingly, the emperor had limited access to the town, which allowed Prudence to lessen her guard and enjoy a good time with Ryan, just like before when she was in London.

Once in the inn, the princess realized that she had no money on her. Ryan then pulled his wallet out of his pocket and took out a ten pence coin. It was made of silver and round. Nash knew it had poor value in London but it was worth a try.

'As you can see, its value is worth ten silver coins. The lion represents a royal coin,' Ryan said with a convincing act.

'Oh yes, I can see the lion indeed. Well sir, we do have a room on the first floor.'

'Wicked, Ryan you're a genius!' said Eric.

'Thanks mate but I don't think I need a kiss ar... ' Ryan abstained himself from being rude in front of the princess.

After a long and eventful morning, it was time for Ryan and his friends to rest before boarding Alexandra's boat. The room had only three beds. Prudence proposed to sleep later on, but Ryan and Nash refused. She was the princess after all, and even if they were lost and confused about the place they were in, Prudence was the only one both brothers cared about. Ryan was the most gallant; he grabbed Prudence and delicately placed her on the bed.

'I will not let you sacrifice yourself for me, on anything,' the young man said.

'But Ryan - I... ' she tried to argue with Ryan, but he interrupted her by touching her lips with his finger.

'I care about you. Something I rarely do about the people I meet,' he whispered into the princess's ear, as he got to his feet.

'Man, I'm beat,' Eric moaned before he fell asleep.

'Ryan, would you care to lie down with me?' the princess asked, with her cheeks turning red. 'I mean - only if you are interested.'

'Huh? Won't it be inappropriate for a princess?' asked Ryan.

'I would feel much safer... if it's only you who rest next to me... ' Prudence was completely red, and she kept on looking down on the sheets. 'So, will you?'

Ryan looked at Nash with a rather satisfied look; he smiled and lay down next to the princess, before putting his left arm around her left shoulder.

Nash had decided to guard the room by standing outside. He wanted to have a tour of the town. But above all, he wanted to get out of the room, furious about Prudence choosing his brother.

Ryan and Prudence's eyes were slowly and gently closing, they did not realize how exhausted they truly were. But it felt good, warm and reassuring for Prudence to be in her knight's arms. As she closed her eyes, she was smiling as if she was happier than ever.

Chapter Twelve
Megalodonus

It was sunset; the princess and her friends were all in the inn apart from Nash, who had decided to take fresh air. Alexandra was outside in the port, loading up a boat with the help of her pirates. The boat was immense; it was made of wood and had long branches which made it look like it could fly. The design of it was rather interesting; the boat looked as if it was a giant wooden shark with wings.

Alexandra was smoking a pipe while observing her men filling up the boat with tonnes of goods. Water, bread, wine, meat, all of it was being stocked inside different barrels. A much bigger and intimidating pirate charged the boat; he was struggling to load up the barrel inside.

'Blimey! This is hard work!' he grunted, while pushing the barrel.

'Stop your whimpers. Have I not taught you how to be a pirate?'

'Yes Lady Alexandra – please do accept me apologies.'

'Load up the gunpowder and do shut up,' ordered Alexandra.

The men were all pushing themselves to abide by their captain's orders. They did not wish to be harmed or killed in such pitiable circumstances. One of them was drinking a bottle of rum. He did not seem bothered by the work that was given to him.

Alexandra was a fierce, cold woman, she caught him and gave him a good beating.

'Gary, tie him up and make sure once in the sky he gets what he deserves,' she said, after pushing her hair back.

'I have a question me lady?' asked one of the pirates.

'What is it that you question?'

'Why did you agree to work with these people?' demanded the pirate. 'They look like incapable idiots.'

'Mmhm... they are not incapable; they did manage to beat up Gary and the rest. I plan on getting the reward I covet.' Alexandra paused, before she smiled darkly. 'You see, the woman who seems to be taking the lead of their team, pretends to be the Princess of Heartsas.' She laughed evilly.

'Fools they are, the princess is dead.'

'It is said so, yes.' Alexandra paused; she seemed deep in her thoughts. 'But I am fairly convinced that she is telling the truth, the emperor is intelligent and strategic... I do not question this. But he seems unstable, and she possesses the necklace of the Fulgura family.' She chuckled, as if she was up to something.

'We are pirates, why should we help a princess?' asked the pirate.

'We are not, we'll help her to get the sword and then it shall be mine. We'll dispose of her and her friends' bodies once the job's done. Then Vita is ours for the taking, even the emperor will have to bow to us,' Alexandra sniggered evilly.

'Brilliant!'

The boat had been fully loaded up; the woman spat on the port, before putting a jacket around her. She then finished smoking her pipe quietly with a rather satisfied look on her face.

Meanwhile, outside the inn, Nash was annoyed that the princess had chosen Ryan to lay down with her. He liked Prudence very much but with Ryan around, it was hard to get her attention. He had to find a way to get his brother out of the picture without hurting or killing him; they had their differences but he would never do something as extreme as putting his brother's life at risk. No, he needed to play fair and win her heart. But it was a tough competition for him. Deep inside, Nash was insecure and scared. He kept a brave face but he was terrified about everything that was happening around him. Ryan however, seemed so strong and so sure about himself, even if his choices were rushed and impulsive. Ryan was hard to compete with, especially when he had the admiration of half of the team and mostly Prudence's.

But Nash had other plans on his mind. He knew Ryan's main preoccupations were to find a way home and protect Prudence. His brother never had the intention of staying on Vita, whilst he desired to live in this world and stay with Prudence. Nash was fairly convinced that the princess would stay, it just made sense. She would find the sword, eliminate the threat and rule as a princess. Knowing his brother, he would never abide by this way of life. No, he would choose his friends and his loving life in London. This ultimately gave him the advantage in seducing the princess; he would not hesitate in playing with her mind if he had to. After all, all is fair in love and war.

It was night time, the young man had enough time to think. He went back at the inn where everyone was supposedly awakened by now. The door of the room was open; Eric was still asleep and snorted loudly. Mia had had enough of the young man's noises; he was infuriating her. She grabbed a pillow and hit him hard, but he was still asleep. It was as if he refused to open his eyes.

'He makes me mad!' Mia yelled, while hitting him.

'Let him be – at least his problems disappear for a while,' said Ryan.

'I guess so – how can she sleep so well with that idiot here making so much noise?'

'I don't know Mia – I guess she was exhausted.' Ryan glanced at Prudence's angelic face. 'She really is something,' his voice turned soft.

'Or maybe she feels so good in your arms,' Mia giggled.

'Who wouldn't?' Ryan boasted.

'Enough, this is rubbish,' Nash snapped. 'We have to go to meet Alexandra at the port; I think it's time, isn't it?' he grunted. 'Make that idiot wake up, we need to go.'

'Mia, wake him up please, I need to wake up Prudence.'

'Ugh – I tried, he just won't wake up,' Mia moaned.

Nash took the pillow and fiercely smashed Eric's face with it. The young man was so disoriented by the hit that he felt lost as he opened his eyes. He could not remember where he was for a few seconds.

Ryan knew his brother was mad for some reason. It sure involved Prudence, but he did not care. It was not his fault if the princess loved his company. Instead, he provoked Nash by caressing Prudence's hair as he woke her up. Ryan was not going to back down for anyone when it came to confrontations. He was aware of Nash liking Prudence, but if he wanted her, he would have to go through him. There was no way he would let him have her. She was the only woman Ryan would never let go of. It was strange, he had never felt this way and he wanted her so badly that whenever she looked away, he had to do something to get her attention. Whenever Nash was around, he would feel somehow threatened, thus the reason he could not bear to see her around him.

'Ryan – can I sleep a bit more?' The princess yawned.

'We have to go – but I reckon you'll be able to sleep on Alexandra's boat.'

'I wish to sleep in your arms again. It felt surprisingly good.'

Nash had had enough of all of this; he decided to get out of the inn after slamming the door.

Ryan was really courteous with the princess; he made sure she did not need anything. But it was time for them to go on their journey; Prudence would never be at peace whilst her kingdom was ruled by an impostor. Ryan was decided; he secretly swore to free Prudence's kingdom no matter what he had to sacrifice. However, he was too proud to say it out loud.

Eric was rather angry; Nash had interrupted a nice dream he was having. But he knew he had to withstand it if he desired to go back to his world. He and Mia had no choice but to go through the quest that was given to the princess. Hopefully, within the journey, they would find a way to get back home.

Nash and the teenagers had left the inn; they were in the port where Alexandra was meant to meet them. She was late and the impatience of Ryan was growing, he started to throw little rocks in the sea. It was occupying him enough to keep his mind off a lot of things. Prudence joined him and found this game rather amusing. She kept on throwing the rocks too close, which sometimes hit Eric's head instead of getting in the sea.

'You keep on hitting that poor bloke!' Ryan laughed.

'Arr! That's the fourth time you hit me on the head!'

'Oh I am so sorry. I do not mean to hurt you,' she giggled.

'I'll show you how to do it – you take the rock and you make a big movement of the arm, do not be scared to throw it as if it was a lance,' explained Ryan.

The princess gave it a try, and it worked. She had managed to throw a couple of rocks in the water without hitting Eric; Ryan congratulated her and looked at the starry sky. The princess did the same by curiosity; she looked up and saw a shooting star. Was it a comet? What was it? It was just so beautiful.

She had never seen or witnessed a shooting star; she had only read about them in books and imagined them. It was a magnificent and ephemeral spectacle; Ryan gently grabbed her right hand and told her to make a wish. A wish… but what could she wish for? She was in danger; her kingdom was ruled by an evil person. She could wish for everything to be sorted out, but what then? Prudence thought of many things, and then she realized something. She did not have to be afraid of making a wish, because she knew exactly where she wished to be. No matter the circumstances, it was Ryan she would choose to be with.

The princess closed her eyes and with all her heart, she made her wish. It felt amazingly good, even if it was only a simple wish. Maybe that was the magic of the shooting star, wishing on something and relying on this symbolic moment to remember what truly matters.

'So what did you wish for?' asked Ryan.

'I wished that...'

'Aha, nearly got you there... if you say it out loud, it won't happen. That's what everyone says of course. But if you want to tell me?'

'I will tell you once you tell me what you wished for.'

'You will know – not now but later on.' He chuckled.

Mia and Eric were observing the two teenagers; they were both captivated by the growing romance that was taking place right in front of their eyes. Eric was not surprised; he knew how girls reacted toward Ryan. Even when he was a child, he always had the attention when it came to girls or women. Mia was smiling in happiness; of course this was something Eric could not understand. He then politely tapped Mia's shoulder and demanded her why she looked so happy.

'This is the first good thing I've seen so far since we came to that world... they look so perfect for each other...'

'Yes that is true, but is that the only reason you're being so joyful?'

'They are the picture I have of a happy couple.' Mia replied with a smile.

'Oh I see...' said Eric. 'One who is too proud to say out loud how he feels... and another one who thinks making someone else jealous works. Mmm...' the young man laughed. 'I suppose everyone got their own little garden, eh...'

'Shut up,' Mia scoffed.

Alexandra had arrived. She had a bottle of rum in her left hand, and with nerve she smoked her pipe in front of the princess and her friends. She acted as if she did not care how late she was. It was as if she had done nothing wrong and people waiting on her behalf had no meaning to her. She then pulled her hair back and advanced toward the teenagers who were looking impatient, especially Ryan.

'*Megalodonus* will be here shortly, it has been taken for a little tour before we begin our trip...'

'*Megalodonus*?' asked Prudence. 'What is that?'

'You shall understand soon enough.'

'And you are not sorry for making us wait?' asked Ryan.

'Why should I be?' Alexandra scoffed.

'You really are something… a truly rude woman,' said Ryan. 'It feels like I'm speaking with a guy.'

'Shut up.'

A boat had arrived, surprisingly it was not coming from the water but from the sky. How was that even possible? A boat is meant to be in the water and not the sky. It was a shock but Vita was like a fairytale, and not believing in crazy things would be unwise. Magic was what drove this world, it was something not to forget, and it was rather hard since in Ryan's world technology had replaced all the magic.

Eric gasped after seeing the boat, it looked monstrous. It was as if a shark had left the ocean and was able to fly in the sky, which was terrifying to look at it. He was not the only one to find it intimidating, even his friends were so shocked that their jaws dropped.

While Ryan and his friends were mesmerized by the boat, something was bothering the princess. There was magic in her world, yet people were not allowed to make use of it… why? She stood silent, but this thought was troubling her.

Ryan slapped his face to make sure that he was not dreaming. He then took a deep breath and smiled. It was time for them to embark the magnificent flying boat. 'How are we supposed to get inside the boat?' he demanded, as he was looking up.

'It's not a boat… ' Alexandra said calmly.

'Then what is it?'

'It's my most precious heritage – *Megalodonus*.'

'Right… Anyway – how do we get on the boat?' asked Ryan.

'Just use the rope, duh,' said Alexandra.

Prudence was scared, she was not adventurous at all, even grabbing a rope and scaling a boat was a challenge to her. Nash then advanced toward her and gently offered his hand. 'I will not drop you – just trust me.'

'I am scared – I am supposed to be brave, but I am not.'

'What a cry baby,' Alexandra scoffed. 'Guys, lower *Megalodonus*, seems like we'll have to take a good impulse before flying.'

'Aye captain!' the pirates shouted, after dropping an immense anchor in the sea.

The impact of the anchor hitting the water was so extraordinary that an immense quantity of water splashed on Prudence and her friends. They were soaked wet from their faces to their feet. 'Aw blimey!' Eric gasped loudly.

'That woman is seriously disturbed,' said Ryan.

'Stop your whimpers, and get on *Megalodonus* now that it's reachable!' shouted Alexandra.

The pirates dropped a board for Prudence and her friends to embark; it was the easiest way for her. Of course, the pirates were all laughing about the lack of courage of the princess. The mockery of the pirates was getting on the brothers' nerves. Nash, who wanted to impress Prudence, did not hesitate and once on board, he punched a pirate who fell down over the boat. All the pirates stood up to the brothers and got out their swords. All seemed furious and impatient.

'Eh, nice to see I have a good influence on you,' Ryan chuckled, as he was drawing out his sword. 'Wow, there are fifteen of them – against two of us. Bring it on then!'

'Enough you imbeciles, we are not here to fight,' Alexandra shouted. 'I want my reward and you want your way out of this chaos. Control your men and I will control mine,' Alexandra turned to Prudence with a serious tone.

'I am sorry, I do apologize on their behalf,' said the princess.

Prudence then told the brothers to control themselves and not to get involved in fights that did not need attention.

The boat had left the port of Parisia, which symbolized the beginning of a long and dangerous journey. Prudence knew things were just starting for her. Outside Parisia it was not safe to travel, especially with the emperor going after the sword. She knew it was inevitable to encounter his troops who would not hesitate to kill her and her friends. But she did not have a choice. She only had about two days left before her kingdom banished her.

As the boat gained enough speed, it left the water and started to fly. The view was mesmerizing; it was as if Prudence was leaving the ocean and starting to fly beside the birds. The fresh breeze was caressing her face, she felt so good that she closed her eyes for a while. She wanted to enjoy at the fullest this nice and sweet breeze of the night.

Mia was exploring; it was the first time in her life she had been on a boat. It was scary but at the same time interesting. Everything she read in books or watched on TV described exactly how pirates were and how their boat was undertaken. She never believed in the stories of the books, or even the films she was watching, she always thought that pirates were just a tale for children. But they were not, and the behaviour of the pirates was unpredictable. One thing she was sure of, was that she would not trust Alexandra or her men. They were up to something, and she could feel it.

'So, enjoying staring at Alexandra?'

Ryan interrupted Mia, who was deep in her thoughts.

'Huh what? Oh… yes, I mean I was just looking around.'

'I know what you're thinking, lady.'

'Really? And what is that?'

'How did I get in this mess? And should I trust those pirates?' Ryan chuckled.

'Nearly this, but yes… can you?' asked Mia.

'I don't know – you know how pirates are described in books. Let's just say, that I will keep a close attention on Alexandra,' Ryan whispered.

Mia and Ryan were talking quietly about the pirates. Then, after a short conversation that led to more questions than answers, they decided to end the topic of pirates. Mia was looking down, and then she looked at Ryan.

'Listen, about before… I'm sorry. I know I acted so childishly, but I was so scared. And you act like you have everything under control… it's remarkable.'

'I have a confession… ' Ryan paused. 'I'm not sure about anything. Truth be told, I'm actually petrified… but then I think of Nash who seems so confident, and I try my best to actually keep up with him – heck, even surpass his confidence… but to be honest… I'm just following my heart.'

Mia smiled; she then elbowed the young man softly.

'Hey, why are you acting like a player?' asked Mia. 'I know you well… and you are so not the type of guy to chase random women… so why now?'

Ryan became red. His cheeks were the colour of a tomato, and his eyes were looking down. His pupils were moving left to right at a fast pace. He was embarrassed and started to sweat.

'The thing is… ' he began, but then went silent. 'I think I'm falling in love… '

'Oh… ' Mia smiled. 'Is it the princess who stole your heart?'

Ryan smiled and nodded.

'Before I met her… I used to think that I had everything figured it out. But since she came in my life… ' he paused and smiled. 'I don't know, I just want to be the perfect guy for her… I guess when I came to Vita… I wanted to impress her. It was the moment for me to show her what I'm worth so she would choose me… ' Ryan then looked down and sighed. 'The truth is… I don't even know if she feels the way I feel about her and it terrifies me… '

'Well, going around women won't make her like you… you have to tell her.'

'Yeah, but only when it's the right time… '

The night was the perfect time to travel without being spotted. Alexandra had much experience as a pirate and she knew how to dodge squadrons or legions boats. Since being a pirate, means potentially being brought down on sight, it was the best strategy she could use to move without any suspicious.

However, her perfect plan was soon to be questioned. She did not know it but the princess was the highest priority of the emperor, before the sword itself. It was true that Prudence was presumed dead. But it was also very true that Reaper and the emperor's men were the ones to spread the rumours. In addition, their quiet and calm journey to the Dragon's Realm was about to take an ugly twist.

Chapter Thirteen
The Tears Of A Princess

Ryan went to look for Prudence; he wanted to share a moment with her under the starry sky the night was offering. The young man tried to approach the princess but Nash outran him, he was talking to Prudence and stealing the moment Ryan wanted to have with her. Alexandra saw this; she secretly laughed before approaching Ryan, who stared at Prudence and his brother with anger. His fist was clenched; he was so angry that he seemed like a bomb ready to blow up. But he took a deep breath and calmed himself down, he did not wish to cause a scene or embarrass the princess.

Alexandra did not hesitate, she went near Ryan and started to mock him. It was as if she was heartless and did not care about how others felt. 'You look so miserable, it is such an amusing sight,' said Alexandra.

'Really?' Ryan scoffed sarcastically. 'Really, you're going to get on my bad side?' he said irritably.

'I'm already on your bad side, just like you are on mine. Feel better?'

'Gee, thanks.'

'You're very welcome.'

'Look, I don't have time with your little flirt right now. I know you force yourself to resist me, I get it. But right now, as you can see *chérie*… I have someone I wish to beat up so badly. That guy over there.' Ryan pointed out Nash. 'Go annoy him.'

Suddenly, as Ryan was talking to Alexandra, the boat suffered a jolt. It was unusual and Alexandra dashed to check what had happened.

'I did not see what it was captain!' a pirate shouted.

'It couldn't be a griffon. It's way too late for them to fly... ' Alexandra muttered.

'Captain! It's the emperor's boat!' the pirate on the turret yelled.

Prudence had heard the pirate. She went immediately to see Alexandra, to advise her of the wisest option they had. The princess gave two solutions, either they tried to outrun the boat of the emperor or they should hide from it.

However, no captain would take orders from an outsider. Alexandra refused and prepared her boat for battle; she was not afraid since she was a pirate, and collecting a bigger bounty on her head would only make things better for her.

'Men, make sure you're ready to unleash our special weapon!'

The boat had been hit again by a canon, it was losing altitude. Ryan could feel the boat jolting a lot more, it was severely damaged but the captain refused to surrender. No, she only cared about bringing down the emperor's boat, no matter what. The young man was certainly not going to let him and his friends die in such a pathetic way. He grabbed his sword and pointed the edge of his blade in front of Alexandra's throat.

'Stop with the attack, we will all die. Find a way to hide us or get us out of here,' ordered Ryan.

'Men! Release the special weapon!' Alexandra shouted.

'Darn! Do you really want to die?' Ryan threatened the captain.

'You will not dare to kill me.'

'You think?'

Ryan took Alexandra's revolver and pointed it at her head.

'Now, I'll do this again... follow Prudence's orders.'

The woman was not disposed to taking orders from Ryan; she pretended to cooperate but knocked him down with a sweep kick. She then drew out her rapier and pointed the edge of her blade at the boy's throat. The situation was reversed but the boat was still under attack. It was not long before it caught fire and it started to head down to the ground.

'Men! Release our special weapon now!' Alexandra yelled.

The pirates did as they were told and shot a bomb toward the emperor's boat. Everyone thought they were doomed, a normal bomb being the special weapon of a pirate? That was rather a joke, since every pirate possesses bombs. However, the bomb then changed into a blazing shark, acting like a shark would. Eating the other boat was its speciality. Alexandra laughed, and to everyone's greatest surprise, they could see a lot of goblins and trolls jumping out of their boat or being eaten alive.

'Now it's time for the last blow!' Alexandra raised her rapier.

The bomb then concentrated a magnificent quantity of energy and exploded. The impact was so strong that the emperor's boat literally got destroyed. As Alexandra was distracted by the explosion, Ryan pushed her to the ground. He then immobilized her by getting a hold on her arms and upper body; he then realized the boat was rapidly crashing down. Mia and Eric were stuck on the left side of the boat; they tried to move but could not manage to get out.

'Ryan! Help us!' Mia yelled, panicked.

'Try something funny and you'll regret it,' Ryan said to Alexandra, before he ran to help his friends.

Prudence wanted to go with Ryan but Nash stopped her, he grabbed her arm and prevented her from moving. 'I will not let you die!'

'I do not care! I want to help Ryan!' she said, as she was debating herself.

'I will keep you safe, no matter what,' Nash insisted.

Ryan had gotten to his friends; a metal shard was preventing Mia from moving her left foot. Eric was alright, he could manage to get out, he ripped a small piece of his jeans but he was fine. Ryan ordered him to go to Nash and Prudence while he tried to get Mia out.

The young man was brave, he was not scared at all. However the speed of the boat crashing was imminent, he tried his best but he had not enough time. Ryan saw the trees getting near; he knew they would crash before he could get Mia out.

'Go Ryan! Leave me!' Mia cried.

'There's no way I will let you die!'

'You have to! Just go!'

'Shush! Grumpy, let me do what I have to do!' Ryan hugged Mia tightly. And then…

BOOM!

When Prudence opened her eyes, it was an inconceivable sight that was being offered to her. The forest was ravaged, tops of trees were on fire and a lot of corpses were piled up on the grass. One body was even slashed in half, and the strange thing was that the man's nerves were trembling and shaking his dying body. Prudence's stomach was turning, she felt sick from all the blood and the smell of death. She restrained herself but her face was turning green. She then heard Mia shrieking in horror. Prudence thought of Ryan and the sick feeling was immediately gone… she looked around to find him, without even thinking of Nash, Eric or others. She just wanted to see Ryan.

Then she saw him… he was holding Mia but… when Prudence looked closely, she could see an immense piece of wood that had pierced his back. The wood maculated in Ryan's blood and the princess's eyes were opening in horror; she could not believe what was happening. Her heart was shattering because of the image that was presented to her. Ryan dying… no! Prudence refused to believe it true. It must have been Mia's blood… it had to be! But it was not…

It was Ryan's blood spilling. Mia held her friend who was severally injured and placed him on the grass, after removing the piece of wood.

Prudence did not wait; she ran toward Ryan in despair, she could see the young man covered in blood. He was breathing heavily as if he was trying his best to withstand the pain. Prudence refused to believe it, she could not handle this. Not Ryan, it was just impossible. She even wished that it could have been Nash or someone else laying on the ground. It was a horrible thing to wish, but she did not care.

'Pru... Prudence?' Ryan moaned in pain.

His body seemed heavy and his arms were trembling. Even his voice and his eyes seemed to shake, but Ryan was doing his best to fight it. Prudence could see the one she loved, shaking and struggling to survive, he was weak. His blood was spilling so much that his white shirt turned to red.

'I... I'm here... Ryan! Ryan, why...' Prudence started to cry, as she was holding Ryan's hand.

'Don't – I'm not dead... see... I am... here.' Ryan placed his shaking hand on Prudence's left breast. 'I'm here... right here. Don't be afraid...' he struggled to talk.

His hand was trembling and his eyes were becoming heavier. Prudence and Mia were both kneeling next to the young man who was losing consciousness.

'Is he... is he going to die?' Eric's voice shivered.

Nash went silent; he could not believe what was happening. His wish had been granted but the price was huge. He refused to look at his dying brother. It was not conceivable, he who was always sure about himself and gifted with incredible luck... dying? No, that was not happening.

'We have to leave,' Alexandra said calmly. 'The boat has caught fire... it's rare that a squad of the emperor is sent alone.' She paused, after glancing at the injured young man. 'We have to move, otherwise they will find us,' she said coolly.

'Quiet!' Prudence cried in tears.

'Go... I will be fine.' Ryan coughed. 'Just think of me... it'll be like a dream to me.' He paused. 'But promise me – that you'll make it... and... bring... them home... for me.'

'I... I don't want to leave you here,' Prudence sobbed.

'Please...'

'I... I promise.' Prudence sobbed. 'Ryan... you have to know...'

she kept on sobbing. 'I love you!' she cried, before placing her head on his bloody chest.

When Ryan heard those words, he could not help feeling like his ears were betraying him. He must have been dreaming for her to say such sweet words. A warm and intense feeling burnt down inside of him. His heart was pounding behind his chest. He felt as if he had reached another world. Was he dreaming? Why did he feel so good suddenly? The pain was gone… he could only focus on what his heart felt… his mind was shattering everything he had lived to focus on this instant. He could not forget the sweetness of those words that made him fly to another world. He was hesitating to let go of the princess, but he eventually did it. His eyes were getting blurry and tired. The young man knew he did not have long before he succumbed to his wounds. Still… she had to know too… even if it would be the last words of his. But he could not speak… his sight turned to darkness… and… he realized… he was gone…

It was not long before bushes and other noises were heard. Alexandra assumed it was the emperor's troops; she took out her pistol and pointed it out toward the bushes. 'We have to go!' Alexandra shouted, while grabbing Prudence's arm, who refused to move.

Alexandra then lost patience and knocked out the princess, before letting Nash holding her.

'But we can't leave Ryan here!' Mia sobbed.

'Shut up!' Alexandra yelled at Mia and ordered one of her pirate to escort her. 'He is dead already!'

'No!' Eric protested. 'He cannot die! Not like this!'

Alexandra scoffed and kicked Ryan around the ribs. The young man did not move or say anything… not a single sound came from him.

'See… ' Alexandra said quietly. 'He is dead.'

Eric looked down and tears dropped off his face. He followed the lead of Alexandra, but upon leaving he could not help but to look at his friend one last time.

Everyone left, leaving Ryan's unconscious body on the grass. The goblins did not wait long before finding him. 'Look, a nice dinner we have here!' one of them said, salivating in hunger.

'Move aside you imbeciles!' a woman's voice was heard.

'It's the Humolf!'

'A traitor to the emperor!' a goblin shrieked.

It was Cheryl. She came out of nowhere, and, with an unnatural speed, she killed all the goblins that stood in her way.

'I am traitor to the emperor, yes,' she chuckled. 'But this one is mine for the taking.' She approached Ryan. 'What is it with you that I cannot seem to stay away from?'

Cheryl caressed Ryan's cold face. She then grabbed him and disappeared in the darkness of the night.

Chapter Fourteen
The Forest Of Nox

It was the middle of the night; Prudence slowly opened her eyes and realized that someone was carrying her.

'I had a terrible nightmare… ' she said, as she regained consciousness. She then saw the face of the person who was carrying her. It was Nash.

'You are awake… here… ' he said, after gently dropping her on her feet.

'Where – where is Ryan?' she asked worried.

'He – I think you know,' answered Nash.

'It was… not a dream… ' her voice started to shake.

Prudence started to fall apart; she began to cry and could feel an immense and terrible pain inside her heart. She knew she was alive but it was hard to breathe. She started to ask herself why breathing was harder than before. Why did she want to give up? Why did she feel so incomplete? And why did it feel so right, yet so wrong, to have shared her heart with someone? All she could think of was Ryan's smile and his last moment. It was haunting her, and her heart felt heavy and burdened by him.

Alexandra did not have time with all the whimpers and sad faces, she knew of the forest and it was not a pleasant thought. They might have escaped the squadron of the emperor but they were not off the hook. The forests of Vita were commonly known for the dangers and secrets they held. But this particular forest had something that seemed to scare Alexandra. She did not wish to tell it because of her pride, but there was definitely something within those woods that made her body tremble.

'Captain… it is the… ' a pirate swallowed nervously.

'The Forest of Nox… ' Alexandra said grimly.

'Excuse me… but why are you so tense?' asked Eric.

'Why so tense? I don't know, maybe because you fools have no idea of what is going on… this forest, is like our doom.' Alexandra seemed to panic. 'If we don't hurry out of here… then we're dead. All of us. I do not wish to die, so I suggest you shut up and follow me!' Alexandra snapped.

The forest was indeed dangerous; there was a dark reason behind its name, of course, Nash, Eric and Mia did not know what. They were not even sure about where they were going. Alexandra was leading the way but that was all. How they were going to get to the Dragon's Realm? They had no idea. They could only follow and try to stay alive.

Prudence stopped walking and looked down in tears. She was inconsolable; Ryan had died, her kingdom was a mess, her life was meaningless, and her will to carry on was gone. She just wanted to die. It was a terrible thing to think, but without Ryan, she did not have the strength to fight.

However, Alexandra was not going to let Prudence give up so easily. Not because she was caring, but mainly because of her ambitions. With the princess dead, she would have no way of getting what she desired, so Prudence had better not die until she had what she wanted. She ordered one of her pirates to tie her up and make her follow them, but Nash was against it, he would not let Prudence be mistreated.

'I know you miss him… I do too,' said Mia. 'But I lost him too you know… and I know he would not want us to give up… so don't. Just don't ruin his memory by giving up Prudence… I won't allow it… '

'Shut up!' Prudence shouted angrily. 'You are the reason he died!'

Everyone went silent.

'I wish it had been you!' Prudence's voice was trembling in anger.

Mia looked down and did not say anything back.

'Ryan was my best friend… we shared a lot together, so trust me Prudence when I say this, he would not want you to give up, especially because of him,' said Eric. 'And you promised him…'

Prudence thought of what Eric said to her. She closed her eyes and thought of Ryan. He was right; Ryan would never let her give up. She could not give up, for his sake.

'You're right… I have to keep my promises… for him.' The princess looked down, convinced. 'I have to be strong…' she said, while wiping her tears.

'Much better, can we go now?' Alexandra grunted.

'Yes… let's go,' Prudence answered, with a strong expression.

The princess secretly promised herself that she would live and fight. But deep inside, she knew it was easier to make this promise than to keep it. Nonetheless, a promise is a promise. She had to fight until the end for Ryan… everything was for him and only for him.

As they were advancing inside the woods, everyone felt as if something was following them. It was dark, cold and the atmosphere lugubrious. The wind seemed as if someone or something was breathing, the trees had scary silhouettes, the grass was cold and dense, and the fog was intense. They could barely distinguish anything and only braves ones, like Alexandra and Nash, were at the front, leading the way.

Eric was scared, these woods made him think of horror films. It was so frightening that he kept on looking around when he heard a simple noise. And then he heard it, the first noise that made him jump out. It was the noise of a goblin shrieking in pain. Alexandra heard it as well, she halted in fear. She could feel her skin shaking, it was getting colder and the tension was dramatically building up on her shoulders. Soon, she could even feel her nerves pumping. The nervous sweat and the awful sensation were building up. She knew what was out there and she knew it was getting closer with every step she took.

Another noise had been heard, it was a branch that cracked, the woman aimed with her pistol toward the noise. But nothing seemed to approach; it was only a much unpleasant feeling. But the noise would not stop at the branch, no, as they were adventuring themselves in the woods, a silhouette appeared out of nowhere. It was quite far from the group. It had a dark black hood but it was difficult to see if it was human.

'We should hurry and find a place to hide until morning… ' Alexandra said nervously.

'What is in those woods? You – who seem so sure – what are you not telling us, what is it that you are afraid of?' Nash questioned the woman curiously.

A creature then moaned in agony.

'Shush… did you hear that?' Alexandra pointed her pistol toward the bushes.

'Captain, we should get out of here!'

'Yes I know, but do you see a place we can find refuge?'

Alexandra then heard something, it was a faint noise but she could feel the grass being disrupted. The woods were becoming much gloomier, the trees were moving and the wind became stronger. 'Whatever you do, everyone, don't look back,' Alexandra ordered darkly.

She pointed her pistol in front of her and advanced quickly. She seemed so afraid that she did not wish to argue on anything and just wanted to get on with finding a hide. Nash and his friends were confused, they did not know what it was that scared the pirate, but one thing was sure; they did not wish to face it.

Shortly after, Alexandra had managed to find light inside the woods. It was a small wooden house but it seemed rather welcoming. 'Okay, we'll be safe once inside.'

She did not wish to wait long in the woods, she ran to the house without even looking behind her. That thing hiding in the woods terrified her so much, that from a strong woman, she seemed weak and insecure. Everyone, of course, followed her, she knew better the way to the Dragon's Realm and Vita for that matter. Everyone yes…

except Eric, who saw a woman; she had a dark black robe and dark hair. Her skin was of a white comparable to the snow, she seemed alone and frightened.

'I wouldn't go there if I were you,' said Mia, who also saw the woman.

'But if it's as dangerous as Alexandra says… then she is in danger.'

'We should hurry; I trust that you will not be a fool,' Mia said, as she resumed her march to the wooden house.

Eric wanted to listen to Mia, but something inside of him was attracted to that woman which he could barely distinguish. She then turned around. Although she was far, Eric could see how beautiful she looked. Her face seemed like an angel and her eyes were so innocent, he could not resist her. 'I will be back; it's just to say hi…' he said, thinking everyone was there.

However, everyone had left already; they were in front of the wooden house knocking at the door. 'Is anyone here?' Alexandra asked, while knocking on the door.

'Go away – you are not welcome here.' An old woman's voice was heard.

'We need a refuge, it is late and the woods are dangerous,' said Alexandra.

'I know of you – I will not allow you to enter.'

'What do you mean you know of us?' demanded Nash.

'Your tricks will not fool me,' the old woman said sharply.

Alexandra got out her pistol, she then told everyone to take a step back as she was going to shoot the lock of the door. 'On the count of three, the door goes down,' she said.

'Wait, you might harm her!' Prudence stood on the way.

'We have no choice, if we don't get in; we're as good as dead.'

'I will not allow it – as a princess, I have to protect everyone…'

'It is not the time for this! Out of my way, or I will shoot you down too!'

'I will not let it happen.' Nash moved in front of Alexandra.

The old woman then unlocked her door, she seemed to cooperate. Prudence opened the door and she could see the woman armed with a crossbow. 'We mean no harm to you,' Prudence said with a gentle tone.

'You are not what I thought you'd be… thank goodness,' the old woman said, as she lowered her crossbow.

Alexandra did not wait long before entering the house; she even pushed her way in. It was a small house, with a bed and a table; there were about two chairs and a tablecloth. The woman seemed very poor. Her clothes were of low quality and she kept on shivering. But her heart was noble and rich; she offered to share her bread with the princess and her friends, even if she could barely afford it.

Once settled, Nash had questions about what was out there in the woods. The old woman went silent for a while. She grabbed a chair and sat down; she seemed to know what was in the woods. It was as if she had experienced crossing paths with this creature or this thing that scared Alexandra.

'A long time ago… ' she began. 'There was a man who was madly in love with the princess of this forest. She was an elf, and he was a human. Therefore, their relationship was doomed from the beginning. He looked hideous and she was the most beautiful creature of the forest. Their worlds were completely different, yet she loved him back. And when an elf loves a human, he or she becomes one.'

'Quite cliché but go ahead… ' said Nash.

'She felt sick, it was an incurable illness. Of course, the young man who loved her did his best to find a cure, but he failed. He even went to speak to the elves of the forest, but they all ignored him. For them, the princess was dead the day she loved the man back. Not long after, when he was back from his quest, he found her dead. It was an unbearable pain.'

'What happened then?' Prudence demanded, intrigued by the story.

'He started to learn magic, dark craft, anything that could bring his love back from the dead. He sought the spell of life. Of course, magic was a forbidden art, anyone using magic or being gifted in it was considered unlawful. So, he could not find what he searched for, and his efforts were vain. However… one day, he saved a man who was badly injured. That man was a wizard, and as a token of his gratitude, he told him a solution.' The woman coughed, she was cold but she resumed the story. 'There is a place in Vita that allows the dead to come back to life. Only once can they be revived. The young man did not wait long and adventured to this place… he begged for the soul of his loved one… and there she was… by his side. But there was a price to pay, if he wished to live with her, he had to fulfil a quest or a task he had been given…'

'What kind of task?' Nash asked curiously.

'He had to bring the Sword of the Lion; a sword coveted by many. This sword has the capacity of fire, and can even conquer a kingdom by itself…'

'Did he find it?' demanded Mia.

'No – as soon as he had the woman he loved, he deceived the magic that helped him and left the place. The Sword of the Lion was the type of quest only fools would agree to fulfil… he had what he wanted… or so he thought. To punish him for his betrayal, a powerful curse devoured him. He was changed into a creature that would never be able to understand love, a creature with a thirst for blood… I do not think I need to tell the rest of the story for you to understand what happened next. But the woman was the first victim of his foolishness and was devoured by it.'

'So whatever is outside in those woods… is that man?' Nash was shocked.

'Yes – it can take the appearances of its victims to lure out any fools who found themselves in his forest. Nox was the name given to this monster, but it has its weaknesses. It fears light and cannot enter the house of anyone without invitations. I have seen countless victims being eaten alive by it… I managed to flee once, but with luck…'

The old woman had finished her story. Prudence and everyone in the house were shocked about the discovery they had made. Nox was a man like others, but he ended up as a monster because he loved a woman more than anything. Was it fair? Prudence kept on questioning herself, and then she realized something. If Nox could find a way to bring the woman he loved back to life, then she could too. She could bring Ryan back to life; it was the only thing she cared about.

'Where did Nox go? To revive the woman he loved?' demanded Prudence.

'Do not be foolish child – you would end up like Nox,' the woman replied.

'I – I wish to know… please… I know you do know of the location of this place. And I can tell in your eyes there is more you want to tell us…' Prudence insisted.

'You do not know anything about me, dear…'

'The boy I love died… he died because of me – I want to make things right… no matter what I have to do… I will never be able to live with myself knowing that there is a way to bring him back yet I did not find it… please, I beg you…'

'Nox was my father – and he killed my mother without even realizing it… I am only sparing you grief and pain. But… I shall tell you the location of this place. It's in the valley of Wolf Glace. You will have to cross the forest and head up north where the mountains are. It is not far from here – but it's dangerous. Since Nox, the magicians of Wolf Glace have become indulgent with anyone who dares entering their home… you will probably have to face griffons and other monsters…'

'I will not escort you there – the Dragon's Realm is on the south east of the forest. We do not have time to waste with side quests!' Alexandra said loudly. 'You only have two days left; if you go to Wolf Glace, then by the time you get to the Dragon's Realm, the time limit will have been reached.'

'How do you know about this?' Prudence wondered.

'I am a pirate. I have seen the world, read all sorts of legends. I know that if a princess deserts her kingdom, then Vita will allow a certain limit of time for her to claim her rights before they are gone forever…' Alexandra scoffed. 'I am no ignorant like you…'

Prudence thought of her kingdom and her role as a princess. But then, she thought of her heart's desire, and what her heart desired more than anything, was Ryan.

'Then you are free to leave… I will not force you to stay with us,' said the princess.

'You need me if you want the sword…'

'I need Ryan more than the sword… for him; I will even sacrifice my kingdom.' Prudence smiled. 'Vita can go to hell…'

'Darn, could we at least proceed with a vote?' asked Alexandra.

'There are four of us and only three of you…' Nash chuckled.

'Look around you imbecile; it looks like your friend Eric has taken the liberty of doing a tour on his own,' Alexandra laughed.

'What?' Nash gasped. 'That idiot – grr, he really gets on my nerves!' he grunted.

'Your friend might already be dead, or taken by Nox. I would not expect him to come back…' the old woman said grimly, before falling asleep.

Prudence and her two friends were panicking; Eric could certainly be dead by the time they had realized he was missing. The princess felt as if it was her fault; she was so busy thinking of a way to bring Ryan back, that she completely forgot about those following her on her journey. Ryan trusted her with his friends, yet she had failed already. She was so nervous that she kept on scratching her nails and biting her lips.

'What would Ryan do if he was here?' asked Mia.

'He would venture out to save his friend…' Nash answered coolly.

'Then I shall honour him…' said Prudence.

'No, too dangerous, that moron might already be dead anyway…' said Nash.

'He is Ryan's friend… I cannot fail Ryan once again… I won't allow it.'

'Jo, go with her,' Alexandra ordered to one of her pirates.

'But captain… I… I don't want… ' he stuttered.

'Shut up or I will kill you myself!' Alexandra shouted.

'Aye captain!'

'I won't take any chances… I'm coming with you,' said Nash.

'Fine, but do not put yourself at risk… '

Chapter Fifteen
The Silhouette Behind The Fire

While the princess and a small escort were out looking for Eric, the young man was quite near the wooden house. He was so mesmerized by the beauty of the woman he saw, that he had forgotten everything around him: his friend who had died earlier, the dangers of Vita, how would he find a way back. He was only focusing on the woman.

'Excuse me – miss?' Eric gently tapped the woman's shoulder. 'Are you alone by yourself?'

'Hello – my dear sir, I am, I have lost my way home. Would you be kind enough to show me the way?' the woman politely asked.

'Of course – but I do not know of the way…'

'Walk me to my house, please?'

'Yes, OK… you can count on me!'

Eric was so hypnotised by the woman, that he was not thinking enough to realize that something was amiss. Instead, he kept on walking farther from the house. A good five minutes had passed since then; the young man was talking to the woman, who kept silent throughout the whole march. The woods were becoming calmer the deeper he walked with the woman; it was as if no living creatures were present. Soon, he stomped on a branch that cracked under the impact of his foot.

Eric looked down at his feet, then he slowly looked at the woman's feet. But something was off, she was not walking… she was floating, and the sort of dark black robe was slightly ripped off around the legs, just like ghosts. Eric understood his error; he swallowed in terror and slowly but surely looked higher and higher until he could see the woman's face.

Terrified, the young man started to take a few steps back. The thing that was in front of him did not seem to notice the boy retreating. Eric slowly but gradually was building up a good distance from what he had taken for a woman. And then, it turned around... its face was no more the face of the woman, but a spectre. A black hood covered everything; Eric could only see enormous teeth with blood spilling from its mouth. It was ridiculously fearsome; Eric gasped and ran for his life.

The creature was too fast, it was not walking but floating, which gave it a great advantage. Eric tried his best to flee, but he was slower than the creature and with terror he slipped on the grass. He tried to get back on his feet but the creature had taken a hold of his right leg and started to pull it.

'Argg! Help!' Eric screamed, while being dragged toward a tree.

The young man tried to crawl or kick the claws of the monster but it did not work. He struggled to the very end of it. He then heard the sound of fire burning, and without understanding it, the creature started to burn.

When he turned around, he could see the silhouette of a young man approaching him. But it was too dark to distinguish who it was. It looked just like Ryan, but that was impossible since he was dead. Caught up with all the emotions and the fear he had felt, Eric fainted before he could see the face of the person.

When Eric opened his eyes, he was in front of the wooden house. Nash, Prudence and the pirate had found him and brought him to the house. He tried to explain about what had happened, but Nash was making fun of him and treating him like an idiot. He felt down, but at the same time he was relieved to be in the house and not in the creature's stomach. That is if the creature had a stomach...

And then, out of nowhere, when he was asked about how he managed to flee, he could not answer. Even he did not know how he managed to get to the house; he could only remember the fire and the silhouette of the man looking like Ryan.

'It will sound absurd… but Ryan saved me,' Eric said, feeling out of his mind.

'I think you got hit in the head when falling,' said Nash.

'I'm serious! This silhouette looked so much like Ryan… '

No one believed him; they all thought he had fallen down and started to imagine things. It was probably the shock that made him see things that were completely absurd, such as Ryan saving him. All believed he was out of his mind, except Prudence, who wanted so badly to trust in the fact that Ryan had survived. The boy had no reason to lie, after all, he was a complete stranger in a world he did not know and above all, it was a world full of magic. But she could not afford the doubts. She had to find out for sure if the one she loved survived or if he truly was dead. Wolf Glace would be her next destination; it was there she would have the answers to her questions.

It was not long before everyone fell asleep; they were all tired from the misadventures they had been living. Eric, however, could not close his eyes; he was still terrified about his encounter with Nox. For him, as long as they were in the woods, they were in danger. He went near to a window and stared at the forest where he could see Nox's shadow flying around trees. It was near and waiting for someone to venture into the forest. Eric took a deep breath and looked away. He had had enough. It was the scariest night of his life. He looked around and when no one looked, he started to cry. He was a man and his pride had prevented him from crying earlier. But he could not believe his friend's death, it was something too painful to feel.

Someone else was also crying; he could hear the whimpers of a girl, it was Mia. She was not sleeping, she could not. When Eric approached her, he could see she was blowing her nose and wiping away her tears. The young man conducted himself as a gentleman and hugged her. He was doing his best to console her but it was hard.

'It is my fault Ryan died… ' she sobbed.

'What are you on about now?' whispered Eric.

'If I – I had not been stuck, he would not have come to save me… and he would be… alive… it's my entire fault.' She kept sobbing.

'It is yes, but he chose to save you. So don't cry, I'm sure we'll find a way… Prudence wants to save him… he can still come back to us.'

'I'm scared… we are in a world we know nothing about… ' Mia whimpered.

'We'll find a way… I promise you.' Eric held her tightly.

It was not long before the two of them fell asleep; they felt reassured in each other's arms.

The night had passed. It was morning, and everyone in the house woke up and packed up their stuff. Prudence was grateful to the woman who took her and her friends in when they were in grave danger. She offered the old woman her scarf and her gloves to keep her warm. Nash wanted to make a good impression, but mostly he was really caring and could not walk away without giving something to that lady who helped him. He took out his wallet and gave her a coin of one pound and another of fifty pence. It had low value in London, but in this world, she could manage to get a lot from it. Eric did the same as Nash; he was the most thankful since he could have died. The old woman was grateful; she hugged the princess and offered bread to the teenagers.

The route to the valley of Wolf Glace was not long from where they were. But the dangers they would have to face were imminent. However, together they were stronger than what was to come.

Chapter XV

Chapter Sixteen
Wolf Glace

The forest was safer to cross during the daylight, however, Prudence could not afford to drop or lower her guard. She was still the target of the emperor and she knew he would stop at nothing until she was dead.

She had a short time to breathe before facing dangers she never thought she would have to face. It was much easier and more pleasant to face them when she was reading the books written by knights and adventurers; now it was her turn to experience it, and frankly she was not fond of it. It was rather scary and stressful, especially for a princess who had been living in a comfortable manner since she was a baby.

After a fine twenty minutes of walking, they had arrived in front of the valley. It was a nice place to look at from the outside, and the griffons could clearly be seen flying in the sky. They were amazing creatures, just as described in books. They were parts of many animals. The head of a lion, wings of eagles, claws of dragons, the body of a tiger, and a snake for a tail.

It was a marvellous spectacle and it was the first time Prudence had seen a griffon with her own eyes. She had read many books about them and was fascinated just by reading. Seeing them was something rather extraordinary. It was an inexplicable feeling that warmed her heart and made her adrenaline pump fast. She could even jump out of excitement but she did her best to avoid looking childish and so she abstained herself.

'Let's go… ' Alexandra grunted.

The captain of the pirates was not in a good mood; she seemed annoyed with this quest the princess was going on. Just by looking at Alexandra, it was an easy task to tell what was on her mind. She did not seem to care about Ryan. To her, he was rather dispensable and not important enough. The sword however was something to go after. The power to rule all over Vita was something worth all the troubles and the dangers. But the princess was needed for Alexandra to get her hands on the sword; without her, there would be no way of getting what she was after. And it was with annoyance that she abided by the princess's wish.

As they were approaching Wolf Glace, the griffons were flying over the heads of Prudence and her friends. They were like vultures waiting for a prey to be weak enough before attacking.

Nevertheless, they had to advance if they wished to get to Wolf Glace, and looking at the griffons was something rather foolish to do once close enough. It was recommended to keep walking and avoid any interactions with them. These creatures were unpredictable, and dealing with them was a delicate task.

'Whatever you do – don't look at them. Keep walking as if they were not here… ' Alexandra whispered to everyone, as she was leading the way.

'What will happen if we look at them?' asked Mia.

'Then we'll run for our lives and pray for someone to stop these creatures.'

Eric gasped after seeing how numerous the griffons were compared to them.

The steps were heavy, slow and the nerve of keeping quiet was arduous. Nash stayed closed to the princess. Protecting her was his main priority. He did not trust Alexandra and so he made sure to keep a close eye on her. But even if Alexandra was a mysterious and untruthful woman, she was the best leader Prudence could have hoped for. She knew Vita like the palm of her hands, and her knowledge on the creatures and the different dangers gave a good idea of what to expect ahead. Alexandra was simply the best member of the small group, something not even Ryan could have topped.

The closer they were getting to their destination, the more the atmosphere was cold and the oxygen was getting heavier to breath. Suddenly it was a lot colder, and even the griffons were reticent in the idea of getting closer, as if a cold barrier repulsed them somehow.

'We're safe – griffons hate coldness,' said Alexandra.

'Thank goodness… I was actually thinking we would not make it… ' Eric said, relieved.

'So is it Wolf Glace?' asked Nash.

'A few steps more and yes we'll be there. I have to warn you though, magicians are not to be trusted. Everyone knows they are always up to something,' Alexandra said grimly.

'What do you mean?' demanded Mia.

'I don't have the time to give you a history class… let's go.'

'Wait… are you referring to this story that happened fifteen years ago?' asked Prudence.

'So you do know something… yes I am… but a princess like you wouldn't know what it was like to be ruled by a magician… ' Alexandra said aggressively.

'You don't need to take it out on Prudence,' said Nash.

'Please – do tell me what happened… '

'Later… we have company,' Alexandra said, as she armed herself.

'What? Where?' Eric looked around.

After a few seconds, a group of ten hooded persons appeared out of nowhere. They were all wearing the same outfit as if it was a uniform, and all of them had hoods that hid half of their faces. They all had black robes with blue embroidery around the sleeves and a sort of amulet hanging around their neck. It was unusual to see people dressed up like this; it was as if they were priests or part of a religious organization. And they all had staffs, which were of different colours. The staffs were the only thing different, blue, red, yellow, green and brown. It was as if each colours had significance; maybe it was the magic they were using that varied depending on their grades, or perhaps it was the level of hierarchy. No matter, it was not the reason why Prudence had come to Wolf Glace.

'Do state your business,' one of the hooded people said, while holding his staff.

'We are sorry we have bothered you,' Alexandra bowed.

'What is she?' Eric was confused.

'Bow before them you idiots!' Alexandra yelled at Eric and his friends.

Everyone did as asked, the hooded people then advanced toward them.

'I am sorry for troubling you – but I am here because I need a favour only you are known to be able to accomplish…' Prudence calmly and gently said, as she was still bowing.

'We are not in position to grant you anything… but come with us, our master will hear you out and will decide if we will help you or not.'

The magicians escorted Prudence and her companions to meet with their leader. It was a beautiful place and all the walls were made of ice. Everything seemed alive. The snowmen were battling with children and the statues were moving: it was a place where magic was fully exploited.

Every person constituting this place was gifted of a magical power, and some were even capable of manipulating different elements. For them it was a blessing, but for others, it was rather a curse. For the princess, being gifted with magic was not a curse, it was more something to cherish and love. Being able to use something so rare and so formidable as magic was a privilege and sometimes she even wished she could be a magician.

Everything in the city of Wolf Glace was shining; the children were all practicing their talents while playing with the snow. One of them even formed a dragon of ice just by using telekinesis. It was a show that left Eric and Mia speechless; they never in their wildest dreams imagined a world such as Vita. Magic was something they had only read in books or watched on TV. It was supposed to be a trick to amaze children, but now it was real, there were no strings lifting the cards in the air, or no other tools used to create the effects of illusion. Magic was something Eric loved, but it was frightening him. He used to always believe that it had been invented to please the believers.

'Hey sir! You are dressed in a funny way!' One of the children laughed, as he shook Eric's hand. 'Do you want to come and play with us?' asked the young boy.

'Erm, no… I have something to do… ' Eric nervously replied.

'Promise you'll come play with us after?' demanded a young girl.

Eric nodded silently; he was so nervous and uncomfortable with everything he was seeing that he could not answer without stuttering.

'Looks like you got yourself a girlfriend after all these years of being single!' Nash sneered.

'Sh… shut up man!' Eric looked down of embarrassment. 'I have a girlfriend! Her name is Alice you idiot!'

'Aha, the girl from the webcam… yes I remember her,' Nash laughed.

'At least I have one! You are flirting with a girl who loves Ryan!'

Nash went silent and clenched his fist. Eric knew things were about to get ugly and did not wait long before hiding behind Mia.

'You are such a coward!' Nash snarled.

'Are you for real? Hiding behind a woman?' Mia scoffed.

'Stop with your childish games!' Alexandra shouted at Nash and Eric. 'We have to be serious if we want them to consider Prudence's request, you imbeciles.'

'Geez she's scary!' Eric jumped out, afraid.

'Mhmph but she's right… ' Nash scoffed with annoyance.

After a little distraction, Prudence and her friends were brought toward a long and extraordinary tower. The tower was so long and so big that it felt as if it was a never ending monument. 'It looks like the Eiffel Tower!' Eric gasped, as he looked above.

The tower was splendid; it was made of ice and crystals, a beautiful piece of work that probably took centuries before being completed. 'Our proudest *oeuvre*...' one of the magicians said, while admiring the tower.

Prudence had never read of this tower in any books, it was the first time she'd seen or heard of it. It was not surprising that knights would avoid places where magicians lived, but it was such a shame not to share this discovery. Such a beautiful tower, yet no one would ever suspect it exists.

After admiring the tower from the outside, it was time for them to go on and meet the master of the place. They entered the tower and once again, they were pleasantly surprised with all the beautiful things inside. It was as magnificent on the inside as the outside, and everything was shining. Unexpectedly it was warm and agreeable to stay in the interior. Prudence closed her eyes and breathed in the welcome atmosphere of the place, before carrying on with her quest.

The magicians led the way to a room and opened a door within a wall. Pretty soon countless stairs appeared. They were transparent, they could barely see them, and the only thing that allowed Prudence and her friends to distinguish the steps of the stairs was a beautiful and radiant blue line that glowed.

'Wait... we are actually going to climb all the way up?' Eric moaned.

'That would indeed be preposterous... the tower is immense... let us chant to bring us to the chamber of the master.'

All the magicians gathered in front of the stairs and started to chant a beautiful incantation. It was not clear what they were saying. It was a complete and foreign language but it was harmonic and beautiful to hear. They then raised their hands and lights shined out of nowhere; it was a radiant and blinding light that shone intensely. The princess and her companions could not help themselves but to close their eyes for a short period, but once opened, they could see a beautiful chamber right in front of them.

The chamber was immense, it had no furniture and only stairs toward a throne; it was an odd place for someone to stay. It did not need any windows as it was ridiculously bright inside and the air was fresh, yet at the same time warm.

An old man was sitting on a throne. He wore a strange and long hat, and his robe was different from the others. It was a golden robe and the embroidery on the sleeves was glowing; his amulet was different from the others and shone a lot more. A sort of blue pearl was encrusted in the middle and it had little fragments of ice.

He had a long beard and tired eyes; his skin was of a pale grey and a lot of wrinkles were present around his face and his hands. He seemed really old and weak. His hairs were long and badly maintained; they were so white that they could barely believe that they were natural. He seemed fragile and dying. Nash thought he could even die at that instant, but he did not say anything. It was more than recommended to stay quiet and talk only when needed in Vita, of course that was something Eric could not do.

'Oh my God! You look dead mate!' Eric yelled, surprised at the old man's state. He then put his hand over his mouth after realizing how out of order he had been.

'Imbecile! You will get us killed!' Nash grunted, as he punched Eric.

'Sorry! I did not mean it like that! It's just the first time in my life that I met Santa Claus! Please don't hit me!' Eric whimpered.

'Aha, I do not know who Santa Claus is, but I do admire your open mind young man.' The old man laughed. 'It is not a surprise for me to hear this, every magician here does not wish to make me feel bad about my age, and so they do not say anything. But honesty is what is important to me.' He chuckled. 'I am the master of this place, and the founder of it. My name is… '

'Merlin?' Eric interrupted the old man. 'Did I guess it right?'

Nash and Alexandra glared at Eric, as if they wanted to punch him.

'Aha, no… I do not know of any Merlin, but it is pretty close. My name is Marvin Furizius.'

'Huh... that's it? Marvin? Usually in all the books and all the TV or video games they use long and uncommon names for magicians...' Eric scoffed.

'Forgive our guest here; he has no idea of courtesy or the meaning of good manners...' said Nash.

'Guest? I thought I was your friend...'

'I am Nash Snowangel and the idiot who is rude is Eric Miheing.'

'I am Mia Takeshitori... it is nice to meet you.'

'Alexandra Delacroix, I have heard many things about you and it is a pleasure to make your acquaintance.' Alexandra bowed, as she introduced herself.

'And you are?' Marvin asked, as he looked at Prudence.

'I am...'

'Prudence Fulgura, I presume...' the old man interrupted the princess.

'How did you know?' Prudence asked puzzled.

'Aha... it is because you look a lot like your mother.' He chuckled. 'Now child, what can I do for you? I do not believe you would come all the way here just to see magic or an old man like me.'

'I wish to bring someone I love back to life...'

'Oh...' the old man sighed with disappointment. 'I would have wished that you, above all, would not dwell with the dead. It is a magic that I refuse to use. I am sorry my dear, but this is for your own sake,' he said with a gentle and apologizing tone.

'But you're like the most powerful magician and all that! Just help us! Please, it's my friend... he died protecting me... and I... I wish I could do something for him...' Mia insisted.

'The master has spoken... we will not grant your wish.'

'My brother knew what he was doing... we'll miss him, but Prudence has higher obligations... sorry guys, but this is it... we've come this far and we got an answer...'

'How dare you!' Prudence glared at Nash angrily. 'How dare you for one second speak to me as if you wish my well being?'

'Princess... I... I do wish your success and happiness... but Ryan is dead... just forget about him and move on... ' Nash said nervously.

'Calm down please children... it is not the time for you to fight between each other. The emperor is becoming stronger by the minute... you will need each other in this journey if you wish to beat him... ' Marvin said calmly.

'It is an order... I wish you to tell us of a way to bring the man I love back to life.' Prudence looked at Marvin and insisted with a firm tone.

The magicians all gathered around the princess and her friends, in a threatening position. Alexandra drew her rapier and was shortly followed by Nash and the others.

'Fine... I shall help you,' Marvin quietly said.

'Thank you... it means a lot to me.'

'But your Majesty... ' one of the magicians said before being interrupted.

'Do not contest the decision of the princess... if she wants to bring her friend back to life, then so be it. However, I will demand something from you.'

'What is it that you wish?' asked Prudence.

'There are two things I desire more than anything in this world before my demise. I wish to see one authentic weapon that was created by my best friend. He had created four of these weapons. They all got dispersed all over Vita, but there is one that I have found. It is hidden in the undergrounds of Wolf Glace.' Marvin paused. 'If you are worthy of my help then you will be able to bring me the sword, even if guarded by werewolves. It has been forty years and I have not seen it with my own eyes... The Sword of the Moon... '

'We... werewolves?' Eric gasped. 'But I thought you wanted the Sword of the Lion?'

'Oh, so you do have heard of this one too? I could never get my hands on this one, it was my friend's favourite weapon... ' Marvin chuckled. 'But this one is out of reach. So, will you go after the Sword of the Moon?'

'Fine, how can I go down in the undergrounds?' Prudence demanded, with determination in her eyes.

'My apprentices will show you the way...'

'And what is the second thing that you wish for?' asked Prudence.

'You shall know soon enough,' Marvin said darkly. 'Feel free to rest if you must. Wolf Glace is secured from the dark forces...'

'I shall leave for the undergrounds at once,' said Prudence. 'And, I am sorry for putting you through all of this trouble... but he is the one my heart beats for,' she said, while putting both of her hands on her left breast.

Nash looked away in annoyance, even when he was gone, it was all about Ryan. Whether it was Prudence or Eric, they were all talking about the same person as if he was the greatest guy in the world. Nash did not hate his brother, but the more time he spent on Vita, the more he could not stand the fact that he always came after Ryan. It was a jealousy that was devouring him on the inside. Why was Ryan so loved?

The princess bowed to Marvin to demonstrate her gratitude and followed the apprentices to the undergrounds. She was so determined and so focused on saving Ryan, that she was not scared at all of the werewolves lying in the cave. It was admirable, but at the same time a really foolish thing to do. Alexandra knew it was too risky and Prudence would die before even getting near to the sword, so she decided to accompany her. Nash did not think twice, he would have gone anywhere he could to protect the princess and if a couple of werewolves wanted a fight, then he would let them have it.

The pirates escorting Alexandra declined and stayed inside the tower where they felt safer. It was out of the question to go on and confront werewolves, and if Alexandra wished to die, then she could die for all they cared. She was the captain, but lately, she seemed too friendly with the princess, and endangering herself to look after Prudence was a sign of weakness to them.

Eric refused to go with Nash and Prudence; it was too perilous and imprudent. He was not going to lose his life over a sword. No, he decided to stay where he was protected and wait for his friends to come back victorious. Mia chose to follow Eric on that one, she had faith in her friends but she was too scared.

The magicians escorted the princess toward a door in the underground. Then they started to chant an incantation and another door appeared on the wall. It was an impressive demonstration, and it was not long before the door opened itself to the princess and her two followers.

'If you find the sword, get out. Don't even look back,' Alexandra muttered.

'We will be fine… as long as we stay together.'

'Yes, you are right princess, we will be fine.' Nash held Prudence's hand, but as soon as he did, she dropped his hand and advanced to the cave.

'Aha – I'm beginning to like that girl,' Alexandra laughed, as she went inside.

'Good luck,' the magicians said, as Nash entered the cave.

Chapter Seventeen
The Sword Of The Moon

The cave was sombre, and only small fragments of blue crystals allowed the three individuals to distinguish what was ahead of them. The walls of the cave were old and covered in humidity. The ground was cold and it was hard to breathe. Alexandra was shivering. It was colder than outside of Wolf Glace, and because no one had been there for a long time, cones of ice had been accumulating on the roof of the cave.

The more they advanced in the cave, the more they felt observed and followed. It was dark and hard to circulate without hitting a rock or a wall. But for someone or something that had been living for a long time in this place, it would be rather easy to move around. At certain times, Prudence and her friends could even hear faint growling and the sound of paws running.

'They're near… be careful, they could be behind us for all we know,' Alexandra said, as she drew out her rapier and her pistol.

'Don't worry, I will protect you… both of you,' Nash said, as he took the lead.

'If you wish to play the hero then do as you please,' Alexandra scoffed.

Nash was unsure about where he was going, or if he would be in position to protect the two ladies. But just once he wanted so badly to be like Ryan, trusted and respected. If Prudence could trust her life with him, then he would be able to charm her and there would be a chance for him to have her love. With his mind set only on Prudence, he forgot about all the dangers around him and he did not even care about Alexandra's fate.

The cave was dense and it was dark, but after a while it was becoming warmer and clearer ahead. It was as if the werewolves possessed a city within the cave itself. Soon, they arrived in front of two tunnels. The tunnels were engraved with claws marks. It was as if the werewolves had created their own alphabet which was completely foreign to Prudence and her friends.

'I will go on the left tunnel…' said Alexandra.

'No… we should not separate…'

'Actually, I'm with Alexandra on that one,' said Nash. 'If we can find the sword quickly, then we'll be out of this cave.' He paused. 'If we all go the same way and we realize it leads to nowhere… then we would have wasted a hell of a lot time and endangered ourselves in vain,' explained Nash.

'Do not worry about me, princess, I have my pistol and my lovely rapier with me. Nothing will happen to me.'

'Thank you, Alexandra…'

'Huh? I beg your pardon?'

'Risking your life for me… it means a lot.'

'Save it for later,' Alexandra chuckled. 'I'm just doing it because you remind me of someone…' She looked down with sad eyes. 'Just remember that I have my own reasons for making sure you stay alive.'

'If you say so…'

'All right, let's go,' said Nash.

'Good luck, princess,' Alexandra whispered, as she went inside the left tunnel.

It was a long and scary tunnel; the texture of the ground was uneven. The rocks scratched by claws and the irritable noise of water spilling made the walk stressful. The princess kept on looking around as she was advancing; it was unpleasant. The growling noises were getting closer and pretty soon the princess saw the silhouette of a werewolf running around them. Nash firmly grabbed his sword and guarded the princess; he was leading the way but he kept a close distance to the young woman. He then saw a werewolf. It was quietly inspecting around while sniffing out the ground.

It was a tall creature, skinny with long claws and long teeth; it was completely hairy just like a normal wolf, but the body structure was a lot like a human. The werewolf seemed strong and fast. Just by looking at it, Nash shivered. Prudence took a deep breath of uncertainly and approached the creature, but Nash stopped her. He got in front of her and made sure she was staying behind him.

The werewolf sniffed out the two individuals. It abruptly turned around and growled in rage. Its eyes were of a golden yellow and its jaw was wide open, saliva was spilling out of it. It had an odd posture, with its claws adjusted in the front and its legs slightly lifted up. By the look of it, it seemed as if it was going to jump on Prudence and Nash, but instead, it was angrily staring at the two individuals.

'It does not look hostile...' Prudence gently made her move.

'Wait, what are you doing?' Nash grabbed the princess's arm. 'Do you have some kind of death wish? It's just waiting for us to come closer!' he barked.

'Do let go of me!' Prudence pulled out her arm. 'If you are so uncertain, then you can leave... I will not stop you.'

She was decided; she did not wish to harm the creature and advanced toward it. The princess was courageous. She knew it could be dangerous and she could be bitten or eaten alive, but killing was not something she could do and so she tried to pacify the creature.

'H... hello,' she said nervously.

'Grrrr...' the werewolf growled, as it bent its back.

'It is a bad idea! Please listen to me...' Nash tried to reason with Prudence.

The creature started to approach the princess, it seemed calmer but Nash stood up in front of it. He was still armed but did not attack the werewolf. 'Humans...' scoffed the creature.

'You speak our language?' gasped Prudence.

'You have to leave,' said the werewolf. 'We smelled you earlier.

A princess has no business here… we respect you and will not harm you or your friends, thus the reason we have not attacked… ' It seemed aggressive but caring.

'I am sorry, but I require the sword… '

'We will lead the way, but the cave is not safe… ' it said darkly.

Nash was curious; he did not understand why the only creatures living in the cave would say this. What could possibly be more dangerous than them? He did not wait long and questioned the creature.

'The magicians did not tell you about it… did they?'

'Tell us about what?' questioned Nash.

'Well, the reason no one ever got out of this cave is because… ' The wolf then went silent and started to sniff out the air. 'It is coming… follow me, quick!' ordered the wolf.

Prudence and Nash did not know what the creature was talking about, but they seemed to trust it. If something was scaring off even the wolves, then the cave was even more dangerous than they had previously thought.

The werewolf was leading the way and soon Nash could hear a loud and scary scream. When the young man looked behind him, he could see a sort of shadow growing. It looked a lot like how Eric described Nox. What was it? Was it Nox? But that was in the forest. What did the magicians do? Countless questions were on Nash's mind but he did not have the time to focus on them.

When Prudence and Nash arrived, the werewolves were all assembled; they were reunited around a sort of rock. This rock had the handle of a sword protruding. All the wolves were praying to it and idolizing this rock. One of them even wore a robe; it was as if a hierarchy was set up within the pack. A beautiful blue light enlightened the whole chamber within the cave and suppressed the darkness of it.

'Wait here,' said the werewolf.

It went to speak to its congeners, who all stared at the princess as if she were a piece of meat they would devour. The one with the robe then approached Prudence. It was a grey wolf with thicker fur and a bigger body, and it had a longer tail and a scar around its eye. It looked scary and really intimidating, but calm. When Prudence tried to speak, it interrupted her and introduced itself as the master of the pack and the eldest werewolf. It then took a dark tone, and warned the princess of a presence that lived within the walls of the cave.

A spectre, or most likely a victim of magic, it was the same magic that made Nox what it was. It was a monster that had lost all possible feelings and thoughts. It was there just to devour anything or anyone that met its path. The princess questioned its origins and how it ended up in the cave. The werewolves all looked at each other and the elder answered her question.

'Marvin Fuzirius…' it said darkly. 'Punishing that fool Nox was not enough. No – he transformed the man and his lover into two creatures that would eternally live a miserable existence. And to make sure we would not escape, he trapped us with this creature…'

'Wait… are you saying that Marvin is…'

'He is a man not to be trusted!' the werewolf grunted in rage.

'Why did he make us go after the Sword of the Moon?' asked Nash.

'He wants it for himself… but no one can ever get the sword out, only the chosen one. This sword will only obey and be wielded by the descendant of the white wolf.'

'But I am in need of it…' Prudence sighed.

'We are all confident that you will get it out of the rock. Now, you shall take it.'

Prudence was worried; she did not think she was the chosen one. What would happen if she could not get the sword out and mostly, what were Marvin's intentions once the sword was in his possession?

She felt bad and looked down on herself. She was a princess, yet she was weak and always on the run. What sword would choose her? Nevertheless, she had to give it a try and so she advanced toward the rock. It was a much bigger rock once near to it.

The rock was made of crystal ice and it shined like the moon. Prudence took a deep breath and tried to pull the sword out of the rock, but it did not work. It had not moved one inch. All the werewolves gasped. They were all convinced of Prudence being the chosen one. The elder then approached Prudence and told her to give it another go, she might have missed. But it was not the case. When she tried to pull it again, she fell on the ground miserably. She was not the one chosen to lift the sword.

'Let me have a try,' said Nash, as he approached the sword. 'I don't understand why... but I feel attracted to it.'

All the wolves started to sneer. They believed Nash was yet another fool, but they let him have a go. If he desired to ridicule himself, then he was welcome to amuse them. Nash was used to being underestimated. Since his childhood he had been looked down upon and walked over; so it did not matter how the werewolves were mocking him, he was used to it. All he knew is that he could feel the sword calling out to him; it was as if it wanted Nash to get it out the rock. The elder wolf was the only one silent. It seemed to trust Nash on his attempt and so it encouraged the young man to try.

Nash looked at the sword. He then grabbed the handle of it, and with no efforts he pulled the sword out of the rock. The sword was magnificent. It was made of crystal and ice just like Wolf Glace, and a beautiful sapphire was incrusted in the middle of the handle. The sword was so beautiful that all the wolves stared at it for a while. Prudence smiled, relieved. With the sword in their hands they would be able to bring Ryan back to life. All the wolves bowed to Nash, including the elder.

'We have found our master,' said the elder. 'Everyone... praise him!'

'Let's be on our way and eliminate that old fool!' Nash said loudly, with excitement in his voice.

'But we need him to bring Ryan back...'

When Prudence said that, all the wolves started to talk

indistinctly between themselves. The elder then approached Prudence and told her about their story. It appeared that all the werewolves used to be Humolfs before Marvin and his apprentices turned them into complete wolves. Prudence did not know what to do; it was the only way for her to see Ryan again. But what if Marvin betrayed her like he did with the wolves? She did not know what to do or think.

'I trust you will make the right decision,' said the elder.

Nash could not stop looking at his sword. Then, two wolves arrived dragging a bloody corpse. They approached the elder and told him they had managed to scare off the demon, but they were too late. When Prudence and Nash looked at the body, it was Alexandra.

Prudence hastened to check up on the woman who was barely alive. She was breathing and still conscious, but her arms and her legs were in a shocking state. A lot of scratches covered her body and she was losing a lot of blood.

'Alexandra!' yelled the princess.

'Pru... Prudence...' Alexandra struggled in pain. 'For... forgive me.'

'No! Why? Don't die!' Prudence started to fall apart.

'Don't... cry on... my behalf...' Alexandra groaned. 'I wanted... I wanted the... sword for... myself,' she confessed.

'What?' Prudence gasped, in tears.

'I did not... like you... and wished... the sword for me...'

'Then... why did you come to the cave?' Prudence asked tearfully.

'Because...' Alexandra paused. 'Because you look like... someone dear... to me... and... it... was too much... to let you... endanger yourself...' she groaned in agony.

'Alexandra... please... don't die! I will get you out of here!' Prudence's lips were trembling. 'Just hang in there! Please!' she desperately tried to comfort the woman.

'Take this...' Alexandra could barely move her arm, but she managed to offer her pistol to the princess. 'It was my father's gift...

before he died… I wish… you to have it… before my… demise.' She coughed blood.

Prudence took the pistol with shaking hands.

'One more thing… please… ' Alexandra was struggling to stay alive.

Prudence nodded her head.

'You… have to… save your kingdom… for me… and tell… Ryan… I'm sorry… I won't be able… to annoy him… ' Alexandra laughed in pain. 'Promise me… '

'I promise… '

Nash could see Alexandra was hurting. He asked the princess to move aside.

'Please… make it stop… the pain… I beg you… '

'I'm so sorry… ' Prudence cried.

Nash lifted his sword. His eyes were full of regrets and barely open.

'*Adieu*… Prudence,' Alexandra smiled. 'I am glad… I have met you.'

'May you find peace… ' said Nash.

The young man then stabbed Alexandra with his sword. The impact of the blade was so strong that Alexandra died instantaneously.

The loss the princess suffered was immense; it was her fault that Alexandra died. It should not have happened and the anger, the pain and the sadness were overwhelming her. She clenched her fist and swore on the body of her friend that she would liberate Heartsas from the emperor and make Marvin pay for this.

The werewolves gathered around Nash and lifted him up. 'Our king is reborn!' one of them shouted.

It was sad for Prudence to lose a friend. The elder tried its best to abstain himself and his kind from jumping enthusiastically, but their deliverance day had finally come. With the sword in the king's hands, they would be able to rise up from the darkness and eliminate Marvin and his apprentices for all the sins and the malice they had committed. Prudence agreed to help the werewolves, if they helped her to escort the body of Alexandra out so she could bury her in an honourable way.

Everything was well thought, however, there was still a menace to overcome within the cave itself. The darkness and the hunger of the spectre that was wandering around were still present. If only they could manage to leave without having to confront it, but that was impossible in such a dark place. It feared light and darkness reigned within the cave, which was the most fitting place for it to exist. It seemed difficult, but Nash had an idea; with the sword glowing, they could manage to scare it off for enough time. That way, all of the werewolves could escape from the cave and submerge Wolf Glace's tower. It was tricky, but the only chance for them to escape in numbers enough to surprise the magicians.

Chapter Eighteen
Loyal To Her Heart

Nash approached the princess, who was mourning the lifeless corpse of her friend. With a gentle gesture, he offered her a tissue he had kept in his pocket. 'Listen… there's something I have to tell you,' said Nash.

'Yes? What is it?' Prudence asked, while wiping her tears away.

'We may not survive this – I mean, if we manage to get out from this cave that'd be good… ' Nash said, while hesitating with his words. 'But we might die against the magicians… their magic is powerful.' He paused and got closer to the princess. 'So there is something I wish for you to know… ' he approached her face, and deeply looked into Prudence's eyes. 'I love you,' he said. 'I know you love my brother… but for you, I will fight until my very end.' He then tried to kiss her, but she rejected him.

'I cannot… my lips are only meant for one person and you have said it yourself. It is Ryan and it will always be Ryan,' said Prudence. 'I am sorry for the way you feel about me, but I cannot give you the love you seek.' Prudence sighed. 'I am sorry. Please, understand that my heart will always belong to Ryan.'

Nash looked away as if he had made a fool out of himself. His efforts were in vain. Prudence loved Ryan and was loyal to him. She followed her heart and he was nowhere near within hers.

'I will always protect you… ' said Nash. 'Even when darkness is the only thing left for you… I will be there to protect you.'

'I shall not need you… ' responded Prudence. 'Nor shall I want you to ever hope for my love back.'

Nash's eyes were wide open in shock, and watery. His lips were trembling and his body was frozen. He was staring at the ground as if he could not move. His heart was shattered into pieces. Nash knew he was alive, but he felt dead. The way the princess had broken his heart made him realize the pain of life itself.

The princess walked away toward the elder wolf. She needed information, but she mostly desired to stay away from the young man.

Prudence knew she was hurting Nash. It was horrible for her to speak in such a way, but she wished for him to move on. She didn't hate him or dislike him at all, but if she gave him hope, then he would never move on. She had to be cruel, so he would understand.

A short time had elapsed; it was time for Prudence and her companions to attempt an escape from the cave, while confronting the shadow. The werewolves were impatient; it had been fifty years since they became trapped inside this sombre cave.

Being the slave of the darkness was miserable, and the light of the sun was something they had not seen for such a long time. The youngest wolves were running happily in circles. They could not wait for this liberating moment to take place.

Nash took the lead. He went in front of all the wolves and in front of Prudence. Then, he lifted up his crystal sword and with a cry of war; he led his companions toward the door of the cave.

The shadow could feel the group of werewolves leaving their hide. And so, it approached them. However, it did not expect the shining light coming out from the sword. The monster could not come any closer, and when it tried, Nash edged the blade of his weapon toward it. The shadow could not attack and was retreating. It was the only thing it could do in presence of the Sword of the Moon.

Finally, after a fine ten minutes, they had arrived in front of the door. The wolves were impatiently waiting for Nash to open it, so they could rip out the hearts of the magicians. 'On your positions…' Nash whispered, while lifting up his sword. 'Go!' he yelled, as he destroyed the door with his blade.

Chapter Nineteen
A Troubling Thought

The door was smashed. An enormous horde of werewolves were rushing toward the unprepared magicians. Blood was splattering, giving place to a massacre. All the magicians were gathering toward the door, but most of them were outrun by the wolves. The magicians did not stand a chance when it came to close combat.

The wolves were uncontrollable. The hatred and rage they felt was overwhelming. It was raining blood. The magicians did their best to defend themselves and managed to eliminate some of their assailants, but they were eventually losing the battle.

Prudence carried out Alexandra's body with her, then left it somewhere so she would not receive any attacks from the wolves or the magicians.

'Stay close to me… something tells me Marvin won't be playing fair,' said Nash.

The young man rushed toward a magician and coldly killed him; he then ran toward another one and slashed his throat. Nash did not seem to feel anything when killing, no regrets, no sentiment, and no remorse. It was as if he became as cold as the wolves. Prudence was scared, but she did not have the time to think about it. She ran toward the chamber where Marvin was.

'What the… where is that stupid girl?' Nash grunted, before he stabbed another magician. 'She really is getting on my nerves!' he shouted.

Prudence ran to the throne. It was long and tiring, but she knew Marvin was up to something. He had wanted her dead the moment she came to Wolf Glace. It must have been the reason why he sent her to the undergrounds, without telling her about the spectre.

As she climbed up the stairs, she could hear the cries of agony and the butchery getting louder and echoing in the very walls of Wolf Glace. A magician then appeared in front of her and threw a fireball with his right hand. Prudence dodged it, but she had not the strength to kill him.

'This is for your betrayal!' the magician shouted, as he concentrated an enormous mass of energy on his hand. 'Die!' He threw a much bigger fireball.

As a reflex, Prudence moved her left arm in front of her face to protect her, but surprisingly after a few seconds, she realized that she was not harmed. Perhaps she was dead. But when she lowered her arm, she could see the ball and the magician frozen. They were changed into a statue of ice. She immediately turned around, and saw Nash staring at his hands, perplexed by what happened.

'Are you... are you the creator of this magic?' she quietly asked.

'I... I guess so... looks like, Ryan was not the only one with a crazy power.'

'Let us go... ' said Prudence.

'Ye... yeah,' Nash said, as he followed the princess.

The stairs took at least ten minutes for Nash and Prudence to reach the chamber of the throne. When they had arrived, the door was wide opened, presenting the old man waiting on his throne as if he feared not. He was sitting down as if nothing was happening around him, with a calm and frozen image; he did not make any movement and patiently waited for Prudence and Nash to come closer.

Prudence was shrinking; she advanced carefully, while maniacally looking around her, in case of an attack or an ambush.

'Why are you so tense?' The old man chuckled, as Prudence and Nash got nearer.

'It is over,' said Nash.

'Ah... it is but a pity... I had plans for you... ' the old man said darkly.

'Abandon Sir Fuzirius... you had no intention in fulfilling our request. And nor shall I,' Prudence said calmly.

'I wish for the sword... as I can see, you have indeed found it. Hand it over and no harm will be done to you... or your friends,' Marvin tried to negotiate.

'Forget it, I keep the sword! It is mine!'

'I am willing to make an arrangement... ' said Prudence. 'We will hand over the sword if you revive two of the people I have lost... ' she paused. 'Then we will convince the werewolves to leave. That way you will have the sword and no more of your apprentices dying.'

Marvin was laughing hysterically. He stood up from his throne.

'It is impossible to revive the dead,' he laughed evilly. 'That fool Nox begged for his lover back. I only managed to bring her for a short while before she was changed into this horrific creature that lies in the undergrounds,' he said darkly. 'I want the sword now... or I will kill two more of the people you care about.'

Marvin clicked his fingers and Eric and Mia appeared chained up. He then laughed as if he had become mad and insisted on getting the sword. However, Nash was never going to hand the sword to Marvin. He loved, too much, the power he had acquired from it and so he refused to hand it over. Instead, he even encouraged the old man to kill the two individuals, as if he did not care at all about their fates.

Marvin's plan was ruined. His leverage was not good enough to Nash, and so he had nothing that would make the young man hand over the sword.

Nothing... except the princess. The old man did not wait long, and with a powerful magic, he created a multitude of swords that gathered around the princess. 'Hand over the sword or the girl dies!' he shouted impatiently.

Nash grunted furiously. He then threw the sword to the old man's feet. Marvin could not believe his fortune. He had finally got his hands on the Sword of the Moon.

'After years… it is finally mine.' Marvin stared at the sword.

'Free my friends!' Prudence shouted.

'Oh… but I have to test the power of the sword. What better way, than to test it on the princess of Heartsas?' Marvin laughed evilly.

'You scum!' yelled Nash.

'The heads of Vita will finally understand that their hypocrisy will cost their lives!'

'Hypocrisy?' asked Prudence.

'We magicians have suffered because we were born with magic… but so are all the people of Vita!' Marvin shouted. 'Even you weak beings are gifted with magic, yet you do not know of it!' he kept on going. 'But because we have multiple gifts we are considered dangerous. This is the reason why the heads wanted us dead! But I shall kill them myself!' Marvin stared at the sword. 'With this they shall not stand a chance!'

'That explains the ice… ' Nash whispered.

'Only when an emotion has reached a certain level can a being activate their gift, depending on what it is. Fire for instance, is triggered by anger,' said Marvin. 'Anyway… this shall not matter, as you shall be my first victims!'

Marvin made the swords around Prudence disappear.

'Come and face the sword, little girl!'

Prudence took her sword out. It was the sword that Nash had lent her back in London.

'Let me… ' Nash demanded the sword.

'No… have I not told you – I do not wish for you to protect me.'

Prudence ran to attack Marvin, but with one gesture of his hands, he destroyed the blade of the young woman. There were no doubts; the Sword of the Moon was superior. Prudence fell on the ground. Marvin was approaching her dangerously.

'Die!'

Marvin was about to slash Prudence's throat, but something strange happened. Marvin could not do it. His hands were no more his to control.

The sword was moving around slightly; Marvin did not understand why and was literally controlled by the weapon. Then, Nash ordered the sword to cut out Marvin's throat and so it did. Only one wield and one person could be the master of the sword. Horrified by this discovery, the old man tried to flee, but it was too late.

Marvin's throat was slashed and his blood was emptying from it. The old man dropped the weapon and placed his hands around his gory throat. He tried to heal his cut with magic, but the sword's power did not allow him to perform his enchantment. Soon, Marvin could feel his body freezing out; ice was covering his hands and his legs. 'What is this curse!' he screamed, with blood spilling out of his throat. His body then turned into ice. Marvin the great magician was no more but a mere statue of ice.

The battle was won and soon enough the magicians surrendered to the werewolves. Their fates lay in Nash's hands. Only the true ruler of Wolf Glace had the right to decide on the sentence given.

The werewolves wished for revenge, and wiping out the magicians would satisfy them, whilst the magicians begged for a fair sentence and to be spared. Nash had a kind heart, and so he decreed that both would share an equal and respected life.

The werewolves were disappointed but abided by it; it was the right thing to do. The elder wolf did not mind it; his feud began with Marvin and ended when he died.

To show their gratitude, the magicians all gathered around Nash and praised him. They had lost many of their members, but they knew Nash would be a fair ruler. Sparing their lives, even after all the atrocities they had performed, showed how great a leader he would be. He had compassion, kindness, and a good sense of justice: things that were of a completely foreign concept to Marvin. With Nash, they knew they would be guided to the right path.

It was true that Nash had conquered the hearts and respects of many, but he had also lost some. Eric and Mia could not believe that Nash chose his sword over them. They could have died because of a sword.

Mia snapped. She refused to stay any longer with Nash around. His selfishness was too much. She advanced toward the new ruler of Wolf Glace and slapped him; it was such a hard slap that the walls of the tower echoed with the sound of it.

'Are you out of your mind?' she shouted furiously.

Of course, every follower of the new ruler stood up to attack Mia, but Nash stopped them; the young man knew the reason why the girl slapped him. She had every right; even he did not understand why he had neglected the lives of the two individuals.

The young man then kneeled before Mia and asked for forgiveness from his friends. Eric accepted and granted the pardon Nash was seeking. However, Mia refused; she needed time to forgive such a selfish man. Instead, she walked away toward Prudence and refused to look at Nash.

Nash turned to Prudence. He did not know if she would forgive him, but the princess was of a good heart. She was not mad at Nash. How could she be mad? He had saved her earlier when Marvin tried to kill her.

'What should we do now?' asked Eric.

'We have to…' Prudence sighed with sadness. 'We have to bury the body of Alexandra. It is the fairest thing to do.'

'What? Alexandra is dead?' Mia gasped in shock.

'We will continue to the Dragon's Realm – I have a promise to fulfill,' Prudence said, in a serious and mature tone.

'But… what about Ryan?' demanded Eric.

'I cannot bring the dead back to life…' the princess paused. 'I wish I could…' she started to whimper, 'but I cannot… I shall only grant what I promised to the two of them.'

'What's next then?' asked Nash. 'I mean after we bury Alexandra…'

'We will have to cross Nox's forest again, then from there we could reach the south east like Alexandra told us before. The Dragon's Realm is there.'

'But we won't make it before the time elapsed… I mean… you only have a day left… ' Nash paused. 'It will easily take us a whole day to cross Nox's forest.'

Prudence looked down and bit her lips.

'Excuse me,' one of the magicians interrupted the conversation. 'But if you wish to travel in Vita in a much faster way, we could effortlessly arrange that,' he claimed.

'What do you mean?' asked Prudence.

'This tower is transformable, thus the reason why no one ever noticed it. It is in reality a ship used in times of war. We could get you to the Dragon's Realm in less than an hour.'

This revelation was of a great relief. With this vehicle, they would be able to reach their destination in no time. As soon as Prudence had the Sword of the King, then the attack on Heartsas was the next step of the plan. Of course, the sword was yet to be found since it was a myth.

Nash wanted to waste no more time and go straight toward Heartsas to eliminate the emperor. With the sword he had found he was powerful, and he felt confident enough to take on the emperor, and liberate Prudence's kingdom from his influence.

But the princess refused. Nash may have become powerful, but he was not invincible. If the emperor had enough influence to recruit dangerous men like Reaper, that meant he was extremely dominant. Prudence did not wish to take up useless risks, and precipitate toward an imminent defeat.

Chapter Twenty
The First Kiss

The magicians needed time to be able to move the tower, and transform it into its original purpose. While they were working on moving the tower, Prudence buried the body of Alexandra outside of Wolf Glace with the help of some magicians and werewolves. The two pirates that accompanied her decided to go back to their lives as pirates. Without Alexandra, their purposes on this journey had no more meaning, and so they left.

A short time after, the magicians were encountering difficulties into transforming the tower and so they required at least two hours before making it function. It was enough time for Prudence and her friends to rest, before venturing in the Dragon's Realm, where their journey would take a decisive twist of fate.

The princess was nervous; she knew she would have to face dangers like she had never faced before. The Dragon's Realm was a place that only allowed royal blood to enter. And so, she would be by herself there. The pressure was building up inside of her, it would be the second time she had been alone in her journey. She isolated herself from the group, because she needed to rest for a short time. However, the conditions were soon to be unfavourable for her…

It was not to be forgotten that griffons were flying around Wolf Glace. And with Marvin gone, the magic that sustained a cold barrier disappeared, leaving the griffons with an opportunity to invade Wolf Glace.

Cries of terror were heard outside of the tower, and soon the walls were attacked. The windows were shattering and the creatures entered in mass. It was impossible to judge how fast and powerful they were, and in a matter of seconds they had pulverised many of the werewolves and the magicians.

'Everyone, leave them to me!' Nash shouted, as he got his sword out. 'Only I have the power to destroy them!' he claimed, with a fierce attitude.

Nash was overconfident with the sword, but in this case he was right to be. As griffons hated coldness, he had an absolute advantage over these creatures. And shortly after defeating many of them, the lot started to retreat. Many retreated, but not all of them.

Prudence was lying in a bed, deeply in her thoughts. She forgot about everything that was happening around her and did not pay attention to the griffons' attack. She kept thinking of Ryan and how she wished he could be with her. Then, when she least expected it, she heard the noise of a person getting close to her. She turned around and with horror, she saw a griffon approaching her, with a murderous intention. Panicked, she jumped out of the bed and ran toward the door, but another griffon appeared and ambushed her in the middle of the room. She was scared. She did not know what to do, so she got out Alexandra's pistol and with shaking hands she fired out, but missed.

The griffons were vicious, and were taking their time before attacking the princess; it was as if they enjoyed the terror they were inflicting. Prudence was petrified in fear, she could not move and she felt as if she would faint.

Soon, one of the griffons jumped on the princess with its claws out. Prudence thought she was done for. But the sound of a sword was heard and blood splattered. Prudence fainted, she was too emotionally affected and all she could hear was the noises of the griffons fighting against someone with a sword. The sound of the metal battling with the hard skin of the creature and the shrieks of agony they were emitting, were piercing and scary. She then heard a final blow and one last cry of agony; it was the very last thing she could remember before everything went dark.

Ten minutes later, Prudence was regaining consciousness. She could hear joyful steps jumping around the room she was in. What was happening?

When she opened her eyes, it was Mia and Eric dancing happily around, and laughing with excitement. 'I knew he'd make it!' Eric yelled enthusiastically.

'Shush! You will wake Prudence up,' Mia whispered.

'What is going on?' Prudence moaned, as she got up from her bed.

Eric and Mia ceased dancing and started to look at each other with happy faces. They were for some reason happier than ever. It was the first time on Vita, that Prudence had seen the two of them being that joyful.

'Can you remember what happened?' asked Eric.

'All I can remember is those griffons…' Prudence tried to recall the attack. 'And I fainted… I could only hear the noises of someone battling the creatures…'

'Well, someone did fight them!' Mia chuckled. 'And he saved you! And he was so gracious!' she kept on going with excitement.

'Who was it? Nash?' Prudence tried to guess.

'Aha…' Eric laughed. 'Guess again!'

Prudence gave a lot of names. But they kept on laughing and made her guess even more. It was fun to them, but really exasperating for her. 'Enough, I demand to know who saved me… do not play games please.' said Prudence.

'He is waiting for you outside the tower…' responded Eric. 'That's all he allowed us to tell you.'

The princess could not understand why the two had to make her saviour seem so mysterious; nevertheless, she had to thank him, and so she hasted herself out of the tower to meet with the mysterious person.

Once outside, she could see a hooded person. He was standing on his own and looking toward the forest. And then the wind blew out his hood, which lowered itself, presenting a blonde haired young man. Prudence was shocked; he looked so much like Ryan from behind. She approached him, slowly but surely, and when she was near enough, she took a gentle tone and bowed to him.

'I thank you sir, for this courageous act you have performed against the griffons. It has saved me and earned you my gratitude. Please do accept it,' she said, while bowing courteously.

'Ah… ' he laughed. 'I thought we already had this conversation about you bowing,' he chuckled. 'For you, I would risk anything,' he said, while turning around.

Prudence could not believe it. It was Ryan. He was alive and in front of her.

'R… Ryan?' she stuttered, as she could barely trust that it was real.

'I thought you'd hug me and tell me how much you've missed me,' Ryan laughed. 'But "R..Ryan" is good enough, I guess.' He chuckled.

She did not wait any longer to hug him, and she started to cry, relieved by him being alive. Ryan gently breathed in her perfume and smiled. He then caressed her hair, while closing his eyes. It felt good to find comfort in each other's arms, and after a fine minute, the young man took one step back and stared at Prudence's eyes.

'Gosh… I could spend forever looking into your eyes,' he whispered.

'And I could eternally stay in your arms… ' Prudence smiled.

Their eyes met… Prudence could not help but to stare at Ryan's beautiful and mysterious eyes. Then, slowly, her lips started to shiver. She wanted to kiss him so much, but she did not know how he felt about her. Her heart was beating faster. She knew she was blushing, because she felt so intimidated by Ryan's eyes, and her palms were getting sweaty. His lips were getting nearer and seemed so soft. His hands were bringing her closer to him… the closer she was getting, the faster her heart was pounding behind her chest. And then, when they were close enough, Ryan approached her face and delicately touched her lips with his. It was a soft touch…

Prudence could feel Ryan's hesitation before kissing her. Maybe it was because she was not kissable?

'I missed the kiss didn't I?'

'I am sorry, what do you mean?' asked Prudence.

'It was my first kiss. I just didn't know how to do it right…'

'It was my first kiss too.'

'Let's not count it and start over, what you think?' asked Ryan.

'Kiss me.'

Ryan smiled and kissed her. His lips were nice and perfect. He did not use too much of his mouth and he knew how to gently touch her lips. Her eyes were closed. Prudence did not seem to wish to let go of him. She could kiss him forever. His kiss felt even safer than his arms. It was a sensation she could never forget… it was as if all her problems had disappeared, and being with Ryan was the only thing that mattered.

'You two are disgusting!' Eric shouted.

Ryan ceased to kiss Prudence and laughed. He then held her hand, and together they advanced toward Eric and the others. Everyone who knew Ryan was thrilled. He was back, and more importantly he was alive. Mia even had tears of happiness dropping from her eyes. She was happy and like Prudence, she felt safer with her friend around. Everyone was happy, even Nash, who was jealous of his brother at first, came to shake his hand and scolded him off for almost dying. Ryan was much loved, and his presence was enough for all of his friends to stop worrying and find the strength to go on.

'I trust you have comforted them?' a young woman said.

'Oh, everyone – this is Cheryl, the woman from the train.' Ryan paused. 'She is the one who healed me, and together we protected you from the emperor's troops.' He chuckled.

'What?' Eric asked confusedly.

'The goblins and the trolls were after you. They followed the trails you were leaving, but Cheryl and I had managed to confuse them and point them west.'

'You were the one who saved me in the forest that night!' Eric gasped.

'It is a trick I've learnt to do.' Ryan chuckled. 'Look… ' he showed his hand, and a flame appeared on it.

'I taught him how to use magic, of course,' said Cheryl.

Nash and everyone were amazed by Ryan's capacity for using fire, they could tell he had become a much more stronger and reliable ally. Nash seemed a bit jealous of the trust and the warmth his brother had, but he also was dazzled in wonder of him. Ryan had by himself managed to protect everyone from a distance, and learnt how to combat in a world full of dangers. Sure there was Cheryl, but still, it was remarkable.

Ryan then turned toward his brother and congratulated him on the finding of the Sword of the Moon, and his new place as a ruler.

The brothers seemed as if they had surmounted their differences during the time they had been separated; it was rather interesting how distance could bring people closer in each other's hearts.

'We should rest… the journey to the Dragon's Realm has yet to come,' Cheryl said darkly.

'Usually she is more fun, trust me guys.' Ryan laughed. 'But she is also quite jealous of my love for Prudence… it got us in some little fights during our journey.'

'Quiet! I am not jealous at all,' Cheryl said sharply. 'But we have no time to waste in useless moments like these… '

'I do believe you are wrong. It is for these moments we are fighting… to make sure we can preserve the peace around us and allow love to grow in a world full of happiness… ' Prudence said, before placing her head on Ryan's shoulder.

'I have known you for a short time, yet you are already getting on my nerves,' Cheryl scoffed. 'I will be resting. I, contrary to you, have no intention of dying.' She paused. 'The Dragon's Realm is the most unknown place on Vita; it is so frightening that no souls would venture there,' Cheryl said grimly. 'I shall see to your success or demise,' she said, before leaving.

'Never mind her, Prudence. You should go rest, you are tired and emotionally overwhelmed,' said Ryan. 'Don't worry, I will be there when you open your eyes,' he murmured in her ear.

Although she was terrified that once awakened he would be gone, and everyone would tell her it was only a dream, she chose to believe Ryan's words and left. Mia did as the two ladies; she went to rest, relieved of Ryan being there to surmount this last quest awaiting them.

Nash and Eric wished to speak with Ryan. They wanted to hear everything. How he managed to survive, how he handled his power, and everything that happened since. One after the other, the questions piled up. Ryan knew it was inevitable and soon there were too many questions that he could not answer. Nash and Eric did not give him any breaks and they kept popping out a new topic every time he was about to say something.

Finally, after draining all possible questions and answers, the two young men ceased to demand anything. Ryan was feeling much satisfied with them being finished and began to talk of something much more important.

'There is something that's been bothering me,' Ryan said darkly. 'Reaper managed to find Prudence so easily when we were in London, yet once in Vita, the emperor himself has not made a move,' he said, with an intrigued tone.

Nash and Eric went silent. They did not know what Ryan was saying, however, he was in the right direction, and once thought was given about it, it seemed unusual. Nash asked him for further information on what he meant. Ryan sighed after looking down.

'I don't know, that is the thing.' He bit his lips. 'But something is off... '

'Man... now I'm worried,' Eric mumbled.

'Ah... don't look so glum. It's not like you're the one who will have to go through whatever challenges Prudence will have to face,' Nash scoffed.

Ryan laughed. He felt happy to be around his loved ones but he kept on thinking about what was missing. The emperor was meant to be powerful and yet he had not seen one movement made by him. All he had done so far was send troops of goblins and trolls after Prudence, but that was it. And if she was really a threat to him, then he would have sent Reaper or the other dangerous men he hired. It would have made much sense.

'You worry way too much, brother,' Nash chuckled, as he got his sword out. 'With this, I will be able to protect the princess… no matter what.'

'You trust this sword too much… ' Ryan scoffed. 'But fine, whatever, as long as you protect her.'

'I'm out of here guys, I feel tired,' Eric moaned.

'Yes, me too,' Ryan stretched out his arms. 'Nash, be careful not to trust this weapon too much,' said Ryan, as he was leaving with Eric.

Nash looked at his sword and scoffed.

'This weapon is the only thing that I have, brother,' he sighed.

'You have love and everyone by your side,' he whispered.

Nash was left to contemplate the sky and the sunset. He scoffed and took a deep breath of disappointment, before lying down on the grass.

Nash stared at the clouds and the orange sky before he felt the earth trembling. When he turned around, he could see the tower moving out from the ground, and changing itself into an enormous warship. He gasped out of surprise, and enjoyed the astonishing spectacle that was being projected right in front of his eyes.

'We are ready my Lord!' one of the magicians shouted.

'Splendid! Impeccable timing, I must say!' Nash gasped excitedly.

The ship was ready; they could finally head toward the Dragon's Realm, where Prudence's destiny was to be fulfilled.

Chapter Twenty-One
The Things That Matter

Prudence was asleep; she was snoring softly out of fatigue. Ryan was by her side looking at her passionately; he could not take his eyes off her and was wrapped in wonder. Her face was so innocent and the smile she had made her look like an angel. The young man was breathless before such a beauty. He then kissed her on the forehead and headed out toward the chamber of the throne.

'Ryan?' Prudence said delicately, as she opened her eyes. There was no one, and so she thought she was dreaming. With tiredness, she went back to sleep.

On his way to the chamber, the young man was interrupted by Cheryl, who was dressed in a rather attractive outfit. It was a white maiden shirt with long black tights; she had a mini skirt with it and black heeled boots. Her wolf tail was unnatural but it did not stop her from attracting men.

'How do I look?' she giggled.

Ryan answered her favourably, while trying to get to the chamber. But she was persistent and stood in his way; she even pushed him toward a wall and moved her red lips toward his. 'You should rest,' said Ryan with a gentle tone.

'Why? Am I so hideous to you?'

'No… you are really attractive,' Ryan said softly. 'But my heart belongs to another woman, as I've told you since we met.'

'You know how my wolfie side can be quite persistent, don't you?' Cheryl chuckled, as she put her arms around his neck. 'Plus you know you do not have much time… you should make the best out of what's left for you…'

Ryan removed her arms from his neck and smiled, then ignored her advances and went to see Nash, who was preparing everything before the departure of the ship. Cheryl grunted out of anger and followed Ryan, who seemed more concerned about the next destination than her.

Once in the chamber of the throne, Nash had a round table put in the middle of the room, with a lot of chairs around it. A long map was set upon it, and different people were reviewing the plan. Whether they were magicians or werewolves, everyone contributed to helping Nash.

'Such a nice sight I am witnessing here,' Ryan shouted, as he advanced toward the round table. 'And would you be kind enough to enlighten me why I was not aware of this little gathering?' he asked.

'Ah… the annoying one could not help himself but come here.' Nash chuckled. 'We are currently discussing the attack on Heartsas.'

Were Ryan's ears betraying him? He thought Nash had mentioned an attack. But when he asked, Nash confirmed his plan. Nash had no intention in letting Prudence risk her life. Even if she was so willing to face the dangers, it was a risk he would not allow her to take.

'You moron!' Ryan yelled at Nash. 'Who are you to make decisions for her?'

'Maybe you want her to try hard and die, but I have other plans for her. I will keep her alive, contrary to you,' Nash scoffed.

The two brothers stood up at each other's face, both in complete disagreement. Cheryl did not wait long and stood up by Ryan's side, however, all the magicians and all the werewolves were at Nash's side.

'What a gorgeous lady you have here,' Nash chuckled. 'What's with the tail?'

'This is none of your concern – leave my tail alone.'

'Phew… ' Nash whistled. 'Learn to control your ladies, young man.'

'Ah... something you wish you could do, eh?' Cheryl mocked Nash.

All the werewolves and the magicians stared at Cheryl. They started to talk indistinctly to each others. According to them, those yellow eyes and this tail made her a unique race, commonly known as a Humolf, a mix between a werewolf and a human. The elder and its congeners used to be Humolfs once, but they were meant to be the last linear of this race. It was unexpected to meet with one, as they had all died from extinction. Curious about her, the elder werewolf and a magician approached her, but as soon as they did, Ryan drew his sword and stood up against them.

'Don't attack that idiot,' Nash laughed. 'See how much I am respected?'

'This world is not yours; you shall understand your misfortune,' Cheryl scoffed. 'This sword you wield is cursed with death on it... only a fool like you can be chosen to wield such a plague.'

Nash stared at Cheryl. He did not seem to understand her saying.

'Meaning?' he asked.

'You take pleasure in killing with this sword...' Cheryl paused. 'The more you kill, the more you feel satisfied. But one day, killing one won't be enough and a hundred will be a much convincing score... and then a thousand. I could go on and on...' she paused again. 'You will kill until Death itself won't come to you – this is why you have come into a misfortune...'

'Excuse me, my lady? Misfortune?' Nash laughed darkly. 'Ahaha! I am the ruler of a kingdom!' he shouted diabolically. 'I have powers I would never have dreamed of! This "misfortune" is just the very beginning of it. This world is mine for the taking!'

'Just as I said... your thirst to conquer is already beginning...'

'You can go to the emperor, if it fits you to get killed pitiably. But do leave Prudence the choice and let her decide. Heartsas is her kingdom after all,' Ryan said sharply, with his sword still in his hands.

'What are you going to do? Take us all?' Nash laughed confidently.

'Psh...' Ryan scoffed. 'That won't be a hard task, you and your little ice toy will get a real taste of power,' he said arrogantly, as he assimilated fire into the blade of his sword.

Ryan's sword was blazing in fire, and smoke was coming out from the blade. It felt hot just to look at the sword itself. Ryan knew Nash had gotten a lot of powers since he had found the sword, but Nash was being overconfident and foolish. If Ryan could get sense into him, then maybe he would reconsider about going after the emperor. However, Nash had no intention of fighting, instead he ordered his followers to attack his brother.

A werewolf immediately jumped on Ryan, but the young man kicked it around the stomach before knocking it out, with the back of his sword.

'If you don't kill then you will be killed!' Cheryl yelled at Ryan, as she created an enormous dragon made of water. The Humolf was very powerful. It only took her about ten seconds, before wiping out the whole lot, with one hand wave. Ryan then created a ring of fire and trapped all of them inside. All except Nash.

Nash clapped his hands, congratulating his brother and his friend sarcastically. 'Nice one... but you two will have a real taste of a fight,' he said, as he got his sword out.

'Come and get it!' Ryan dashed with his sword in hands. 'You will be begging for mercy!'

The two brothers were about to cross blades, but as soon as they did, someone shouted 'Enough!' out of nowhere. It was Prudence; she was out of breath, since she had to run all the way to the chamber. As soon as she got close enough to the two brothers, she slapped Nash.

'Aha...' Ryan laughed, before he got slapped too.

Ryan then explained Nash's plan for defeating the emperor without getting the Sword of the King.

Prudence could not believe her ears. Nash, who seemed more

reasonable than Ryan, had gone foolish; perhaps it was the sword's influence on him. Ever since he had his hands on the sword, he had been acting bizarre and overconfident about his abilities. She then demanded him to hand over the sword or to separate from it, but the young man refused.

'See… crazy already,' said Cheryl.

'Shut up!' Nash snarled.

'Fine, I will leave you with it,' Prudence sighed. 'But I have my destiny to fulfil. I intend to go to the Dragon's Realm and obtain the sword that is rightfully mine,' she said nobly. 'And I trust that you will take me there before going after the emperor?' she asked.

'Sure. For you I will do anything,' Nash said, as he held Prudence's hand.

Ryan looked away with frowned eyebrows and fire in his eyes. His brother was selfish and he was not stopping his attempts to charm Prudence, even when she told him where he stood. He knew how Nash was and once he had an idea in his mind, he would not stop. But Ryan did not care, he loved Prudence and Prudence loved him. That was all that mattered, and if Nash wanted to waste his efforts in vain, then so be it. At least he knew something mattered more for Nash than a sword.

After a short conflict that was quickly dealt with, Ryan left to speak with Eric. Cheryl wanted to go with him, but Prudence stopped her. The princess dragged the young Humolf into a corner and abruptly engaged in conversation with her.

Prudence desired to know of her. What was she doing with the emperor and why did she save Ryan? However, Cheryl did not answer any questions Prudence asked. Instead, she kept on laughing arrogantly, as if she could not take Prudence seriously. Then she grabbed the princess, and violently pushed her to the wall.

'Listen to me, "Your Highness", I despise you and your family,' Cheryl said with hatred in her eyes.

She then began to strangle the princess.

'I have had my eyes on Ryan for a very long time and I plan on taking your place in his heart,' Cheryl said evilly, as she was pressuring Prudence's neck. 'I suggest you stay out of my way, as I will not hesitate in ripping your guts out.' Cheryl pushed the princess to the floor.

'So you wish for Ryan... ' said Prudence, as she placed her hands around her throat.

'Yes. See, us Humolfs are really complex when it comes to love, but once we find someone who makes our heart beat faster then that person is ours to couple with.'

Prudence stood up. She was trembling a bit and her throat was hurting.

'I am sorry but I will not lose Ryan to you. He is the one my heart chose and even if I have to die... ' she paused. 'Then I will die remaining true to my heart.'

'You little... '

Cheryl wanted to attack Prudence. She advanced toward the princess with a threatening posture. But before she attempted anything, Ryan stopped her. He and Eric were both walking around when he surprised her whilst trying to harm Prudence. Eric was puzzled by what was happening. He stood there silent, but he could see Cheryl's anger. Prudence immediately went near Ryan and stood by his side. She was frightened about Cheryl, but was too proud to say it.

'Look at your love, she is so scared she cannot even face me,' Cheryl scoffed arrogantly.

'Leave her alone. I thought we had that discussion before coming to Wolf Glace?'

'For you Ryan, I will even go against my nature and support that weak woman.'

'I will not tolerate you insulting her... ' Ryan said calmly but menacingly.

'What's up with this story? Nash who loves Prudence and now that Cheryl wolfgirl who loves Ryan... phew... seriously... ' Eric sighed. 'People, make up your damn mind.'

'Shut up little boy!' Cheryl yelled at Eric, who immediately jumped behind Ryan like a scared cat.

'Cheryl... please...' Ryan sighed.

'I will take my leave for now. But Ryan, remember that I am not afraid to die for you unlike someone here...' Cheryl laughed evilly, before she left.

Eric waited for Cheryl to be far away before manning up.

'Yeah, it's better for you to leave, eh!' said Eric.

'You know she's half wolf... she can hear you...'

'What?' Eric whimpered.

'Relax, she's too far to hear what you're saying anyway...' said Ryan.

'What a bloody weirdo she is,' Eric scoffed. 'Wonder how you could have put up with her...'

Ryan sighed, and explained that he was in debt to her. She had saved him when he was about to die. Ryan was a maniac when it came to trust and honesty, but also loyalty. And Cheryl had shown all of it by going up against the emperor himself. Ryan could not just ignore her after all she had done for him.

Prudence understood Ryan. She was scared of Cheryl, who was someone she could not trust or appreciate because of her vile and impulsive behaviour. But without her, Ryan would have been dead. So, Prudence was deeply grateful to her for saving him.

But one thing was sure, the princess was not going to let go of Ryan because of Cheryl. She was frightened, but she was not planning on renouncing on her love.

Suddenly, the tower that was now a warship started to move. It was shaking slightly, which made Ryan and his friends aware of something happening.

'That idiot, what is he doing now?' Ryan snarled, before he headed toward the throne room.

Once there, he could see Nash leading a team of magicians and werewolves. They were controlling the warship and heading toward an unknown location. Ryan jumped out in front of his brother and questioned his doing.

Of course, Nash was not obliged to answer to his brother, and so he blanked him. Ryan got upset and punched Nash in the face before asking him again what he was doing.

'We are heading toward the Dragon's Realm you utter imbecile!' Nash shouted. 'Oh yes, before I forget.' He then punched Ryan in the face. 'Never hit me again, or next time that will be worse than this.'

Ryan was destabilized by the punch, but quickly regained his balance.

'Oh, you're going to get it good!' Ryan tried to punch his brother, but Prudence and Eric stopped him.

'Don't break yourself a nail, bro... ' Nash laughed. 'Girly hands... '

'Let go of me!'

'Nash... stop it please,' said Prudence.

Nash laughed but stopped his mockery. He then informed the princess of the duration of the journey before they reached the Dragon's Realm. Two to three hours were to be expected according to the magicians. Prudence was much satisfied to hear that Nash would not go up against the emperor for now, and lead her to her original destination.

'I trust you will inform us once we have arrived?' Prudence gently asked.

'You can count on me... ' said Nash, before he offered his hand. 'Would you give me the honour of escorting you outside, on the deck?' he asked courteously. 'The view is beautiful, in particular, about an hour from now, we will be able to contemplate the stars,' he insisted. 'I mean... so I've heard.'

Prudence did not want to be rude or mean to Nash, however, he did not seem to understand that she was not interested in his advances. She knew that what she would do next would hurt Nash, but something had to be done for him to let go of her.

'Would you be kind enough to escort me?' she turned to Ryan, after completely ignoring Nash.

'Aha,' Ryan laughed. 'Of course my lady. Let us be on our way.' He chuckled, as he gracefully and chivalrously took the princess's hand.

Nash bit his lips. He seemed annoyed by Prudence's gesture. He then stomped the ground angrily.

'They look so good together,' Eric said, while staring at the couple leaving.

'Do shut up,' Nash grunted.

The couple were on the deck of the ship. It was beautiful and the air was fresh. The view gave a good glimpse of a bird's life; flying amongst the clouds was an astonishing sight. Prudence closed her eyes, and spread her arms as if she had wings. 'I feel like I am flying,' she said, with the wind blowing in her face.

'It is normal for an angel to fly,' Ryan said, while holding Prudence's waist from behind. 'Just don't jump, OK?'

'Would you catch me?'

'No.'

Prudence's eyes opened widely. She did not think Ryan would say no.

'I would fly with you,' Ryan delicately pressed his cheek next to Prudence's. 'Together, we would fly with the angels… and the birds of course… and any other flying things that live on Vita… '

Prudence smiled and closed her eyes. It was a beautiful thing to say.

An hour later, the couple were still outside, enjoying the fresh air and the view the ship was offering from the deck. The night had arisen and the stars were shining so beautifully. Prudence was facing the scenery, whilst Ryan was behind her, with his arms around her waist.

Prudence did not wish to say anything, but something was bothering her. She was thinking of what Marvin had said earlier: the heads of Vita were hypocrites. Was it true? She never, ever, suspected that she could be capable of using magic in her life. And she still never saw magic coming from her hands. So was Marvin lying? But then again she saw Ryan, and Nash using magic, yet they were not even from Vita to begin with.

If it was true, and the heads were using peer pressure on the people, to hide or even disguise themselves from magic, then Marvin was not entirely evil. He wished to make use of something that he did not feel ashamed to possess. It was not a crime to wish for freedom, maybe somehow, somewhere, she was starting to understand better those so called enemies of Vita. Whether it was Marvin, Daemn or those from the past, all they tried to do was to bring what they believed right to see the light…

Prudence could not forgive Daemn for what he had done to Heartsas, but he did bring freedom to the orcs, goblins and other dark creatures that everyone banished on Vita. Was he wrong for bringing every race to walk together? No, but trying to make the world live in fear was something she could not abide to. A world of fear is not a world that anyone would want to live in…

'Are you OK, my love?' asked Ryan. 'You have been quiet for a while.'

'Oh… sorry – I was thinking… '

'Would you care to share?'

Prudence told Ryan about what was on her mind. She then thought of something else. It was a scary thought. What if she would end up like the heads of Vita? If she was successful and managed to beat Daemn, would she end up bringing back the old ways? The ways where orcs, goblins and others are oppressed because of what they are?

'No of course not, my love.'

'How can you be so sure?' asked Prudence.

'Because you have a kind heart – and that is what will make you the difference between the old and the new ways. Always remember that.'

Prudence felt slightly better.

'As long as you are with me, I suppose I should not worry.'

Ryan went silent.

'I suppose,' he said with a weak tone.

The princess then asked Ryan about Cheryl. She wanted to know why Cheryl seemed so angry against her and her family. Ryan said he knew nothing of it. Prudence knew Ryan was lying because his voice was slightly shaking and he was quite evasive on the subject. However, she did not insist. He may have promised Cheryl that he would not say anything. Or perhaps he truly did not know. It did not matter much anyway, Cheryl was not important to her.

Ryan then turned Prudence around. He made her face him.

'What is it?' she stared at his eyes.

'I wanted to ask you – why...' Ryan paused. 'Why did you go to Wolf Glace instead of the Dragon's Realm?'

'For you.'

'You could have lost everything because of me.' Ryan seemed to feel guilty. 'If I was truly dead and...'

Prudence kissed him before he said anything else.

'I did what my heart thought was right.' Prudence smiled. 'I love you more than anything else Ryan and I needed you by my side.'

'I was only gone for a day.'

'A day without you felt like forever to me.'

Ryan went silent. His eyes were focused on his feet. He was hiding something...

'There is something you have to know...' Ryan paused, his voice was calm but she could see how troubled he seemed to be. His eyes could not face hers. 'I...'

Ryan was about to say something when Prudence felt a jolt. The ship had been hit by something. When she looked at the sky, she could see the silhouette of a dragon.

'We have arrived!' a magician shouted.

'What did you wish to say?'

'Oh – it can wait!' Ryan said enthusiastically. 'I mean, wow, look at the dragons!'

The Dragon's Realm had been reached. Even at night, they could distinguish the silhouettes of many dragons flying around. They were scary and immense; their very structure was intimidating. Ryan's jaw dropped at the sight of one. The dragon had long wings and was as described in books. The creature possessed small spikes from its neck to the edge of its tail. It had a long tail that could destroy a wall of rock with one movement, and massive muscles around the legs and the arms. It even possessed a solid cuirass which could easily endure swords or many weapons. Its face and jaw were similar to a dinosaur but more impressive, and the bloody red which served as a skin colour, gave it a devilish appearance. At last they had arrived: the Dragon's Realm…

Chapter Twenty-Two
The Dragon's Realm

The dragon was following the ship very closely, maybe too close; it looked as if its intentions were to bring the ship down. Ryan held Prudence tightly and took a few steps back to protect her. Both adolescents were amazed by the imposing presence the dragon had. Its big wings and its massive body were terrifying. Ryan trembled for a moment. It was a spectacular view they had but a scary one too. Nothing would stop the dragon from attacking the ship, and if it did, then he and Prudence were the first ones who would suffer the impact.

'Prudence, you should go back inside,' Ryan said calmly yet with concern.

'Do not be afraid my love –' Prudence said with excitement in her eyes, '– it is only guiding us to its king.'

'How do you know that?' Ryan gasped as the dragon got near.

'It told me so,' Prudence replied. 'Have you not heard it?' she asked.

'No… I don't speak dragon,' Ryan replied.

'Only royal blood can hear them.'

'Cheryl,' Prudence sighed in annoyance, after seeing the Humolf. 'Are you not safer inside?'

'I could not miss the spectacle your lowness,' Cheryl answered arrogantly.

Ryan then asked Cheryl about what she meant, when she said that only royal blood could hear the dragons' voices.

'Seventeen years ago dragons were the guardians of all the places around Vita, but one day, they were considered too dangerous by the people and so they were hunted down,' Cheryl said darkly. 'Only a few royal families refused to annihilate the species. Heartsas, Infernos, and Wolf Glace were the only ones to stand against the hunt. The three kingdoms allied themselves and offered a safe place for the dragons, which is commonly known as the Dragon's Realm.'

'That doesn't answer what I've asked.'

'In guise of gratitude, the dragons allowed only those three kingdoms to ever step in their home. And so, they offered the capacity of communicating with them. The dragons and the three royal families can share thoughts. That way, they can be recognized and not attacked. Thus, the reason only royal families can venture to this realm.'

'But I don't understand.' Ryan went silent, he was deep in his thoughts. 'How could they be hunted down? They are so powerful looking…'

'They used to be smaller than this, trust me,' replied Cheryl.

'Oh, fair enough…' said Ryan.

Prudence knew her parents were good people. Hearing about the tale of the dragons made her smile. She somehow felt closer to her parents. Ryan looked at Prudence; he could see how proud she was on the inside.

He understood the feeling she felt. His mother was someone he was proud of, even if she had not saved dragons or fought against powerful magicians. He understood how important parents were. He felt lucky; he had the chance of having both parents there for him. But he could see how painful it was for Prudence to hear about her parents, and not to have gotten the chance of knowing them.

'That said, I still hate you and your family,' Cheryl said rudely before taking her leave.

'Why do you?' Prudence asked Cheryl, but was ignored by her.

'Let her be, she has her own personal reasons,' Ryan said calmly.

Another dragon appeared along with ten others; they were all holding the ship and gently descending it to the ground.

The ship was placed in front of a gigantic castle, and anyone who wished to leave the ship was invited to go through the colossal gates.

Prudence was the first to leave the ship, accompanied by Ryan who kept a cold and strong posture. The young man had his eyes and jaw wide open, and he kept on looking around. He and his friends seemed miniscule in comparison to the dragons and their realm; it was as if they had been reduced to a bug size.

Eric was shaking. Just like Ryan, he could not stop looking around and felt somehow small compared to everything that surrounded him. He swallowed his breath after seeing the countless number of dragons flying over his head and staring at him.

'Gosh,' Eric whimpered, after he saw two dragons armed with swords waiting near the gates. The swords were of the same size as their tails. One wave of it and everyone would be wiped out.

Mia's hands were shaking. Her mouth was shivering and her teeth were making noises. The pupils of her eyes kept going left, right, up and down. She got closer to Ryan and stayed right behind him, with Eric by her side.

Cheryl was behind Mia and did not seem to care at all about the creatures around her; she walked straight, with an arrogant expression.

'You lot stay in the ship,' Nash ordered the magicians and the werewolves. 'It's better if you stay and ensure that we will be ready to leave once Prudence finds her sword,' he said calmly.

'Very well, my Lord,' the elder wolf bowed to Nash.

'Mhmp... ' Nash chuckled. 'I really enjoy this new me.' He laughed quietly, before resuming his walk to the gates of the castle.

Nash was walking with a fearless posture. The way he stood and the way his eyes were focused straight on the gates, and not on the dragons, made him arrogant in the presence of the creatures.

Nash caught up with Ryan, and then he placed his left arm around Prudence's shoulder nervously. 'See, princess, as a promise keeper, here we are in the Dragon's Realm,' he said.

'I thank you,' said Prudence, after removing Nash's arm. 'And I am pleased to share this moment with you.' She turned to Ryan.

'What can I say?' Ryan placed his right arm around Prudence's waist, to rub it in Nash's face. 'You're mine… and I'm yours, my darling.'

'Typical.' Nash grunted. 'At least there's still Mia and Cheryl who are free.'

'Sorry but I am in the same boat as you when it comes to love,' Cheryl smiled wryly.

'Don't count on me to be your replacement girlfriend, I like someone else,' said Mia.

'You guys should keep it serious!' Eric said loudly. 'We are in front of these impressive creatures and you guys talk about love!'

Suddenly, one of the dragons guarding the gates of the castle got near to Eric and started to smell him. 'Why me?' Eric whimpered.

'He is non-royal blood –' the dragon snarled. 'Can he still pass?'

'The master will decide,' the other dragon replied. 'Smell the others, except the Humolf, the princess and the one with the Sword of the Moon.'

'At least some recognize my power,' Cheryl scoffed.

The Humolf advanced without fear; she did not even look at the dragons as she got inside the castle. Prudence's eyes were focused on Cheryl. How could she enter the domain?

Nash laughed with pride as he entered the castle; he glanced at Ryan and mocked him. Ryan could not waste time with his brother being childish, and so he just ignored him and focused on what was happening in front of him.

'You are allowed to enter, Princess of Heartsas,' one of the dragons bowed to her.

Prudence entered the castle; she was surprised how courteous and organized the dragons could be.

Ryan was puzzled. Only royal blood could speak or hear the dragons. Then how come those two were granted the possibility of speech?

'How come you two can talk?' he asked loudly.

One of the guards then answered him. Some dragons had the capacity of learning the language of the humans. It was however, something dragons did not consider a privilege, but a curse. Ryan tried to argue with the fact that not all humans are evil, but the dragons laughed at him.

'This one is a bit of a talker,' one of the dragons snarled. 'You are all free to come in the castle – should the master think you unworthy, you will be ordered to leave the premises.'

'Gee… thanks, I guess,' Ryan scoffed, as he walked toward the gates.

'Ryan, what are you crazy?' Eric whispered to the young man. 'They could eat us in one bite and you are being grumpy!' he whimpered.

'You loved dragons before, so how come you are afraid?' Ryan asked, puzzled.

'In books, yes!' Eric said loudly. 'Not in reality! I never thought I'd meet one!' he whimpered, after looking behind him. 'They're too scary!' his voice trembled.

Ryan ignored his friend, and just walked inside of the castle. He knew deep inside that Eric was brave, but it would take time for him to realize it.

The castle was immense. Just to touch the roof of it Ryan would have needed at least five double deck buses. It was well decorated apart from the low luminosity. They only had low quantity of torches. But it was more than enough for the friends to distinguish what was ahead of them.

A dragon, smaller than Ryan, advanced toward him and his friends. It did not look impressive at all compared to its kind. The dragon was rather skinny with a cute face and small hands. Its skin was of a light blue. It had a small jaw with small teeth, which gave it the look of a teddy bear instead of a monster.

'I am Dragonus; I shall be your guide to meet the master. Please make yourselves comfortable around me, I know you are threatened by my form but I will not bite,' it said proudly.

'Oh, he is so cute!' Prudence pinched the left cheek of Dragonus.

'Hands off lady!' Dragonus said with embarrassment. 'I am not cute! I am terrifying!' it said as loud as it could, but with a small voice, it made it look cuter.

'I thought all the dragons were scary,' Mia sighed in relief.

'I give up! I will never have the same respect as the others!' Dragonus started to sob.

'Oh please do not cry,' Prudence tried to comfort the dragon, by hugging it.

'Eh... it feels good!' Dragonus chuckled. 'Anyway!' it said loudly, before starting to walk. 'Let us be on our way.'

Dragonus led the way.

The walls were all made of bricks and the castle was vast. It was as if it had taken centuries to build. The corridors were dark, but in presence of the dragon it was much more pleasant to cross them.

A lot of portraits of dragons and families of the three kingdoms were displayed in the gallery room, which led to the throne. According to Dragonus, the king loved to spend his time contemplating the portraits of the families that saved it and its kind. Prudence saw a lot of portraits. But then, a certain portrait took out all of her attention.

'Isn't that...' Prudence gasped, as she saw the portrait of a woman, 'my mother?'

'It is indeed,' Dragonus said. 'She was the fairest woman of all.'

'Psh,' Cheryl scoffed.

'I am aware that you have issues against me,' Prudence said calmly. 'But I will not abide by your preposterous behaviour when it comes to my mother.'

'How ridiculous, you do not scare me at all.'

'Ladies, please,' Ryan stood between the two women.

'Huh?' Eric gasped, as he looked closely to the portrait of the woman. 'Her eyes are dark yellow. And... ' Eric looked closely to the portrait. 'She has the same smile as Cheryl... '

Cheryl went silent and turned around.

Prudence looked closely at her mother's portrait, and she could see a troubling resemblance with the Humolf. 'What is the meaning of all of this?' she asked loudly.

'Let us be on our way,' Cheryl said tranquilly.

'What are you not telling me?' Prudence abruptly turned Cheryl around to face her.

'Prudence… ' Ryan tried to calm down the princess.

'How naive can you be?' Cheryl scoffed. 'Your mother was a Humolf,' she said coolly. 'More importantly… ' she paused, as if she enjoyed the moment. 'She was my mother.'

Prudence was dazed by Cheryl's revelation. She took a few steps back and swallowed her breath. She could not breathe at a normal pace and she was in shock. She even thought that she was hallucinating, but it was real…

'You are –' Prudence swallowed her breath one more time, '– my sister?' she asked with a trembling voice.

'We share blood, that is all there is,' Cheryl responded coolly.

'Why did Mother…' Prudence seemed lost in thoughts. 'Why did she abandon you?'

'I don't know,' Cheryl scoffed, 'but I don't care,' she paused. 'The woman means nothing to me.'

Prudence clenched her fists.

'Dragonus, why?' Prudence looked at the dragon. 'Why did no one tell me that I had a sister?' Prudence shouted.

'No one knew… ' Dragonus paused. 'No humans knew that Keira's eldest child was a Humolf.' Dragonus looked down. 'Everyone thought that Keira's first child was dead because of an illness… but we dragons knew that it was not the case.'

Prudence's face turned to horror. Her eyes were wide open, and she stood silent. Ryan tried to comfort her, but Prudence seemed emotionally frozen.

Dragonus felt bad about Prudence discovering her link with Cheryl. He led the way to the throne without wasting any more time on the gallery.

They had arrived in the throne room; it was the highest and biggest chamber of the entire castle. Everything was well lit up compared to the other chambers, and gold was used in every single brick. It was a marvellous room with a giant golden throne and a red carpet. It was a long room, which was about the size of two football pitches.

'I don't see any kings… ' Eric said, as he was approaching the throne.

'Quiet! The king is right over there!'

Eric looked closely and could see a small creature sitting in the throne; it was smaller than Dragonus itself. By the looks of it, it was inconceivable that this small creature was the king of that extraordinary species. 'I still don't see any kings… ' said Eric while looking around. 'Maybe that little worm will tell us where it is.'

'You imbecile,' Cheryl scoffed. 'He is right here.'

'What?' Eric asked confusedly.

'I am the king of the Dragon's Realm!' it jumped out of its throne, after hearing Eric.

'You are the king?' Eric laughed. 'Well, if that's the case then I am the King of Paris,' he mocked the small creature.

'He is not with us,' Ryan said with embarrassment. 'And there's no royalty in France. Not anymore… '

'You,' the king looked closely at Ryan. 'You have decided to come back.'

'I beg your pardon?' Ryan asked, baffled. 'I have never been here before,' he said quietly.

'No matter, I must have you confused with Solarius's son,' the king said calmly. 'Ah… ' it turned its regard toward Prudence and Cheryl. 'The daughters of my dearest friend… I see that you've both grown up since then.'

'So you are my sister.' Prudence glanced at Cheryl. 'I strongly wished that it was a lie… '

'We are here to collect the Sword of the King,' Cheryl said in a direct manner to the king. 'We have no time to waste in useless blabber,' she said coolly.

'I see. You are a lot like your mother was,' the king said, while looking at Cheryl. 'Well, I am sorry, but I am meant to put you through three different trials before you can claim the sword.'

Cheryl and Prudence looked at each other. Prudence's tongue was strongly tied, her eyes were focused on the Humolf and her fist clenched. The Humolf however, did not seem to care of her sister and advanced toward the king.

'I am the one who will claim the sword,' she said, with confidence in her words.

Prudence could not let that happen. She stood up in front of the king and demanded to be put through the trials without any delay.

'Then so be it… ' the king said softly. 'Dragonus – summon the elders,' the king ordered.

'Yes Your Majesty.' Dragonus bowed.

'I have to protect Prudence,' said Ryan. 'I wish to participate in the trials.'

'Aha,' the king laughed. 'You are indeed Solarius's son… ' The king paused. 'However, only Keira's daughters are to be tested.'

'But… I,' Ryan protested.

'Ryan… it is fine, I will be fine.' Prudence held Ryan's hand.

Ryan had to abide by the rules; the king looked at him with a soft look as Ryan's eyebrows were frowning. Dragonus called out the ancient spirits of the dragons.

The dragons that appeared in front of Prudence and her companions were translucent. It was as if they were ghosts, only their heads were shown and half of their body. They looked intimidating and scary; one of them even stared at Eric with an aggressive look. Eric did his best to avoid any eye contact and bent down. He was pretending to do his shoelace.

'At least one of them shows respect,' one of the spirits grunted. 'Why have you summoned us?' the spirit asked.

'Keira Fulgura's daughters are here to be tested for the sword,' said the king, as he pointed out the two girls.

'One sword for two pretenders,' one of them chuckled. 'It shall be interesting.'

'Who is the oldest?' another spirit asked.

'I am.' Cheryl stood before them.

'Then you shall be the first to enter, before being followed by your sister.'

Cheryl smiled in satisfaction; she seemed pleased with the advantages given to her. The spirits of the dragons began an incantation and soon, two doors appeared. One of the two doors opened in front of Cheryl. The door had a strange symbol above it; a sort of lightning bolt was engraved.

'Good luck,' Ryan wished to Cheryl, as she headed inside.

'Thank you,' she replied to him.

Once the Humolf entered the door, it closed itself behind her and disappeared, everyone gasped. Their jaws and their eyes were wide open.

'Prudence... don't go. Please,' Nash said with a worried look.

'I will be fine,' Prudence replied. 'I have to beat my sister. She will not use the sword for the right reasons,' she said determinedly. 'Only I can stop her.'

The second door opened shortly after. Wings were engraved above it. Prudence took a deep breath; she could feel her body shaking slightly and her palms getting sweaty.

'Prudence,' Ryan called out to her. 'Here, you will need this more than I,' he offered his sword to her.

'Thank you, my love.' She took the sword while looking at him; she could see how worried he was.

'Whenever you feel alone, remember that you are not. I am here with you,' he said, as he kissed her hand.

Prudence then smiled. She turned around and resumed toward the door, but at the moment she was about to cross the door, the young man held her hand and made her face him.

'Yes?' she asked.

Ryan kissed her and wished her good luck. Prudence felt a lot better and after looking at Ryan one more time, she crossed the door. The door then closed itself behind the princess and disappeared. The first trial was about to begin for her.

'She will be fine, don't worry mate,' said Eric, as he placed his hand on Ryan's shoulder. 'She's in love, she will not renounce in fighting.' He paused. 'Actually both the ladies are in love... and with you, haha...'

'This is why I liked Alexandra better, at least she hated Ryan,' Nash said annoyingly.

Ryan was silent.

'Rather interesting...' one of the spirits said, as it looked at Ryan. 'Solarius's son has fallen for Keira's daughter.'

'Solarius... that is the third time I've heard about this. Who is that guy?' Ryan questioned the spirit.

'Clearly your mind has been erased since you have been reincarnated,' the spirit said. 'Two brothers were blessed with extraordinary powers; however, their minds were unstable because they were the sons of the sun and the moon.'

Ryan was confused, he had never heard of such a tale. He had grown up on Earth. It was his first time on Vita, yet even he realized some things were amiss, such as the power of fire that was gifted to him or the Sword of the Moon choosing Nash.

There were a lot of things he could not understand. The spirits then told them about the story of Solarius and Lunaria, two lovers who were forbidden to be together. One was the sun and one the moon.

'Their two sons battled each other once in maturity; the oldest had the gift of ice, whilst the youngest had fire. They were to fight to death, and one day, they both died. The clash of their swords had brought their demises.' The spirit paused. 'Fenri was the wielder of the Sword of the Moon, or Lunaria's sword if preferred. Leo was the wielder of Solarius's sword, also known as the Sword of the Lion.'

'Wait...' Ryan interrupted the spirit. 'Are you saying that I am Leo and Nash is Fenri?' he asked.

'Have you not been following?' asked Nash.

'You are indeed. It is no mere coincidence that your brother has found the Sword of the Moon,' the spirit affirmed. 'However, the Sword of the Lion has been sealed in another world, to make sure this feud would cease once the two brothers arrived back on Vita.'

'Gee, you're too late, old spirits,' Eric laughed. 'The two brothers are now fighting over a woman.'

'We foresaw this matter,' another spirit said. 'Interesting indeed that Leo's reincarnation…'

'The name is Ryan,' Ryan interrupted the spirit.

'Oh, as feisty as he used to be,' the spirit chuckled. 'As I was saying, it is interesting that you have fallen for Keira's daughter…'

'Why is that?' asked Nash.

'Keira was in love with Leo, but he died before she could confess her love to him.' The spirit paused. 'She married, she had two daughters. But she could never forget her love for Leo.'

'Fenri loved Keira if I recall, but she never looked at him,' another spirit added. 'It is indeed funny how story is repeating itself…'

'No, it is not,' said Nash.

Everyone stared at Nash.

'Because no matter how much I hate my brother, I will never kill him,' said Nash. 'The bond of brotherhood is always stronger than it looks. No matter how much we hate it or love it.' He paused and smiled. 'But I don't like him, that's for sure.' Nash turned to Ryan. 'So don't get your hopes up Ryry. I won't kill you, but it doesn't mean that I will drink tea with you.'

Ryan's eyes opened in wonder. Nash's words were strong towards him. Even if his brother did not like him, Ryan felt good knowing that their rivalry was not as extreme as Solarius's sons.

'You cannot ignore the facts, but it will be funny to see what will happen to you two,' a spirit laughed. 'A new chapter is indeed writing itself for Leo and Fenri…'

Ryan decided to ignore what he had heard; this story must have been a coincidence and nothing else.

He was born in Belgium during a family trip, and then he grew up for three years in India before his mother brought him to France. He could still remember the last day of Paris before he came to England. He was fourteen and excited to live in his mother's homeland. Nowhere in this history of his had he been to Vita, until now. It was just absurd. The spirit must have been wrong, it was just inconceivable.

But it did not matter; all Ryan was thinking about was Prudence. His heart was beating fast and his thoughts were fixed on her. He had horrible images that kept on coming into his mind where he could see the woman he loved dying. 'Come on Prudence… come back in one piece,' he whispered quietly.

Chapter Twenty-Three
The Trials Begin

Prudence was inside of a dark corridor. Different torches were lit with a bright red flame. Her body was shaking slightly. She had an unpleasant feeling, and her heart was beating faster at every step she took.

This ill feeling she felt was overwhelming her. The nerves of her body were screaming out and her eyes were looking everywhere. One noise, one whisper of the wind, was enough to frighten her.

A door was in front of her and a sword was engraved above it. She swallowed and pushed the door with shaking hands.

It was a gigantic chamber; two stairs were dressed up with a magical light in the middle. It was a red glowing flame that burnt greater than the other flames; the princess approached it. She did not know why, but she wanted to touch it.

Once close enough, she moved her hand forward and the flame changed into the form of a knight. A flaming red knight: it was covered in fire and its body was glowing red.

'Who dares disrupt my rest?' he said with an intolerant tone.

'It is I, the Princess of Heartsas... Pru... Prudence Fulgura.' The princess introduced herself with a trembling voice. 'I... I am... here... to collect...' she stuttered.

'Mhmp,' the blazing knight scoffed. 'You do not seem prepared child. The trials are dangerous... ' he mocked the princess. 'I shall assist you to your very demise.'

Prudence was frightened, but then she thought of Cheryl. The knight was wrong; she was ready. No matter what, Prudence had to claim the sword before her sister.

'No, my kingdom needs me,' she said firmly. 'I understand… that I am not the strongest woman on Vita, but I… ' she looked down and closed her eyes. 'I am not alone. I will get through with it because I have love by my side.' She smiled, while thinking of Ryan.

'You do speak well, however, will you truly succeed?' the knight asked sharply. 'Behind those doors is the very first trial you will be demanded to complete.' The knight pointed out a door with his sword. 'Sharing memories with loved ones is such a pleasant feeling. However, fighting those memories will not be easy tasks,' he said, with a mysterious tone. 'You may still return to the Dragon's Realm, if you do not feel ready enough.'

'I will triumph in this,' said Prudence. 'I have to, for a promise I made.'

'Very well, you shall be an entertainment to me,' the knight said with amusement in his voice. He then opened a door. 'Remember to conquer fear, doubts and your enemy,' he said to her before disappearing.

Prudence took a deep breath; she armed herself with the sword that Ryan had lent her, and crossed through the door.

It was a sinister chamber: dark, windy, with a freezing atmosphere. A lot of webs were present; it was as if tonnes of spiders had woven their webs. Prudence swallowed her breath as she looked around. Her visibility was poor and she felt strangely observed.

She walked slowly, the sword in her hands, her eyes going left to right and her ears focused on anything that could betray the presence of a possible enemy.

It seemed that no one or nothing was around. It was not a long chamber. It certainly was dark, but there was a door right in front of her. As she walked toward the door, she could feel her feet crushing the rubble. It was as if she was walking on someone's skeleton and she was destroying it bit by bit. Her white teeth clenched as she was walking; the noise the rubble was making was piercing and irritating.

She had reached the door. She sighed with relief as she held the handle of the door. However, at the moment she was about to pull it, a web stuck her hand to the handle. The princess turned around in horror, and there it was, an enormous spider.

It looked exactly the same as Tarantula. It had the same eyes, the same legs, the same body, the same colour, and the same hungry look in its eyes. Prudence shrieked and managed to get her hand off the handle.

The spider did not waste time and jumped on her to crush her body and devour her, but Prudence was fast enough and ran back to the middle of the chamber. With shaking hands and an unbalanced stance, she got in guard and faced the creature.

But the circumstances were not favourable for the princess. It was too dark for her to have a clear view on where the spider was, and its dark colour it made it even harder for her to distinguish a silhouette.

Then, when she looked up, she could see those bloody red, devilish eyes. Prudence screamed and ran around the chamber. Her heartbeats were getting louder; she could feel her heart beating faster with the seconds. She was breathing loud and fast. The spider then crawled toward her; it was playing with the princess's nerves.

It was terrifying. The spider was fast and enormous. Prudence tried to run again, but she realized the spider had cornered her. She was paralysed with fear. She did not know what to do and the creature was approaching with its monstrous fangs.

There was no way out; she only had one chance of defeating the creature. Prudence swallowed her breath. She could feel her heart hammering her left breast, and the cold sweat of her nerves submerging her body. But she had only one way of getting to the door… she had to confront it, no matter what.

Armed with courage, she ran towards the spider with her sword. The spider waited for her to come closer so it could catch her and rip her to pieces. However, the princess was much cleverer, and once near it she glided below its horrifying jaw, and pierced its enormous furry body when she got to the middle of it. The spider shrieked in agony, and Prudence immediately rolled on the ground before dashing towards the door.

'Forgive me!' she shouted.

She then opened the door with haste and immediately went to the next chamber without looking behind. She was not even sure if she had killed the spider, and did not wish to think of it. She was out of breath and could not believe she had managed to fight it.

She took a deep breath and realized her black cotton tights were slightly ripped; she had cut herself on the rubble on the ground. She was all right though, it was stinging a bit but it did not stop her from moving.

'Be strong, Prudence,' she murmured, as she looked around the chamber.

Chapter Twenty-four
The Inner Thoughts

The chamber was different from the previous one, it was dark but a sort of fountain was spilling from a beautiful crystal wall. Prudence advanced towards the wall and saw her reflexion. Then, it changed. She could see herself with a crown and a beautiful dress. It was the dress of a princess. She was sitting in a throne. Then she saw Cheryl. The Humolf was chained up and tortured.

'My God…' Prudence gasped in shock.

The princess could see herself enjoying the pain that Cheryl was being put through. She could not believe it: why was she so evil? She then saw a pile of dead bodies. All the bodies were humans, elves, dwarves, orcs, trolls and any other species that lived throughout Vita. The princess gasped, and took few steps back. 'Impossible!' she said in horror.

'But it is what your thoughts desire…' a voice said out of nowhere.

Prudence turned around and saw no one.

'I am right here.'

Prudence looked at the wall, and she could see herself standing right in front of her.

'What are you?' Prudence asked loudly.

'I am your deepest thoughts.'

'You cannot be!'

Her other self was starting to laugh.

'I know everything about you,' she said. 'You shameful woman, wanting only to follow your mother's steps because you wish for glory. Have you no shame?'

Prudence took a step back. She seemed lost in thought.

'I have never wished for such things!' she tried to argue.

'This was not enough indeed. You wished to stab Cheryl with this very sword you are wielding,' the doppelgänger said. 'Have you no shame?'

'Stop it!' Prudence yelled. 'I am no murderer! Do not speak ill of me!'

'What about the time you wished for Ryan to bathe you? Deep inside, you wished him to take pleasure in seeing your naked body. To bed him, is what you wished. Have you no shame?'

'I am a princess! I would never do such things!' Prudence exploded. 'I do lust after Ryan's love, but marriage is what is important to me. You speak nonsense,' she shouted in anger. 'You not know of me!'

'Do not reject your deepest thoughts.' The doppelgänger approached Prudence. 'What you saw in the water was the reflection of your thoughts. You wish to govern and annihilate anyone or anything that stands in your way. Have you no shame?'

Prudence fell down on her knees. She suddenly felt weak. The more she thought about it, the more she realized that it was true. She was a horrible person. She was selfish and only cared about her own interests.

As Prudence was looking down in shame, the doppelgänger made a sword appear in her hands, and approached Prudence. 'I shall set you free,' said the doppelgänger.

Prudence closed her eyes. She was defeated by her own self. All that was said, was true. Her inner thoughts wished for all of this. A woman like her had no place, she was evil. A hateful being… yes, she deserved to die.

The doppelgänger lifted her sword and was about to slash Prudence's throat when the princess heard someone calling out to her.

'That was your thoughts… but what about your heart's desires?' the voice said.

Prudence's eyes opened in surprise.

'Ryan told you – it is your heart that will make the difference, not your thoughts.'

After hearing this, Prudence looked up, and rapidly took her sword and countered the attempt of her doppelgänger. She then pushed her doppelgänger and stood up.

'I have shame, for I had those thoughts,' Prudence said. 'But my heart is what will make the difference between those thoughts and my acts.'

After those words, the doppelgänger dropped her sword and smiled. 'You have indeed accepted yourself. No shame can be found in this.'

Prudence could see her other self disappear, and the wall of water changing into a door. The princess was perplexed by who had made her stand up for herself, but she had no time to think about it. She ran to the door and opened it.

Chapter Twenty-Five
The Cold Knife

It was a much more pleasant chamber. It was less dark and the visibility was great. Prudence could distinguish everything in front of her. A long and strange chamber it was, though. Everything was decorated as if she was in London. The furniture was of a noble choice. The texture of the objects and the walls were quite modern. It was a lot like Ryan's house. There was even one of those mirrors called a "television".

Prudence was confused. Where was she? It was a lot like Ryan's house, but it was not it. She had never been to this house, yet it felt familiar to her.

No matter, she advanced toward the door. It seemed rather easy. There were no challenges whatsoever. She then placed her hand on the handle, and unlike earlier, she looked behind her before attempting in opening it.

There was nothing or no one. She then turned the handle and pulled it. But the door was not moving. It was locked.

'Tut tut,' said the voice of an old man. 'Leaving before even greeting me? Such pitiable manners.' He laughed manically.

'Reaper!' Prudence snarled, as she saw her enemy. 'I will end you here,' she firmly held her sword's handle.

'You shall understand your misfortune.' Reaper laughed. 'And I shall enjoy the pleasure of ripping through your skin,' he said, before getting out a big machete.

The old man then ran toward the princess with the huge knife in his hand. He attempted to cut her but she dodged him. He quickly took another knife out of his other pocket, and with both blades, he was trying to stab her. Prudence was really agile and managed to evade Reaper's hits. She blocked many of them with her sword. But because of her lack in experience, she was quite shaken.

'DIE DIE DIE!' he shouted, as he tried to stab Prudence.

Soon, he had managed to make her lose balance and disarmed her.

Prudence was against a wall and without her sword; she had no way of defending herself. She could see the man approaching while licking the blade of his machete.

'I will enjoy this,' he said grimly. 'Do not worry; it will only hurt when I take out your eyes,' he said calmly.

Prudence was breathing loudly and heavily. She could see his evil smile getting larger. His long tongue was licking the edge of the razor sharp blade. He was vicious and strange. Prudence was panicking. It was just like with the spider. But then she thought about it: the spider was much more terrifying and more imposing compared to him.

She took her chances. She knew she could die, but once he got close enough, she speared him and brought him down. He was an old man after all, and with a fragile body he was quite easy to take down.

Once on the ground, Prudence ran toward the sword that she had dropped earlier, but Reaper got a hold on her ankle.

'You will not escape!' he grunted, as he tried to pull her back.

'Let me go!' she gasped for air, as she tried her best to kick his hand.

'It is futile to run from your fate!' he held her right ankle firmly.

Reaper then lifted his right hand, and stabbed her right leg.

'ARRGH!' Prudence yelled in pain. She could feel the blade piercing through the skin of her leg.

'Ahaha!' Reaper laughed, as he saw Prudence not attempting to move. 'I love this part!' he stabbed her again in the same place.

'ARRRRGH!' Prudence shouted in agony.

It was horrible, the pain was unbearable. She could feel the cold blade ripping through her muscles. Her blood was flowing over the coldness of the steel. Her heart was beating fast, and her nerves were reacting against the pain. But the shock of losing her blood and losing control made her panic. Reaper then pulled her and turned her around.

'It is so good!' he yelled with enthusiasm, as he lifted his knife in the air.

Prudence knew she was done for. She was too hurt, and she was out of strength. He had both his knees on her waist. She could not move her lower body. She only had her arms to defend herself, and when he tried to cut her throat, she managed to get a hold on his hands. She was doing her best to fight back, but he was too strong and soon the cold blade was getting near to her throat. The princess closed her eyes, she could not fight anymore.

'It is time to die!' Reaper shouted, as he got closer to her throat.

'Fight it!' Prudence heard the voice of a woman.

She opened her eyes. It was strange, but a light appeared out of nowhere, and there she was. Alexandra Delacroix.

'Do you remember the promise you made to me?' Alexandra shouted. 'If you die here, then everything you have fought for will die with you. Including me,' she said loudly. 'Don't betray my memory!'

Prudence could not let it happen; she closed her eyes and emitted a loud scream. The princess gave all she had in her. She made use of all of her energy and all her adrenaline to push away Reaper. Lights were appearing in her hands and soon, it changed into lightning. Reaper could not understand what was going on, and was electrocuted before being brutally crushed against a wall.

'Im… Impossible.' Reaper faded away as he said that.

Prudence tried to get back on her feet, but her right leg was injured. She could not move it well and it was hurting a lot. She was limping. But even if it was hard, she had to withstand the pain.

'I am glad to see that you did not let me down,' said Alexandra.

'It is thanks to you,' Prudence said, while biting her lips, and with pain in her eyes.

'No, it is thanks to you.' Alexandra chuckled. 'You always had it in you. The strength to fight back. Remember to fight till the end, princess,' she said, as she was disappearing. 'Good luck… '

'No, please… don't go.' Prudence's voice trembled.

Alexandra was gone, but the princess could never forget what she had done for her. Alexandra had helped her when she was alive, and she kept on helping her even when she had joined the dead. Prudence had no right in failing this woman who had sacrificed her life for her. She had a promise to keep to Alexandra.

Prudence held her sword and used it as a support to facilitate her painful walk. As she advanced toward the door, she could hear it being unlocked. The princess took a lot of time to get to the door due to her injury, but she eventually managed to reach it. Before entering the door, she could see angelic wings being engraved above it. She looked at the symbol before going through to the next trial.

Chapter Twenty-Six
The Two Gargoyles

It was a room similar to the one she had been in when she had met the blazing knight. The only difference was that the red glowing flame had turned to a sky blue one. It was a much prettier sight to see.

Just as before, she felt tempted to touch the flame and ended up doing so. As soon as she did, a blazing angel appeared from it; it was burning with a blue fire, exactly as the knight did, only with a different colour. Prudence gasped at the sight of the angel; it looked more intimidating than the knight.

'I see you have managed to conquer your three enemies,' the angel said calmly. 'But strength of the mind is a much harder trial…'

'Strength of the mind?' Prudence asked with confusion.

'You will need to understand and accept what you seek.'

It made no sense; Prudence did not understand what the angel was saying to her. Accept what you seek? Why would she not?

'It shall start now, of course, if you desire to leave?' the angel proposed.

'No, I cannot look back,' Prudence said, nervously sweating.

The injury was affecting her. Her mind was getting blurry and soon, she felt dizzy. She had lost quite a lot of blood and the condition of her leg was worsening. Nevertheless, she had to carry on with what she had been given to do. She could not let down Alexandra, or anyone for that matter. The angel made a door appear out of nowhere.

The princess groaned and limped over to it. It was hard. Just feeling her blood spilling with every step she took, made her feel even more uncomfortable. She then recalled Ryan giving her a bandage when she first met him. She grabbed a small piece of her cottons tights and ripped it; she then covered her wound with it, putting a lot of pressure on it, before tying it up tightly. The wound was still hurting but a little less than before. At least that way she would not have to feel too much of her blood spilling.

Her body was shaking slightly as she approached the door, and her breathing was loud and rigid. She took a deep breath, closed her eyes for a little time and opened the door.

She opened her eyes and saw a goblet in the middle of an altar. It was empty. She looked around, clueless about what it was that she was meant to accomplish with it. There was nothing in this room, only the goblet and an altar.

She then felt her blood spilling from her wounded leg. It was too obvious, and she had nothing else in the room that could help her to fill the goblet. The princess painfully removed the bandage she had previously applied, and placed the goblet right below her leg. The bandage had slowed down the bleeding, but the wound was still open.

Two drops of blood were spilled inside and suddenly, the room turned to a bloody red. Prudence gasped, and placed her right hand on her left breast. She could feel her heart pumping faster as the room was transforming itself.

'What is the meaning of this?' she said, as she looked around.

Two statues appeared out of nowhere, more precisely, it was two gargoyles. Both of them stared at the princess with open hands. It was as if they were begging for charity.

Prudence thought of it but she had no money with her. She tied up her wounded leg again and limped to the two gargoyles. A strange inscription was engraved above their heads. *Thou shall compensate the thirst of one. Equality will be the price to the path of awakening.* She read it in her mind. What was the equality that was mentioned? She had only one cup with her, she could not share it.

It was a confusing and nerve wracking enigma. Prudence was increasingly affected by her injury. Her vision was becoming blurrier and she could feel a massive headache. She was suffering from a fever.

Twenty minutes had passed since then. The princess had tried everything she could, but it was vain. Out of fatigue, she fell down on her knees. She was tired and she could not continue.

'I am sorry!' she panted. 'I... I cannot achieve it!' she whimpered. She was out of strength and out of faith; this enigma had taken away all her will.

She then felt her blood spilling again. She stared at the goblet. And then she saw it, another phrase that was engraved around the goblet. *Each drop has its meaning. With one drop I shall calm the thirst of thee.* Prudence started to think hard about it.

'One drop...' she muttered to herself. 'Oh! That must be it!' she said loudly.

Prudence took the goblet and gently poured one drop of blood into each gargoyle's hand.

'Please be it!' she mumbled desperately, as she waited for something to happen.

However, nothing was happening. She looked down and started to cry; she placed her hands in front of her face but could not stop crying. Without realizing it, the tears were falling into the hands of the statues.

The walls started to tremble. Prudence gasped and looked around. She did not understand what was happening. Soon, a wall moved and the two gargoyles grunted. When Prudence looked at their hands, she could see her blood being turned into water. Both statues moved apart, giving place to a portal within the wall.

'I have succeeded!' Prudence said, before stepping inside the portal.

Chapter Twenty-Seven
Cheryl

Prudence was brought to a garden; she looked around and saw nothing but the green grass, beautiful flowers and the magnificent blue sky. What was this place? Prudence then felt someone's presence; she turned around and saw a glowing light appearing out of nowhere.

When the light ceased to glow, it took on the appearance of a woman, and not any woman. 'Mother!' Prudence gasped.

'I prayed for this day to come,' the woman said.

She was breathtaking. Her face was angelic and her eyes of a mesmerizing dark yellow. Her skin colour was white and as pure as the snow, and her brown hair was well coiffed. She looked like an angel. Even her voice was adorable, and just by looking at her, Prudence started to cry. Her mother was just the most beautiful woman that she had ever seen in her life.

Prudence then tried to hug her, but her arms went through her mother; she was there, but in the form of a spirit.

'Mother... I have missed you.'

'Do not cry my daughter,' Prudence's mother said gently. 'I am proud to have witnessed your courage, you and your sister.'

'I do not like the thought of that woman being related to me.' Prudence looked down.

'You have to understand what she has been through. I hope you will look past all the rivalry you two possess and you will learn to love her.' Her mother paused. 'Thus, the reason I have summoned you here.'

'You have?' asked Prudence.

'I wish for you to understand your sister.'

Prudence did not understand what her mother meant.

'Do not worry, you shall understand soon enough.'

Her mother cast an incantation and a sort of mirror appeared. A small Humolf, fragile, skinny and frightened, was presented to Prudence. She seemed so scared and so insecure. Was it Cheryl?

'Your sister has suffered a lot.'

Prudence could see her sister being beaten up and mistreated by lots of people. Cheryl was trying her best to survive and she had tough times. The princess felt sorry for her sister; she looked down with watery eyes.

'Do you now understand my shame?'

'What do you mean Mother?' asked the princess.

'It is my fault that she suffered.'

'I cannot believe that... ' Prudence paused. 'You love her... just as much as you love me,' she said softly. 'I can see it in your eyes.'

'Still, it was my shame to abandon her.'

'Why did you?' asked Prudence.

'Your father and the kingdom could not tolerate having a Humolf as an heir.' Her mother paused. 'I listened to him... and abandoned my child.'

'It is not your fault Mother... ' Prudence paused, she then thought of something. 'But you were a Humolf as well... '

'I only had the eyes and the small fangs – I was lucky not to have the tail, which was the ultimate proof of being a Humolf. But your sister... '

'I see.'

'Just promise me... promise me that you will love her for me.'

Prudence took a deep breath. She then sighed.

'I need to know one thing before I can see her as a sister.'

'Why she is in love with the same man as you are?' her mother guessed.

'How did you?' Prudence asked, puzzled.

'I have been watching over you,' her mother smiled. 'I cannot tell you the reason for Cheryl loving Ryan.'

Prudence sighed in disappointment.

'But I shall show you…'

The mirror presented another scene. Cheryl looked about eight years old; she was lying in the street, cold, shivering, with barely any strength to survive. She was covered in bruises and dirt.

Prudence could not believe what she was seeing; Cheryl had been so unfortunate all these years. The princess could see her sister trying to sleep in ripped clothes. It was snowing, and she had no shelter or decent clothes for such conditions.

A group of five teenagers accompanied by a man began to disturb her; they spat on her and surrounded her. 'Look, it is a Humolf! Look at her tail!' one of the teenagers said, while touching her.

'Disgusting sight it is, eh?' The man laughed.

'Please… leave me alone.' Cheryl shivered.

'Creatures don't mix with humans!' one of the teenagers yelled.

'Fetch!' another one said, while throwing a wooden stick.

'She is boring, she does not even fetch!'

Cheryl started to cry. The man and the five teenagers kept laughing of the misfortune of the young Humolf.

'She is boring!'

One of the five teenagers then punched Cheryl in the face; she fell down and hit her arm on the wall. Prudence moved with anger at the sight of it, she wanted to inflict pain on those six people.

Suddenly, as she kept watching, a knight pushed aside the five teenagers and the man. His armour made him look strong and intimidating. He had a helmet on. Prudence could not deduct his identity.

One thing was sure, he was feared by everyone and just his presence was enough for the six men to kneel before him.

'Move aside, you miserable creatures,' he said sharply, as he looked at the six persons.

'Y… yes my Lord,' the man stuttered in fear, before leaving with the five teenagers.

'Do not fear, child,' the knight said. 'I mean you no harm.'

He bent down toward the young Humolf and took out a small biscuit from his pocket. 'Please.' He gently offered her the biscuit.

Cheryl jumped on his hand and ate the biscuit in one go. She was starving. The knight offered her more biscuits, but eventually he ran out of them. 'What is your name?' he asked, as he stared at Cheryl.

'Cheryl…' she said softly.

'Cheryl… a beautiful name indeed.' The knight chuckled. 'I am sorry, I have not much to offer you. It is but a shame to witness such an unfair life…'

'Please sire…' Cheryl advanced toward the knight with watery eyes and a shrinking expression. 'Take me with you, please.' She started to cry. 'I have no one…'

The knight stayed silent for a while. He did not seem to want Cheryl by his side. But then he stared at her and he could see how sad and alone she was. He kneeled before her and took her hand. 'Very well, my child… you shall come with me,' the knight said delicately.

He then removed his helmet. His blond hair was well coiffed and gorgeous. Prudence knew this hairstyle, and when he turned around, she could see it was Ryan. She gasped in shock and called out to him.

'He cannot hear you, my love,' Prudence's mother informed her.

'You are really handsome sire,' said Cheryl.

'Aha… you are the beauty. I, compared to you, am a beast,' the knight chuckled. 'Let us rest for tonight. And at dawn, we will dress you with suitable clothes before we venture into a new quest,' he said with a nice and comforting tone.

The mirror then disappeared. Prudence was baffled by what she had witnessed. He looked exactly like Ryan, but it could not be him. She stayed silent but eventually started to question her mother.

However, her mother either had no answers to it, or she did not wish to tell the truth.

No matter, Prudence started to understand her sister and even began to admire her.

'I will look after her, Mother,' she said gently. 'I promise.'

'Thank you my child...' her mother said tearfully. 'I love you so much.'

'I love you too Mother...' Prudence started to cry.

'I shall take my leave.'

'No Mother, please... I have wished all my life to speak with you.'

'Remember Prudence, things are not as they always seem to be. Remember this.'

'I do not seem to understand Mother. What are you talking about?'

'When you feel that darkness has won, remember that there is always light...'

Prudence's mother then started to fade away. The princess could see her mother becoming more and more distant, and her body disappearing slowly.

'I will always be by your side and in your heart my darling,' said her mother. 'I am glad to know that you and your sister are no more alone,' she said, as she disappeared.

Prudence was silent and wiped away her tears. It was the first time she had spoken to her mother. She then smiled in happiness. Everyone was right; she was as gracious as they described her to be. Suddenly a portal appeared. Prudence knew it was her next trial and even if she still limped, she crossed it with no second thoughts.

Chapter Twenty-Eight
The Burden Of The Sword

It was a gigantic chamber, quite dark with a lot of torches lit up with different colour flames. A colossal statue of a dragon was in the middle of the chamber. Prudence then perceived a silhouette; it was Cheryl. As she approached the Humolf, she felt an unbearable pain and fell down. She had not the strength to walk toward Cheryl, and so she crawled to her. Cheryl turned around with contempt as she saw Prudence crawling in pain.

'I am indeed surprised that you have passed the trials,' Cheryl scoffed. 'To tell you the truth, I was expecting you to fail and die in the very first bravery test.'

'I... I made it this far... because I am meant to... have the sword,' Prudence panted.

'You do not look well, princess.' Cheryl laughed. 'What a troubling injury,' she mocked her sister, as she looked at her leg. 'I shall put an end to your misery.' She took out her sword and approached Prudence.

'I cannot fail here!' Prudence tried to get back on her feet but miserably failed.

'Aha... what an amusement you are,' Cheryl laughed.

'I cannot fight you, sister,' Prudence groaned.

'Indeed,' Cheryl said calmly. 'You are weak.'

'No... I cannot fight you...' Prudence said gently, 'because I have already won.' She chuckled. 'I have love by my side... and I am glad I have gotten to know that I have a sister... because... I love that you and I are related.' She smiled. 'I always wished for a big sister...'

Cheryl's eyebrows lifted in surprise. Her eyes were wide open as she heard Prudence's speech. She went silent for a while and seemed lost in her thoughts. Cheryl then approached her weak sister, and lifted her sword as she was going to kill her, but ended up putting the sword back in its sheath.

'Let me take care of this...' Cheryl said softly, as she placed her hands on Prudence's wound.

A bright green light glowed; Prudence was blinded by it and was forced to close her eyes. When it stopped glowing, she opened her eyes and felt no more pain. She immediately looked at her wound and noticed that it was healed. She could stand on her feet again; her fever had gone and she felt great.

'Why?' Prudence asked softly.

'Do not think of this as a sign of affection,' Cheryl said sharply. 'It is only a way for me to watch you suffer once Ryan becomes mine,' she scoffed, as she looked away.

Prudence flinched before smiling. 'Thank you, sister,' she said gently.

'I told you before, I am not your sister,' Cheryl replied rudely. 'Let us solve this enigma, then I can go back to hating you.'

Though Cheryl seemed to mean what she said, she could not stop smiling whenever Prudence called her sister.

After walking near to the dragon's statue, both sisters stared at it. It looked intimidating. Prudence turned to Cheryl, who was biting her lips with her eyes focused on the statue.

'The sword is right there,' Cheryl said darkly, as she pointed out the statue.

'It is but a dragon, sister,' Prudence said confusedly.

'Only an ignorant like you would see it for what it is,' Cheryl said offensively.

Suddenly, the sisters could hear faint laughing behind them. Cheryl turned around immediately, and with one wave of her hand, she threw a powerful water ball that exploded. Two small and bright flying creatures came out of their hide.

'What are they?' Prudence shrieked.

'Fairies,' Cheryl said indifferently.

The fairies were little beings and were easy to perceive due to their glowing wings. They were magnificent creatures, though they seemed deceitful. Judging by Cheryl's vigilant stance, she did not seem to like them.

'Wow, she is good!' one of the fairies said enthusiastically.

'Indeed!' the other one shouted.

'What are fairies doing here?' Cheryl asked. 'We have no time to waste with fairies, so get out of here,' she said sharply.

'It is the very first time I've met a fairy,' Prudence said passionately.

'Do not be fond of them.' Cheryl paused. 'They spend most of their existence playing tricks on the people they meet. I would not trust them.'

'Grumpy one she is!' one of the fairies said loudly.

'We know you wish for the sword!'

'How do you… ' Prudence started her question, but she was interrupted by the fairies.

'We know,' one sneered. 'If you desire to claim it then you have one more trial to complete!'

'Only one can claim the sword.'

The fairies then laughed together. They flew around the chamber for a short instant before coming back with their amusing behaviour.

'To succeed, you will have to understand each other through fighting.'

'The royal one will be worthy of the sword,' one of the fairies sneered.

'Only the true heir of the sword shall rise victorious.'

Prudence could then hear a sort of hymn being sung. *'Through the dark ages I have lifted my burdens on my shoulders… Through the dark ages I have sinned in selfishness… Through the dark ages… Shall my decision be my pride or my shame.'*

What was this beautiful hymn? And what did it mean?

Prudence looked at Cheryl and could see her smiling. The fairies, however, did not seem to hear the hymn.

'Did you hear it?' Prudence asked Cheryl.

'Of course – and if you could, it means you have Humolf genes.'

'What do you mean?'

'Only Humolfs can understand the hymn or hear it, and if I have understood correctly...' Cheryl paused. 'This means that the sword will impose a condition on the wielder.'

'How does she know?' one of the fairies whispered.

'So it is true?' Cheryl looked at the fairies.

'Yes – the sword has been created in order to save Vita, or to destroy it. However, to save it you will have to sacrifice your soul, making you the ultimate hero of Vita's history at the price of death...'

Prudence was shocked to hear about this.

'And what happens if you choose to live?' Prudence asked, with a trembling voice.

'Survive and you shall become the plague of Vita, the one who allowed the demons to roam free,' the fairies said darkly. 'Only the wielder of the sword shall decide when the time will come.'

As soon as the fairies said this, Cheryl turned to Prudence and drew out her sword.

'*En garde*,' she said, before taking a combat stance.

'You wish to cross steel with me? Why?'

'Only one will be worthy of the sword,' replied Cheryl. 'It shall be me.'

Prudence went silent but drew out her sword. She wanted to make her mother proud and get the sword, but what if she did get the weapon? Prudence saw the sword as a curse rather than a solution. She would have to make a choice: whether to live as the plague who destroyed her world, but at least she'd be with Ryan; or die a hero and make everyone happy, but she would be separated from the one she loved. Both choices left her perplexed and Cheryl wanting to fight was not helping her.

Prudence's heart was beating fast. Cheryl was used to fighting and she seemed so confident. The princess was reticent but still engaged the battle; she had no choice, as her sister seemed decided to fight.

'Only one can have the sword… and you do know what my choice will be once I have it!' Cheryl laughed evilly.

Those words were enough to convince the princess not to give the sword away to Cheryl. She was her sister, but Cheryl would use the sword for destruction only: something Prudence could not let happen, even if deep inside she was still deciding on what she would do once the sword was acquired.

Chapter Twenty-Nine
The Sword Of The King

The two swords reasoned. The clash of the steel was loud and ferocious. Soon the chamber's walls seemed to be shaking under the impact of the two weapons. The two sisters were violently battling each other; a bolt of lightning could be seen from a distance, and the sound of a wave crashing down on the ground could be heard. The shrieks and the groans of the two women were echoing around the whole chamber.

'I am so glad we were given this task!' one of the fairies yelled happily.

'I do understand what you mean,' the other one sneered. 'I would have been unlucky if I had missed this intense combat.'

Prudence and Cheryl were both equally impressive; the princess was showing an unexpected demonstration of her will, while Cheryl was trying to prove her superiority. It was as if two lions were battling each other and none of them was taking the advantage.

The young princess was becoming very agile in the battlefield; she was very talented, and learnt fast. From dodging a sword attack to throwing lightning with her hands, she was captivating and each second she seemed to be getting stronger. Cheryl seemed surprised and at the same time frustrated. She could not understand how Prudence had become strong.

'Sister, please, let us end this charade!' Prudence panted. 'I do not wish for us to hurt each other!' she said loudly, as she was dodging the hits of her sister.

'You are a coward!' Cheryl yelled in anger. 'I shall end you!' she raised her voice, while attempting to hit Prudence.

Prudence blocked Cheryl's blade with hers. She could feel her sister using all of her weight and strength to make her lose balance. The princess then used her own weight and gently bent her knees, she then pushed the ground with her feet and Cheryl's strength was reversed. The Humolf had lost balance and had been pushed back; she almost fell, but immediately retrieved her equilibrium.

'Impressive,' Cheryl whispered.

'I beg you to listen to me,' Prudence said softly. 'I do not wish to harm you.'

'Do you wish for the sword?' Cheryl shouted.

'Y… yes,' Prudence said with a trembling voice.

'Then why are you not fighting your all for it?'

'Because… ' Prudence paused. 'You matter more to me than this sword!' she shouted at her turn.

Cheryl sighed; she then looked at her younger sister. The Humolf went silent and was biting her lips, she seemed to struggle with the way she felt about Prudence. Whenever she was around Prudence, she seemed conflicted in her thoughts.

'I wish… ' she started to say, but ended up going back on her words. The Humolf regained her stance and looked at her sister as if she was an enemy.

Cheryl was ferocious; her hits were making Prudence's sword tremble and the young princess lost balance. Cheryl was splendid, the way she used her sword, it was as if she was dancing with it and the blade was her slave.

'Do fight!' Cheryl yelled at Prudence as she tried to stab her.

The young princess managed to dodge the hits but had no time to strike back; Cheryl was way too fast for her. Prudence took a few steps back and electrocuted her sister, who was forced to the ground. It was a low charge since she did not wish to harm Cheryl, but it was enough for Prudence to speak her mind and try to reason with her sister.

'I know you have suffered sister,' Prudence began. 'But hear me out would you?'

'Grr… ' Cheryl groaned, as she stood up on her feet. 'Stop talking!'

'No, I will not stop!' Prudence paused. 'I know how much you have suffered, but I did too.' She sighed. 'I was raised to be a princess, yes, but I was lonely and I had nothing. It was always written and dictated what I had to do.' She paused, trying to find the right words. 'You have suffered a lot more than I, but you found someone who believed in you and who took you to live a life full of excitement and magic.'

'You do not know anything!' Cheryl shouted.

'Yes I do,' replied Prudence. 'I saw you, and it pained me to see how you've been treated.' She paused again. 'But you have to understand that Ryan is not the knight who saved you from loneliness.'

'It does sound absurd, but it was Ryan,' Cheryl softly said. 'And I will always love him. So you can stop trying to convince me to let go.'

Cheryl then resumed battling with her younger sister. She did not hesitate in stunning Prudence with a magical water ball. It was water, but the pressure contained inside the sphere was enormous. It was as if a metal ball had hit Prudence's head at full speed.

Cheryl then punched Prudence in the face and violently knocked her down; she then tried to stab her, but failed since Prudence was quite talented in evading or dodging attacks. The princess was still on the ground and kicked Cheryl in the stomach. The Humolf took a few steps back and groaned in pain. It was a strong kick, but not enough to stop her. Prudence was back on her feet and back in a defensive stance.

'Tired already?' Cheryl laughed.

'Mother loved you,' Prudence said calmly. 'She still does.'

'Stop it!' Cheryl yelled furiously.

'She wished she had never put you through all of this,' Prudence carried on. 'I spoke to her. She needs us to love each other.' She paused. 'Don't you understand? We are sisters… we should not fight against each other!' Prudence said loudly.

'Mother abandoned me!' Cheryl shouted angrily.

'She did not. A mother's love can never abandon her child.'

'You would not know any of it! You have been raised and treated as a princess from the very beginning!' Cheryl raised her voice. 'What would you know of me?' she yelled.

'I do not know of your suffering,' Prudence calmly replied. 'But I know that I will love you as a sister if you give me a chance.'

Cheryl went silent; she wondered why Prudence was so willing to hold on to that bond.

'Why?' Cheryl asked quietly. 'Why are you holding on to me?'

'Because you are my sister and you will always be, no matter what happens.'

Prudence then dropped her weapon and spread her arms. 'I have said all that I have in my heart. The choice is yours to make. My love –' she paused '– or the sword?'

'Your foolishness will never cease to surprise me!' Cheryl laughed. 'Now the sword is mine for the taking and so is your life!'

Cheryl dashed to Prudence with murderous intention. She was like a monster jumping on her prey. Prudence closed her eyes in tears; she then smiled as if she was welcoming death.

The princess then heard the sound of a sword being dropped. The steel crashing in the ground echoed in the chamber. 'Darn you!' Cheryl groaned.

Prudence could feel someone hugging her. When she opened her eyes full of water, she could see it was her sister's arms. 'Cheryl?' Prudence said weakly.

'I am sorry.' Cheryl's voice was breaking.

'Do not be,' Prudence sighed in relief.

Cheryl then took a few steps back, her eyes full of water and her cheeks moist. Her chin was slightly lifted and her lips wavy. A look of sincerity had replaced her previous expression of anger. Prudence wiped away her tears and smiled.

'I cannot let you look at me.' Cheryl turned away.

'No, please… ' Prudence placed her right hand on Cheryl's left shoulder. 'Do not feel ashamed of your tears,' she said softly.

'I hate you,' Cheryl said, as she turned around to face Prudence. 'At least… ' she paused. 'That was the way I felt about you.'

Prudence hugged her sister; both of them closed their eyes and gently smiled.

'Sisters,' one of the fairies whimpered. 'Get me a violin!'

'It is so beautiful!' the other fairy said.

Both fairies then held each other and cried.

Suddenly, the statue of the dragon began to shake. The ground of the room and the walls were shaking. A sort of faint earthquake was happening. The two sisters looked around, alarmed. They were both shaking.

'Do not let go of me, whatever happens!' Cheryl said sharply.

'I won't!' Prudence shrieked.

It was shaking a lot more; soon the two sisters could barely stand on their feet and they fell down on the shaky ground. The statue then started to change colour. The pale grey was turning to silver. The texture of the statue was metamorphosing into a much alive and reptile skin. Soon, they could distinguish the arms and the legs slightly moving. An imposing scream came from the dragon. When Prudence and Cheryl looked up to it, they could see that it was no more a mere statue, but a real and scary dragon.

It had a silver body. Its claws, eyes, wings, and its fangs were of a blinding white, whilst its skin was of the colour of a sword's blade. It approached the two sisters with a curious and menacing look. Prudence held Cheryl's hand; she was shaking at the very sight of the dragon that did not seem to wish them well. Cheryl stared at its eyes; she did not show any sign of emotions, whether it was fear, courage, or even curiosity. She just stared at the dragon.

The dragon then lifted its colossal jaw. Prudence could see it was preparing for an attack. Immediately she moved Cheryl out of the range of the dragon, by electrocuting her. It was the only way she could protect her sister.

'Prudence!' Cheryl yelled, as she saw the dragon commencing its attack.

The creature then breathed out its extraordinary fire and burnt the princess. 'ARGH!' Prudence yelled in agony, as she was being burnt alive. The princess could feel her skin melting and her body stinging. It was not long before she succumbed to the infernal blaze.

'NO!' Cheryl shouted, powerless in front of this horrible spectacle.

Cheryl then tried to throw a wave of water, but the fire was too strong. Her magic was not strong enough to extinguish the flames.

The dragon had finished breathing fire; it disappeared along with its flames. Cheryl ran towards her sister, who had been burnt to death. Prudence was not moving; her skin had been turned completely to the colour of coal. Her clothes were burnt to ashes. A lot of smoke came from the lifeless body of the princess.

'No… Prudence… ' Cheryl sobbed.

Prudence's hand then moved. Cheryl gasped with surprise.

A second had elapsed. The dark body of the princess was taking its former colour, and a sword appeared in her right hand. 'AH!' Prudence shouted as she opened her eyes full of terror. She was alive. It was as if the dragon had not burnt her at all. Beautiful armour made of crystals replaced her burnt clothes. It was shining, and it even had a cape with the design of a dragon's wings.

'Ch… Cheryl,' Prudence said with a trembling voice.

'You are alive!' Cheryl hugged Prudence. 'I am so glad! '

'I thought I had lost you… ' Prudence said softly.

Both sisters were crying in each other's arms. They were both emotionally touched. Cheryl even held tightly her sister as she wept. 'You two need a room.' They heard a familiar voice say. When both sisters looked around, they could see Ryan and his friends staring at them happily.

'Oh no!' Cheryl stood up and wiped her tears away.

'It was Eric who suggested you two get a room,' Ryan chuckled. 'What is wrong Cheryl? Why are you ashamed of your tears?'

'Shut up!' Cheryl shouted.

Cheryl's cheeks were turning red; she looked away from everyone and did her best to pretend that she was not crying.

'What happened to your clothes?' Mia asked Prudence.

'I… I do not know… ' Prudence responded, puzzled.

'You found the sword!' Nash said loudly.

Prudence immediately looked at her right hand and saw the weapon. It was a mesmerizing sword. It was made of crystals. The sword was shining like the stars, and its blade was made of a magnificent and intense white mirror. Prudence could clearly see her reflection in the blade. When she looked closer, she distinguished small words engraved upon the blade. *Only a true king will be worthy of cleansing the darkness.* But she was no king… she was a woman, and even if she got married, she would end up as a queen. She stayed silent and contented herself in smiling proudly. She'd made it… she had the sword.

Everyone was congratulating the princess. The spirits of the dragons all smiled and gave their blessings to the young woman.

'We bid you farewell, may you be successful in defeating your enemies,' one of the spirits said, as they disappeared.

Ryan jumped in front of Cheryl and approached Prudence; he then held her hand and said, 'I am glad that you're okay.'

'I am glad that I have you.' Prudence wrapped her arms around her lover.

Cheryl glanced at the happy couple. She sighed and looked away. The Humolf then started to walk away from everyone.

'Sister,' Prudence called out to Cheryl. 'Why are you leaving?'

'It is not my story, it is yours,' said Cheryl. 'I wish you luck, but I shall take my leave now.' She looked down.

'Will I see you again?' Prudence asked sadly.

'That will depend on the path you shall take.'

Everyone looked at each other, not understanding Cheryl's words.

'You will do the right thing, though…'

Prudence looked at Cheryl. Her sister was smiling with pride. Prudence knew what Cheryl was talking about: she would have to make a choice. Protect everyone and die like a hero, or be with Ryan and become the plague of Vita. A terrible choice she had to make, but Cheryl looked at her with a deep and trustful expression.

'Just be strong and take care of him.' Cheryl looked at Ryan. 'He is a big talker but he can easily put himself in risky situations.' She giggled. 'Oh and by the way – it is time to tell her.'

'Tell me what?' asked Prudence.

'I'll tell you later…' Ryan said quietly.

'You better give her that thing you've been carrying around with you.'

'Thank you, Cheryl…' Ryan groaned. 'It was supposed to be a surprise.'

'Ahah!' Cheryl laughed wryly. 'Goodbye,' she said before taking her leave.

Everyone stared at the Humolf leaving; they all had their opinions on the individual, but none of them knew what she had been through or what made her who she was. No one knew, except her sister, who would love her no matter what happened.

'What is next?' Nash asked Prudence.

'It is time for me to take what is rightfully mine,' Prudence said with fire in her eyes.

The emperor was her next target; it was time for her to fulfil her destiny once and for all. She would either become a hero or a plague…

Armed with courage and with determination by her side, the princess and her friends left the Dragon's Realm. They were heading toward the end of their journey: Heartsas.

Chapter Thirty

The Decision

Prudence was on the deck of the warship. She was staring at the moon. The wind was caressing her face and her hair; she closed her eyes for a few minutes. In less than an hour, she would have to confront the emperor. She knew nothing about that man, what he was like, or how dangerous he was. She knew absolutely nothing. But it did not matter, Heartsas was her kingdom and it was her duty to liberate her home from this evil individual.

The sword was hers, but the curse was also there. She still had to make a decision.

The night was not only the best opportunity for a surprise attack; it was also the best time to contemplate the emptiness ahead and to clear out the doubts from her mind. The princess looked to her left; she could see Eric and Mia running around like children. Perhaps they were trying to amuse themselves before the finale. Prudence smiled, but then she realized she was wrong. She should have taken them home instead of dragging them into her perilous journey. If she knew of any other portal that led to London, she would have focused on it, but she did not. She felt a lot of guilt. Who was she to endanger others?

Ryan was near Prudence. He could see her standing on her own. He wanted to talk to her but he decided to talk to his brother first. Nash had been quiet for some time and Ryan wanted to make sure what his brother had in mind once the battle was over.

'What's up?'

Nash turned around and ignored Ryan.

'What's your plan once everything is over?' asked Ryan. 'I mean, once we're home.'

'I'm not going home. At least, if you're referring to Earth as home.'

'Why?'

'Because I don't want to,' Nash said, with a calm but strict tone. 'What's waiting for me there? A world were innocent animals are being slaughtered each day because of their skin? A world where some humans think of themselves as God and destroy everything around them? Is that where you want me to go back?'

'You don't belong in Vita.' Ryan paused. 'Cheryl said you'll be cursed by death,'

'Then so be it,' Nash answered coolly.

'Seriously, do you even mean what you're saying? What about Mom and Dad? What about… '

Ryan was trying to think of anyone waiting for Nash in England, but he could not find anyone else except his parents.

'I've given a lot of thought to it. I have no one there, and nothing waiting for me.' Nash went silent. 'I have always been living in stress, everyone is always pushing things on me. "You're the big brother, you have to be responsible! Look at your brother… " It is always the same thing, "Look at your perfect brother." He scoffed. 'Sometimes I wish I was you… I wish I had all the things you have.'

Ryan went silent. For the first time, he could see how sincere Nash was.

'Are you drunk?' asked Ryan.

'You know I don't drink! Stop acting stupid,' Nash snapped. 'In London, I don't live – but you do. And that makes me envy you! You have the simplest things which are necessary in life… friendship, respect, and most importantly you have love.' Nash then looked away and sighed. 'I've loved – but I failed, because you're the one she chose. It is always about you, Ryan here and Ryan there. Whether it's Prudence or Eric or anyone for that matter… it's always you.' He paused and scoffed. 'Heck, a part of me was happy when we thought you were dead… '

Ryan stood silent and looked at his feet.

'I've got my share of problems too.'

Nash turned to Ryan with anger.

'Shut up – you know nothing about problems. People would actually kill to have your luck.' Nash then bit his lips and clenched his fist. 'Seeing you with Prudence makes me so angry. It devours me on the inside not to touch her or to feel her lips. I was there for her when you were not – I even protected her the best I could, but she never chose me!' Nash then looked at Eric and Mia. 'Everyone here, they're all here because of you! Not for me! For you only – nobody is waiting for me in London or on Earth for that matter. Here at least I have a position as a ruler and I can make a difference with my life… I'm special!'

Ryan went silent and did not say anything.

'So yes – whatever curse I'm meant to get from staying here, then give me this curse, because I'm not leaving Vita. And that's my final decision!'

'What will I tell our parents when they realize you are missing?' Ryan asked loudly. 'They will search for you,' he paused. 'What will I tell them?'

'Tell them I left home, and I'm not coming back,' replied Nash.

'But… '

'Don't try to convince me.'

Ryan sighed.

'Fine, if it's what you want.'

Ryan started to walk away but then he stopped.

'I just wanted to say that I was surprised by you earlier,' Ryan said quietly.

'For what?'

'Well, for one thing I always thought that you would let me rot and die if I was in danger – but hearing you saying that you would never go as extreme as Fenri and Leo… well, it made me think that you have my back.' Ryan smiled.

'I'm your brother – of course I do.' Nash looked away. 'Now get out.'

'Thank you,' Ryan whispered as he walked away towards Prudence.

Prudence could not look at them and decided to stare at the stars. She closed her eyes once again to try and hear the whisper of the wind.

'Beautiful night, it is.'

Prudence opened her eyes, and looked to her right. It was Ryan.

'It is,' she said calmly.

'Do you think of her?' Ryan asked.

'Do I think of whom?'

'Cheryl.'

'I do – but I am not to worry about her,' said Prudence.

'Are you scared of what's ahead of us?' Ryan asked quietly.

'I would be a traitor to myself if I said no,' replied Prudence. 'But it is my duty to end this nightmare.'

'I hope I'm not troubling you. You seemed deep in your thoughts.'

'No…' Prudence paused. 'You can never trouble me – I was just thinking of what I will do once the time comes. If, of course, I am still breathing.' She chuckled.

'When the time comes?' asked Ryan.

'Oh it is nothing my love – nothing for you to worry. I just meant that If I'm still alive…'

Ryan placed his hands around Prudence's waist. He then approached her with lifted eyebrows and wavy lips. He glanced at Prudence intently. His dark eyes were piercings hers.

'I cannot afford to think of losing you,' Ryan said softly. 'You are the only one I wish to live with. I forbid you to think of death…' His voice was trembling.

Prudence touched Ryan's lips with her fingers. She closed her eyes.

'I adore this sentiment I am feeling,' she said with a soft voice. 'Ryan…' she opened her eyes. 'I wish to always be with you,' the princess said with a gentle tone.

'It's reciprocal, my love… '

Prudence smiled; she knew what her choice would be. As selfish as it was, she decided to choose to live as the plague. As long as she had Ryan, she did not care for Vita. Vita was her birthplace, but Ryan was her new home. Love was the place she chose to reside in forever, no matter what the story of Vita will write about her.

But it was strange. Ryan looked down and sad. Prudence then recalled Cheryl's words before she left. '*It is time to tell her…*' The princess asked Ryan about it. Perhaps it was the reason why he looked so down.

'I – I wish things would be easy,' Ryan said calmly but with a trembling voice. 'The truth is… I won't probably make it.'

Prudence gasped in shock; she asked him what he meant and why he was saying such a terrible thing. Ryan then unbuttoned his shirt and a faint green light was surrounding his fatal injury. He explained to the princess that Cheryl's magic was keeping him alive, but it would surely stop working. And once the magic ceased to work, he would die. Prudence bit her lips in anger; she clenched her fists and scolded Ryan for not telling her earlier. The princess felt a lot of pain knowing that Ryan would die. Her heart was shattering and an ill feeling was replacing her happiness. Ryan was dying… no… why did this nightmare have to happen again?

'I wish I'd had the strength to tell you – but I could not… ' Ryan's voice was breaking. 'I just wished that… when I spoke about being with you forever… that it would come true. But I am dying, and that is the reality.'

'I will save you,' Prudence said firmly. 'I have to… '

'No – you have to save your kingdom.'

'Ryan I… you are my new home… ' Prudence looked at Ryan with watery eyes.

'Stop it – I want to die knowing that you made it… '

Prudence looked down. Death seemed a much happier choice after hearing Ryan's confession. The princess sighed, but deep inside she had decided on what she would choose to do. She would not die a plague anymore… no… she would die a hero and join Ryan in the other world. It was a charming thought to die with the one she loved. Yes… Ryan and her would be together forever…

'I forgot.' Ryan took out a small box from his pocket. 'I bought you this – two days ago, before coming to Vita. But yeah… I know it's not a lot… ' he stuttered in embarrassment. 'Here, I'm not sure if it fits, it was meant to be a bracelet, but they made a mistake… I mean, they mixed up my order with someone else's. These things happen.'

Prudence looked at Ryan as if she did not believe him.

'OK, I admit,' said Ryan. 'They did not make any mistakes… '

When Prudence looked at what Ryan gave her, she saw a beautiful ring. It was not made of diamonds or expensive materials, but it was just beautiful to think that it came from something priceless. It came from love, and that was the most valuable gift ever given to her. Hers and Ryan's initials were even engraved on it. She smiled, and presented her left hand to him.

Ryan was about to put the ring on her index, but she told him to put it on her ring finger.

'Prudence, you… ' Ryan went silent and stared at her eyes.

'I wish to know that we died engaged to one other… ' Prudence paused and looked at the ring. 'This ring shall be the symbol of our love… and who knows, if we survive… we will get married.' She smiled happily.

Ryan smiled and tears dropped from his face.

'Why are you crying my love?'

'It is just a beautiful thing to hope for a tomorrow,' Ryan sighed, before he kneeled to her. 'Prudence Fulgura – will you marry me?'

Will you marry me? How beautiful and sweet those words were. Prudence took her time before answering, not because she was hesitating, but because she wanted to live this moment to the fullest she could.

'Yes – forever,' Prudence said tearfully.

Ryan then got back on his feet and kissed her. They then turned toward the scenery, and observed the beautiful stars shining in their millions. Prudence was engaged to the one she loved. She had accomplished the duty of a princess by choosing her prince. They had known each other for one week and half, but the love they shared was worth a million lifetimes.

It was not long until Prudence could distinguish the castle from the distance they were at. Heartsas was right ahead.

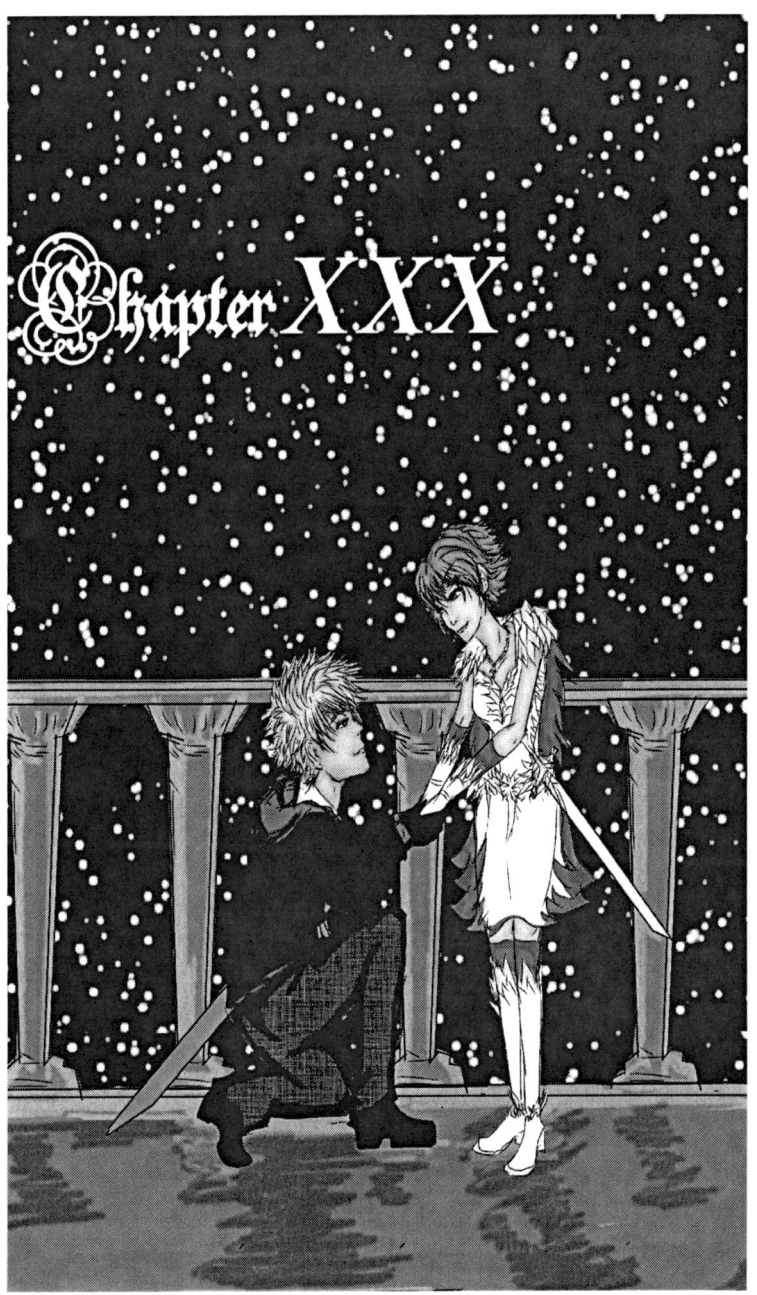

Chapter Thirty-One

The Assault Begins

Meanwhile in Heartsas, the emperor was sitting on the throne. His black armour was as sinister as his person. He was breathing slowly and gently, yet he seemed to be aware of Prudence coming toward him with the sword. Soon, the red hooded man appeared.

'My Lord… ' he said.

'They are coming,' the emperor said slowly. 'Soon, I shall retake what I have lost.'

'Are you not afraid my Lord?'

'How dare you speak of fear to me?' the emperor groaned evilly.

'Pardon me, my Lord… ' the red hooded man bowed.

'No matter. Keira shall witness my revenge.' The emperor laughed darkly. 'Her daughter will be the one to bring me what I need.' He paused and his body and voice started to shake. 'Fifteen years ago only one memory was remembered – Keira Fulgura, the queen. But they had all forgotten about my existence!' The emperor's fists then clenched. 'For fifteen years I have lived in the shadow of my name – behind a fragile and pathetic girl. I shall retake everything today and Vita shall understand my wrath and remember me forever!'

'What about the heads? They are the ones who… '

'We shall deal with them later on – once I have enough power to face them,' the emperor said darkly. 'They actually ignore what my true ambitions are… '

'A betrayal… interesting.'

The red hooded man then moved towards a window. He stared

at the dark sky and saw the silhouette of a warship approaching. 'It shall begin now,' he said calmly.

'Prepare everyone,' the emperor said, as he got up from the throne. 'I shall await her in a most convenient place.'

'You mean the roof?'

'Yes... I do like to enjoy the sight of blood splattering,' said the emperor. 'From here, I can only hear the cries of the battle...'

'She shall not pass through my defences,' the red hooded man claimed. 'I shall annihilate her myself.'

The emperor went silent for a while, then laughed in a manic way.

'Do as you please.' He laughed. 'But you shall understand your very misfortune.'

The emperor then disappeared.

The battle finale was about to take place. Thousands of goblins and orcs were standing in front of the castle's gates. It was an impressive sight, but a worrying one too.

'Nevermind their numbers! We shall crush them!' Nash shouted, as he lifted his sword up in the air.

All the werewolves and magicians pushed a war cry before descending the ship to the ground.

'This is it,' Ryan looked at Prudence. 'Stay by my side,' he kissed her hand.

'Let us end this,' said Prudence.

Ryan was shaking; however, he tried his best not to show it. He grabbed a sword he had found earlier in the weapon room of the ship. And once near the ground, he jumped off to have a good head start.

'Ryan!' Prudence shouted.

She then in turn grabbed her sword and jumped to follow the one she loved.

Eric gasped after he saw the two lovers jumping out of the ship to battle the massive horde of goblins and orcs. He then took a pack of arrows and a bow.

'What are you doing?' Mia yelled.

'It is time for me to man up like Ryan,' Eric said with a trembling voice. 'I have to make sure I can protect my friends.'

'You'll get yourself killed! Ryan has powers and so does Prudence!' Mia tried to reason Eric. 'You will die without powers and you're not even good with the bow!'

'I don't care; I will not be a coward,' Eric said loudly.

Mia then turned Eric around and kissed him. Eric was surprised and stared at her eyes for a short while. 'What… what was that for?' he stuttered with his cheeks turning red.

'In case we don't make it,' Mia sighed. 'I thought the kiss would give me confidence… just like Prudence has whenever she is with Ryan.'

'Oh, fair enough. Here… '

Eric kissed Mia; he then advanced toward the front of the ship and swallowed, before jumping out of the warship. Mia then saw another bow and a set of arrows. She grunted and took the bow with the arrows. Just like her friends, she jumped out of the ship and headed towards the final step of her journey.

Chapter Thirty-Two
The Man Behind The Hood

Slash, and the sound of two steels crossing paths was heard. The sound of blood spilling was echoing through a long distance. Cries, heavy thumps, armour being crushed, pierced flesh, it was all there was.

The battle was raging. The werewolves and magicians were unifying themselves to combat the orcs and the goblins. However, both sides were suffering collateral damages. It was hard to distinguish which was taking the advantage. But the emperor had other tricks under his sleeves. When Ryan and Prudence looked up to the dark sky, they could see griffons attacking the warship and their allies.

Ryan stabbed one of the goblins that was coming his way and burnt down a whole troop of orcs. 'Go ahead Prudence! I will make way for you!' he shouted, as he stabbed another goblin.

'Ryan!' Prudence said loudly. 'Please, come with me!'

'Darn,' Ryan groaned. 'OK! Let's do this together!' He slashed another one of his enemies.

Ryan and Prudence ran toward the gates of the castle, but hundreds of goblins and orcs were standing in their way. The young man threw a powerful fireball, and an enormous number of them were smashed to the ground. The noise of their skulls crushing echoed in the dark night.

'How cool did I look?' Ryan shouted as he dashed to the gates.

'You were cool!' Prudence giggled, as she held his hand.

The two lovers were impressive; they could not be stopped by any of their enemies. Ryan was not shy anymore when it came to stabbing a goblin or an orc, or whenever he had to burn them down. He was going for it, no matter what.

Pretty soon, the creatures standing in the couple's way realized the futile battle they were leading. They ran away at the sight of the couple.

'That's the power of love, baby!' Ryan laughed.

The couple were near the entrance; a fine twenty seconds were separating Prudence and Ryan from the castle's gates. But at the moment they were about to cross the entry, five griffons stood in their way. All of them looked vicious and dangerous. They were slightly different from the ones met in Wolf Glace.

They possessed a crocodile head, the body of a dragon, and the arms and legs of a human being. Their tails were no more a snake but a gigantic anaconda, and their wings were the same as the dragons. There were no doubts, these griffons were not just griffons, but an army the emperor had been leading.

No creatures like those were ever spotted on Vita before. Even the goblins and the orcs were frightened and stood a good distance from them.

Ryan tried to stab the monster in front of him, but as soon as he did his blade shattered into pieces. 'Darn!' he shouted before throwing a fireball. The griffon was hit by the fire, but nothing happened. No bruise, not a single trace was shown.

'What the heck!' Ryan gasped in horror. 'Prudence, head to the castle! I will try and make a diversion!'

'You will get yourself killed! Ryan!'

Prudence could not allow Ryan to fight these creatures with no possible way to damage them. She fought against one of the griffons and with a swing of her sword, she slashed it in half. Ryan's jaw dropped, and his eyes were full of wonder at the woman he loved.

'So this is the power of the sword, eh?' Ryan chuckled. 'Show off!'

With Prudence armed with this incredible weapon, they feared no creatures. The four griffons that remained took a few steps back and flew away from the two lovers. Ryan then took the sword of one of the dead bodies lying on the red grass. Then, together, he and Prudence entered the castle.

While the couple went inside the castle, Eric and Mia were struggling to survive the attacks of the emperor's army. Dodging, squatting, crouching, crawling, Eric was trying everything to avoid being hit by an arrow or stabbed by a sword. It was a rather difficult task and most of the time it was his ridiculous clumsiness that got him out of danger.

'Use your bow!' Mia yelled at him, as she shot down an orc with hers.

'It's easy for you to say – ah!' Eric said loudly, as he dodged an arrow.

The young man was lost; he did not know what to do in the battlefield. Sure, he could make use of his bow, but he did not even know how to use it properly and might end up killing one of his allies. Instead of fighting back, he kept on running away, until he got surrounded.

Eric was cornered; five goblins and two orcs were coming at him with their evil eyes and their horrible faces. The young man whimpered, just like a child would do if they were in trouble.

'I have to take at least one down,' he whimpered, as he struggled to arm himself with the bow. 'Take this, loser!' he yelled as he shot one arrow.

He missed.

'He cannot even aim!' one of the goblins laughed, after seeing the arrow piercing a tree. The goblins were all laughing as they approached the young man.

Then, out of nowhere, the sound of an arrow stabbing flesh was heard. When Eric looked closely, it was one of the goblin's heads that had been pierced. The monster fell down lamentably before emitting one last groan. All the goblins looked around, but soon they were all brought down one by one.

'Thank God I've been taking archery lessons back home,' Mia chuckled, after killing the last goblin that was cornering Eric.

'There's still two!' Eric shouted, as he pointed out the two orcs.

'Die!' One of the orcs tried to stab Mia.

'Look out!' Eric jumped out fearfully; then a powerful wind blew away the two orcs.

The young man was stunned; he did not understand how he had done it. He stared at his hands for a while, forgetting about the chaos around him.

'Look out you idiot!' Mia shot down a goblin that tried to stab Eric in his back.

'Gee, thanks!' Eric chuckled. 'Did you see what I did earlier?' he asked loudly.

'Yes.'

'Man I can't believe it!' Eric chuckled with excitement. 'I've got powers! Yay!'

'Let's just get inside the castle! It is way too dangerous here!'

'Erm… yes, let's go!'

The two teenagers ran to the castle, just like Ryan and Prudence did. However, they were followed by two griffons. Mia turned around and tried to shoot one, but the arrow destroyed itself after touching the skin of the griffon.

'Get inside the castle!' Eric yelled at her. 'I will try something!'

'If you die, then I'll be mad at you!' Mia said loudly, before passing inside of the castle's gates.

Eric seemed more confident. He glanced at his hands and took a deep breath, before trying to blow the griffons away with the same attack he did previously. But it did not work. The wind was there and was even strong enough to push two to three orcs, but the griffons seemed immune to his powers. Eric swallowed his breath. He understood how much trouble he had just put himself in.

Both griffons were snarling viciously as they approached the young man. Their demonic faces were enough to paralyze Eric in one place with fear.

Eric closed his eyes, feeling his demise approaching. Then, out of nowhere, he heard a slash and a cry of agony. When he opened his eyes again, he could see the two griffons half cut, lying on the ground motionless.

'Everyone has to keep an eye on you... tch,' Nash scoffed.

Nash looked at the griffons before he stared at his sword.

'Seems like these creatures are immune to everything except magical weapons...'

'Mate, you just saved me!' Eric jumped out happily.

'Yeah... well, you owe me one now,' Nash said calmly. 'Anyway... Prudence and Ryan are already inside the castle.'

'Yeah, let's go!'

'I'm the one who says it!' Nash grunted. 'Let's go!' he said loudly.

The two young men ran inside of the castle. They could feel the intensity of the battle outside, echoing inside the walls of the premises.

Once inside, Nash could not help himself but to look around him. The walls were beautiful, the red carpet was well placed and the portraits around him gave life to the place.

'Prudence had a great life!' Eric said loudly, as he looked around. He then approached one of the portraits and noticed a familiar face. 'Look,' he said to Nash, as he pointed out a man. 'He looks so familiar...'

'We don't have time to play who's who,' Nash grunted. 'I can hear footsteps approaching,' he whispered. '*En garde*!' he told Eric, as he took a fighting stance.

'But... I don't want... to fight you!' Eric stuttered, afraid.

'Idiot, I will not fight against you!' Nash moaned. 'Can't you hear people approaching?'

Eric then paid attention and Nash was right. He could hear the sound of armour thumping on the ground. It was the sound of metal marching in coordination. Soon, Eric could perceive a horde of ten soldiers walking towards them.

'Since you are a nuisance on the battlefield,' Nash said calmly. 'I will let you take your leave.'

'Erm… OK… but If I do that, Ryan is going to call me a coward.'

'Then aim!' Nash ordered to Eric abruptly.

Eric was so panicked by Nash that he was struggling to get his bow. By the time he could get his weapon, Nash had frozen all the soldiers with one gesture from his sword. The young man was extraordinary; he looked heroic, yet really pretentious.

'Like I said,' Nash scoffed. 'You are a nuisance on the battlefield.'

Eric clenched his fist.

'I will not take any more of your lip mate!' he said loudly.

'Do shut up,' replied Nash.

'Grr… anyway… ' Eric took a deep breath. 'Check this out! That old man on the picture! He was the one who wanted Prudence in Hook Road!'

'Huh?' Nash wondered. 'What is it that you… ' The young man interrupted himself. He was shocked by the discovery Eric had made. 'That's… ' He looked closely and saw Reaper in the picture.

Prudence's mother was there too, with a baby in her arms, it must have been Prudence. There was a middle aged knight on the left and a man with a crown next to the princess's mother. Nash assumed it was the king. Reaper was next to him. What was he doing in the picture?

'What is the meaning of this?' demanded Eric.

'I have no idea,' Nash answered, baffled. 'We have to find Prudence and tell her.'

'Yes. Let's hurry up!'

Nash and Eric ran in the corridors. They did not know where the throne was or where they were meant to go since it was an enormous castle. But they had no time to waste; Prudence had to know about the portrait before going up against the emperor. It did not mean much, but still, Nash felt it was important for Prudence to know.

While the two young men were looking for Prudence, Ryan and the princess were near the throne chamber. A lot of soldiers were guarding the entrance, but with the new sword the princess had acquired it was not a hard task for her to wipe them out of her way. One swing was enough to eliminate the whole lot of them.

'We have arrived!' Prudence panted. 'It is right behind this door!'

'Let me make an entrance!' Ryan chuckled. 'One… two… three.' He pushed the doors and jumped stupidly. 'Surrender evil doer!' he said loudly.

Ryan looked ridiculous, but Prudence did not want to say anything. It made her laugh and no matter how stupid Ryan could act, he always looked gorgeous and sweet to her.

'I look idiotic don't I?'

'Yes,' Prudence giggled.

'Anyway… erm.' Ryan was scratching the back of his head with red cheeks. 'Let's look around, eh?'

The couple looked around, but they could see no one. It was an empty throne and an empty chamber that greeted them.

'Wow,' Ryan whistled. 'It's sure is crowded here,' he said sarcastically.

The young man then approached the throne; he could feel that something was amiss.

'Prudence, stay close to me,' he told the princess, as he looked carefully around. 'I feel like someone is watching us.'

Prudence's sword was glowing. From a normal white blade, it changed into a shining light. She could barely distinguish the shape of the blade, and Prudence could feel the warmth of the light intensifying. 'What is the meaning of this?' she asked, mystified.

Soon, the light started to leave the sword; it fired itself out of the weapon as if it was an arrow. Prudence had no knowledge whatsoever of what was happening, but the blade aimed itself toward the darkness of the chamber. It was so fast that she could barely keep up with her eyes, and when it stopped, an unknown individual appeared out of nowhere.

'Such a magnificent weapon.' It was a man's voice.

The blade of the sword came back to its original place. Prudence sighed, reassured.

The man then left the darkness. Prudence could not tell of his identity because of the red hood he wore.

'Who are you?' Ryan asked the man.

'I am the one who will put an end to your very futile quest.' The man laughed darkly.

'Aha, no,' said Ryan. 'If you wished us dead, you would have done so the moment we entered the chamber.' The young man paused and smiled. 'If I had to guess… ' he paused again. 'You were trying to fool the sword, but you could not – which means that you may be powerful… but not as powerful as the sword.'

'It is indeed really foolish of you to speak of me.'

'Prudence!' Nash yelled, as he entered the throne chamber. 'There you are! '

Ryan turned to his brother and his friend. He was happy to see them. He firstly mocked the fact that Eric had managed to fight back, but he was glad to see they were fine.

However, after seeing them, the young man started to worry about Mia. He had not seen or heard from her since the battle had begun. He was so preoccupied by what was ahead, that he had forgotten about who he had left behind.

'We saw a portrait of Reaper in the corridors!' Nash said loudly.

'I beg your pardon?' Prudence snapped.

'He was in your family portrait!' Eric added. 'And I am the one who discovered it.'

'Reaper… but… ' Prudence was dazed.

At the same moment, they could hear someone clapping their hands from behind. When they turned around, they could see Reaper, who had taken Mia as a hostage.

'Well played gentlemen,' Reaper chuckled with his evil smile.

'Mia!' Ryan shouted, as he saw his friend trapped under Reaper's magic. 'I'll get you out of this!' he snapped in anger and ran toward Reaper.

'Ha! ' Reaper laughed. 'Move closer and I will snap her neck.'

'Ry… Ryan! Make it stop! It hurts!' Mia was shrieking in pain.

'Do shut up!' Reaper intensified his magic, and soon Ryan could hear Mia's arm cracking.

Ryan did not know what to do. His desire to kill Reaper was overwhelming, but if he moved any closer, he knew Reaper would snap Mia's neck. What could he do? Mia was being tortured in front of him. What was he supposed to do to make the pain go away?

'Please Ryan!' Mia cried in pain. 'Make it stop!'

'What do you want, old freak?' Ryan asked loudly.

'The sword. Hand it over,' Reaper said calmly.

Ryan immediately turned to Prudence; his eyes were begging for the princess to do as told. 'Please… ' he said.

Prudence threw her sword toward Reaper, for Mia's sake.

'Such an ugly twist,' the red hooded man said with amusement in his voice.

'Alas,' Reaper said calmly. 'I suppose do-gooders are truly fools.' He laughed.

'Free her now!' Ryan shouted.

'Yes, indeed.' Reaper laughed and cracked Mia's neck. 'Now she is free.'

'MIA!' Ryan shouted in horror.

'The bastard!' Eric snarled.

Ryan snapped. He dashed toward Reaper with fire in his eyes and went berserk. Reaper tried to stop him with his magic, but it did not work and soon Ryan was surrounded by a burning aura. It was a sort of burning shadow that was surrounding the young man's body. The shadow was taking a lion's silhouette.

'Impossible!' Reaper shouted in terror, understanding the error he had committed in enraging Ryan.

The young man speared Reaper to the ground and with rage he punched him to death. Reaper's face was so brutally disfigured that no one would have been able to identify him. His pale grey skin turned to red, and his beaked nose was completely swallowed. The only thing that remained intact was his evil smile.

The red hooded man turned around, 'The spirit of fire,' he muttered indistinctly.

Ryan's body was back to normal. The fire surrounding him was gone.

'Grr,' Ryan panted. 'Mia!' he turned to his friend's lifeless body.

Not long after, Eric ran toward Ryan and could not help himself from bursting into tears as he contemplated Mia's unmoving body. 'Not you!' Eric moaned in tears.

'I beg you to forgive me Ryan,' Prudence said softly. 'But…' she paused, trying to find the right words to say. 'But I have to free my kingdom,' the princess said, as she took her sword back.

Prudence then approached the man in the red hood.

'Surrender now,' she said calmly. 'And no harm shall come to you.'

Surprisingly, the person in front of the princess began to laugh. He then turned around and clapped his hands.

'You have grown into a confident woman,' he laughed. 'It is not long since you were crying like a baby!' He kept laughing manically.

Prudence was dazed. What did he mean? She had never met him before. However, the more she listened to him, the more his voice sounded familiar.

'Who are you?' she asked.

The man did not reply and drew out a sword that was hidden inside his robe.

'Only the steel shall talk from now on,' he said darkly.

'If you so wish, this sword shall guide your way to hell,' said Prudence.

'Let me have him,' Nash said, as he got between Prudence and the hooded man. 'Ryan needs you.' He paused. 'Now…'

'But I…'

'Do as I say – don't worry, that idiot in front of us will begin to talk once I have finished with him,' Nash said with a confident tone.

'You and your brother are foolish,' the man said. 'It will be a pleasure to end this life of yours.'

Nash smiled; he delicately pushed Prudence so she would not stand in his way. Then, he jumped out with his sword pointing toward the hooded man. 'Take this!' he shouted, as he tried to lacerate his opponent.

'Rather stubborn of you – to think you ought to beat me!'

The steels crossed paths. Sparks of metal were shining in the chamber. It was a beautiful spectacle, both were fast and accurate. However, it was not long before the effects of Nash's sword began to affect his adversary's weapon.

The ice was progressively freezing the other blade, rendering it weak and fragile. Nash sneered gently, before harshly hitting his adversary's sword. One hit was enough to shatter the blade into pieces.

'Argh!' the man grunted, as he fell down lamentably.

Nash then edged the blade of his sword towards the man's throat.

'Do reveal yourself,' the young man said calmly. 'Or I will cut you before discovering your identity,' he added sharply.

'Failing against a child… tcht,' the man scoffed miserably. 'I have indeed lost my way in the battlefield.'

'I don't care about your life,' Nash scoffed. 'Reveal your identity and surrender, or die like a miserable bug.'

The man held his hood. His hands were shaking. Slowly and gently, he lowered his hood and his grey coiffure was the first thing Nash saw.

Prudence was by Ryan's side. He seemed inconsolable, and tears were falling from his eyes. The princess gently kissed him on the cheek, and stayed by his side for a short time.

'I am sorry, Ryan,' she said kindly.

Prudence then glanced at Nash; he had been triumphant over

his opponent quite rapidly. She then looked closely, and with horror, she discovered who was behind the hood. She forgot about Ryan and ran towards the man. There were no doubts, it was him.

'Sir Slade!' she said with a trembling voice.

'Ha ha,' Slade faintly laughed.

'I let you decide his fate,' said Nash.

'Sir Slade – but – I do not understand the meaning of this!' Prudence snapped. 'I thought you dead – what has happened?' she questioned the man. 'Why have you succumbed to the emperor?'

'The emperor is true ruler of Heartsas and Vita!' Slade said loudly.

'Do be quiet!' Prudence raised her voice and thumped the ground. 'How could you betray my parents?' she asked furiously.

'You are a child!' the man laughed maniacally. 'Soon, you shall be granted the eternal rest!' he said loudly. 'I shall enjoy your demise!'

'Where is your commander?' Nash demanded.

'He is waiting on the castle's roof,' Slade laughed. 'The dark scenery is the perfect setting for your end!' he said loudly, as he glared at Prudence.

Prudence's desire to discover the true identity of the Emperor Daemn was devouring her on the inside. She remained calm, but deep inside she was impatient to know of her enemy and defeat him.

While she was deep in her thoughts, Slade kept on laughing and cursing the princess. She did not pay attention to him, but he was going on and on about how she would die and how useless she was.

Finally, after a fine minute, Nash had enough of the man's lips; he hit the man in the face with the back of his sword.

'Bloody idiot,' Nash chuckled. 'Do not listen to him, you are the true ruler.'

'I do not know,' Prudence looked down. 'Regardless – Daemn must be defeated.'

'And he will be!' Ryan shouted, as he got back on his feet with anger. 'It is because of him that my friend died!' he groaned in rage. 'I will show no mercy to him!'

'Let us go,' Prudence said calmly.

'What about Mia?' Eric asked.

'We have no choice but to leave her here until our enemy is defeated,' answered Nash.

'Let us end this before it is too late for me!' Ryan snarled.

Prudence and her friends ran to the stairs. Their final battle was about to take place.

Chapter Thirty-Three

The Promise

One step, two steps. She was counting each one of them as she was walking up the stairs. She knew by heart how many stairs there were, five hundred of them. She had grown up in these very walls without ever suspecting the circumstances to be different. After all, how was she supposed to forsee being thrown out of her own house?

It was strange to her: feeling her nerves kicking in, the ill feeling around her stomach, the adrenaline pumping her blood faster by the second. She used to mount the stairs and descend them joyfully, but now it was all different. It was a dark feeling and an angry one too.

It was a shame, having to mount these stairs feeling that way. Especially as it would be the last time she was to mount them. Once everything was over, she would die with Ryan and become a hero, having fulfilled her parents' wish. It was a great motivation to her. But she was not naive; she knew that it would not be that simple. Her enemy was unknown to her, yet by himself he had managed to influence Sir Slade in betraying her family. He was a powerful foe; it was the only thing she was certain of. Who was hiding behind that name? Daemn…

'Daemn,' she murmured as she was climbing up the stairs.

'The man doesn't even have a good name,' Ryan scoffed. 'Of all the names, he chose "darn"… Can you believe it?'

'I admit it's kind of a rubbish name if you ask me,' Nash sneered.

'If I was an emperor, I would call myself a name that is catchy!' Eric said loudly.

'Do not mock him,' Prudence said darkly. 'If Sir Slade was convinced of his being able to beat even the sword… ' she swallowed nervously. 'Then we ought to take him seriously.'

Four hundred steps they had climbed. Soon, Eric started to feel tired and his body felt heavy, he was breathing lamentably and harshly.

'How far is it?' Eric panted.

'We have a hundred more stairs to climb.'

'Grr!' Ryan grunted furiously before dashing to the top.

'Wait for me!' Prudence shouted.

The young man was fast, he was determined to make the emperor pay for his friend's death. In a matter of seconds, he was the first one to reach the top followed by his brother and the princess. Eric was the slowest one; he took his time and was breathless halfway from the top.

The view on the top of the castle overlooked dark scenery. It was the night, but even then they could perceive the chaos submerging Heartsas. Prudence had difficulties in accepting this chaotic image of her kingdom.

'You have done well,' a voice said out of nowhere.

When Prudence and her friends looked ahead, it was the emperor. His monstrous armour made him look inhuman. He was facing the forest and did not seem concerned by possible attacks from Prudence or her companions.

'We meet at last,' he said calmly. 'After fifteen years… '

Prudence wondered what he meant by fifteen years. But she did not care. She hated him. Having him in front of her made her blood boil.

'It is over! Surrender now!'

'I shall not surrender.' Daemn turned around.

'Fool, you are,' Prudence scoffed. 'I shall discover the face of betrayal hiding behind this helmet of yours!' she said loudly. 'Your very sight sickens me!'

'Aha,' he laughed. 'You really are like your mother.'

'Do not speak of my mother!' Prudence yelled.

'It's your fault, if Mia… '

Ryan's voice and hands were trembling.

'I'll never forgive you!'

The young man did not wait for anyone to give him permission. He ran with his sword in his hands, wanting to slice the emperor in half. However, the moment he got near to him, the emperor threw a powerful bolt of lightning. The young man was brutally projected to the ground and half of his body was covered in bruises and burns.

'Darn – it hurts!' Ryan groaned.

'Fool! ' The emperor laughed evilly.

Prudence advanced toward Daemn. She edged her blade toward her enemy and calmly, she took a guarding stance.

'Your presence is a disgrace to royalty. Yet… ' Prudence paused. 'I shall grant you a noble duel.'

'How courteous of you… ' The emperor bowed, before drawing out a massive red sword.

The brothers tried to interfere, but Prudence ordered them not to.

'It is my fight,' she said calmly. '*En garde!*'

Prudence did not want to admit or say anything, but she was copying her sister and Alexandra's way of talking in battle.

'Your very sight is a disgrace to behold!' the emperor said loudly.

Daemn ran towards the princess and magically disappeared. Prudence gasped; she did not know what magic he was using. How did he disappear? Where was he? The princess's body was trembling. Panicked, she looked around her. To her right, then her left, perhaps behind? She held her sword tightly.

There it was, the first sound of steel striking steel. Luckily for Prudence, the Sword of the King protected her and acted by itself when she was being attacked. It was as if someone or something was guiding her hands whenever she was attacked.

'Such an irritating weapon you wield!' the emperor grunted, as he became visible again. 'No matter,' he said darkly. 'Soon it shall be mine.'

'Never shall I think of giving it to you!' Prudence raised her voice.

Ryan's body was tingling to move. He wanted to stab the emperor or snap his neck, but Prudence was loyal and a bit big headed. She would never allow him to interfere with this battle, when it was clear that she was winning. However, if she was losing, Ryan would not think twice before jumping in.

'Prudence! Do not give him any chances! Kill him when you can!' Ryan shouted.

'This sword shall seal your existence.'

'I do not think so… ' the emperor laughed evilly.

He then tried to stab Prudence, but the sword moved again and slashed him around the ribs. Blood spilled from the dark armour. 'Ugh… ' he grunted, as he took few steps back. 'Impressive sword, indeed… '

'I shall end you here – unless you surrender and answer my questions.'

'I have no obligation to do so!' Daemn shouted.

'What an idiot,' Ryan groaned. 'He does not admit defeat against the ruler of all swords! '

Nash looked preoccupied by this battle. His eyes were focused upon Prudence's sword and the emperor.

'Something's up,' Nash said darkly.

Prudence sighed. She then advanced towards the emperor with the intention of killing him. She raised her sword in the air.

'I shall discover your identity, dead or alive.'

The emperor laughed darkly, he seemed out of his mind. He then clicked his finger and a sort of monstrous blazing bird appeared out of nowhere. It was a colossal bird, the size of a dragon. Its face was devilish with fangs and long claws. Everyone gasped out of surprise; they were shocked by the immense creature.

The emperor did not wait any longer and jumped on the back of the blazing monster. They flew in the sky, and stopped halfway to the castle, staring at the princess and her friends.

'The sword is the ruler of all blades!' the emperor shouted, as he was in midair. 'Let us see if it can dodge the cry of a phoenix!'

The princess's first initiative was to run, but the emperor taunted her. 'Let us see if the Fulgura blood has enough bravery.' He paused with an arrogant posture. 'Or if they are cowards!'

Prudence turned to her friends with wide eyes. 'Run!' she shouted.

Eric had just managed to reach the top, when he saw the immense creature. 'God no!' he shouted, as he ran back to the stairs.

Nash and Ryan looked at each other. One was waiting for the other to run away. 'She is mine,' Ryan glared at Nash.

'Yes, but can you protect her?' Nash scoffed.

'Have you not heard what I ordered you to do?' Prudence snapped. 'Do not stay here!'

The phoenix lifted its long beak up in the air. Soon, fire glowed from its beak; it was preparing for a powerful attack. Prudence pushed Ryan to the stairs. 'I cannot lose you,' she said softly.

'Do come with me then!' Ryan grabbed her hand.

'I cannot. It is my duty to defend my family's honour and I have to stop him.' Prudence removed her hand.

The phoenix snarled; it was ready to attack.

'Please!'

Ryan did as demanded; he went to the stairs, just like Eric. Nash wanted to play the hero and so he stayed with Prudence on the roof.

'Come and get it!' Nash yelled, as the phoenix lowered its beak full of fire.

'I shall grant you your demise!' the emperor shouted.

Five seconds ticked by, and the phoenix spat all its fire on the roof of the castle. A tsunami of fire was submerging the place. Prudence was holding on to her life with the sword protecting her. It was deflecting the fire.

However, the more the sword deflected, the more it absorbed the heat. Prudence's armour gloves started to melt. The sword's handle was boiling up.

'ARRGH!' she grunted in pain.

Her hands started to bleed. The heat was insupportable. However, if she let go of the sword that was it for her, she would end up burnt alive. What could she do? Her hands felt as if they would melt.

'I'm here princess!' Nash approached her, surrounded by ice.

He did not seem affected by the heat; his sword had the capacity of incessant ice, which granted him a perfect guard against fire. His body was surrounded by ice, which fully protected him. Prudence felt her hands about to slip... she could not hold on to the sword any longer. It was unbearable. 'RYAN!' she shouted. 'FORGIVE ME!'

She was about to let go of the sword, but at the same time Nash grabbed her and surrounded her with ice. She was safe and protected. The Sword of the Moon was surprisingly powerful.

'Don't worry, I'm here,' Nash chuckled.

'You have saved me.'

'Yes,' Nash said softly.

'Thank you.'

'I want you to know – that you will make it.' Nash paused. 'And even if Ryan has little to offer you... he is the right one for you.' He looked down. 'You know I'm running away from the trouble and the boring life we live in England, but he is not. He is courageous and he faces his destiny no matter what, just like you do. And that's what makes him the right one for you. Just know that.'

'I am sorry for the pain I have caused you,' Prudence said quietly.

'Ah... look at us talking about our lives in those circumstances.' Nash laughed wryly.

'Please... try to accept what is going to happen.'

Nash looked at Prudence, not understanding what she meant.

'I know now that it is my fate to seal the portal for good. I shall die for my world...' Prudence looked down. 'I wish I could spend my life with Ryan, God knows I even envisaged giving up my duties as a princess for him.' She paused and looked determined. 'But I have to protect my world. It is my destiny, to complete what my mother started.'

'Shut up,' said Nash. 'Neither me, nor Ryan will let you die.'

'I do not ask your permission... I just wish for you to be prepared for what is to come.'

Nash looked intrigued. He stared at her, and demanded to know what else she was hiding from him. Prudence looked at Nash before looking down.

'Ryan should have been the one to tell you – but he is also dying... '

Nash's expression turned to horror. He demanded an explanation to this. His voice was shaking and his eyes were lost in terror. Prudence knew it was not the right time, but since they were stuck in the ice, she decided to tell him about Ryan's condition.

Meanwhile, Eric and Ryan were both staying on the stairs, safe from the flames of the phoenix. Ryan was concerned about Prudence. He cared about his brother too, but Prudence was the only one on his mind.

'I saw her ring, you know,' Eric said quietly, knowing it was not the right time or place for this discussion.

'Yes, so?' Ryan seemed somewhere else.

'You've only known her for a week and a couple of days... don't you think it's absurd?'

'Mate – whether I've known her for one day, one month or one year... ' Ryan paused. 'It makes no difference to me.' He looked down with wonder in his eyes. 'Whenever I am around her, my heart beats faster. Whenever I'm far from her, I miss her like hell.' He smiled. 'I only needed to look at her, to know that she is the one I am meant to be with.' Ryan paused and sighed. 'I could spend eternity looking at her eyes, feeling the warmth of her skin and smelling the softness of her perfume... ' he closed his eyes and seemed sad.

'Wow… you really are a crazy romantic bloke.'

'Love makes me feel alive, but I know it won't be long now,' Ryan sighed in sadness. 'I am relieved to know that I will die with my ring upon her finger.'

'What?' Eric jumped in shock. 'What did you not tell me?'

Ryan explained his situation to Eric; what would happen to him once Cheryl's magic ceases to work.

'Promise me mate… if I don't make it, you will defeat the emperor and you will go home safely.' Ryan looked serious. 'Because I can't lose another friend of mine… '

'I promise… ' Eric looked down with sad eyes.

Ryan stared at the top of the stairs. He could see the sparkles and the intense fire burning. He was crouching but was quite close to the incessant flames. Ryan just wanted to be ready to jump on the roof as soon as the attack was over.

After a long ten minutes of flames, the attack had finally ceased. The ice surrounding Nash and the princess melted. Both individuals were fine, and glanced at the emperor, who was sitting on the phoenix's back.

'Glad you kept her safe.'

'Ryan! ' Nash turned to his brother.

Ryan and Eric were both standing there, staring at the emperor.

'It's time to die!' the emperor snarled, as he ordered the phoenix to throw a fireball.

Prudence was the one targeted. Nash tried to take the attack instead of her, but Ryan got in front of the two and received the ball right in the upper body. However, the fire started to be absorbed by his body.

'It looks like the fire does not affect me!' Ryan gasped.

'The spirit of fire… ' the emperor seemed concerned. 'I had not expected this. So you have decided to come back, Leo… '

Ryan stared at the emperor. He did not understand why he was called Leo. He remembered the story of the two brothers, but he was not Leo. He was Ryan Snowangel, a simple man from Earth.

The young man then felt a piercing pain around his chest. It was stinging and his flesh was itching. He could feel the same pain he had felt when he had nearly died.

'Ugh...' Ryan placed his hands on his chest and coughed blood. 'Ryan?'

Prudence could see the green light around Ryan's chest glowing.

'I guess I don't have much time...' Ryan said weakly.

'No – Ryan, no...' Prudence's voice trembled.

'We have to end this Prudence... for your kingdom's sake,' Ryan said gloomily. 'We knew we did not have enough time for me...'

'No! You knew!' Prudence snapped.

'We don't have time to argue! Daemn is still here!'

Daemn looked rather satisfied.

'How touching – the one you love is dying...' he laughed. 'Allow me to abridge his suffering!' Daemn then paused. 'No, actually, allow me to tell him a small tale before I kill him.' He sneered. 'The burden of the sword.'

Ryan looked at Prudence but then he looked back at the emperor. He did not understand what Daemn meant by the burden of the sword.

'No! Don't!' Prudence shouted.

'Do you not know? Whether I open the portal or not, she has the intention of sealing it?'

Ryan looked at Prudence.

'What does he mean?'

'Her mother has trusted your beloved princess to sacrifice herself for Vita, and Prudence here will grant her mother's wish.' Daemn laughed. 'In about a couple of hours, the portal leading to the demons' world will open and it is the duty of the wielder of the sword to make a choice: either the wielder chooses to accept the demons' powers and at the same time, allows them to walk through Vita and exterminate everything...' Daemn paused before he laughed maniacally. 'Or the wielder can make the ultimate sacrifice and save everyone, including Vita itself!' His voice trembled in excitement. 'I shall only make one of these two choices! Like your beautiful princess.'

'Why is that?' Eric asked.

'The sword is a form of magnet,' Daemn replied. 'On Vita, the sword has only a few utilities when it comes to the demons. It shall only guide them.' He paused. 'But once the sword gets to the demons' world, then it will actually act as a cataclysm and explode, so that the wielder, the demons and the portal are gone forever, preserving the peace and the safety of Vita.'

'What?' Ryan shouted at Prudence. 'You can't accept that I'm dying but you're willing to die for everyone, thinking I will be OK with it?' he snapped. 'If I had the chance of living with you… I would! And you… you wish to throw away the gift of life for a bunch of fools who could not stand up for themselves during dark times?'

Prudence stared at him. Her eyes seemed full of determination.

'We shall be together, my love… '

Ryan went silent. 'But I… ' he started.

'We shall be together and that is all that matters.'

'Indeed you shall be together… all of you!' the emperor laughed. 'I shall end you all here!'

Daemn swung his sword. The blazing bird dashed toward the castle with an evil look in its eyes.

'Watch out!' Nash said loudly before he took a guarding stance.

The bird was approaching viciously. It was ready to crush the princess and her friends. Everyone could see its monstrous claws adjusting so that they could destroy the roof. It was coming at full speed and seemed unstoppable.

Suddenly, an arrow was fired out of nowhere and hit the emperor's left shoulder. Daemn fell down from the bird and crashed on the ground.

'I succeeded!' Eric yelled happily. 'I brought him down!'

'Argh… curse you… '

The phoenix started to act strangely. After Daemn was brought down, the blazing bird started to move around itself. It seemed, somehow, trapped inside a prison. After a short minute, it broke free from an invisible cage.

'You have my gratitude, humans,' the phoenix said. 'I shall take my leave, as my kind are not to be involved in such things.' It paused and flew higher. 'I am sorry for the trouble caused by me... it will be the last time I shall be under the spell of anyone,' the phoenix said, as it was leaving in the dark sky.

The emperor was grunting in pain, but he was slowly getting to one knee. His dark armour was half shattered. His helmet was broken, and soon his face was to be revealed. Prudence and her friends advanced toward him.

'Such a dire situation you are in,' Nash scoffed.

'It is at my advantage.' The emperor laughed maniacally.

He then looked at the princess and her friends. Prudence eye's opened in horror; the man in front of her, it was no one else than the King of Heartsas.

He had barely aged since the pictures upon the castle's wall. He was a handsome man, with long dark hair and brown eyes. His skin was of a pale white and he was quite intimidating. Prudence's jaw dropped, she was speechless. What was the meaning of all of this?

'Hello daughter,' he laughed evilly.

'Father...' Prudence said softly.

'Father – what?' Eric jumped out after hearing this.

'You have grown well...' Daemn laughed. 'You look like your mother...'

'Do not talk of my mother!' Prudence raised her voice.

'Aha... Prudence... such a naive girl you are... I am ashamed to know that my blood runs through your veins.'

Ryan could see how Prudence was broken by this horrible betrayal. He looked at her, and saw how hurt she was. Ryan could not tolerate Prudence hurting.

'Shut up!' he snarled. 'You're a dead man!'

Daemn looked at Ryan and started to smile.

'Yet you are the one dying...'

'What happened?' Prudence asked quietly. 'Fifteen years ago, when mother and you disappeared. What truly happened?'

'Since you shall die soon enough…' Daemn got back on his feet. 'Fifteen years ago – I faked my own death. The powerful magician, Filius, wanted the army of the demons. A noble decision, yet a low minded man,' he grunted. 'I killed him, and then your mother, but before he died,' the emperor's fist clenched, 'Filius went to the demons' world – and he sealed the portal from there.'

Ryan was confused. If the portal was sealed, then it could not be opened. So why was Daemn so eager to waste his efforts in opening a portal that cannot be opened?

'Aha – I can see that you wonder what else I am hiding,' Daemn chuckled. 'Well, just like with the stones there is always a portal from one world to another. Filius could only seal the portal from the demons' world to Vita – but what he failed to consider was that Keira would not be strong enough to seal the portal from Vita to the demons' world.'

Daemn then started to walk around and his wounds were healing.

'Keira wanted to seal the portal, but I stabbed her right in the stomach…'

Prudence thumped the ground and clenched her fists after hearing this. However, she had to listen to Daemn before she could kill him.

'She was dying – but before I finished her – she made sure to use the energy she had left to seal the portal from Vita to the demons' world for fifteen years.' Daemn then turned to Prudence and her friends. 'Fifteen years later and the portal will open once again in a matter of hours. Keira's last chance of sealing the portal resides in you…'

'I shall succeed!' Prudence said loudly.

Daemn laughed.

'Allow me to finish my story, child… the best part is to come.'

'There is more?' Prudence gasped.

'Your mother needed something that could serve as a means to preserve the seal…' Daemn paused. 'And so, she took a certain relic… a relic which was offered to me when I became king. My own sword.' The emperor went silent.

'What?' Ryan jumped out in shock.

'Keira was clever. She used her soul to seal the sword in the Dragon's Realm, so that even I would not be able to collect it.' Daemn smiled. 'But her daughters…'

'I do not understand!' Prudence's voice trembled.

'Only in the fifteenth year, would the demons' portal open…' the emperor laughed. 'I needed one thing to make the demons mine, which was the sword. Since I could not get it myself… I used you to collect it for me.'

Prudence's eyes opened widely. She looked at the sword.

'No… that is not possible!' Prudence's voice was shaking in horror.

'All the dangers you faced… the goblins, the orcs, and Reaper! They were a motivation for you to go after the sword and to bring it to me.' Daemn laughed hysterically. 'I even used that stupid pirate to go after the sword!' he sneered. 'Who do you think was the author of the sword's rumour?'

'Bastard!' Ryan grunted.

Prudence fell on her knees. She had fought so many battles, for this ultimate deception. Her father was no man but a monster. It felt as if the sword had used Prudence more than she used it. With one gesture of his hand, the sword flew away from Prudence's hands and appeared in Daemn's. The bright shining white of the sword, turned to the colour of the night.

Everyone was shocked. Ryan stood silent and began to think about everything that had happened. Everything made sense now…

'That is the reason why it was so easy for you to find her in London!' Ryan snapped.

'Yes… the sword Slade had lent her was a mere measure for us to know of her location.' Daemn laughed evilly. 'We have been keeping our eyes on you… knowing everything you were doing.'

Prudence's teeth were shaking.

'How could mother love a monster like you?' she asked with a broken voice.

Daemn laughed again.

'Just like you, she was naive,' his voice was trembling in amusement. 'And I made her disappear… now… I shall make you disappear too!' he kept on laughing with his dark voice. 'But before this I shall thank the one who helped me through this entire charade,' he excitedly raised his voice. 'A daughter I had rejected at birth… Cheryl.'

The emperor clapped his hands, and Cheryl appeared in front of Prudence and her friends. She was smiling with a face that showed no remorse.

'You bitch!' Nash shouted.

Everyone was staring at the Humolf with anger. Prudence, however, seemed even more broken, especially after Cheryl's implication in Daemn's ambitions.

'You have betrayed mother and me… ' she looked at Cheryl.

Cheryl stood silent. Her eyes were focused on Prudence and she seemed serious.

'Remember – things are not as they always seem to be… ' Cheryl said calmly, as she stared at Prudence.

Prudence did not understand why Cheryl stared at her with a serious face. She had won… she had successfully fooled her and her friends throughout the whole journey. So why was she acting all serious? And where had Prudence heard those words… *Things are not as they always seems to be…* Her mother had told her that, but it did not make sense back then… and it still did not make sense even now.

'I only had until the 24th before the portal opened by itself. All the powers would have gone to waste and the demons would have killed everyone on Vita, including me… ' Daemn said quietly. 'A miracle, you have managed to make this naive child succeed before the clock runs out.'

'It does not matter how I fooled her,' Cheryl said calmly. 'You should kill the one who motivated her to go through with it… Ryan,' she said coldly.

Ryan was on his guard, he grunted after seeing how deceitful Cheryl was. He hated her, but deep inside, he hated himself for trusting someone like her. Nash and Eric followed Ryan's gesture and were firmly holding on to their weapons. The three of them were trembling. The sword the emperor was wielding was the strongest of all. Nash, who seemed confident and cocky before, reverted to a worried and serious person.

'Mhmph… ' the emperor chuckled. 'Since you have helped me to achieve my goal, I shall grant you your wish and kill this rat.'

Daemn turned to Ryan and approached him with a menacing look. Eric aimed at Daemn and fired a lot of arrows; however, all his attacks were deflected by the sword. Ryan told Eric to move out of the way, and to take care of Prudence. The young man then assimilated fire in his blade and dashed toward the emperor. His brother was assisting him in his attack and together, they faced the emperor.

'It is because of you!' Ryan cursed Daemn as he ran to him. 'I will destroy you for Prudence's sake!'

'Fool… ' the emperor mumbled.

Ryan tried to stab the emperor, but his attacks were vain, and his blade shattered into pieces after one collision with the Sword of the King. Ryan gasped in horror before being stabbed in the chest. It was so fast that even Nash could not do anything. No one could perceive the sword's speed as it pierced Ryan's chest.

'Ryan!'

Nash snapped in anger and tried to stab the emperor, but even with the powerful Sword of the Moon, the young man was quickly brought down to the ground and knocked out with one powerful lightning bolt.

Prudence could not believe what had happened. She ran to Ryan, and once near him she fell down on her knees and held his body, which was emptying itself of all its blood. 'NO!' she shouted in anger and sadness, as she realized that he was no longer breathing.

'No! Not you my love!' she cried in tears. 'I am so sorry! It is my fault!' she sobbed. 'Forgive me my love! Please! Do forgive me!' she kept crying.

'Now you shall die...' the emperor approached Prudence.

He looked at Prudence one more time, then, he lifted his sword in the air.

'Die!'

Daemn was about to slash Prudence's throat, but Cheryl jumped on him and attacked him.

'You traitor!' Daemn snarled, as he blocked Cheryl's sword.

'I shall not let you kill my sister!'

'You are right, foolish child – I shall begin with you and make extinct your species!' Daemn shouted with an evil voice.

Prudence was shocked at Cheryl standing up for her. The princess could not understand Cheryl at all. She betrayed her, but then, she saved her... why? What did she expect from her?

Cheryl dragged the emperor far from Prudence.

'Remember Prudence! Do not give up hope... things are not as they always seem to be!' Cheryl shouted, as she was battling against Daemn. 'Trust in Ryan's love!'

'Ryan...' Prudence softly caressed Ryan's cold face.

'Aha! The rat is dead – trust in despair!' Daemn said sharply.

The emperor laughed as he battled Cheryl with one hand. Cheryl tried to block the hits, but it was a rather hard task to do. The sword of her enemy was the most powerful one, and soon, she could feel the steel of her blade tremble. It was becoming unstable, and after shaking from left to right, the emperor destroyed her blade with one blast. Cheryl was thrown brutally to the ground; her forehead was cut, and a lot of blood was spilling from it.

'Cheryl!' Prudence shouted as she stood up.

'Foolish to believe in surpassing the ultimate sword!' Daemn laughed.

'Ugh…' Cheryl panted, as she placed her hand on her injury. Cheryl then fainted.

Daemn lifted his sword, ready to end the life of the Humolf, but Prudence grabbed Ryan's shattered sword and ran to him. She tried to stab him, but once again, the sword moved by itself and protected him.

'Yet another bug to crush,' he grunted. 'I am indeed getting tired of this charade…I shall end you two together!'

'You killed my mother…' Prudence paused. 'You killed the one I love,' she looked down with watery eyes. 'You shall not kill my sister!' Prudence said loudly.

The emperor did not wait long and attacked Prudence. He was even more aggressive than when he fought Cheryl, and with an implausible speed, he disarmed Prudence and brought her down on her knees.

'Time to die!'

'No! He's going to kill her!' Eric was muttering to himself with a shaking voice. 'I…I have to do something! But…but if I do that… he's – he's going to…kill me!' he stuttered.

Eric was shaking; he was petrified by everything happening around him. Still, he took out his bow and aimed toward the emperor. 'Leave my friends alone!' Eric shouted before he shot an arrow. He had aimed well, but the sword countered the attempt of the young man.

'Too many insects…' Daemn groaned as he noticed Eric.

The emperor then threw a lightning bolt that brutally electrocuted Eric. The young man crashed to the ground and lost consciousness.

While chaos was reigning in the battlefield, Ryan was in a dark room. Everything was dark; it was all black inside, and there was nothing. No flowers, no sky, no animals, no one… nothing, except this infernal darkness. *I failed her…* Ryan thought to himself.

'You only failed her if you give up.'

He heard the voice of a woman.

'Huh?' Ryan opened his eyes. He was in a garden, with tons of flowers and animals around him. 'Am I in heaven?'

'No…you are in my garden.'

Ryan turned around and saw the woman he had seen in London. It was the one who had warned him of his destiny. 'But I thought it was Cheryl…' he mumbled.

'Yes…my daughter and I look alike,' the woman said as she lowered her hood.

It was Prudence's mother. She was mesmerizing, a true beauty. She had nearly the same face as Cheryl, with dark yellow eyes. She removed her mysterious clothes and a beautiful white gown appeared on her. Ryan gasped in wonder; he stood up and bowed to her.

'You are Prudence's…'

'Yes I am,' she interrupted him. 'We have little time…'

'What do you mean?'

'You have to save my daughter and Vita.'

'How can I?' Ryan asked confusedly.

'Remember the inscription on the blade?'

Ryan tried to recall what was engraved in the blade, but he failed to remember.

Only a true king will be worthy of cleansing the darkness…

'Oh yes I remember now!' Ryan gasped. 'But I am no king… '

'The Sword of the King was meant for only a king to wield… Prudence's father is a king, however… he fails to understand the true strength of a king.'

'The true strength of a king?' Ryan asked puzzled.

'Yes… '

'What is it?'

'Love… this is the true strength of a king. And a king needs his queen in order to use his strength to the maximum. When you proposed to Prudence and she accepted your ring, she united her heart with yours,' Keira paused. 'You became a king the day she loved you back, Ryan.'

Ryan could not believe what he was hearing. He who was just a citizen from London… he, a king? It was hard to conceive but Keira was serious. Ryan had only one problem left. How could he save Prudence when he was already dead?

'Vita means "life" in Latin… The reason for this world to be named so – is because it allows the impossible to be made possible. Hence, bringing the dead back to life… ' Keira then took Ryan's hand. 'Only one in a million is chosen by the world, to be granted this privilege… '

'And I have been chosen… ' Ryan said softly.

'Yes. The world has its own soul, it is not always clear, but Vita offers you a chance to stand up again and eliminate the emperor.'

'What's the catch?' Ryan asked, as if he suspected something.

'You will have to accept my daughter's destiny,' Keira said quietly.

'Alas… something I can't promise… '

'The decision is in your hands. Know that every man has an opportunity to shape his destiny. Know that defying what has been written will have an impact on everything… ' Keira paused. 'Are you willing to risk everything for the one you love? Even the existence of others?'

'I cannot be selfish… ' Ryan said calmly. 'But I cannot let Prudence die either.'

'Will you make her a plague?'

Ryan stayed silent.

'No – I will find another way to protect her honour, while protecting her… '

'Then you shall.' Keira paused. 'But remember that the price will be deep… no matter the decision you shall make.'

Ryan could not refuse such an opportunity. He had a chance to save the one he loved, and save his friends. With the sword in his possession, he would be able to vanquish Daemn for good. But above all, he would be able to defy the tragic destiny that was written for Prudence.

He took a deep breath and closed his eyes.

'I accept what has been granted to me.'

'Good luck,' Keira said softly.

A powerful blue and bright light surrounded Ryan.

The young man could feel his body being restored. Air was refreshing his lungs and his heart started to beat. He was alive, once again. When he looked around, he could see Prudence on her knees. She was facing Daemn, who was about to swing his sword to cut her throat.

'No one is going to save you now – princess.'

Ryan immediately threw a fireball at the emperor. The sword protected the man but Daemn gasped out of surprised when he saw Ryan. He was shocked to see the young man alive and well.

'Ryan!' Prudence gasped, with a happy expression on her face.

'Your mother asked me to get you out of this mess! '

Ryan's body was glowing with an angelic light; he was not a man anymore, but more of an angel.

'Impossible!' the emperor yelled in frustration.

'The sword is mine!'

Ryan called out to the weapon. It took only a second before the sword changed master. Ryan had a grip of the dark blade, which was restored to its former light.

'The devil!' the emperor could not believe what was happening. 'Curse you, Keira!' he yelled. 'I shall end all of you here!' he shouted. 'The army of the demons shall be mine!'

Ryan threw another fireball that brutally crashed the emperor to the ground. The young man then approached his enemy, and pointed the edge of the blade toward his throat.

'Surrender… ' Ryan said quietly.

Daemn stood up heavily.

'I'd rather die!' he snarled. 'Vita shall feel the burden of my death!'

The emperor tried to throw a lightning bolt at Ryan. However, the sword deflected the attack. Ryan then stabbed him around his right ribs. Daemn was coughing blood and took a few steps back. He then started to laugh maniacally.

'Do you believe this is over?' he coughed more blood. 'I have not – told you about… ' he coughed again. 'I shall use myself to open the demons' world!' Daemn yelled.

'What?'

'With my soul – the demons will be able to walk free!'

The emperor's body started to glow with a purple aura. Soon, his armour cracked and his body was surrounded by red flames.

'You shall witness the end of everything!' Daemn said loudly. 'You only have one way of stopping it!'

Ryan looked at the sword, and then at Prudence.

'That's right… ' Daemn's body started to dissolve. 'Alas – the demons' world… ' the emperor laughed before his whole person was drowned inside the flames. Ryan and Prudence could see the flames turning into a portal, and demons were appearing inside of it.

The portal was opening itself, slowly but surely. Ryan turned to the princess, his eyes were open weakly, his eyebrows were wavy and his mouth was trembling. Prudence could see the sorrow in the eyes of the one she loved.

'It is time for me to accomplish my duty.'

'Yes… ' said Ryan.

'Hand me the sword, my love.'

Ryan was not giving the sword to her. What was he planning on doing? She asked herself. He then smiled weakly and his voice shook. 'Prudence,' he said with a weak tone. 'Remember that I love you. No matter what.' A tear fell off from his face.

'Ryan… ' Prudence said calmly.

He was taking a few steps away from her.

'It's the reason why I cannot let you sacrifice your life,' he said quietly.

'But I…' Prudence tried to speak but he would not let her.

'I won't let you become a plague either – the people should remember you as a saviour or a hero, not a plague my darling.'

Prudence approached Ryan, but he edged the sword's blade toward her. He did not seem to want to listen to her.

'I will seal the portal that way no demons will be able to come to Vita,' Ryan paused, trying to find the right words. 'It sucks that I have to die when I have just been brought back.' He looked down with watery eyes. 'But I'll do this for you – for us.'

No... why was Ryan not listening? Prudence tried her best to talk him out of this, but he refused to listen to her. She did not care at all about Vita or what the people would say about her. She only wanted Ryan. Now that he could live, they could be together... so why? Why was he not listening? He gazed at her.

'Thank you...' he said.

Prudence looked at him with confusion. Why was he thanking her? She was the reason why he would die... it was all her fault. He should curse her instead of thanking her.

'I always wondered if I had something big written for me,' he smiled wryly. 'Now I know – I was meant to love you and die for you.' He looked happy. 'To die for the one I love – there is nothing more beautiful.'

'Do not do this, please my love...'

'I have to...' Ryan sighed. 'If there's something I could wish for...' He paused. 'It's to know that you are safe and well... and that your honour is intact.'

Prudence thumped the ground as her voice broke.

'I shall never be well without you! My honour can go to hell!'

'Don't say that...' Ryan said calmly. 'The world must know what an incredible woman you are – you cannot be selfish because of me.' His eyes were struggling to not cry.

The portal was nearly complete; soon, the ground was trembling and lightning pierced the sky. Ryan could feel the sword calling out to him. It was as if it whispered to him what he had to do. 'Goodbye...' he said loudly.

He turned around and walked toward the final step of his journey. Prudence ran to him.

'No…' she stopped him.

The princess then held him from behind. Her head was against his back and her arms around his waist. She was holding him tightly.

'Prudence…' Ryan's voice was breaking.

'Promise me…' Prudence paused. 'Promise me that you will come back to me.'

Ryan knew that it was a hard promise to make. He was not even sure about what was out there. He knew that he was probably going to die, still, he promised her that he would come back to her, one way or another. He then turned around and faced Prudence. The princess kissed him and wrapped her necklace around his neck.

'This necklace shall remind you of our promise,' she said in tears. 'I shall wait for you to make it back to me.'

'I love you.' Ryan closed his eyes and kissed her one more time.

The portal was complete. It was an infernal circle of fire, and a sort of dark red scenery appeared. Ryan approached the portal with the sword glowing brighter.

Nash and the two others had regained their consciousness and did not understand what was happening. 'Ryan!' Eric shouted. He tried to approach his friend, but Ryan told him not to. If any of them came close to him, he would attack. With the Sword of the King in his hands, it was more than enough for his friends to obey.

'Make it home!' Ryan said loudly, as he walked toward the portal.

'I don't get it. Why are you saying this to me?' Eric asked, puzzled.

'Ryan…' Cheryl said worriedly. 'Do not go…'

'Brother!'

It was becoming hard for Ryan, just to hear his friends calling out to him. The pain of leaving behind the ones he loved was overwhelming his heart. It was without haste that he ran and jumped inside the portal.

It took around fifteen seconds before the portal closed itself and disappeared in the sky.

'Ryan!' Eric yelled. 'He… he is inside that… '

Prudence fell on her knees. She was devastated. An aching feeling was piercing her heart. She was alive, but it was so painful. She looked up, and millions of stars shone in the sky. The red turned back to blue. It was dark because it was night time, but Heartsas was shining back to its former glory. Light had vanquished darkness once again. But was it truly a victory for Prudence? She stared at the starry sky, and tears started to drop from her eyes.

'Thank you,' she said weakly, as she was crying.

Cheryl knew what Ryan had done, she turned around, and a tear fell from her eye. 'Imbecile… ' She bit her lips.

Nash did not say a word. He was trying to be strong but everyone could see his eyes struggling not to cry. He then sighed and looked down.

'Will he ever be able to come back?' he asked the princess.

Prudence did not wish to answer. It pained her too much.

Then, out of nowhere, she could see a shooting star. She smiled and with relief she stood up. This star… it was there to remind her of the wish she made before, back in Parisia. It was the wish of hope. She will be with Ryan, yes. When the time will be right, they will be reunited.

'He has gone, but he will come back… ' Prudence smiled. 'To me… '

Nash stood silent and looked at Prudence.

'What's going on now?' he asked.

'It is time for me to take what's mine,' Prudence replied quietly. 'And when Ryan is back, we shall leave for London… together.'

Cheryl looked at Prudence as if she had gone mad. But then, she smiled.

'Maybe love will conquer all,' she whispered quietly. 'Even death… '

'There is so much to do now,' said Prudence. 'We shall get rid of the goblins and the other creatures that allied with Daemn.'

'Leave it to me,' said Nash.

Eric could not believe it. He had managed to be the only one, with Nash, to survive the journey. He never thought he would live through something like this, ever, let alone survive it. He looked down at his feet, and there was only one thing he wanted more than anything. He wished to go home. Feel the warmth of his apartment, and be with his family. Yes, it was finally time for him to go home. Not in London, where he was meant to spend Christmas with Ryan, but back in Paris, where he had a family waiting for him.

Prudence and her friends headed down to the castle's gates. Something strange had happened. Slade had disappeared, and so had the bodies of Mia and Reaper. What was the meaning of this? Prudence questioned herself, but she did not have time for this.

She had to put an end to the war by presenting herself as the unique ruler of Heartsas. It was time for the princess to take what was hers. Nash pushed the gates, and when they opened, Prudence witnessed the dragons all bowing to her.

They had come to aid her in her war. All the goblins and orcs had been crushed; Daemn's army was no more. The remaining monsters had dropped their weapons and surrendered to the princess. The age of peace had finally started for Heartsas.

Chapter Thirty-four
A New Journey Begins

Three years had passed since Daemn's demise. Prudence was still a princess because she had not been officially wed. However, it did not matter to her.

Princess Prudence Fulgura had decreed the right of all Humolfs, dragons and other species to walk as equals. It was a whole new system that had been devised. Prudence was known as the fairest princess in every kingdom of Vita. But despite the new law, a lot of dragons preferred to remain in their realm.

Prudence was the most prosperous woman in all Vita. She had books written about her, and everyone knew of her. She was the woman who had fought back when the darkness had risen up. A lot of princes had come to take her hand, but returned to their kingdoms alone. She was true to her heart and was waiting for one man only to wed her. And every night, she stood on the roof of the castle. She stared at the starry sky, thinking of him until he came home to her. Someday, somehow…

Cheryl was recognized as the daughter of Keira Fulgura. However, she could not live as a princess. She was too adventurous to just sit back and live her life inside a castle. She went around Vita, and with her new name, she was more feared and respected than before. It was the opportunity for her to mark the history of Vita. And so, she embarked upon a new journey.

Nash had decided to stay on Vita, as he wished. In three years he had lived a happier life than when he was on Earth. He loved London; it was his home, but he loved Vita even more. He was a ruler, and a good one. History was quickly marked by him. He was known as a fair leader and a noble one. Just like Cheryl, he had begun a new journey. It was time for him to discover all places on Vita. His life was just starting, and Nash was planning on making the best out of it.

Eric was back to his normal life in Paris. His experience on Vita had changed his way of seeing things, and the way he wished to live. He had become a much more mature and responsible man. Of course, he could not forget about Vita, and tried to speak about it. But who would believe him? They would all think he had gone mad. A world with dragons and goblins… no one would believe him. And so, he decided to keep secret what he had lived.

However, Mia's disappearance lead to investigations. Eric was interrogated for days. But how could Eric tell Mia's parents that their daughter was dead? Or that they would never find her body? It was the same for the missing brothers. Ryan's parents went to look everywhere they could, but they never found anything. Shortly after, Ryan's mother fell terribly sick. Ryan's father could not tolerate seeing his wife hurting so much. He decided to cease with the investigations. Eric hated himself for not being able to tell the truth, but he did not feel that the truth would be good enough.

It took time, but everyone was moving on with their lives, whether it was on Earth or on Vita. But something was about to change everything…

'It is as I've heard.'

'Are you sure sister?' Prudence asked, as she was standing on her castle's roof.

'It is as said. A certain demon has been killing innocents around Vita… '

'What is happening?'

'That I don't know, but something bothered me.' Cheryl went silent.

'What?'

'The demon was described as beautiful and is praised like a god by those who survived. And… he had… ' Cheryl paused. 'He had the necklace of the family around his neck.'

Both sisters remained silent. Prudence's thoughts were only focusing on Ryan.

'Could it be Ryan?' Prudence wondered. 'We have to go. We have to find out. I have to know… please… '

'Then let us go,' Cheryl smiled. 'Together, we will find out what is happening and who this beautiful demon is.'

A new journey was awaiting Prudence and Cheryl. The beautiful demon: who was he? Why did he have the Fulgura's family necklace around his neck? Was it Ryan? If so… what had happened to him? Prudence had to know.

And so it was on this fateful night, that a new journey was opened to her…

Meanwhile, in the darkest place of Vita, five people wearing dark robes were sitting around a long table.

'Three years since Daemn has failed us.'

'Yes – everything was going according to plan, except the princess not dying.'

'Who would have thought that Leo would take her place?'

'What do you think happened to him?'

The five were discussing in the darkness of the room. No one could distinguish their faces. They were hidden within the darkness of their souls. A young woman then stepped into the room. She was accompanied by a middle age knight.

'It does not matter – the demon is our priority,' she said.

'Indeed,' one of the five said calmly.

'We'll be on our way to capture him – he has been spotted on Oceanus.' The woman was about to leave.

'Wait… '

She turned around.

'Be sure to kill anyone who would dare stand in our way. Anyone but the princess.'

The woman laughed.

'If you refer to the Princess of Heartsas – I shall only wait for her to cross my path… ' the woman paused, 'so I can see her beg for death once I kill her loved ones.'

The five went silent.

'My lords – fear not,' the knight said. 'No one would dare to stand up against the heads of Vita.'

'Indeed… ' one of the five paused. 'Just make sure to kill anyone but the princess and him. We will need them.'

The woman laughed darkly before walking away.

'One more thing… '

The woman halted and turned around.

'Make sure she thinks that we will kill her… '

'Ha! ' the woman laughed.

She then left with the knight.

'Can we trust in her success?'

'She is driven by vengeance… of course we can.'

A big thanks to:
My family for their support
Everyone who read the story
Bubblecow for the useful guidance and edit
Matador team for making *Regnum Vita* come true
Amy Statham for the proofread
Jennifer Liptrot for the great work she did
Chris Sansom and Gareth Howard
And to her, the girl from the train.

The story is not over yet. To thank you for reading Regnum Vita, here is a short preview of

Regnum Vita II

Chapter One
A Dangerous Quest

Inside a boat, a young girl was sitting down on a wooden chair. She had her back slightly bent toward a wooden table. She was writing in a diary with a feather. It was Prudence.

It has been three months… we went looking for you but we could not find you anywhere. There have been different rumours about a demon with blond hair, and my family's necklace around its neck, killing people…

Prudence was writing. She then heard someone approaching.
'Oh, Cheryl…' she looked on her left.
'Still writing to him?'
Prudence looked down at her diary and nodded.
'When we find him, I want him to read what he has missed.'
Cheryl cleared her throat.
'You know, if we find him, we might be surprised…'
Prudence sighed.
'Ryan is not a killer,' Prudence said quietly. 'I know what people say, but you and I both know Ryan…' she paused. 'He would never commit what this "demon" did.'

'All I'm saying is we should be prepared to face the worst.'

Prudence then closed her diary and stood up.

'I know,' she said. 'But I'd rather think of the best case scenario.'

'Where should we go now?' asked Cheryl.

'We should gather information about this demon,' replied Prudence. 'We still have places we have not searched.'

Cheryl shook her head.

'Fine, I will tell –'

Cheryl and Prudence felt a jolt and both fell down.

'What is going on?' Prudence stood up, alarmed.

'Your Majesties!'

A young man dressed like a soldier pushed the door.

'We are under attack!' the soldier said. 'We need to… '

Before the soldier could say anything, an arrow pierced his heart. Prudence and Cheryl looked up and saw a man smiling at them. The man had a hood on.

'Let me have him, sister!' Cheryl pushed Prudence and got out her sword. 'They might be pirates.'

Cheryl ran to the man after dodging his arrows. She punched him and stabbed him in the chest.

'A brigand… ' Cheryl looked at the man's corpse. 'Sister, follow me!'

Prudence and Cheryl ran to the deck.

When they arrived, they could only see dead soldiers. There was no one else. Cheryl clenched her fist.

'That man I just killed,' she paused. 'He couldn't have done that.'

'What do you mean?' asked Prudence.

'I killed him so easily,' Cheryl grunted. 'Yet there is no one else here… '

Someone clapped their hands.

Both sisters looked around, but saw no one. Then, they looked up and saw a woman floating in the air. A mask was hiding her face. She had long chestnut hair.

'They got me… '

Cheryl turned around, shocked.

'You're alive!'

The man laughed and shook the dust from his clothes.

'It is such a pathetic boat for princesses,' he chuckled.

Prudence and Cheryl held their swords firmly. Both sisters were on guard.

'Who are you?' asked Prudence. 'And what do you want?'

The woman who was floating then disappeared and reappeared next to the hooded man. She slowly put her feet on the ground.

'We are two faces, sent to stop you on your research.'

'Our research?' Prudence looked down. 'You mean Ryan?'

The woman and the hooded man looked at each other but did not reply.

'Call it what you want,' she said. 'The demon is ours for the taking.'

'Shut up!' Prudence shouted.

Prudence threw a powerful lightning bolt to the woman, but she dodged it with one finger. She then laughed.

'Why so touchy?' she chuckled. 'The demon would kill you as soon as it gets a chance.'

'We are here to kill them,' the man grunted. 'So let's kill them!'

The man ran to the sisters with a sword in his hands. He tried to stab Cheryl but she dodged his hit and kicked him in the stomach. Prudence immediately saw an opportunity and electrocuted the man. It was a powerful hit, and the impact made him fly out of the boat.

'Good job, sister!' Cheryl chuckled.

The masked woman created a flaming circle. The boat was burning fast because it was made of wood.

'We shall meet again,' she chuckled. 'Today I spare your lives, but remember that as long as you're looking for the demon, then you're doomed,' she laughed. 'They don't want you to find him, and they will make sure of this.'

The woman then disappeared.

Cheryl created an enormous wave to extinguish the fire, but the boat had suffered too much damage. It was sinking.

'Prudence, come, quick!'

Prudence was deep in her thoughts. Cheryl then slapped her and held her hand.

'Let's find a lifeboat and head to the nearest town!'

Prudence nodded and with her sister, she ran to the nearest lifeboat.

They were out of danger, but Prudence could not stop thinking about the two individuals. Some people were after the demon. Why? What did they have in mind? The masked woman was extraordinary. But she was an enemy. From this moment on, Prudence knew that there was a lot more to this quest than finding Ryan.

It took an hour for Cheryl and Prudence to reach a port. They were both exhausted and out of breath. But the sisters knew that they had to gather information and move fast. The people after the demon were powerful… extremely powerful.

When Prudence and Cheryl looked at the port's signboard, they could read *Ventus Port*. The sisters had visited this town earlier that day, to buy provisions. They did some research in the city, but they did not find anything that could lead to the demon.

'We should find a boat,' Prudence said quietly.

'Sure,' Cheryl paused. 'But then what?' She sighed. 'A boat is great for visiting places, but not good enough if we wish to travel fast.'

'What do you suggest then?'

'Let us visit the tavern, and see if we can get our hands on a pirate,' said Cheryl. 'They possess flying boats, which are ten times faster than a normal boat.'

Prudence stood quietly.

'They cannot be trusted,' said Prudence.

'But you worked with a pirate,' said Cheryl. 'Alexandra, was it?'

Prudence did not reply.

'Fine, we could just visit the town and get a boat,' Cheryl sighed.

'No, you are right,' said Prudence. 'Let us find a pirate.'

The two sisters went to the city's tavern. They knew that pirates frequented those kind of places. After all, it was there that Prudence had met her first pirate. Just walking inside the tavern made Prudence think of the first time she met Alexandra. Surprisingly, Prudence's first journey formed the best memories she had of herself.

'Hello?' Cheryl waved her hand in front of Prudence's face. 'Are you dreaming again?'

'Oh... ' Prudence snapped out of her thoughts. 'Sorry, I was thinking of something.'

Cheryl smiled and held her sister's hand.

'Come on,' Cheryl dragged Prudence toward the barman.

When Prudence looked at the barman's face, she recognized him. It was the same barman she met in Parisia. What was he doing here?

'Ah,' he said in wonder. 'Princesses,' he paused. 'Prudence Fulgura, the same one I met three years ago.'

Prudence swallowed her breath.

'You remember,' she said quietly.

'Of course, Your Highness,' the barman chuckled. 'Back then, I didn't know who you were, but since you defeated Daemn, everyone knows you.' He took a glass and cleaned it. 'What can I get ya?'

'We are not here to drink,' said Cheryl. 'We need a pirate.' She paused. 'Or someone who would be willing to lend us a flying boat.'

'Straight to the point,' the barman laughed. 'I only know of one person who could help you,' he said. 'The young Delacroix.'

Prudence's eyes opened wide. Did she hear him right? Delacroix? As in Alexandra Delacroix?

'Who is this Delacroix?' asked Prudence.

'Why don't you go and meet her?' The barman pointed out a backdoor. 'She hates loud people, so she isolates herself in that room.'

'I see.' Prudence stared at the door.

'Well, that's good enough for me.' Cheryl walked toward the door. 'You're coming?' she looked at Prudence.

'Yes, of course.'

Prudence and Cheryl were both behind the door. They knocked but no one responded. Cheryl delicately turned the knob to the left. The door wasn't locked.

'OK,' Cheryl whispered. 'On the count of three… one, two… '

Cheryl slowly opened the door.

'Three… ' she said as she pushed it gently.